PENGUIN BOOKS

A CALCULATING HEART

Caro Fraser was educated in Glasgow and on the Isle of Man. After attending Watford School of Art she worked as a advertising copywriter for three years, then read law at King's College, London. She was called to the Bar of Middle Temple in 1979 and worked as a shipping lawyer, before turning to writing. She is the author of eleven other novels, six of which are part of the highly successful, critically acclaimed Caper Court series. She lives in London with her husband, who is a solicitor, and her four children.

A Calculating Heart

CARO FRASER

PENGUIN BOOKS

PENGUIN BOOKS

Published by the Penguin Group
Penguin Books Ltd, 80 Strand, London WC2R ORL, England
Penguin Group (USA) Inc., 375 Hudson Street, New York, New York 10014, USA
Penguin Group (Canada), 90 Eglinton Avenue East, Suite 700, Toronto, Ontario, Canada M4P 2Y3
(a division of Pearson Penguin Canada Inc.)
Penguin Ireland, 25 St Stephen's Green, Dublin 2, Ireland
(a division of Penguin Books Ltd)
Penguin Group (Australia), 250 Camberwell Road, Camberwell, Victoria 3124, Australia
(a division of Pearson Australia Group Pty Ltd)
Penguin Books India Pvt Ltd, 11 Community Centre, Panchsheel Park, New Delhi – 110 017, India
Penguin Group (NZ), cnr Airborne and Rosedale Roads, Albany, Auckland 1310, New Zealand
(a division of Pearson New Zealand Ltd)
Penguin Books (South Africa) (Pty) Ltd, 24 Sturdee Avenue, Rosebank, Johannesburg 2196, South Africa

Penguin Books Ltd, Registered Offices: 80 Strand, London WC2R ORL, England

www.penguin.com

First published by Michael Joseph 2004
Published by Penguin Books 2006

1

Copyright © Caro Fraser, 2004
All rights reserved

The moral right of the author has been asserted

Set in Monotype Garamond
Typeset by Rowland Phototypesetting Ltd, Bury St Edmunds, Suffolk
Printed in England by Clays Ltd, St Ives plc

ISBN-13: 978–0–141–00824–0
ISBN-10: 0–141–00824–5

This work is dedicated with affectionate
thanks to Timothy Young QC, the Scrutton
of his generation

I

'You know what? I reckon you want to go for something more vibrant next time you have your colour done.'

Ann Halliday said nothing, merely glanced at Charmaine's reflection in the salon mirror. Charmaine stroked Ann's newly-cut hair reflectively. Then she nodded. 'Yeah, go for something a bit more blonde.'

It was an effort for Ann to think of any appropriate response. Her hair didn't interest her a great deal. It had taken her over eighteen months to persuade Charmaine not to blow-dry it into some voluminous style that could not possibly be accommodated under her barrister's wig. She liked it to be cut neatly and sensibly, in a way that wouldn't attract any attention at all. When she was younger, when her light brown hair had had a youthful sheen, she'd worn it long and sleek. But age had faded that lustre, and grey was creeping in. Better short and unobtrusive.

She gazed at her own reflection. Then again, maybe Charmaine was right. Perhaps blonde highlights would brighten things up a bit. But she didn't want to attract comment, and teasing comment, even if kindly meant, she would certainly get from her fellow male barristers, particularly the three she was about to have lunch with. She would hate anyone to think she had gone to trouble over her appearance. Such a thing was suggestive of vanity – and vanity, Ann Halliday thought, was strictly for the young.

Charmaine picked up a square mirror and wagged it back and forth behind Ann's head, as she always did, showing her a reflection of the cut. Ann could never see the point. It meant she had to smile and nod appreciatively, as though she cared what the back of her head looked like.

Charmaine put down the mirror and unfastened the Velcro on the gown, lifting it from Ann's shoulders. 'Off anywhere nice?'

Ann stood up and let Charmaine brush her down. It was a fair enough question, since she normally came in to have her hair cut on Saturday afternoons, never on a weekday such as today. 'I'm meeting some friends for lunch.'

'Lovely. Nice way to cheer up a Monday. A girly get-together, is it?'

'No. Some male friends.' As soon as the words were out, she felt they sounded odd, not what she meant to imply at all. 'Colleagues,' she tried to add, but Charmaine was already off.

'More than one! Now, that's what I call greedy!'

'It's sort of a business lunch. Nothing very exciting.'

She paid the bill and tipped Charmaine, who fetched Ann's jacket and helped her into it. 'Well, you enjoy it, anyway.'

Ann left the salon with mild relief, stepping out into the summer air, focusing her thoughts on lunch. It seemed strangely dislocating, meeting up with Marcus, Roger and Maurice in this way. Like a bunch of outlaws. Last week they had been fellow tenants at 3 Wessex Street, a large and prosperous set of barristers' chambers, but now they were free agents. Well, for the time being. The departure from the chambers where she had worked all her adult life still held an air of unreality for Ann. Looking back over the past few months, it seemed now as though she had been swept along, a victim of forces not of her own creation. A set of barristers' chambers was not like a company, or even a partnership. It had no animus, but was a collection of individuals, each of them paying rent to occupy space in the same building, each in his own employment, answerable to no one, but all relying on the same group of clerks to organize their professional lives, bringing in work and processing fees. Just as the identity of any set of chambers depended on the personalities of the individual tenants, so it was that the stability and smooth running of chambers depended on the tenants' mutual dependency. Where personalities clashed, splits and factions were often the result. It had been Maurice who had started the whole thing. Maurice – ambitious, aggressive, piqued at not having been made head of chambers – had created the split almost as an act of reprisal against those who had opposed him, fomenting little rows and divisions within chambers. He had gradually brought others into his camp – Roger, who had been a protégé of Maurice and who largely tended to take his side no matter what, and then Marcus and herself. She had had her own grievances, of course. She had felt for some time that she wasn't being clerked properly, not getting work of the quality she deserved, but without Maurice's persuasion, she wondered if she might not have stuck it out. It had been a great leap, to leave the chambers where she had been a tenant for twenty-five years. Maurice had flattered her, talked her into it one evening in a wine bar. 'The fact is, Ann,' he'd said, 'Five Caper Court want to expand. They're too small. They need people of your calibre, your expertise.' She'd known then that his own vanity required that he take people with him when making his departure. But she'd agreed. Should she be grateful to him? Should Marcus and Roger, for that matter? Time would tell. By the end of the week they would be newly installed as tenants at 5 Caper Court – not as large in numbers as 3 Wessex Street, but no less prestigious. The word was that the head of chambers there, Roderick Hayter, was destined for the High Court bench in a few months' time. Did Maurice have his once-thwarted ambitions focused on that position in a new set of chambers? Very probably.

It was a five-minute walk to the restaurant in Gray's Inn Road from Bloomsbury, where Ann lived. Marcus and Roger were already there. Marcus, black, beautiful and twenty-five, was lounging in his chair at a table by the window with an air of magnificent boredom, looking as immaculately turned-out in chinos and an open-necked shirt as he ever did in his three-piece suit. Roger, on the other hand, who was sitting studying the menu through his round glasses, was dressed in a Gap T-shirt, scruffy jeans and trainers, and looked as dishevelled as he did in the eternal M&S suit and unironed shirt which he wore for work day in, day out. The attention paid by each to his appearance, Ann always thought, was symptomatic of their peculiarly different, though formidable, intellects. As a lawyer, Marcus Jacobs was fastidious, hard-working and somewhat haughty, fiercely proud of his ability to deliver snap opinions on complex legal problems. Roger Fry was another character altogether. Sweet-natured, kind-faced, with a donnish air which belied his twenty-eight years, Roger conducted his social and his working life in an erratic and eccentric fashion, but seemed somehow to bring both off. His appearance was a matter of general indifference to him, so too his surroundings. Conferences with well-heeled and powerful clients in his room at 3 Wessex Street were generally conducted amid a clutter of books, papers, and cardboard boxes stacked with documents. It was as though Roger was too focused on law, on the case and the facts before him, to pay much attention to his immediate surroundings, unless those surroundings happened to be a pub or a wine bar. But both Roger and Marcus were successful and well regarded in their profession, and each attracted a different kind of client. Like Ann, however, they had begun to feel that the best cases at 3 Wessex Street were being diverted by certain of the clerks to other, less deserving members of chambers. So here they sat today, waiting for Maurice Faber, bound together by their new destiny.

'Hello,' said Roger, glancing up at Ann. Marcus, with his customary impeccable good manners, half rose from his chair. Ann smiled and sat down, and Marcus subsided.

'It's a strange sort of day,' said Ann, taking off her jacket. 'I should be used to working from home, but for some reason I couldn't get down to anything this morning. I went to the hairdresser's instead.'

'I know what you mean,' said Marcus. 'It's odd not having chambers there in the background. Briefs to pick up, mail to open, coffee to drink, people to chat to.'

'Office syndrome,' said Roger. 'It's a security blanket.'

'You think that's why Maurice arranged this lunch?' said Marcus. 'Give us a sense of security?'

'Identity, more like. He thinks this is his show, and he's running it.'

'I find it rather exciting, joining a new set of chambers,' said Ann. 'Like a new school term.'

'You found those exciting?' Roger put down the menu, took off his glasses and rubbed his eyes. 'It honestly doesn't make much odds to me, so long as I've got a desk and a telephone.'

'You look very tired,' said Ann, glancing at Roger with motherly concern. 'Have you been working late on that shipbuilding case?'

Roger laughed and replaced his glasses. 'No, Ann. Kind of you to think so. I went on a pub crawl round South Ken last night with some friends.' He gave an enormous yawn. 'Sorry. Only got out of bed an hour ago.'

'New surroundings are one thing,' said Marcus. 'What about the people?'

'You met them all at that chambers tea a month ago,' remarked Ann.

'Yes, but I can't honestly say I know anyone well. Except Anthony Cross.'

'I'm fairly friendly with David Liphook,' said Roger, 'and Will Cooper, Simon Barron. They're a decent bunch. And Leo Davies, of course – didn't you have a case against him a couple of months ago?'

Marcus winced inwardly. He didn't care to remember his one and only courtroom encounter with Leo, in a dispute concerning the personal liability of freight forwarders. He hadn't exactly come off best. He had to admit to a grudging admiration for Leo Davies' skills of advocacy – not to mention his taste in clothes. Marcus was always prepared to respect anyone who dressed as well as Leo did.

'Ah, yes – Leo Davies. Every woman in the Temple is supposed to be madly in love with him – isn't that right, Ann?' Marcus glanced at her.

'Something of an exaggeration,' said Ann dryly, turning her attention to the menu. She and Leo went back many years, having been at Bar School together. She didn't run across him much nowadays, though she heard a good deal about him. Without being flamboyant, Leo had managed to cultivate a reputation which was unusual in the staid world of the Temple. He was renowned for his brilliant mind and acute professionalism as a barrister, and was regarded as witty and amusing company, but there were always darker rumours circulating about him which, everyone assumed, must have some foundation in truth. Ann harboured a certain curiosity as to whether or not he merited his libidinous reputation – it certainly wasn't the way she remembered him at twenty-one,

even though she had always found something both provocative and beguiling about those sharp blue eyes and gently
modulated Welsh voice. Not that she would have admitted
that to the likes of Marcus and Roger. Besides, she regarded
herself as a hardened professional woman, not given to
weaknesses where other members of the Bar were concerned.

Marcus nodded in the direction of the door. 'Here's
Maurice.'

Maurice Faber was in his early forties, tall, with thick, very
dark hair and heavy eyebrows, which gave him an Italianate
look. His movements, bodily and facial, were brisk and
energetic, his glance and smile quick and keen. Unlike Roger
and Marcus, he was dressed in a suit and tie. He held up
a folded copy of the *Sun* as he came towards their table,
grinning.

'Any of you seen this?'

Ann, who was strictly a *Guardian* reader, shook her head.

'There certainly wasn't anything in *The Times* that got me
going,' said Marcus.

'I haven't been up long enough to look at the papers,' said
Roger. 'What's the scandal?'

'Hah! Scandal is just the word.' Maurice sat down. Ann
could tell from his eyes that whatever it was that had him so
excited was bound to involve downfall or humiliation for
someone else. Such things invariably turned Maurice on. She
felt an anticipatory compassion for whoever the unfortunate
person might be.

Maurice held up the front page for them to see. '*MY
LOVE HELL MADE ME WANT TO END IT ALL*,'
read the headline, and below that, '*TV's Melissa tells how top
QC lover drove her to suicide bid*.' There was a large, glamorous
picture of a blonde woman, familiar to those present as
Melissa Angelicos, presenter of a Channel 4 arts programme.

Below that was a somewhat smaller photograph of the very man they had just been discussing, Leo Davies.

'Bloody hell,' said Roger. He reached out for the paper, and Maurice handed it to him, then sat back, relishing the moment.

'What on earth is that all about?' asked Ann incredulously, as Roger and Marcus huddled together, devouring the story.

'It seems,' said Maurice, 'that Leo Davies was having some intense relationship with this television presenter woman, and it all began to go off the rails. He was knocking her about, having affairs with other women –'

'Other *men* as well, according to this,' said Roger, without looking up.

'– it began to affect her work, she lost her job in television because of it, and in the long run she got so unhappy over him that she wanted to top herself. But before so doing, she decided to tell the world what a shit Davies was by penning a lengthy suicide note, giving intimate insights into their affair and detailing his many failings. Which –' Maurice indicated the paper '– is what you're reading. She posted it off to the *Sun*, then swallowed a large quantity of pills and vodka. Not quite enough, however, because she woke up in hospital the next day.'

'And they've printed it?' marvelled Ann.

'Well, not in its entirety, apparently. But the good bits.'

Marcus shook his head. 'He'll have them. This is pretty strong stuff. He has to sue.'

'If he can. Not much point, really. The damage is done.'

'Listen to this – *"But love rat Leo claims he hardly knew Melissa.* '*I have never been romantically involved with Melissa Angelicos,' said Leo Davies, when our reporter spoke to him on the phone at his chambers in the Temple, from which he conducts his one-and-a-half-million-a-year commercial practice –"'*

'Ha, ha. He wishes.'

'"*She is a neurotic woman who has been pestering me and my family for some months, and her story is a pathetic, delusional fantasy.*' He declined to comment further.'''

'They must be mad to publish it,' said Ann.

'Oh, come on. Think of the increase in circulation. Even if this woman is completely nuts and has made it all up, they hardly lose out.'

'I'd be straight round to Carter-Ruck, if I were Davies,' said Marcus, still poring over the juicier bits of the story.

'Let's have a look.'

Marcus passed the paper to Ann. She scanned the contents, which were admittedly pretty bad, and glanced across at Maurice.

'You and I both know Leo,' she said. 'None of this sounds remotely true.'

Maurice shrugged, but said reluctantly, 'I have to say I agree with you. Much as the story adds to the gaiety of our nation, I suspect that, reading between the lines, most of it is fabricated. There may be some basis to it, perhaps they did have an affair, but certain things don't ring true. I don't believe he's the type to behave violently towards anyone. More to the point, all that stuff she comes out with about his professional insecurity is so much crap. He's one of the best lawyers around. And one thing they fail to mention in that article is that Davies obtained an injunction against her a couple of months beforehand because she'd been harassing him.'

Ann gave a small smile. Maurice had certainly done his homework. He'd probably been ferreting away at this all morning.

'So you believe him when he says that he was never involved with her?'

Maurice grinned. 'Well, to quote another unreliable female – he would say that, wouldn't he?'

While the four of them sat discussing the scandal over lunch, the same topic had been exercising the members of the clerks' room at 5 Caper Court. The *Sun* was not a newspaper which any of the barristers in that august set of chambers would deign to purchase, but everybody, on their way in and out of the clerks' room, normally paused for a few moments to glance at the copy belonging to Robert, the junior clerk. On this particular morning, however, Robert had been at the House of Lords, and didn't come into chambers until ten forty-five, until which time the inhabitants of 5 Caper Court remained blissfully unaware of the events which were about to overtake them. When Robert did finally come in, newspaper in hand, he was agog.

'Have you heard?' he asked Henry, the senior clerk.

Henry, a harassed man in his early thirties, with thinning hair and an expression of almost permanent dejection, looked round from where he sat at his computer screen in his shirtsleeves.

'What?'

Robert dropped his copy of the *Sun* on to Henry's keyboard. Henry glanced down at it, smoothing it out. He gazed at the headline, then at the photograph of Leo, in disbelief.

'I would have thought plenty of people in the Temple would have been on the phone to you about it,' said Robert.

Henry shook his head slowly as he read the story.

'Then again,' said Robert, 'it's so bad they probably didn't like to.'

Oh, Mr Davies, thought Henry – oh, Mr Davies, what have you gone and done? His heart sank as he digested the details. As though this bunch didn't give him enough grief.

It was bad enough trying to keep their work in order, without them getting their sodding love lives all over the papers. *Continued on pages 5, 6, 7 and 8 . . .* He couldn't bear to look. What would this do to business? A scandal like this was bad publicity, whichever way you looked at it. The work was bound to suffer. Clients didn't like seeing their barristers' faces in the papers, especially not a story like this, beating up his girlfriend, driving her to suicide . . . He glanced back at the picture of Melissa Angelicos. No, not Mr Davies. Not his style. Mind you, whether it was true or not was completely beside the point. Henry groaned aloud.

'Pretty bad, isn't it?' said Robert, agreeably thrilled by the sensation. This was about the most exciting thing that had ever happened in chambers. By and large, barristers were a boring bunch, not given to all the stuff this woman claimed Leo got up to. Bunking off with blokes, for instance – mind you, Robert had always thought there was something a bit fruity about Mr Davies.

A third clerk, Felicity Waller, came through the swing doors at that moment and caught Robert's last remark.

'What's bad?' she asked.

Felicity was a buxom and very pretty twenty-three-year-old, with a cheeky, brisk manner which endeared her to most, if not all, of the barristers at 5 Caper Court. Even those who didn't entirely approve of Felicity's plunging necklines and thigh-skimming skirts were appreciative of the fees she negotiated for them, a skill which Felicity put down to genes inherited from her South London market trader father.

Henry had long nursed a silent, hopeless and unrequited passion for Felicity, and would normally have given her his full attention, particularly as she was wearing a figure-hugging summer dress of some brevity, but today he didn't even look up. He just shook his head and stared despondently at the paper.

Felicity put her cup of coffee down on her desk and came over.

Robert indicated the paper and endeavoured to mask his excitement with a tone of regret. 'Mr Davies has got himself into a bit of trouble.'

'Let's have a look.'

Henry's phone began to ring. He answered it, handing the paper to Felicity, who took it over to her desk.

'Bloody hell . . .' She took in the headline, the picture of Leo, and sank slowly into her seat. She looked long and hard at the picture of the faded blonde which dominated the page, then began to read through the sordid list of her allegations against Leo. That he'd hit her. That he'd had affairs with other people during their relationship, men as well as women. That he'd neglected his son by his ex-wife, failing to turn up on access visits. That his professional life was a mess. That he drank. That he rubbished colleagues. She glanced up at Robert, who'd sidled over to assess her reaction.

'This is crap,' said Felicity. 'It's total and utter crap. Mr Davies isn't like that.'

'Not the point, though, is it?'

'He's a lovely man. He wouldn't do any of this.' Felicity's view of Leo was somewhat coloured by the fact that when her erstwhile boyfriend, Vince, had been up on a manslaughter charge two months ago – through no fault of his own, Felicity always averred – Leo had spared no effort to help her and advise her. Not that it had been of much help, since Vince had gone down for eight years. Still, Mr Davies was her champion, he'd got her this job in the first place, and he was bloody lovely to look at as well, so she would hear no ill of him. Like Henry, she knew in her heart that this was not

Mr Davies's style at all. 'Poor bloke. Not going to do his practice much good, is it?'

'Is he in?' asked Robert.

'No, I haven't seen him all morning – thank God,' said Felicity. 'He's probably got wind of this and is steering well clear. Can you imagine having to walk around the Temple, knowing everyone's seen this and is talking about you? He'll probably lie low for a couple of days.'

Henry, engrossed in morose speculation about the way in which this scandal was likely to tarnish the reputation of 5 Caper Court, clicked on his computer screen and brought up, out of curiosity, the list of tenants who were in chambers that morning, witnessed by the swiping of their electronic tags as they came into the building. There was Leo's name.

'He's in,' said Henry, puzzled.

In fact, at five-thirty that morning, as dawn light pearled the eastern sky and crept across the silent cobbles of the lanes and courtyards of the Temple, Leo had come into chambers to do some work on a skeleton argument in one of his cases. He had parked his Aston Martin in the deserted car park at the bottom of King's Bench Walk and, apologizing to the dosser in the doorway of 5 Caper Court for disturbing his slumber, had come into chambers to enjoy a few hours of steady, uninterrupted work before the telephones began to ring and feet and voices to sound on the stairs. Since no one was aware of his presence, no one had troubled him all morning.

Now, at ten to eleven, fatigued even by his own industrious standards, Leo Davies closed his books, rose, stretched and yawned. His lean figure was trim and athletic for a man in his mid-forties, his features clean-cut and handsome, his blue eyes sharp and intelligent. The premature silvery-grey of his thick hair, in the eyes of Felicity and other admirers, only added to his attractiveness. He stood now at his window, gazing down at the figures hurrying to and fro across Caper Court, his mind paused in a rare state of idleness, and decided to have a coffee and go downstairs to collect his mail and catch up on the gossip.

Down in the clerks' room, speculation was rife.

'D'you think he knows about it?' asked Felicity.

'Dunno,' said Robert. 'Depends. What a way to start the week.'

The door of the clerks' room opened at that moment, and all three clerks turned as Leo came in. They looked at him in horrified uncertainty. The cheerful expression on his face suggested that he knew nothing of this calamity.

'Morning, troops,' said Leo mildly, going to his pigeon-hole to extract the bundle of letters which lay there. Then he glanced round at them in puzzlement, surveying their silent faces. 'Some problem?'

Henry took it upon himself to deliver the blow. He rose from his desk. 'Robert's just brought the paper in, sir. You'd better have a look at it.' He picked up the newspaper from Felicity's desk and handed it to Leo, who took it wonderingly.

They stood in stricken fascination as Leo scanned the front page carefully. His expression didn't falter, except for one moment when he raised a brief and quizzical eyebrow. He might as well have been digesting the contents of an interesting, but not very remarkable brief. They waited.

Leo tossed the paper on to Robert's desk and passed a hand across his brow. He looked up at Henry. 'That's a bit of a nuisance, isn't it?'

'Yes, sir,' replied Henry, somewhat nonplussed by Leo's reaction.

'It's a complete load of balls, of course. Some journalist rang me up a week ago and asked me about the contents of this suicide note, whatever it is, that she'd written, and I told them then. I didn't expect them to print it.' As though the import of it had only just hit him, Leo sat down. 'Holy Christ.'

'It's not good, Mr Davies,' said Henry.

'I knew it was rubbish when I read it,' said Felicity. 'I said, none of this is Mr Davies' style.' She glanced at Robert for support. 'Didn't I?'

Leo gave a wan smile. 'Thank you, Felicity.' He drew the paper towards him again and studied the photograph of Melissa Angelicos. That vindictive bitch. It was like being pursued to the very depths of hell by a madwoman. She'd seemed innocuous enough on their first meeting as co-trustees of a recently opened museum of modern art, but what had seemed like a mild crush on her part had turned, over the course of a few months, into a full-blown obsession. She had stalked him, lain in wait for him outside his flat at night, pestered him with letters and gifts, followed him in her car to his country home, turned up during court proceedings . . . The thing had become a nightmare. It was when she began to harass Rachel, his ex-wife, and their baby son that Leo had taken legal steps to obtain an injunction against her. He had thought that, plus a few quiet threats, had done the trick. But no. A failed suicide attempt, this farrago of lies and fantasy committed to paper and sent off to a daily newspaper which was stupid and evil enough to print it, and she was succeeding in wrecking his life once again. In reality, Melissa was no more than a B-list celebrity – a fading personality from television's intellectual hinterland – but that, coupled with the fact that Leo's involvement in a major fraud case had earned him a flattering profile piece in the *Evening Standard* just over a year ago, had been enough to ensure front-page coverage.

He flicked through the pages to where the story continued, embellished by another picture of himself emerging from the Law Courts, and glanced through the contents. That they had actually had the *gall* . . . Didn't they have any respect for privacy or decency, let alone the truth? He felt a hot surge of anger. He would make those bastards, and Melissa Angelicos, pay for every lying word printed here. He'd have a writ issued before the day was out.

The phone rang and Robert went to answer it. Leo folded up the paper and rose. 'I'm sorry,' he said to Felicity and Henry. 'This isn't going to make life very easy for you people.'

'We'll cope, sir,' said Henry. 'Not the first damage-limitation exercise we've had to carry out.'

'What will you do?' Felicity gazed at Leo with big, anxious eyes.

'The first thing I'm going to do,' said Leo, 'is to go home and consider my options. Field my calls. Don't tell anyone where I am.'

As he left the clerks' room, he passed Simon Barron, a junior tenant, without saying a word. Simon, who had heard about the scandal from friends on his way back from a con in Paper Buildings, gazed after him.

'I hadn't expected to see Leo in chambers today. Not after the news.' He glanced at the clerks. 'I take it you've all heard?'

Henry nodded grimly. 'Mr Davies has only just found out himself. He's going home.'

'Best place for him,' sighed Felicity.

Leo drove back to his flat in Belgravia. The summer air was heavy with the threat of thunder, and the first drops of rain were pattering on the leaves of the plane trees in the quiet garden square as he parked his car in the mews garage. In the flat he opened one of the long windows in the drawing room and let the scent of rain, now splashing heavily on to the pavements and parks, fill the room. He stood there, watching, listening, thinking.

He turned from the window, loosened his tie, and sat down in an armchair. The room was large, high-ceilinged, expensively furnished in a restrained, minimalist fashion, the walls hung with works of modern art from Leo's own collection – and to Leo at that moment it felt nothing like home. The place never had. Like the house where he and Rachel had lived during the brief months of their marriage, he had never felt any proper sense of belonging. Neither to the house, nor to Rachel. Only Stanton, his house in Oxfordshire, felt like a safe haven, though pressure of work meant he'd had precious little time to visit it of late. Now, in this moment of isolation and humiliation, with a hungry world outside feasting on fabricated stories of his licentious doings, he badly wished he was there, safe and far away. He closed his eyes, trying to work his way through his anger to thoughts of how best to deal with the situation. The phone rang several times, but he ignored it.

After twenty minutes, the buzzer to his flat sounded. With a sigh, Leo rose and crossed the room and went to the intercom. 'Yes?'

'Leo, it's me – Camilla.' The voice was light and young, charged with anxiety.

'Come up.' He pressed the buzzer to let her in, and went to the front door.

She stepped out of the lift, rain-soaked, and came into his arms, unquestioning and loving, and hugged him. Touched, he passed his hand lightly over her auburn hair.

'You're very wet.'

'It's stopping now. I ran all the way from the Tube.' She took off her raincoat and Leo hung it up.

'Aren't you meant to be in court today?'

'I am. But when I rang chambers and Felicity said you were here, I had to come. I can't stay long. I've got to be back in court at two.' She hugged him again, then looked at him, eyes wide and sad. 'Oh, Leo . . .'

He essayed a smile. 'Not much fun, is it?'

'There was a copy of the paper in the robing room at the Law Courts. I couldn't believe it . . . I still can't.'

'What does that mean? You don't believe it? Or you don't want to?'

Leo turned and went into the kitchen. Camilla followed him.

'Of course I don't believe it! No one who knows anything about it possibly could. You told me all about her, the way she was harassing you. I was in court with you that day she showed up with her camera – remember? I just don't want other people to believe it.'

'Yes, well . . . there's not a lot you can do about that, unfortunately.'

'But you can.'

'Issue proceedings, you mean? It's not something I ever advise anyone to do lightly. Litigation is a mug's game, as well you know, which is why the mugs pay people like you and me so handsomely to conduct it.' He opened the fridge. 'Can I make you a sandwich or something? Can't sit around in the Court of Appeal on an empty stomach.'

'No, thanks. I'll get something on the way back.' She came over, closed the fridge, and hugged him again.

He sighed and put his arms round her, giving himself up to her ardour and sympathy. 'You are the sweetest thing in the world. I'm glad you came.'

'I called you on my mobile. Why didn't you answer?'

'I assumed it might be some journalist.'

'How would they get your number? Henry wouldn't give it out.'

'True.' He sighed. 'I'm getting paranoid, fairly understandably. Come on –' he took her hand and led her from the kitchen '– I want to sit down and hold you.'

He stretched out on the sofa, Camilla nestling against him. They talked for a while about the newspaper article, about what Leo could do about it. 'The trouble is,' he said, 'I still feel rather numb. It's hard to think properly. The best thing for me right now is you.' He kissed her. 'It seems absurd that you still haven't moved in. I could do with a bit of domestic security.'

'Leo, it's not that easy. I can't just pack up and leave. Jane has to find a new flatmate, and that takes time.'

'I've told you that I'll happily pay dear Jane as much rent as –'

'It's not just that. It's not just money. And it's not just Jane. There are my parents to think about.'

'Oh, God.'

'Leo, look at it from their point of view. How will it sound if I tell them I'm shacking up with some forty-six-year-old? I'm twenty-two. You're older than my mother, for heaven's sake.'

'You could point out to them that I'm a perfectly respectable commercial lawyer, who's –' He paused. 'No, I suppose the respectable bit is shot to pieces, isn't it?' Leo ran his fingers through his silver hair in exasperation. 'Christ, if a libel action is what it takes, then so be it. But you're grown up, for God's sake. Why worry about what your parents think?'

'Because they are my parents! And I love them. I don't

want to upset them.' Leo gazed at her. Twenty-two. From a parental point of view, still not much more than a child. She kissed him. 'I do love you – you know that?'

Leo returned her kiss gently. 'Yes, I believe you do.'

She got up. 'I have to get back to court. Sorry it's such a fleeting visit. I'll see you this evening.'

He lay on the sofa, listening to the sound of the front door closing. He thought about the evening a week ago when he had gone round to her flat. He'd been afraid that he'd lost her, fearful that all the things she'd heard – about his bisexuality, his fling with Anthony, and God knows what else – had estranged her from him for good. Did he now regret the impulse which had prompted him to propose marriage to her? It wasn't a question of not loving her enough. God knows he did . . . But if anyone had told him a few years ago that at forty-six he would be on the point of marrying for a second time, he would have laughed in disbelief. Someone whose sexual appetite ran to men as well as women wasn't exactly ideal husband material. He had spent twenty years cultivating for himself a private life utterly detached from his professional existence, one in which he enjoyed spending the considerable sums he earned in his practice at the Bar, indulging his tastes in clothing, works of art, wine and ridiculously expensive cars. Being tied to someone, unable to do exactly as he pleased, with whomever he pleased, was not his style at all. Which, naturally, was why his marriage to Rachel had come unstuck. One homosexual affair and a fumble with the nanny was probably more than most wives would tolerate in their husbands. Not that his marriage to Rachel had ever been more than one of convenience – his own, at any rate – something to scotch rumours about his sexuality which had, at the time, threatened to harm his professional reputation. And she'd been pregnant. Oliver, his two-year-old son, was the one good thing to have come out of that mess. He had never thought it possible to love another being as much as he did Oliver . . . Beyond Oliver and his own mother, Leo didn't care much for the idea of family.

At least with Rachel he hadn't had to contend with anything more than her mother, and those encounters, while she'd been alive, had been mercifully few. With Camilla, however, he was going to get the full works, he could see that. He rubbed his hands across his face. Parents. He was going to have to meet them. Oh, Lord . . . he really wasn't up for this. It was already beginning to feel oppressive. Not Camilla herself, who was delightful, clever, astonishingly sensuous and touchingly young, but the set-up, the encroaching involvement of other people. A wedding. Relations. She would want babies, eventually. Shades of the family prison-house begin to close upon the ageing rake, thought Leo – and a lot of people would doubtless say it served him bloody well right.

He shouldn't have asked her to marry him. Just to move in. But in thinking that, wasn't he admitting that the thing wasn't necessarily going to be long-term? It was possible that she would grow tired first, feel the need of someone younger, closer to her own age, but in all honesty, the doubts lay with him. He knew himself too well. How long until his notoriously restless gaze fell upon someone – male or female – and he found himself unable to resist the temptation? He loved Camilla, but he didn't trust himself. Just a couple of months ago certain episodes with that departed wretch, Gideon, had forced Leo to the decision that some clean, respectable living was what he needed at his age. For Oliver's sake, if not his own.

He closed his eyes at the recollection of that narrowly

averted scandal. Gideon, now mercifully deceased, had been a rising young star in the Civil Service, and he and Leo had become close for a while. Far too close, in hindsight. Gideon, besides being a heavy gambler with a taste for expensive living which far outstripped his means, had also turned out to have a nice little sideline in blackmail. Leo, it ultimately transpired, had been one of his intended victims, and only Gideon's untimely demise had relieved Leo of the obligation of forking out a hundred thousand pounds to the young wretch. Yes, that incident had certainly served as a reminder that Leo was capable of living far too dangerously. Camilla had seemed the answer to that. Marry her, settle down, live quietly . . . Now, as the reality of what it all involved began to dawn on him, he felt less certain.

With a groan of exasperation, he stood up and paced around the room. Forget Camilla for the moment. Forget about marrying anybody. That could wait. The pressing issue at the moment was what he should do about this hellish thing in the papers, and limiting the damage it was bound to cause. The one person to whom he very much needed to talk was Anthony. There was no one closer. But he had succeeded in damaging that precious relationship through his own irresponsible behaviour. The mistake had been to sleep with him, to let Anthony think there was something more to it than . . . What? Friendship? He doubted if there was any of that left. A week ago Anthony had been ready to leave chambers just to get away from Leo, so hurt and disillusioned was he, and Leo, having spoken to him only once since then – a brief, unhappy exchange which had resolved nothing – had no idea if that was still his firm intention.

He needed to speak to him, to sound him out, to help him decide what to do. He had never gone to Anthony in that way before. Maybe it would help to resolve more than one troublesome issue. He went to the phone and picked it up, and rang chambers, asking to speak to Anthony.

2

After taking Leo's call, Anthony stood up and paced round his room to stretch his long legs. The dark, sensuous good looks which had so attracted Leo four years ago, when Anthony had first come to 5 Caper Court as a raw and nervous pupil, had taken on something of a hard edge over the last year or so. He paused at the window, as he did countless times each day, and gazed with troubled and brooding eyes at the sundial set in the stones of the wall opposite. The conversation with Leo had been brief, perfunctory, and a little puzzling. First Leo had asked if Anthony had seen the papers.

'No,' Anthony had said. 'Not yet. Why?'

'Nothing that need worry you. It's my problem, I'm afraid.' A pause. 'I – I need to talk to someone about it. Which is why I'm ringing you. Have you got an hour or two to spare at the end of the day?'

That was where Anthony had hesitated. He'd told himself not long ago that he wanted nothing more to do with Leo, that that was it, finished. But . . .

'Yes, I suppose so.' He hardly knew why he said it.

'Thanks. I'm at home at the moment. I'll come into chambers around seven, if you don't mind hanging on till then. I don't particularly want to see anyone else.'

That had been the end of the conversation.

Anthony moved away from the window and paced around again. He knew in his heart that he should have said no. How was he ever going to make good his resolution to dissolve the relationship if he was so instantly willing to sit down and discuss Leo's personal problems with him? He wasn't sure he cared to know about any of Leo's problems, anyway. They usually signified the messing-up of other people's lives. The trouble with Leo's fatal attraction was that everyone who got involved with him ended up getting hurt. He himself was no exception. It seemed that four years of the best, the most intense and stimulating friendship he had ever known with another man, had been wrecked by a combination of his own naiveté and Leo's cruelty. Staying the night at Leo's, letting Leo make love to him – he had thought it signalled some transition in their relationship, a step towards something secure and lasting. What a fool he'd been. *'It's only sex, Anthony.'* He recalled Leo casually tapping his cigar on his case before lighting it, narrowing his eyes against the smoke, throwing away the words. Throwing away Anthony's very heart, destroying his belief in Leo. Muscles in Anthony's stomach tightened reflexively as he steeled himself against the memory. He was only one in a long line of victims, after all. No big deal, no big surprise. How long did Camilla think she was going to last? Another nice bit of footwork on Leo's part, moving in on Anthony's ex-girlfriend when he knew he still had feelings for her . . . That was one good reason to leave 5 Caper Court. The place was becoming incestuous, emotionally claustrophobic. But there, too, was another instance of his own vacillation. Having made up his mind to leave and find a tenancy in another set of chambers where he wouldn't have to see Leo every day, here he still was, undecided. It was pathetic. He hated himself.

If he'd had any sense, let alone strength of purpose, he would have told Leo to stick his problems, find some other fool to lay them off on – Sarah, for instance. She was always eager and willing where Leo was concerned. But an unquenchable part of him longed to see Leo, to be for just a little while the sole focus of his time and attention. That was the real reason why he'd said yes. In spite of everything, it pleased Anthony to be needed by Leo. He reached out to his computer, saved the work he'd been doing, and shut it down. Better go and rustle up a newspaper and find out more about this problem, whatever it might be.

On the way downstairs he ran into Jeremy Vane, a senior member of chambers, a loud and self-important individual for whom Anthony didn't care a great deal.

Jeremy stopped him. 'Heard the latest scandal about Leo, have you? Got himself splashed all over the front of the tabloids – some woman who tried to top herself on his account.' Jeremy thrust fat fingers into the tight pockets of his waistcoat. 'Whole thing's bloody ghastly. Doesn't reflect at all well on chambers.'

Anthony's mind reeled a little at this information, but he managed to reply, 'I shouldn't imagine it's doing Leo a lot of good, either.' What woman could this be? Knowing Leo, one of many. It must be pretty grim if it had made the front pages.

'Man's only got himself to blame. The kind of unregulated life he leads. It was always going to rebound on his professional standing some day.'

'Jeremy, if I didn't know how much you cared about the image of chambers, I'd say you actually sound pleased.'

Jeremy raised his eyebrows. 'Merely saying that it's about time Leo had his come-uppance.' He marched on upstairs to his room.

Anthony went into the clerks' room, and found a huddle of barristers mulling over Robert's copy of the *Sun*.

'Seen this?' David Liphook, a stocky blond man in his mid-thirties, passed the paper to Anthony.

Anthony took the paper and scanned the front page,

absorbing the contents. He flicked through quickly to the inside pages. How much of this could possibly be true? He felt cold at the possibility. No, it couldn't be . . . But he'd thought he'd known Leo, and just look how far he'd been deceived. Come to think of it, he remembered a conversation with Leo several months ago, one in which he'd admitted knowing this woman Angelicos, having some kind of a fling with her . . .

'I haven't a clue what to make of it,' said David, and shook his head.

'I personally think the woman's off her head,' said Michael Gibbon, leaning his thin frame against Robert's desk and folding his arms.

'Very possibly,' said Will Cooper. He looked languidly round at the others. 'But how much close scrutiny does Leo's private life bear?' He shrugged.

'The fact is,' said Michael, 'one month ago Leo took out an injunction against Melissa Angelicos to stop her harassing him. Doesn't that tell you something?'

Will raised his eyebrows. 'It tells me there's no smoke without fire.'

'They were co-trustees of Chay Cross's museum,' said Michael. 'Anthony knows all about it.' This was a reference to Anthony's father, ex-hippy and waster, who had managed, thanks to the caprices of the modern art world, to reinvent himself as one of the leading postmodernists of the day. The wealth attendant upon such fashionable success had enabled Chay Cross, with the help of some local authority funding, to open a museum of modern art in a defunct Shoreditch brewery, of which Melissa Angelicos and Leo had been trustees, along with others.

'I'd hardly say that,' said Anthony. 'I barely knew the woman.'

'What about Leo?' asked David.

'Well, he *knew* her, obviously . . .'

'Do we mean in the biblical sense?'

Anthony was at a loss. Before he could find words, Michael Gibbon cut in. 'Look, whatever the nature of the relationship, I'm pretty much sure from what Leo told me that these allegations against him are pure fabrication.' He tapped the paper. 'Leo is quoted as saying as much.'

'What d'you reckon?' David asked Anthony.

Anthony folded the paper and handed it back to David. 'I don't know any more about it than the rest of you – not as much as Michael, at any rate – but I don't believe a single word this woman has written. If Leo says she's lying, then that's good enough for me.'

'Too bloody right! Good for you, Mr Cross!' Felicity, who had been listening, banged down her pen and got up from her desk. 'I don't know how anyone can think otherwise, frankly. You lot should stick up for one another.'

'It's not a question of loyalty,' said Will, 'so much as veracity. I doubt if even the *Sun* would print this kind of thing if there wasn't something behind it.'

'That's rather a naive point of view, if I may say so,' said David. At that moment Henry came through the swing doors, balancing his lunchtime packet of sandwiches on top of a steep bundle of papers. 'What's your take on all this, Henry?' asked David, tapping the paper.

Henry waved the paper away wearily and took off his jacket. He sat down, adjusted his red braces, opened his sandwiches and sighed. 'I don't know where he finds the time, to be honest. Not with the amount of work he has.'

'You're not saying you believe this rubbish they've written, are you?' Felicity rounded on Henry.

Henry held up his hands in defence. 'I'm not saying

28

anything. I don't care one way or the other, frankly. Mr Davies's personal life is his own – it's when it starts damaging business that I mind.' He shook his head. 'This isn't going to do his practice any good.'

'I think that's where you're wrong,' said Felicity. 'Even bad publicity is publicity. You wait and see.'

Henry shook his head. 'Anyway, I've got enough on my plate without worrying about Mr Davies' practice. We've got four new tenants and a clerk landing on us tomorrow morning, don't forget.'

'As if I needed reminding.' And then Felicity swore with such unladylike vehemence that Henry was quite startled. He had yet to fathom why she was getting so worked up about the arrival of this new clerk, Peter Weir. So far as Henry could see, he was a perfectly nice bloke.

Anthony spent the afternoon considering the applicability of the Brussels Convention to a French arbitration dispute, spinning out the time, punctuating it with cups of coffee. From half past five onwards, people drifted out of chambers, and by seven the building was empty. Anthony, whose sash window was open to the summer evening air, swivelled round and glanced down into Caper Court. Sure enough, punctual as ever, Leo appeared from the cloisters and crossed the flag-stones. He was wearing dark blue trousers and an open-necked shirt, and carried a copy of the evening paper. Anthony swiv-elled back round and waited, listening for the sound of Leo's feet on the stair. He remembered a time when that swift, springing tread, taking the stairs an unmistakable two at a time, had set his heart racing, when he couldn't wait to see Leo's face, hear his voice. It had been a happy anticipation then. Now, the anticipation was dark, tainted. The love he had felt for Leo had lost its innocence, just as he had.

A few moments later Leo rapped on the door and came in. 'Hi.'

Anthony merely nodded by way of reply. Leo sat down in one of the chairs at the long conference table which abutted Anthony's desk, chucking his copy of the *Standard* on to the polished surface. 'I take it you saw the *Sun* earlier today?'

'I saw it at lunchtime.'

'There's nothing in the evening paper, thank God. I've no idea if any of the dailies will follow it up tomorrow.' He glanced at Anthony. 'I suppose it's all over the place?'

Anthony nodded. 'You're the talk of chambers.'

'And the entire Inns of Court, no doubt,' sighed Leo.

'Have you done anything about it yet?'

'I haven't issued any writs, if that's what you mean. That's what I wanted to talk to you about.'

'Why me?' asked Anthony. He gazed frankly at Leo. 'Libel isn't my specialism. There are plenty of other people better equipped to advise you than I am.'

Leo stood up and thrust his hands into his pockets. 'You know I don't need advice on the law, Anthony. I need to speak to you as a friend.'

'And you think I'm your friend?'

Leo paced the room, tapping the spines of books, inspecting the pictures which lined the walls. Long moments passed.

Leo turned at last. 'You tell me. Are you?'

It was Anthony's turn to be silent. He swivelled his chair slowly from side to side, looking at Leo long and hard. It exasperated him, infuriated him, that Leo should take him so much for granted.

'I don't think you can ever know what it cost me to –' He stopped. Leo could never understand. Leo was so cool with his sexuality. He wouldn't ever understand how it was to grow up thinking you were a nice, straight boy, only to find out that things weren't that simple, that someone like Leo could lead you down another path, confusing you, making you think and want things you had never dreamed of, then leaving you high and dry. A lost boy.

He tried again. 'Put it this way, Leo – I haven't got anything to thank you for.'

'I know.' The shadows in the corner of the room where Leo stood made his face look tired and grim. 'I shouldn't have let it happen. And I'm sorry.'

'Sorry?'

'That it's caused this – this bad feeling between us. It was never my intention to hurt you. I thought you knew the terms.'

Anthony shook his head. 'No, it turns out I didn't. But it doesn't matter. I don't want to go back over that. It's in the past now, and it's going to stay there.' He paused. 'Don't ask about friendship. We're both here now. If you want my advice, you can have it, for what it's worth.'

'Thank you.' Leo crossed the room and sat down again. 'I've been going over the whole thing all afternoon, trying to decide what to do.' He let out a sigh. 'Eight hours ago I was all set to sue. The entire story is the most pathetic pack of lies, after all. The woman is not only obsessive and deluded, she's also a calculating and vindictive bitch. This is a deliberate act of personal sabotage.'

Anthony shrugged. 'She must have a motive. And I assume there's a basis in truth, that you had some kind of relationship with her. I seem to remember you telling me a few months ago that you'd gone back to her place after a few drinks – something like that.'

'Not one of the cleverest things I've ever done, admittedly. But absolutely nothing happened. Quite the opposite. She had ideas, but I wasn't interested. And that, I suspect, is where it all started. I won't go into details, but I imagine she found the episode somewhat humiliating, and never quite forgave me. Hence the vendetta.'

'Hence the suicide attempt?'

'Hardly. Still, if you ask me, it's a pity she failed.'

'Except that that would have damned you completely.'

'True.'

'So there's no truth in anything she says?'

'Not a single word. She has a diseased imagination.' He glanced at Anthony. 'Did you believe there was any truth in it?'

Anthony shook his head. 'No. I don't think anyone who knows you could possibly believe it.'

'Which only leaves the great British public. A few million good reasons to sue her and the paper.'

'Or not, as the case may be.'

'Meaning?'

Anthony picked up a length of red tape from the brief he'd been working on, and wound it round his fingers. 'Think about it. In a few days' time, the great British public will have other preoccupations. The *Sun* will be shafting some other poor bastard. Things move on, people's memories are short.'

'Not in the microcosmic world that you and I work in.'

'That's something you may just have to live with. The alternative, as I see it, is infinitely worse. Imagine. You sue for libel. Fine. Nothing happens for a few months. Then bang, just when everyone had more or less forgotten the original story, the case comes up for trial, and the publicity starts all over again. Only this time your private life comes in for some serious, *real* scrutiny. For each and every one of that woman's allegations that you deny, the other side will try to find some basis in truth. Affairs with other men? Well, ask yourself, Leo – do you really want the best lawyers the *Sun* can buy investigating that particular aspect of your life? Then there are all the things she says about how you neglected Oliver, didn't show up on visits – that means the spotlight gets turned on Rachel and Oliver. The allegations about your professional life – all untrue, but do you think your clients are going to enjoy seeing their QC held up to the light and given a thorough inspection and overhaul?' Anthony chucked the red ribbon on to his desk. 'I don't know why I'm bothering to tell you all this. You already know it.'

Leo nodded. 'But the point is, if I do nothing, then everyone assumes that every word she's written is true. Can I afford to let that happen?'

'The people who know you, the people who matter, don't believe it. As for the rest, the tabloid readers, they're not really interested in you. It's just another titillating story to spice up breakfast or the journey to work. They don't actually know or care about you. They won't remember your name this time next week. If you sue, things will be a lot worse in the long run. Come on, Leo, you know it.'

'You think I should just let it lie?'

Anthony nodded.

Leo stood up and began to pace again. 'It makes me feel so bloody impotent.'

'There must be something you can do to make good the damage without actually suing. You must know people. Isn't there some journalist who owes you a favour? Someone who can make sure a little more exposure is given to some truths relating to Melissa Angelicos?'

'Such as?'

'Well, if you're not the reason why her career is on the slide – what's the real reason? Then there's the fact that she's been harassing you to the point where you had to take out an injunction – that's worth a bit of coverage.'

Leo walked to the window, brooding on this. Certainly there were strings that might be pulled. 'Yes . . . Yes, I might be able to do a few things in that direction . . .'

'If someone came to you for advice, you'd counsel them against suing – you know you would.'

Leo nodded slowly. 'Okay, right. I'll explore some other avenues first . . .' He turned and glanced at Anthony. 'Do you feel like going for a drink, or did you have plans?'

Anthony swivelled his chair and looked up at Leo. One glance from the blue eyes, one smile of invitation, and he felt his resolve weakening. Why had he been so hell-bent on keeping Leo at a distance? Fear of getting hurt again. No one was immune to that. He might as well just live for the here and now, enjoy what scraps of Leo's companionship he could. 'All right.' He put away his papers, picked up his jacket, and they went downstairs and left chambers together.

'You've talked me out of issuing a flurry of writs,' said Leo, as they crossed Caper Court. 'What are the chances of my dissuading you from leaving chambers?'

Anthony made no immediate reply. Their discussion about whether or not Leo should sue for libel had been pretty perfunctory; Anthony suspected that Leo's mind had already been made up before he came. He'd wanted an excuse to see Anthony alone, to neutralize the atmosphere so that he could broach this subject. As they came out into Middle Temple Lane, Anthony turned to Leo. 'Feel like braving the stares and whispers of Middle Temple Bar?'

'Not much,' said Leo. 'But it's better than skulking off to some anonymous pub like a guilty man. Come on.'

There was a light buzz and a few more interested glances than usual in the crowded bar when Leo appeared, but no frosty silence or disdainful stares. A number of people went out of their way to greet him, as if in defiance of the scandal. Leo and Anthony took their drinks out to a bench in a quiet corner of the rose garden.

'That wasn't too bad,' said Anthony.

'Members of the Bar are far too civilized to behave in any other way. It's the impact it's going to have on my practice that I'm worried about. Anyway, forget all that.' Leo leaned back and sipped his Scotch. 'You haven't answered my earlier question. Are you still determined to leave chambers?'

'I don't know.' Anthony took a drink of his beer. 'I'm looking around, certainly.'

'I don't want you to go. Nobody does.'

'So you said before,' replied Anthony shortly. 'I've got my reasons for wanting to leave.'

'Can't stand the sight of me?'

Anthony looked very directly at Leo. 'Quite the opposite. As you bloody well know.'

The effect on Leo of that gaze, the depth of feeling in those brown eyes, was profound. But the risks in becoming involved with Anthony were too great for him to contemplate. 'Come on, Anthony, can't we put things back the way they were? For the sake of our friendship? It means a lot to me.'

Anthony looked away. 'It's not just you and me. It's other things. Camilla, for instance. Why did you have to start an affair with her? Of all people, why her?'

Leo took a small silver cigar case from his pocket, and flicked it open. 'I happen to be pretty serious about Camilla.' He lit a cigar and blew out a stream of smoke.

Anthony gave a small, wincing smile. 'Right. For how long, though? You have a famously short emotional attention span.'

Leo said nothing for a few seconds. Then he nodded. 'That's the worst of it. The fact is, I don't know how it'll work out.'

Anthony turned his glass round in his hands for a few seconds, thinking. It was no longer important that Camilla had once been his girlfriend. That was history now. Leo could do as he liked; so could she. 'For God's sake, don't make her suffer the way you made me.'

A brief silence fell between them, broken only by the occasional drowse of insects in the roses, and gusts of chatter and laughter from students further up the garden. Leo thought he detected, in the way Anthony spoke, some suggestion that he was beginning to reconcile recent past events. When he spoke at last, he said, 'In return, promise me you'll reconsider leaving. Nobody wants you to. Especially me. Whatever has happened between us, I need you.'

But not, thought Anthony, in the right way. He sipped his drink and said nothing. 'Anyway,' Leo went on with a smile, 'let's forget about personal problems for a while. Tell me what you think about this new bunch joining us tomorrow.'

Anthony shrugged. 'I only really know Marcus. He's all right. Fancies himself a bit. Then again, he's terrifyingly bright. That's probably his main problem – he's very keen to let you know how much he knows, how right he always is.'

'I think I deflated that particular balloon a couple of months back. He was on the other side in a case involving freight forwarders. Not very significant, not much money involved, but the boy had really gone over the top in preparation. Didn't see the wood for the trees, as it turned out. You're right – he didn't take that particular defeat very well. I put that down to his age. He'll learn that he can't win every case.'

'He'd like to.'

'Well, that's a good sign. Maybe he'll have mellowed a bit by the time he becomes our first black law lord.'

'You think?'

'Oh, yes. If the lords spiritual and temporal still exist in thirty years' time, that is.'

'As for the others, I can't say. Maurice Faber has a pushy reputation, but I don't know him personally. Roger Fry's a decent enough bloke, by all accounts. David gets on well with him, which must be a good sign. Ann Halliday's very able, isn't she?'

Leo nodded. 'She can be quite formidable, the kind of person that others often underestimate. To their cost. I suspect she was under-employed at Three Wessex Street, which is why she's made the move. I've known her a long time. We were at Bar School together. Nice girl. Quite good-looking once, but she's let herself go a bit.' Leo sipped his drink reflectively.

Anthony gave him a wry glance. No doubt Leo had once considered Ann Halliday worth the effort. Perhaps he'd even made the effort. Few people of any passing attraction escaped Leo's promiscuous attentions.

For the next half-hour they talked idly of the respective merits of the new tenants, and exchanged chambers' gossip, until Anthony felt a return of the peaceful, familiar pleasure he had always derived from being with Leo.

By the time they parted, around half past eight, Leo felt pretty sure that he had managed to restore something of the old equilibrium, and that Anthony would think twice about leaving. An interesting exercise in subliminal persuasion, but not exactly a difficult one.

On the kitchen table in the house in Newbury which Leo's ex-wife, Rachel, shared with her lover, Charles Beecham, lay a well-thumbed copy of the *Sun*. Charles had picked it up that morning at the village shop. It was not a paper he would normally have bought, but the headline caught his eye, and when he realized that the story concerned Leo, he hastily purchased a copy and made his way back from the village very slowly indeed, reading as he walked. As a writer and presenter of popular historical television programmes – his latest project was an American commission concerning Anglo-American historical relations, which took him off to the States every couple of weeks – and a not particularly industrious academic, Charles's days at home were spent spasmodically loafing and working. Today all thoughts of work vanished entirely, and it soon became clear that loafing wouldn't be on the agenda, either.

Charles's initial reaction to the story had been one of incredulous amusement. He had once been a client of Leo's and liked him enormously, and didn't believe one word of what he read. It was only when the first importunate journalist arrived at the house and tried to doorstep him with questions about Rachel and Leo that Charles realized how serious the repercussions of the story, false or not, might be. This was bad news not just for Leo, but for anyone close to him. The phone began to ring so incessantly that Charles had to take it off the hook. By lunchtime, four journalists and two photographers were camped outside the gates of the house at the bottom of the drive. Oliver, Rachel's two-year-old son from her marriage to Leo, was due to go to a friend's house down the road for tea, but the nanny was reluctant to run the gauntlet of shouting reporters. The household felt besieged.

As soon as Rachel had arrived home at the end of the day, Charles could tell from her face that she was already aware of the paper and its contents. Unlike Charles, her reaction had been one of indignation and fury. Whether she believed the story or not, Rachel blamed Leo for the fact that it had found its way into the papers. According to her, there had to be some foundation to it. She had been married to Leo; she knew him. Charles thought this all rather unfair, and was inclined to take Leo's part. After all, the poor sod was even quoted as denying all the allegations quite comprehensively. It was now eight-twenty, and they had been talking about it for two hours.

Charles, tall and rangy, paced the kitchen and ran his fingers through the greying-blond curls so beloved by female viewers of his documentaries. 'Talking about it isn't going to make any difference. I'm hungry. I'd like to have some supper.' He turned to Rachel, who stood by the sink like a martyred Madonna, her dark, silky hair framing her pale, angry face. 'It's not really our problem, in the long run.'

'Not our problem? With reporters outside the house all day long?'

'They've gone now. Come on – the story's a one-day wonder. They won't come back. At least, I very much doubt they will.'

'I have to speak to Leo. I'm going to call him now.'

'Why? The poor guy's probably had a bad enough day, and I don't get the impression you intend to offer him your commiserations.'

'Bloody right I don't! This mess is of his making, it's affecting us, and I want to find out what he intends to do about it!' She turned and picked up the phone.

Charles sighed. At times like these, a stiff drink was the only answer. He poured himself a gin and tonic and watched as Rachel stabbed at the phone buttons. He knew why she was calling Leo. There were the ostensible reasons, like finding out what he intended to do, and giving a little vent to her wrath, but the real truth was Rachel hungered for contact with Leo. She wanted to speak to him, for whatever reason. And this gave her a solid pretext. Charles was well aware of all this. He had known it for as long as he had known Rachel. Not that it was something she would ever admit to – not even to herself. She gave Charles love, in that she gave him time and affection, but Leo had always been a dominant presence. Charles had always assumed it was something she would get over, with time. But lately, with their own relationship undergoing difficulties and uncertainties, he had begun to wonder whether Rachel was ever going to fall out of love with Leo.

Leo drove back to Belgravia, feeling worn out. It had been a bastard of a day. He wanted nothing more than to excise the demons of the past twelve hours, even if only on a temporary basis. What he badly needed, he thought, as he parked his car in the mews and walked round to the flat, was to find Camilla sprawled on the long sofa, looking suitably and gravely schoolgirlish, ready to be undressed and made love to over some duration. One of his favourite pastimes, at the moment, was finding novel ways of shocking and exciting her in the same instant. He took particular pleasure in provoking the incredibly sensual expression of wide-eyed perturbation that she wore at such moments, enjoying the sensation of being both aroused and amused by her. That, at any rate, would take his mind off his problems for an hour, at least.

He threw the car keys on to the hall table and went into the drawing room. She was there, as he had hoped she'd be, reclining in a position of innocent invitation, damp and sweet-smelling from a recent shower, flicking with the remote control through the channels on Leo's wide-screen television.

'Just what I need,' murmured Leo, sinking on to the sofa next to her and slipping his hand into her bathrobe to find the comforting, voluptuous softness of her breast. She gave a small sigh of pleasure, arched her body slightly towards him, and then, just as Leo was about to kiss her, said, 'I had a really horrible conversation with my parents just before you came in.'

'Oh?' Leo immediately felt depressed. It wasn't what he wanted to hear at this particular moment. In an attempt to change the subject, he slid his hand down between her thighs.

But she merely wriggled with faint impatience and moved away. She wasn't going to be deflected, he could tell. 'What about?' he sighed.

'Moving in with you. They're not keen.'

'Why worry what they think? You're a big, grown-up girl. And a very sexy one, too . . .' He bent his head to flick his tongue lightly over one nipple, which had the satisfactory effect of making her gasp slightly, but she moved his head gently away and carried on talking.

Leo gave up, closing his eyes to listen.

'I don't like doing anything that upsets them. I'm very close to them. They don't like the fact you're so old.'

'You make me sound like bloody Methuselah. I'm only forty-six.'

'It's not just that. What happens when they put two and two together, and realize you're the same Leo Davies who's just had his name and face all over the papers?'

'Mmm.'

'They want to meet you.'

'Oh, Christ.'

'Well, what's the problem with that? If we're going to be married, you *have* to meet them.'

He was going to have to find a way to tell her that they

should put the marriage idea on hold. Not that he didn't love her . . . She was infinitely lovable, if only she would shut up for a moment and let him get on with it.

'I can't meet them. Not this week. Not next week. Not next month, come to that.'

'Why?'

'You yourself brought up the subject of my *scandalum magnatum*. If the thought of you living with me appals them, they're not exactly going to relish having me as a son-in-law, are they?'

She said nothing. Leo contemplated her, then pushed the soft auburn hair away from her face. 'Can we stop this conversation? I had hoped you were going to take my mind off things for a bit. Something I very badly need.' He brought his mouth to hers, kissed her long and hard, and was gratified when she took his hand from her face and drew it down across her body between her legs, gasping faintly at his touch. Just as he was wondering whether his back could cope with a lovemaking session on the sofa, or whether he should take her through to the bedroom, the phone trilled next to them.

'Oh, God . . .' Camilla reached out a hand.

'Don't answer it.' He kissed her again.

'I can't concentrate.' She reached out and picked the phone up before he could stop her. He suspected she thought it might be her mother. He rolled away.

'Hello?' After a second she handed the phone to Leo.

'Leo? It's Rachel.'

'Rachel.' Leo sighed inwardly. His ex-wife had exquisite timing. 'How are you?'

'Not great. But I don't suppose you are either.'

'You saw the paper.'

'Of course I saw the paper.'

'It's all rubbish.' He glanced up as Camilla rose from the sofa, pulling her dressing-gown around her, and left the room.

'Is it?'

'Oh, Christ, here we go . . . Rachel, you *know* it is. The woman is a fantasist, an obsessive. I had to get an injunction to –'

'Leo, my only concern is for Oliver.'

'What's Oliver got to do with it?'

'I've had reporters outside the house all day! Beth couldn't even take him out for a walk!'

'That is regrettable. For that, I am very sorry. But I had no idea any of this was going to happen.'

'Everyone else has to suffer for the appalling indiscretions you commit in your personal life –'

'Rachel, did you ring me up just to have a go at me? I'm very sorry about the reporters. I'm very sorry your name got into the papers. I'm very sorry that she told such godawful lies about myself and Oliver. All in all, I'm very bloody sorry for myself right at this moment. Okay?' There was silence at the other end. The old story, thought Leo. She had this need to provoke an emotional response in him. It couldn't be love, so anything else would do.

'What are you going to do?' Her voice was quieter.

'I'm not going to do a damn thing.'

'But if it's all as libellous as you say –'

'Thanks for the "if". Believe me, were I to issue proceedings, we'd all be sorrier in the long run. You, me and Oliver. As a lawyer, you should know that.'

'Yes.' She sounded even more subdued. 'Yes, you're right.' He heard her sigh. 'It's so unpleasant. Everyone at work –'

'I know. Believe me, I know. I haven't had the best day myself.'

'You still manage to find yourself a little feminine consolation, I notice.'

'Rachel –'

'Sorry.' She was struggling with something. Tears? Anxiety? He had no idea. She always wound herself up by calling him like this, these futile exchanges . . . 'Look,' she went on, 'can we meet up for lunch sometime soon?'

'If you like. I intend to keep a low profile for the rest of this week, but perhaps we can do something the following week. I'll have a look in my diary and let you know. By the way, I take it I'm having Oliver this weekend?'

'Yes. Can you pick him up before ten on Saturday? Charles and I are going to France for the weekend.'

'Right.' Leo was momentarily surprised by this. 'I thought you and he –'

'That's something I'll tell you about when I see you.'

'Fine. And look – I'm sorry about the publicity, this wretched woman. The last thing in the world I want is for you and Oliver to suffer.'

'I know.' She sighed. 'It's far worse for you. I only hope it isn't going to damage your practice.'

From the maintenance point of view, I'll bet you do, thought Leo. 'No, I hope not. Bye.'

'Bye.'

He hung up the phone and leaned back, closing his eyes. He was aware of Camilla snuggling up next to him. He remained as he was, letting her unfasten his shirt, then the waistband of his trousers. 'Shall we pick up where we left off?' said Camilla, parting her robe and kissing him.

A few moments ago he would have thought himself incapable of arousal for the rest of the evening, but he was wrong. She was turning into a delightfully skilful lover. Given how gauche and unadventurous she had been just a few weeks ago, Leo felt he'd done wonders with her. It was just a question of working out exactly what to do with her in the long run.

Rachel put the phone down. She stood for a moment by the desk, staring out at the glimmering summer dusk, then became aware of her own reflection in the panes, her pale face, dark, sleek hair around her shoulders, the strained and tense expression on her face. She made an effort to relax. She hated so much hearing another woman's voice on the phone when she rang Leo. Another woman sharing his time, his bed, enjoying his company and his affection, all that she had lost.

Charles came through from the kitchen, stood behind her and kissed her neck, adding his reflection to hers. Maybe if he were a bastard, just like Leo, she would love him as much. But it was beyond Charles to be anything but kind and sweet.

'How was he?' he asked.

'Oh, robust as ever.' Rachel sighed. 'Not going to do a thing about it.'

'Did you expect there would be writs flying in all directions?'

'Leo knows that would be worse for us all in the long run. Just imagine what a field day the media would have with a libel action, when it came to trial. No, he intends to ride it out, so far as I can tell. Which is what we'll have to do, too.'

'Poor bastard.'

'Please, don't start feeling sorry for Leo. I know you like him, but I've no doubt this predicament is partly of his own making. He can't be entirely blameless.'

'Oh, come on. He's going to have to suffer the fallout, professionally.'

'I know. I can imagine a lot of potential clients will run a mile from instructing him now.'

In her £2,000-a-night hotel suite, Adriana Papaposilakis, somewhat late in the day, was reading a copy of the *Sun*. She flicked back through the pages and scanned once again the features of the QC who was at the centre of the scandalous story about this poor television presenter. Very handsome. Quite remarkably so. He was also apparently amoral and licentious to an extraordinary degree, if the story was to be believed, but given the average wronged woman's propensity for vengeful hysterics, Adriana doubted if the portrait was strictly accurate. Accurate or not, to her such qualities weren't without their attraction. Dangerous and challenging men were few and far between, in her personal experience. Her own power and wealth – and beauty, of course – seemed to have an emasculating effect upon them, rendering them soft, easy and ultimately tiresome. This man looked more formidable and interesting than most. How useful, too, that he happened to be a commercial barrister of the first rank. She wondered why she hadn't come across him before. He would be a thrilling change from the dry, boring lawyers who generally handled the affairs of her multi-million-pound Greek shipping line. Just the man to help her with the vexing matter of the insurers who were refusing to pay out on the loss of her yacht. She smiled, yawned, ruffled her blonde hair with a small and delicate hand, then reached for a pen to note down the name. Leo Davies.

3

Henry came into chambers especially early the next morning to oversee the smooth settling in of the new tenants. On the steps outside he encountered a small number of journalists and photographers, clamouring for information about Leo.

'I very much doubt if Mr Davies will be in chambers today,' Henry informed them sternly, 'so you can get off my steps and stop wasting your time.'

When he peered out of the waiting-room window half an hour later, they were still there.

'They'll probably wait out there all day, on the off-chance,' remarked Felicity. 'Nothing better to do.'

'Has anyone spoken to Mr Davies since yesterday morning?' asked Henry.

'He rang late yesterday afternoon and said he wouldn't be in for the rest of this week. Asked me to rearrange his cons, and would I look at his diary and see if he could manage –' Felicity stopped suddenly, picked up her papers and turned away.

Henry, surprised by the abrupt truncation of their conversation, looked round to see a tall, sharply dressed man in his early thirties coming into the clerks' room. It was Peter Weir, the new clerk who was joining chambers with the tenants from 3 Wessex Street, and Henry was very glad to see him. Not only had they badly needed a new pair of hands for some months, but Henry also hoped that Peter's confident, assertive manner would be good for business.

'Morning,' said Peter cheerfully. He and Henry shook hands.

'Good to see you,' said Henry. 'We've got a desk all ready for you. Here we are . . .'

It didn't take long for Henry to familiarize Peter with the computer system and take him through the working set-up of the clerks' room, but while doing so he was conscious that Felicity was studiously avoiding any contact with Peter. She hadn't even said hello to him. When Peter eventually went off to take some papers to the new tenants and acquaint himself with the layout of chambers, Henry turned to Felicity. 'What's got into you?'

Felicity looked at him, stony-faced. 'Nothing.' She picked up a bundle of faxes and left the room.

'Will someone tell me,' Henry appealed to Robert, 'what's going on?'

'According to Sarah —' At that instant, Robert's phone began to ring. A blonde girl came into the clerks' room, and Robert gestured in her direction. 'There's Sarah. Ask her about it. She knows.' He picked up the phone.

'Good morning, Henry,' said Sarah Coleman breezily. 'I see the gentlemen of the press are decorating the front steps.' Sarah was one of three pupils in training at 5 Caper Court — though in Sarah's case she had already decided that the amount of time and effort involved in being a barrister was far from worth it. She had only taken up the pupillage because of Leo, with whom she had a long-standing and unorthodox relationship, and because it had seemed an amusing thing to do at the time. Now she was counting the time until her pupillage ended in September, and casting around for other things to do with her life.

'I wish they'd bugger off,' said Henry peevishly. 'Tell me — what's the problem between Felicity and the new clerk, Peter? Robert says you know.'

Sarah smiled. Poor old Henry, doggedly devoted to Fliss,

and always the last to know what she was up to. She raised her eyebrows. 'I must say I was surprised when I heard you'd taken Peter Weir on. Clearly you had no idea.'

'About what?'

'He and Fliss were having a bit of a fling until recently. I don't think she's exactly thrilled that you've recruited him. In fact, I suspect she'll be looking round for another job very soon.'

Henry was stunned. Felicity and Peter Weir? So he was the mysterious man whom she'd been seeing, who'd made her look so radiantly happy all those weeks.

'But he's married.'

Sarah shrugged. 'These things do happen.' She sighed. 'Pity you didn't realize sooner.'

Henry sat down at his desk in dismay, taking it all in. He had no illusions about Felicity, had never really harboured any hopes that she might reciprocate his feelings, but he had always thought better of her than this. An affair with a married man, one with a family, too . . . Not that he wished to sit in judgment on anyone. He just couldn't help feeling disappointed. And miserably jealous, if he was honest. For all her coarse language and immodest dress sense, he loved Felicity. The thought that Peter Weir had –

Felicity came back in at that moment, stopping that particular train of thought. Henry regarded her with a heavy heart. Leaving aside his own feelings, as head clerk he couldn't tolerate an atmosphere. It didn't do to have any animosity in the clerks' room, otherwise things couldn't run smoothly. He went over to Felicity's desk.

'Can we have a word?' Felicity glanced up at him and nodded moodily. 'Let's go and get a coffee,' said Henry, and she got up and followed him out to the privacy of the small kitchen.

'Now,' said Henry, when he had poured them both some

coffee, 'I don't want to know the ins-and-outs of whatever was going on with you and Peter Weir –' Fliss made a face and sipped her coffee '– but I think we need to sort the present situation out. I can't have you going around not talking to him.'

'What d'you expect me to do? How can I behave decently towards someone who did what he did? I'd never have gone near him if I'd known he was married – and with kids. Bastard.'

'You didn't know?'

'Course I didn't. I'm not some kind of home wrecker.' Felicity's eyes grew moist. Henry's ever-tender heart tipped a little. 'I wish you'd told me you were thinking of taking him on,' added Felicity. 'It might have spared us a lot of trouble.'

Henry was about to say something suitably pompous about it being the head clerk's place to make decisions without reference to junior clerks, but he thought better of it. He sighed. 'Perhaps. I'm sorry. He seemed a logical choice. He knows this new lot, and he's very able.'

'Oh, yeah. Sure.'

'Look, I don't want bad feeling in the clerks' room. I can do without that. We all can. I'm asking you to make an effort to be polite to him. Can you do that?'

Felicity shrugged. 'Dunno. For as long as I have to, I suppose.'

'What does that mean?' Henry felt a hollow sense of apprehension. He had often consoled himself with the thought that, even if his love for Felicity was doomed to remain forever unrequited, at least he got to see her every day. If she were to go, his life would become barren, meaningless.

'Henry, I don't think I can stand having to see his smarmy face every day. I might start looking round for another job.'

In that moment, as in so many moments, Henry wished he could take his courage in his hands and tell her how he felt, let a torrent of true and passionate feeling pour forth. But of course he wouldn't. She already knew, anyway – he could see it in her eyes. It wouldn't change the situation. Probably make her more likely to leave, if anything.

'Well, I hope it won't come to that. I value you. Very much.'

Felicity looked at Henry's sad eyes. God, he was a nice bloke. Nicest she knew. She hated to see him look so miserable. 'Don't worry.' She laid a light hand on his shoulder and gave his cheek a quick peck. 'I'll try to be civil to the bastard in the meantime.' She picked up her coffee and went back to the clerks' room.

Later that afternoon, most of the inhabitants of 5 Caper Court drifted in to Inner Temple Common Room for afternoon tea. It was a quaint and useful ritual, a way of relaxing and chatting with people with whom one might normally exchange only the briefest of greetings, in spite of sharing the same chambers.

Marcus, who had spent the day trying to arrange his new room to his exacting tastes and prepare for a three-week hearing coming up the following Monday, looked in on Ann Halliday en route to tea. She was still in a muddle of books and boxes, jacket on the back of her chair, papers spread out before her. Marcus noticed that so far she hadn't made any attempt to brighten the room up with personal belongings, such as pictures or plants.

'How's it going?' he asked.

She looked up and sighed. 'I haven't had a minute to sort things out. Peter's landed me with a new joint-venture case. They want the opinion first thing tomorrow.'

'Don't tell me you're too busy to come to tea. Wouldn't look good on our first day. Got a duty to be sociable.'

'I suppose fifteen minutes won't make any odds. I'm going to be here all evening, anyway.' She closed her books and left chambers with Marcus.

Maurice Faber was comfortably ensconced in one of the armchairs, holding forth to David, William, and Stephen Bishop. Already the centre of attention, thought Marcus.

Roderick Hayter, the head of chambers, came in with Simon Barron and two pupils, a quiet, nervous young man and a girl with dark hair and watchful eyes, both of whom, new and raw, merely sat with their tea on the fringes of the group, listening to the conversation.

Maurice stirred his tea and eyed Roderick Hayter. The word was that he would be a High Court judge before the year was out, and 5 Caper Court would need a new head of chambers. The job was not an easy one, and therefore not to the taste of many barristers, but ever since childhood and the first competitive flush of prep school, Maurice had had an appetite for positions of pre-eminence. The same spark of aspiration which had driven him to be form captain, head of house, head of the debating team, captain of the First XV (but not quite President of the Oxford Union – Maurice had no political inclinations and gauged carefully the likely return on any expended energy) had made him a thrusting and aggressive lawyer, one of the youngest QCs in his year, with an appetite for success. The fact was, Maurice liked to come top. He never asked himself whether it might be some sense of inadequacy which made him so keen to be acclaimed and recognized, or whether his parents might have done better to set less store by the badges and honours and form prizes. He simply strove, from morning to night, as he always had done, eager to win. Cases, women, arguments . . .

He sat weighing up the other likely contenders. Stephen Bishop? Not a chance, too easy-going, probably wouldn't even put himself in the running. Jeremy Vane? A possibility. Jeremy liked nothing better than swanking about, being top dog. Not that he was much liked. Leo Davies? He was a dark horse, universally liked and admired in spite of everything one heard . . . Maurice suspected Leo couldn't care one way or the other about being head of chambers, but that was just the kind of quality one had to watch out for. Still, in the light of this recent scandal, Maurice couldn't see even Leo being a popular choice. If and when the time came, Maurice felt he'd be in with a fairly good chance. It wouldn't be easy, being so new to 5 Caper Court, but Maurice liked a challenge. He had a few months to make his mark.

As Roderick sank into a chair next to him, placing his tea cup carefully on the table, Maurice remarked, 'I was surprised you didn't take the opportunity to take out an ad in *The Times.*'

'Sorry?' said Roderick.

Maurice waved a hand in the direction of Ann and Marcus. 'Expanding chambers. Plenty of chambers seem to seize the chance to advertise. You know the kind of thing. A big box in Legal Appointments pages: "Five Caper Court is pleased to announce, et cetera, et cetera."'

'Sounds like something in the births columns,' said Michael Gibbon. 'I'm not very keen on that kind of self-publicizing. Not quite our style.'

Bristling at the implied criticism in this remark, Maurice replied swiftly, 'I suppose you prefer the other kind of publicity? The kind Leo Davies has been attracting?' He raised an eyebrow.

There was a brief, embarrassed silence. 'No one's much enjoyed that,' said Simon. 'Least of all Leo.'

At that moment Sarah came into the common room with David Liphook, her pupilmaster. She glanced across at the other tenants as she collected her tea. The dark-haired guy next to Roderick must be Maurice Faber. Interesting. She liked the dark, Mediterranean looks, the liquid eyes. Bit old, though, forty at least. Leaving Leo aside, old guys were a bit of a drag. Her gaze shifted to Marcus. His ebony features seemed to stand out amongst the other pallid faces in the common room. Dead, white males, thought Sarah. Just about summed up the Bar. Compared to them, Marcus really was something. At that moment Marcus looked up and met Sarah's gaze. He returned it for a few cool seconds, then looked away. A touch supercilious, perhaps, thought Sarah, but she liked that. She liked something to work on. She smiled as she picked up her tea and followed David over. Maybe this new bunch would make her last couple of months in chambers a little more interesting.

She sat down next to Camilla, who was flicking through a newspaper.

'No further scandal about dearest Leo?' said Sarah. Camilla gave her a cold glance and said nothing. She had no wish to talk to Sarah about anything, particularly Leo. 'I suppose yesterday was bad enough. I don't blame him for going to ground.' Sarah sipped her tea. 'Still, at least now you know just what kind of a person he is. You wouldn't hear it from me.'

Camilla folded up the paper. 'You don't think I believe that woman's pathetic story, do you? Nobody does, Sarah. Nobody in their right mind.'

Sarah crossed her legs and sighed reflectively. 'You mean that you don't have the least – how do we lawyers put it? – the least lurking doubt? Come on, Camilla. There had to be something going on. You know what he's like. Nothing is ever what it seems with Leo. Your trouble is you're too ready to believe anything he says. At least I know better than that. But then, I *do* know Leo. Properly. In ways you never will.'

Camilla got up and left without a word. She'd let Sarah drip enough poison in her ear in the past. She didn't want to hear any more. Anyway, she told herself as she crossed the cobblestones of Mitre Court, Sarah was merely jealous. She couldn't stand the idea that Leo should bother with someone whom Sarah no doubt regarded as her inferior. For Sarah, life was about looks, clothes, possessions and being seen in the right places with the right people. She didn't understand how things were between herself and Leo. He wasn't as bad as everyone thought. All right, he was no saint . . . He'd been frank with her from the start, told her about the kind of life he lived, the things he'd done, the way he was . . . Camilla had to admit that wasn't quite true. He would never have told her about Anthony, if Sarah hadn't. She didn't want to think about that. Leo and Anthony in bed together. No, she wouldn't let her mind go there. She would concentrate on the positive things.

But her determination faltered helplessly. She might as well admit it. She couldn't trust Leo completely. There was still the matter of that letter. He'd said he'd never known Gideon Smallwood, the civil servant who killed himself, and yet she'd seen a letter addressed to the man in Leo's own hand, lying on Robert's desk. A lie she was trying to ignore, trying to pretend didn't matter. Just like yesterday's tabloid front page. Believe enough in Leo, and everything bad would go away . . . But would it? She'd just accepted his complete denial about the *Sun* story. Maybe there was more to it, things he wasn't telling her. Just like the envelope addressed to Gideon Smallwood. Well, she would clear that up. She would ask him about that letter.

*

In the silence of his flat, Leo gave himself up entirely to work. He worked with the same steadfast absorption as in his early days as a Welsh working-class grammar school boy, when he had striven to block out the reality and poverty of his situation by fixing with single-minded determination on escape to a better world. Back in those days, he knew how much harder it would be for someone without the privileges of a public school education to achieve the kind of success he sought at the Bar. That knowledge had bred in him a fixed ambition, a determination never to be anything other than first-rate, and he had early on developed unshakeable habits of industry and purpose. Now, surrounded by the material evidence of his intellectual and professional attainments, he worked as assiduously as he had as a student. He bestowed on every case and every client unstinting care and concentration, and it was a quality which marked him out as being the very best, brilliant in his field.

Yet today he found the seclusion hard to bear. Every lonely sound – the faint hum of the lift, the front door of the building closing as Mrs Gresham took her little dog for a walk, occasional traffic round the leafy square – seemed to highlight his sense of isolation. That story in the paper had made him feel marked out, vilified, and in today's silent aftermath he had a sense of being set apart from humanity. He regularly worked from home, when he wanted utter peace and quiet, but today his solitude was different. It was enforced. He was in hiding, in retreat.

When the phone rang, he felt a welcome relief. It was the journalist friend whom he'd asked to try to run a piece undermining Melissa Angelicos's recent story.

'Just ringing to tell you to check the paper tomorrow. Rather helpfully, the Angelicos woman has apparently had a nervous breakdown. Gone to Italy with her sister for a bit of rest and recuperation. In quite a bad way, people tell me. So what I've written helps to suggest she's an unstable fantasist.'

'Excellent. Thanks for helping me out.'

'I'll call in the favour sometime. See you.'

Leo hung up. So Ms Angelicos had gone off to Italy with her nerves in shreds. The woman should be institutionalized. He glanced at the papers on his desk, and realized he didn't have the heart for any more work. Instead, he wandered through to the pristine silence of the drawing room and went to the long window overlooking the square. There he stared across at the sun-dappled communal garden, where no children played, and where the clang of the metal gates marked the passage of the well-heeled, mainly elderly inhabitants of the Belgravia square. The only child who had ever played there was Oliver, on weekends when he came to stay. At the thought of his son, Leo's heart lifted. He longed to see him on Saturday.

He stood there, reflecting. Babyhood had been the easy part with Oliver. Now the little boy was two, and growing conscious of the world around him, and his place in it. In another couple of years he would be moving into a world where life encompassed school, and sport and weekend activities, and friends grew as important as family. The pattern thus far established – of alternate weekends spent here or at Stanton – would have to expand to accommodate new aspects of Oliver's life beyond nappies and buggies and high chairs. This flat was no good. Leo had never cared that much for it. He'd simply chosen it on impulse when he and Rachel got divorced, probably with the idea that he would go back to his former bachelor existence. A mansion flat in Belgravia wasn't a suitable place to bring up a small boy. What he needed was a house, with a garden. Somewhere just like Stanton, but here in London.

The idea grew in him as he stood there. His sense of inertia vanished. He would find a house for himself and Oliver – and Camilla, for as long as that went on. He had sensed that she didn't feel entirely at ease in the flat, with its pale carpets and high ceilings, tastefully lit pieces of modern art and immaculate furniture. It was no one's idea of a proper home. On impulse, he looked up three local estate agents in Yellow Pages, and rang and asked them to send details of the kind of place he was looking for. A five- or six-bedroomed family house in Kensington or Chelsea, with a decent garden. All right, such a place would cost a fortune, but what was he earning all this money for, if not to provide a home where Oliver would always want to come, and bring his friends to, as he grew up?

Charged with a new sense of domesticity, Leo decided to cook supper for himself and Camilla. He left the flat and headed for Tesco's in Sloane Square. As he strolled along in the late-afternoon sunshine, he realized that ringing the estate agents had rekindled in him the desire for a more settled life. Maybe he and Camilla would work out. Maybe it would be the best thing for him. He would get rid of the flat, find a nice, friendly house, and wait to see if it changed him. In the meantime, he would concentrate on Camilla, on being with her and making her happy. Perhaps if one was single enough of purpose, determined to make it with one person, it could be achieved.

Camilla came to the flat a little after seven, weary from a tedious day spent working on an opinion in a case concerning repudiatory breach of a charterparty. She found Leo in a more buoyant, tranquil mood than she had expected. It vaguely irked her that he should apparently have put the scandal of yesterday behind him so quickly and easily. Was it part of his duplicitous nature that he should jettison problems, be they troublesome events or people, so effortlessly?

He kissed her. 'You look done in. Glass of wine?'

'I'd rather have a cup of tea, thanks.' She followed him through to the kitchen. 'You seem remarkably cheerful, all things considered.'

'My way of dealing with adversity. I've decided to make fundamental changes in my life. I'm getting out of this place, finding somewhere better for you and me and Oliver. A house. Would you like that?'

She should have been relieved that he was so upbeat, not switching off and becoming distant, as he could when beset by problems, but for some perverse reason she couldn't capitalize on his good mood. 'Yes. Of course.' She nodded.

'Don't sound too thrilled.' He glanced at her. 'What's up?'

'Nothing. Bad day. Horrible case from Eversheds. And Sarah, winding me up about you.'

'Ignore Sarah. She has a talent for making trouble. What did she say?'

'Oh, talking about the thing in the papers, suggesting there had to be something behind it.'

'Come on — you know it's a complete fabrication. Everything there is to know about that woman, I've told you.' He handed Camilla her tea.

'I know . . . But the way Sarah talks, that smile of hers . . . as though she knows things about you I don't.' She regarded him with solemn eyes, 'How well do I really know you, Leo?'

He put his hands on either side of her face, smoothing back her hair. 'As well as anyone. As well as anyone I've ever loved. You make me feel I could be a better person.'

'I can't change anything about you, Leo. I'm not that deluded. You're who you are. I just don't think you tell me everything, and that frightens me.'

'We've been through this before.' He sighed. 'Come on. What's brought this on? Not just the thing in yesterday's papers.'

'Partly.' She moved away from him.

'What else?'

'The way you still keep things from me. I think I know it all, and then something else crawls out of the woodwork.'

With a past as chequered as his own, Leo knew there was no point in remotely trying to guess what she'd stumbled upon. 'Such as?'

She hesitated for some seconds before replying. 'That man, that civil servant who died a couple of weeks ago. Gideon something.'

Leo's heart sank. 'Smallwood. Gideon Smallwood.' He had been enough trouble alive. With his death, Leo had hoped never to have to think about him again. 'What about him?'

'You said you hardly knew him, that he was just one of the Lloyd's Names.'

'That's right.'

'Is that the only way in which you knew him? Professionally? Merely as a client?'

In the few seconds in which Leo hesitated, Camilla could tell he was trying to work out what exactly she knew, and whether or not to lie. 'Why does it matter?' he asked. His tone was remote, evasive. She felt heartsick.

'It matters because I need to know how far you're prepared to lie to me. You say you hardly knew him, but on the day the Lloyd's case finished, I saw a letter addressed to him, in your handwriting, on Robert's desk.'

'Oh, for Christ's sake! It was to do with something that happened a while ago, nothing that concerned you. Yes, all right, I knew him personally, not just professionally. He's dead now, and it doesn't matter. You can't be privy to every aspect of my private life, you know.'

She regarded him unhappily. 'I know. It worries me. I don't want you to have to lie to me.'

'The bastard was trying to blackmail me, okay? Are you surprised I didn't particularly want to discuss it with you? When he died, I thought that was the end of it.' Leo opened the fridge, took out a half-drunk bottle of white wine, and poured himself a glass. 'In fact, as far as I'm concerned, it is. Now I'm going to cook us some supper.'

'Leo! Someone dies alone in his flat, in mysterious circumstances, you tell me he was trying to blackmail you – and you expect me to regard that as perfectly reasonable? What else is there that I don't know?'

'You don't have to make it sound as though I killed him. Look, the little sod was screwing me for a hundred thousand pounds. The fact that I was more than a trifle relieved by his untimely death doesn't mean I was responsible for it.'

Camilla stared at him. 'What on earth did you do that was worth a hundred thousand pounds, Leo?'

He returned her stare. 'Believe it or not, sometimes people are blackmailed for things they *haven't* done.'

'All right – what was it you *didn't* do that was worth so much?'

He looked away. These were things he didn't want her to know, mainly because there was no need ... But the conversation had reached a point where there was no possibility of further evasion. 'He had some photographs, taken in – in unfortunate circumstances.'

'Which is a euphemism for – what, exactly?'

Leo set down his wine glass. 'Right. I'll tell you, exactly as it happened – it's not going to sound good, but I want you to believe me that it is the truth. Gideon and I went out for the evening, to dinner, and afterwards he suggested going on somewhere, I had no idea where ... It turned out to be some kind of gay brothel. Nothing happened, I was there for no more than five minutes, I couldn't wait to get the hell out, but some – some boy kissed me. That was all. It happened in seconds, a complete set-up. Gideon got it on camera. The boy was fifteen, in care at the time. A couple of weeks later, Gideon let me know, and demanded a hundred thousand to keep it from the papers.'

Camilla leaned against the sink, gazing at him, absorbing this. 'You were never going to tell me about this, were you?' She shook her head, looking at him with a hopeless, lost look. 'I take it this man Gideon was gay. And you were spending time with him, going out with him? It must have been when you had already begun sleeping with me. What do you *do* when you're not with me, Leo?'

'I told you! Don't you listen? We merely dined together! I had no idea where he was taking me afterwards! It was a set-up, the whole thing was fabricated!'

'Just like the piece in the papers yesterday? Sarah was right. It can't all be false, can it, Leo? There has to be some element of truth in it. Something you don't want me to know. There'll always be something you don't want me to know. You and this man Gideon. You and Anthony. That's another thing you never meant to –'

The violence of Leo's reaction to the mention of Anthony's name astonished her. He threw his half-drunk glass of wine into the sink, smashing it, making Camilla jump. 'Don't bring Anthony into this! Don't mention his name! You will not judge me, do you understand?'

In the silence that ensued, Camilla's fear quickly evaporated, leaving her cold and angry. She could tell from Leo's eyes that he immediately regretted what he had done, but she wasn't going to wait for him to try to make it better.

'I think I'd better go.'

Leo said nothing.

She went out into the hallway and picked up her bag. Leo merely stood leaning in the doorway, watching her. She could read no emotion in his eyes. It would always be like this. She would never really know anything. Stopping now would be for the best.

She closed the door of the flat and went downstairs. At the bottom she paused, waiting, listening. How badly she had wanted him to stop her, to say, 'No. You're not to go. This is my fault. Come back.' But he had simply let her go. She opened the street door and went down the steps. She was better off away from him. He knew it, and so did she. The knowledge made her cry, and she didn't stop crying all the way home to Clapham.

Leo picked the larger pieces of glass from the sink, flushing the rest away into the grinding maw of the waste disposal. He dropped the shards carefully into the bin, then rinsed and wiped his hands. His instinct, as soon as he heard the sound of the front door closing, had been to go after her, bring her back. But Leo was too old a hand, too practised for such a simple display of contrition. Besides, there was nothing to be gained from it right now. She was too young, too bewildered and outraged by what she had learned. She needed some time to work it through, a few days in which to let her feelings get the better of her good sense. She would persuade herself that the Gideon thing didn't matter, that he hadn't sought to deceive her so much as protect her. She was also, he knew, too physically dependent upon him, upon his lovemaking – something she was not presently aware of, but would be acutely so by the time the weekend was up. Give it another couple of days thereafter, and the girl would be such a mixed bag of self-doubt and fraught desire that he would have no difficulty in making everything all right. It was merely a question of leaving her alone for just long enough. Leo knew all too well how to manipulate a young and inexperienced heart. Had he not loved her as much as he did, he might almost have felt ashamed.

4

Rachel Dean came out of the lift on the seventh floor of the offices of Nichols and Co. and headed for her office, picking up a coffee on the way. In her office she slipped off her jacket, and sat sipping her coffee as she checked through her diary. A ten o'clock meeting with Adriana Papaposilakis. That should be interesting. For some time now she had been working on a case concerning an insurance claim on Miss Papaposilakis's private yacht, which had caught fire and sunk two years previously in circumstances which left the insurers disinclined to pay out. Following months of fruitless wrangling between solicitors, the case was due to reach a hearing in a few weeks. Throughout the case Rachel had dealt only with Miss Papaposilakis's PA, Mr Defereras, a small, elderly Greek lawyer who attended to business with scrupulous care and few words. Adriana Papaposilakis herself was something of a mythical creature. All Rachel knew was that she was a Greek beauty with a formidable business reputation, rumoured to be given to occasional underhand dealing and fiscal evasiveness, traits not uncommon in the average Greek shipping tycoon.

Rachel glanced up and caught Fred Fenton's eye as he passed by in the corridor. She called out to him and he sauntered in with his coffee.

'You've met Adriana Papaposilakis, haven't you?'

Fred, a rangy thirty-two-year-old, settled himself in a chair at the other side of her desk. 'The woman with the impossible name. Yes, I worked on a speed and consumption claim involving one of her vessels last year. We won, as I recall. Why?'

'I have a meeting with her in an hour. I'm curious to know what she's like.'

'She's – let's see ... How can I put this? She's very –' Fred hesitated '– very personable.' Fred smiled and took a sip of his coffee. 'Built along Dolly Parton lines, though not quite so pneumatic. Blonde, petite, with something of the short-arse complex – dynamic and aggressive, as though compensating. You know the kind? Having said that, she is remarkably attractive, in a somewhat obvious way. The fact that she's utterly loaded may have some bearing on the way she behaves and is perceived. Probably used to having men eating out of her hand.'

'And leaving aside her physical attributes?'

'Oh, as a client? Typical Greek. Doesn't like handing over information and documents unless absolutely pushed to do so. Always has an eye to the main chance. Not the most straightforward of people. But I don't suppose plain dealing goes hand-in-hand with multi-million-dollar fortunes as a rule, does it? Oh, and of course she looks after the pennies. Tiny claims are just as important as big ones. She certainly knows how to take care of business.'

'I wonder why I'm being favoured with a personal visit,' mused Rachel.

'Perhaps this case is very dear to her heart.' Fred rose from his chair. 'Let me know how you get on.'

Adriana Papaposilakis arrived twenty minutes late for her appointment, and made no apology. She was shown into Rachel's office, with Mr Defereras in tow, and immediately the room was filled with a subtle, enchanting fragrance. Even Rachel, who rarely wore perfume, wanted to be able to ask what it was.

She watched as Miss Papaposilakis settled herself into a chair with a queenly air. She was certainly very beautiful – diminutive, shapely, with short, blonde hair and a heart-shaped face and creamy skin. Her eyes were a dark and velvety brown, dramatically made up. She wore a close-fitting suit of a vibrant pink which might have been verging on vulgar, had it not been so beautifully cut, clearly couture, and a discreet quantity of evidently very expensive jewellery. Too many diamonds for daytime, thought Rachel, but she couldn't help feeling faintly envious of so much serene glamour, and was immediately conscious of her own under-stated appearance, her navy suit and silk blouse, minimalist pearl earrings and lack of make-up.

After the exchange of a few pleasantries concerning the Silakis fleet and the parlous state of the shipping business generally, Miss Papaposilakis came quickly to the matter in hand.

'This case regarding my yacht, Miss Dean. It's coming to court very soon – yes?' Her accent was light and pretty.

Rachel nodded. 'We have a hearing date for July the twenty-fourth. Of course, we're still attempting to reach a settlement with Bentley's, but where a claim of fifteen million dollars is concerned, I don't think there's a great deal of room for manoeuvre. Not after all these months.'

'All these insurance companies are crooks. Why else would they refuse to pay out?'

Rachel glanced down at the papers on her desk. 'I'm afraid the sticking point is the fire which occurred before the vessel sank. Their experts are not convinced that it occurred accidentally.'

'Miss Dean, a deck boy died in that fire. Do they intend to say in court that my crew started the fire themselves? Deliberately? And put at risk their own lives? And the life of a boy, only eighteen years old?' Her dark eyes burned. 'Why should they do such a thing?'

The question might have been posed rhetorically by Miss Papaposilakis, but it merited an honest answer. 'As I'm sure you know, if a crew member scuttles a ship,' replied Rachel, 'he usually only does it for the benefit of the owner.' She glanced at Mr Defereras, but his face remained expressionless.

Miss Papaposilakis's gaze grew stony. 'That *I* would have arranged to have such a thing done? It is outrageous that they should dare to suggest it.'

'Well, they haven't gone as far as actually –'

'It is what they imply!'

'If the other side could establish that the fire was started deliberately, that would be the inference, naturally. But as the expert evidence stands at the moment, I think they'd have an uphill struggle proving any such thing, let alone that it was done with your connivance.'

'Naturally.' Miss Papaposilakis shrugged. 'As though I would allow such a thing to be done for a mere few million dollars!'

'I'm surprised they've maintained such an intransigent position, I must confess. But they do seem to be digging their heels in. I doubt very much if there's any scope left for settlement.'

'If it is to go to court, it is imperative that I win. It is not just because of the money.'

'Naturally, we'll do our utmost –'

'I want the very best barrister.'

'Well, as Mr Defereras knows, we've already instructed Kate Carpenter. She's very able –'

Adriana Papaposilakis gave a sigh of impatience and waved a manicured hand, the nails painted the same shade of fuchsia as her suit. 'No. I already have someone better in mind. A QC called Leo Davies. Have you heard of him?'

Rachel met Miss Papaposilakis's very direct gaze. 'Of course.' She hesitated. 'I appreciate that the case is important to you, but someone like Mr Davies is very expensive –'

'Miss Dean,' interrupted Adriana Papaposilakis, 'two days ago I paid forty million dollars for thirty Pakistani vessels. In cash. I know when to spend money, and to spend it to good advantage. Instructing a QC to handle this case for me may seem expensive to you, but not to me. I understand Leo Davies is very good. In fact, I hear he is the best. I want him.'

'He is, as you say, very good. He's also very busy.'

Adriana nodded. 'I hope he can make time for this case. I would like you to ensure he does. I expect to hear from you by tomorrow.' She stood up, and Mr Defereras followed suit. 'We must go. I have another meeting in quarter of an hour.'

They shook hands, and as Rachel showed Miss Papaposilakis and Mr Defereras to the door, she asked, 'I'm curious – there are lots of good commercial barristers around . . . Was there any particular reason why you wanted to instruct Leo Davies?'

Adriana Papaposilakis smiled. 'He has a reputation. I like men with reputations. They're more interesting than most, don't you think?'

Rachel stood in the doorway till they reached the lift, then closed the door. She went back to her desk and sat down. The delicious scent still hung in the air. She wondered whether Adriana Papaposilakis was aware of the connection between herself and Leo, and if that was why she had come here in person today. To look over Leo's ex-wife, see how his tastes ran. It was clear enough from her parting remarks why Adriana Papaposilakis had chosen to instruct Leo, apart from his skills as an advocate. There were half a dozen other silks in London just as able as he was – but not, of course, with his particular brand of magnetism. Rachel could only hope Leo was already heavily committed to some other matter on July the twenty-fourth, and that Miss Papaposilakis, accustomed as she might be to getting what she wanted, would in this instance find her desires thwarted.

Ten minutes later, the phone interrupted her. 'Mr Davies for you,' said the girl on the switchboard.

'Thank you.' Leo came on the line. 'Leo, how extraordinary. I've just had instructions from a shipowner who has asked particularly for your services. I was about to ring Henry.'

'Well, why don't you tell me about it in person? You said you wanted lunch, and I can do today, if you're free. It'll have to be quick, though. This afternoon is my first in chambers for several days, and I have a con at two.'

Rachel glanced at her watch. 'I'll come over to the Temple. Why don't you book a table at Drake's?'

'Fine. See you there at one.'

Two hours later, as the taxi crawled through the traffic on Ludgate Circus, Rachel wondered what instinct had prompted her to suggest the wine bar where they used to meet in happier times, in the days when she had just met Leo and was utterly in love with him – and he with her, or so she had thought. Because it was easy, somewhere they both knew, that was all. The taxi stopped at the bottom of Fetter Lane, and Rachel got out and paid the driver. As she walked up the busy street towards the narrow, hidden courtyard in which Drake's lay tucked away, she felt the sad pang of re-created past pleasures. The truth was that she had chosen this place because it enabled her to pretend, to make believe things were as they had once been. She went into the cool depths of the wine bar. As she sat and waited at the table which Leo had booked, she could already anticipate the fleeting pain it would give her to see him come in, ducking his head slightly in the low doorway. Pain born of the knowledge that this was now, and that the happy future she had once imagined was now in the past. He would come in, she would look up and smile, all just as it had been three years ago – except that life had moved remorselessly on, and things were now utterly different.

A few moments later, Leo came in just as she had imagined, looking unchanged – lean, fit, electrifyingly handsome, his expression preoccupied, not expectant. The smile he gave when he caught sight of her didn't reach his eyes.

Leo sat down. 'I'm sorry. I haven't got as long as I thought. Robert's brought the con forward to quarter to. I'll have to make this quick.' A waitress came over with a wine list. 'No, just water, thanks.' He glanced at Rachel. 'For you?'

She shook her head. 'Mineral water's fine.'

They ordered some sandwiches. The waitress went away. How different, thought Rachel. There was nothing of the old, restful intimacy that meetings here had once possessed. Leo's manner was charged with restrained impatience.

'So, who's this shipowner?'

'Sorry?'

'The one you mentioned on the phone earlier.'

'Oh, yes . . . Adriana Papaposilakis, head of Silakis Shipping. She came to see me about an insurance claim on some private yacht of hers. There was a fire on board, and Bentley's, who are acting for the insurer, take the view that it didn't start accidentally. Not that they've gone very far in establishing otherwise, but they're still refusing to settle. The hearing's in three weeks' time. We've already instructed Kate Carpenter, but Miss Papaposilakis is insisting that you should be instructed as leader.'

'The less I have to do with Greek women, the better. They seem to be a disaster in my life.'

'I take it you mean the Angelicos woman. Is she Greek? She didn't look it.'

'Parts of her must be, given the name. What did you say this one is called?'

'Papaposilakis.'

'I've never done any work for Silakis. Why does she want me?'

'I asked her that. She said something about your reputation – not that I think she was talking about your professional one, I hasten to add.' Rachel shrugged and picked up a sandwich. 'That was the impression I had, at any rate. Maybe she reads the tabloids. She looked like the kind of girl who would.'

'What's she like?' Leo seemed intrigued, and this surprised and mildly annoyed Rachel.

'Small. Aggressive. Pretty, in a rather obvious way. Clearly not used to the sound of the word "no".'

'Given that she's running one of the largest tanker fleets in the world, that's hardly surprising.'

Rachel said nothing for a few seconds. She'd assumed Leo would want nothing to do with the case, but he seemed interested. In Miss Papaposilakis, no doubt, rather than the case. She said quickly, 'It's a very trivial dispute, probably a waste of your time. It really doesn't merit a leader. I'll say you're tied up on the twenty-fourth, if you like.'

Leo sipped his mineral water, then shook his head. 'I'm not sure that I am. I'll have to check. If she's especially keen to have me, let the lady have her way. Old Henry is going about prophesying doom and the collapse of my practice as a result of this recent scandal, so it might be useful to be able to point to a case that's actually been generated by my adverse publicity. That'll show him. As for Miss Papaposilakis, I'll try not to hold the fact that she's Greek against her.' He glanced at Rachel. 'Another sandwich?' She shook her head. 'So – to change the subject, you said a week or so ago that you had something to tell me about yourself and Charles.'

'I wasn't going to tell you anything about myself and Charles,' replied Rachel with swift defensiveness. 'Only,' she relented, 'insofar as it relates to Oliver.'

'Of course. Fine. Insofar as, then.'

That cool hesitancy of hers – it had been, reflected Leo, the only thing that had ever turned him on about her. Melting the glacial reserve. Once that had gone, there was very little left that was interesting.

'When you and I talked that day at Stanton, I gave you the impression Charles and I might be splitting up. We're not.'

Leo's pulse quickened. 'You mean you're going to the States with him? I thought you said you had no intention of taking Oliver out of the country.' He knew that Charles Beecham had been offered work in the States, and his one fear was that Rachel would go too, taking Oliver where Leo would rarely see him.

'Oh, don't worry,' replied Rachel swiftly. 'I know Oliver is the only one of us you're concerned about. You've always made that perfectly clear.' Leo said nothing. He knew she would be miserably content with the intimacy of a row, but he wouldn't afford her that satisfaction. After a few seconds, she went on, 'Charles is still going to do the documentary series for NBC, but I won't be going with him. That is, he'll go out to the States for six weeks or so, come back for a week or two, then go out again. It's not ideal, from his point of view, but he understands that you and Oliver have to see each other.'

'I'm grateful to him. To both of you. It's very considerate.' Beyond the words lay an unarticulated truth. Leo knew that Rachel was still in love with him, whatever relationship she might have with Charles. She would never voluntarily leave their common sphere of existence and go where she could not see him on a regular basis. This much she had just acknowledged. If she could not have Leo, she would let Charles, and the safety of his adoration for her, suffice.

'I wasn't thinking entirely of you in all this, you know,' added Rachel. 'The firm may make me an equity partner before the end of the year. I don't want to lose that.'

'No, indeed,' said Leo. An equity partnership in a firm such as Nichols and Co. would be an enormous boost to her income, worth at least a couple of hundred thousand a year. 'Congratulations.'

'I haven't got it yet.' Rachel sipped her water. 'Anyway, that's how things stand. Nothing is going to jeopardize your contact with Oliver.'

'I have some plans of my own, where Oliver is concerned,' said Leo. 'I've put the flat in Belgravia on the market. I'm looking for a house, something with a decent garden, somewhere more like a proper home for him as he grows up.'

Rachel nodded. She longed to say – *We had a house like that, once. We could have given Oliver that stability and happiness. You had to chuck it all away. You couldn't do anything as simple as stay faithful, or love us both.*

Instead she asked, 'Does anyone else figure in this sudden change of domestic circumstances?'

'If you're asking about my girlfriend –'

'By which you mean that you've actually managed to last more than six weeks with someone.'

Leo sighed. 'Don't. Please.' He met her unhappy gaze. 'If you're asking about my girlfriend, the answer is – I'm not sure. Aspects of my life have become rather uncertain recently. Oliver is the prime object of my concern, in any event.'

'I know. I just like to know who else is involved in his life, who's around at the weekends when he sees you.'

And in my bed, in my thoughts. 'I can assure you, I'll keep you abreast of any long-term decisions that affect Oliver.'

'I want him to be happy. And safe. I suppose I should be glad it's a woman you're seeing, and not some man.'

Leo glanced at his watch. How wearying these meetings with Rachel could be, in a subtle, relentless way. He replied, 'I suppose you think you should be.' There was a pause. 'I have to be getting back.'

Rachel nodded. 'Let me know how your house-hunting goes.'

'I will.' Leo rose. 'I'll call you in the next few days to arrange about Oliver's weekend.' He gestured to the waitress for the bill, and dropped two ten-pound notes on the table. 'Oh, and send those Silakis papers over. I'll have a look at them.' He bent and kissed her swiftly on one cool, pale cheek. 'Bye.'

'Bye.' She sat and watched as he headed for the door, ducking his head to avoid the low beam on the way out. Then he was gone.

Felicity put the phone down and swore under her breath. Twenty to two, and she still hadn't had a chance to slip out for lunch, not thanks to this bugger Maurice Faber. He'd been bitching on all morning about all the things that were wrong with his new room, and she had spent the last hour trying to get someone to come and sort out the lighting, which he maintained had too much glare. 'I insist that it be altered by the end of the day. I simply can't work in these conditions,' he'd said. She'd like to alter something for him, she knew, and it wouldn't be his lighting.

Sod it. No one was going to come out at such short notice, so he was going to have to lump it. She picked up her bag, and was about to leave, when the phone rang. Since Robert had slipped out for a few minutes, and the other two clerks were at lunch, she had no choice but to answer it.

'Hello – clerks' room.'

'Fliss – is that you? It's me – Sandy.'

At the sound of her brother's voice, Felicity subsided into her chair. She hadn't spoken to him in months. 'Sandy. How are you?' Her tone was apprehensive. Sandy had only once called her at work before, when he needed to borrow money.

'Uh. . . .' There was a long pause, filled with Sandy's breath-ing. 'Not so good, actually, Fliss. Not so good.' The tone was lightly philosophical, but the voice had a broken edge to it, as though not far from tears. 'Can I see you, like? In your lunch hour?'

'Why? Where are you?'

'Just down the road a bit. Not far from you.' There was a bipping sound. 'Shit. My money's running out. I'll be outside McDonald's. The big one. By Charing –'

The dial tone cut him off. Felicity replaced the receiver. He must mean the McDonald's at the end of the Strand, by the station. She picked up her bag and hurried out of chambers.

Fleet Street was so choked with traffic that she abandoned any idea of getting a bus, and walked instead. It was after two by the time she reached McDonald's, and at first she couldn't see Sandy. But there he was, not milling around with the rest of the tourists and shoppers, but sitting against the far end of the wall, hunched up on the pavement. He got up when he saw Felicity, and tried to smile.

'Oh, my God.' Felicity was appalled at the state of him.

He was wearing a stained, grey hooded sweatshirt and filthy jeans and trainers, and his hands and face had the unmistakable grime of a street-sleeper. It was then that she noticed the sleeping bag and bundled-up dirty blankets on the ground next to the place where he'd been sitting. His eyes as he gazed at her were bright and slightly feverish.

'Hi, Fliss.'

'Oh, Sandy. Bloody hell. What's been going on?'

He shrugged. 'Got chucked out of the flat. Couldn't quite manage the rent.'

'How long ago was this? What have you been doing since then?'

Sandy scratched his head. His nails were encrusted with dirt. He simply shrugged again, swallowed hard, and she saw that he was close to tears. Some people passing by jostled him, and she put out a hand to steady him.

'We can't talk here. Come on. Let's go somewhere quieter.'

Sandy picked up his bundle of bedding and together they walked down Villiers Street towards the gardens by Embankment Station. Felicity bought them both a couple of rolls from a sandwich shop on the way, and they sat on the grass in the shade of the plane trees and ate them. She watched as he ate, thinking how much things had changed since the days they had shared the flat in Brixton three years before. They'd left home together to get away from their drunken bastard of a father, off on the big adventure. The flat had been tiny – pretty scummy really, but it had seemed great at first. Fliss had worked as a secretary – probably the world's worst – while Sandy alternated between various casual jobs and long bouts of idleness and dope-smoking. She'd met Vince through Sandy, when he and Vince were working on the same building site. Hadn't taken long for the set-up to turn sour, though. Too many drugs, too little to do, that was Sandy's problem. It got to the point where she couldn't stand coming home each evening to the mess of beer cans and fag ends and idle young men. So she'd moved out to Clapham with Vince, and left Sandy to his own devices. Mistake, big mistake. But how long could you remain responsible for your grown-up brother? She studied his thin, grimy face.

'How long have you been sleeping rough?'

'Not that long. Just over a week.'

'Why didn't you ring me before now?'

'Dunno.' He shrugged again, ate his roll. 'It wasn't that bad at first. Weather's been all right. I dossed in a doorway back up there the first few nights. Then I went down to Waterloo when there was that rain. Had my coat nicked. Nearly got beaten up by some madman.'

'What have you been living on?'

'I've begged a bit. Some of the restaurants give you stuff at the end of the day.'

'Well, you can't carry on like this. What would Mum say? Why haven't you been back home?'

'Didn't fancy seeing the old man. I'd rather sleep on the streets than get messed about by him again.'

Felicity plucked at the grass for a few moments. She couldn't help feeling that all this was her fault. But then, she'd never stopped feeling guilty about Sandy. While they were sharing the flat, she'd been the one who'd held things together, held *him* together. Every time they met up after she'd moved out, he seemed to have gone further downhill. There had been that time eighteen months ago, when he'd landed a job with some office suppliers and things looked as though they might improve, but that had been a one-week wonder. Sandy had simply been incapable of getting up in the mornings. The last time Felicity had visited the Brixton flat, it had been worse than a tip. Grey sheets on the unmade beds, rubbish spilling out of bags in the kitchen, dust and mess everywhere, unwashed dishes, crumpled beer cans, a broken pane in one of the windows. And Sandy hadn't seemed to care. A couple of joints, a few pills, and he just let the world go away.

Felicity glanced at her watch. Two forty-five. She'd better be getting back. 'Look, you'd better stop with me for a while till we get you sorted out. Nothing permanent, mind – I'm not going to let you sponge off me again.' Sandy looked at her warily, saying nothing. 'Well, it's why you rang, isn't it?' She didn't mean to sound so harsh, but frankly the thought of looking after Sandy depressed her. She had to help him – he was her brother. But she couldn't help wishing he could do more to make sense of his own life. 'I've got to get back to work. I'll meet you here at six. Okay?'

Sandy merely nodded. Felicity got to her feet and picked up the roll wrappers to put in the bin. As she reached the gate to Villiers Street she glanced back at the figure sitting alone on the grass in the sunshine, among the rest of human-ity, and felt a pang of pity mixed with irritation. She supposed she was glad he'd rung her. She'd rather he stayed with her than dossed on the streets.

Hurrying through the door to the clerks' room, Felicity bumped into an irate Maurice Faber.

'I hope you've arranged to have something done about my lighting.'

'The earliest I can get someone to look at it is Wednesday morning.'

Maurice glanced at Felicity's bag and realized she had only just returned to chambers. 'Have you been out to lunch till this hour?'

'I went out at ten to two, actually.'

'I suggest you try to take lunch at the conventional time.' Maurice turned to retrieve some papers from his pigeon-hole and Felicity made a face at his back.

When Maurice had gone out, Henry wandered over to Felicity's desk. 'Those bundles came over from Freshfields while you were out – the ones Mr Vane needs for his arbitration tomorrow.'

'Oh, thanks. I was just about to chase them up,' said Felicity.

Henry picked up the cheesed-off note in Felicity's voice and glanced with concern at her dispirited face. 'Some problem? Anything I can help with?'

'Not really, Henry. Just a bit of family hassle. It turns out my brother's been sleeping rough for the past week or so. Got kicked out of his flat for not paying the rent. I met up with him at lunchtime. So of course I had to ask him to come and stay with me for a while. Not that I mind . . .' She paused. 'Well, I do actually. That's awful of me, isn't it?'

Henry shook his head. 'I wouldn't relish having my sister descend on me out of the blue. But when it's family – well, what can you do?'

'Quite.'

Not quite sure what further consolation to offer, Henry changed the subject. 'By the way, we've got a date fixed for the chambers' party.'

'What party?'

'They've decided to have a bash to celebrate the expansion of chambers. The usual PR job. Invite along every commercial solicitor in the City who likes a drink – which is most of them – get them nicely tanked up, and hope the work floods in.'

'When is it?'

'July the twentieth. Not the handiest time of year to be throwing a junket, given that some people will be away on holiday, but then again, it saves on the champagne. Mr Hayter suggests having a marquee in Inner Temple Garden, so I'll have to get busy arranging that. Then there's the food and drink. You, me, Peter and Robert will have to sit down and sort it all out.'

'Not a prospect I relish,' muttered Felicity, as Henry went to answer his phone. Despite what Henry had said about keeping everything harmonious, so far she was doing her best to avoid contact with Peter. The worst of it was, despite having been deceived and strung along by him, she still felt a little pang every time she set eyes on him. But that was love for you. She seemed fated to get it wrong every time.

In Court 17, the afternoon's proceedings in the case of *Rotterdam Diamonds BVBA v. Air Italia* had been underway for a little over an hour. Camilla, acting as a junior in the case, had endeavoured to listen attentively to her leader, Adrian Eder QC, but now she found her attention wandering. It drifted, as it did about twenty times an hour, to Leo. The past six days had been sheer torment, possibly the most wretched of her life. Leo hadn't been in chambers, he hadn't called her, and she had been forced to endure the past weekend in the company of her charmless flatmate, Jane, who was evidently dying to know what had gone wrong between her and Leo, but was behaving like the soul of discretion. The unasked questions hung heavy in the air, and Camilla felt she would have preferred an outright interrogation to Jane's sympathetic, silent glances of concern. She'd thought of going to her parents for the weekend, but didn't dare, in case Leo should ring while she was away. He hadn't. Camilla had come to the inescapable conclusion that he wasn't at all bothered by what had happened. She still felt she'd been right to be upset by the way he concealed things from her, and that he should be the one to make the first move, but he evidently didn't care enough. So much for loving her.

'My Lord,' intoned Adrian Eder, 'my submission is that the phrase "special declaration of interest" is imprecise and does not imply a pre-estimate of the damage that would be suffered in the event of a loss. The special declaration might well be less than the true value of the cargo, as in the case of the diamonds. I would refer your Lordship to the passages marked in Drion's work on *Limitation of Liabilities in International Air Law* at page three hundred and fourteen . . .' Camilla watched as Mr Justice Latham leafed through the volume before him, and tried once more to fasten her attention on the case in hand, which concerned the loss of a cargo of diamonds in air transit. She tried to picture a heap of diamonds, 120,000 dollars' worth. How big or small might that be? She had no idea. Perhaps there had been no more than ten or twelve diamonds involved. Perhaps many more. From here her mind wandered to diamond jewellery, and to rings, and the now forlorn hope which she had once had that Leo might buy her a ring. If he meant to marry her, it was what people did. She doodled unhappily on her notebook, feeling foolish at having entertained such a soppy idea. She very much doubted that he would ever marry her. The idea even seemed faintly ridiculous. The past few days of uncertainty had sapped Camilla of much of her confidence. Her present perception of herself was reduced to that of an unsophisticated, not very interesting girl who had been seduced by someone older and far more skilful into thinking she was loved. She wasn't the kind of girl that Leo would want as a wife. Beyond a certain amount of law, she knew nothing, really. Not about life, or art, or books and films and people – all the things that interested Leo. She didn't even know much about sex. At this, she instantly recalled that way Leo had of touching her, reducing her in seconds to abject desire. He could do it just by looking at her. That kind of thing came with practice, obviously. Sarah was right. She was simply one in a long line of conquests. Why should she think of herself as being special to him?

'. . . and in addition, may I refer your Lordship to two foreign decisions in point? The first is a decision of the United States Court of Appeals for the Second Circuit, *Perera Co Inc v. Varig Brazilian Airlines*, nineteen eighty-five, Aviation Cases seventeen at page eight hundred and ten, where the point was conceded . . .'

Then again, maybe it wasn't mere indifference on Leo's part. This was the first row they'd ever had, and she might have touched some nerve . . . It had been the mention of Anthony that had set him off. That he and Leo had been lovers, however briefly, was something she found almost impossible to contemplate. Perhaps it was more important to Leo than he was prepared to admit. No, she didn't want to think about that. This was between her and Leo. The whole situation was making her so wretchedly unhappy that she had to know where she stood. If Leo wasn't going to make the first move, she would simply have to swallow her pride and do it herself.

With this resolve, she turned her weary attention once more to Article 22 of the Warsaw Convention, as amended by the Hague Protocol of 1955, and tried to fix it there.

5

The following morning Leo established with Felicity that he had no other commitments for 24 July, and the papers in the case concerning Ms Papaposilakis's ill-fated yacht were sent round to Caper Court. Leo spent the afternoon reading through them. It seemed that, before its demise through fire and water, the *Persephone* had been a fine vessel – built in 1988 by Benetti, 280 feet long, with a cruising speed of nineteen knots, manned by a crew of six, and with accommodation for fifteen guests. As he mused on these particulars, Leo wondered what it would be like to have the kind of wealth where an insurance claim for fifteen million fell into the realm of small change. As a QC, his earning power was presently very substantial – provided, of course, that there was no adverse fallout from his recent unpleasant publicity – and he usually spent pretty freely. He generally never gave much thought to the lifestyles of his many superbly wealthy clients. But now, as he sat pondering the papers before him, he felt a new consciousness of the stresses of the work which earned him his money. Perhaps it was age, middle age, reminding him that his energy and intellectual drive must eventually diminish. He had never imagined that idleness might possess attractions – work had always been his passion. He sat back, trying to imagine what it would be like to be immensely rich – so rich that one's notion of work might consist of little more than watching interest accumulate on interest, with fleets of tankers and oil-trading companies busily earning income worldwide. Rich enough to spend idle weeks on board a yacht like the *Persephone*, with its luxurious cabins and excellent chef and crew in attendance, cruising the sunlit waters of the Caribbean in the company of good friends, with the freedom to sail off to new waters when bored, and drop anchor in some fresh, delightful haven . . .

I might go mad, thought Leo. He swivelled idly in his chair, the papers in his lap, and glanced out of his window to the courtyard below. He caught sight of Camilla making her way slowly across Caper Court from the cloisters, her robing bag slung over one shoulder. There was something so disconsolate and naive in the way she walked, like an unhappy child, and he realized with an immediate pang what a bastard he'd been, letting the past week go by without a single word. The trouble was, selfishness became a way of life, if you'd spent years putting yourself first.

Leo sighed, pushed the papers aside, and stood up to stroll round the room and stretch his legs. He thought about the cause of their argument, the fact that he had concealed the truth about Gideon Smallwood from her, and wondered how many more such arguments there would be in the future. Unless he underwent a radical change of character, which seemed unlikely at his age, she would be in for a constant bout of unpleasant surprises. The more he thought about it, the more he realized that he was highly unlikely to live up to Camilla's expectations of probity and decency in a husband. Not judging by his past form, at any rate. As his perambulations brought him back to his desk once more, his eye again fell on the Papaposilakis papers. He thought about the possibility of a golden old age spent island-hopping in the Caribbean. What were the realistic prospects of any form of carefree retirement if Camilla were to have children, as she would presumably want to? The thought was enough to make him sit down again.

He found these new trains of thought mildly disquieting. He had never given much thought to his own old age before. Perhaps this was what happened to everyone in their mid-forties. And she was so young – too young. The marriage question really needed serious revising. And yet, and yet . . . it wasn't as though he didn't love her . . .

Oh, bugger it, thought Leo. Living for the present had always been good enough in the past. All he had to do was maintain the status quo, enjoy her company and the delights of her voluptuous young body, and the future would arrange itself. The point was, he had wasted an entire week and made her unhappy into the bargain. Time to do something about it. He closed the door and went downstairs to Camilla's room.

Leo tapped on the door and went in. Camilla had just dropped her bag in the corner and was putting her papers on her desk. Simon, her room-mate, was out. She looked up and saw Leo, and felt her pulse jump, but said nothing. Leo closed the door and leaned against it.

They looked at each other in silence for a moment, then Leo said, 'I'm sorry. I've been a complete heel these past few days. I should have rung.' Still Camilla said nothing. 'How have you been?'

Camilla shrugged. 'Why the sudden concern?'

Leo moved towards her. 'I said I'm sorry. I've had a lot on my mind.' The look she gave him was wary, defensive. 'Come here.'

She came into his arms and allowed herself to be held. The familiar warmth of him brought instant, easy tears to her eyes. 'This is what I hate most, Leo,' she muttered. 'The capacity you have to make me so unhappy.'

'I don't mean to. That's the last thing I want, believe me.' He kissed her face and stroked her hair.

Believe you, she thought. If only it were that easy.

He drew back and looked at her, kissed her mouth quickly, softly. 'I should have done this days ago.' That wasn't strictly true, he thought to himself. He could tell from the warmth of her physical response that she was all too ready to make up for a week's abstinence. The wait would be well worth it.

'Why didn't you? I've been so miserable.'

'Because I'm a bigger fool than many people suppose.' He kissed her again. 'Look, this isn't quite the time or place. I have a couple of things to prepare for a hearing tomorrow. I'll pick you up around eight and take you somewhere outrageously expensive for dinner. We can talk then.'

'I'd be happy just to stay in,' said Camilla, leaning her body against his.

'You have to eat. I'll see you later.'

He kissed her lightly once more, then went out just as Simon was coming in, post and papers under one arm.

Simon, who was more than a little keen on Camilla himself, could tell within a fraction of a second – from Leo's manner, from the look on Camilla's face – that he had been within a whisker of interrupting something. He said nothing, merely gave Camilla a smile, then sat down and set about opening his mail. At the back of his mind, however, was a certain misgiving about whatever it was Leo was up to. Simon liked the man, found him amusing, clever, but he wasn't at all sure that it was in Camilla's best interests to be getting involved with him.

Leo was too practised, both personally and professionally, in the subtle art of manipulation to have to make much mental preparation for the conversation over dinner that evening. He was careful to re-establish the former levels of intimacy and affection between Camilla and himself before eventually touching on the argument which had led to the glass-smashing and Camilla's week of purgatory.

'I suppose I should have told you about Gideon Smallwood, but the whole thing was such a bloody mess at the time – I really had no idea what was going to happen. It wasn't exactly the kind of thing I wanted to confide in anyone.' Not entirely true, he knew – had relations between them been otherwise, he would probably have told Anthony, above all people.

Camilla sighed. 'I just worry that you don't seem to trust me. The last thing I want to do is start that argument all over again –'

'Of course I trust you,' interrupted Leo. 'That's the least of it. My chief worry concerns your trust in me.'

'What do you mean?'

He reached out a hand to hers. 'You are so sweet, and so special, and you want to think well of me, and to know absolutely everything about me. I love that. But I'm not sure either of those is possible. I'm not a straightforward person. I can't guarantee anything about myself, past, present or future.'

She hesitated, then said, 'You're saying you don't think you can promise to be faithful to me.'

There was an element of truth in this, but now was not the time to admit it. 'I'm saying nothing of the kind. I just realize that I've been unfair in asking you to marry me when you can have no real idea of what sharing my life might be like.'

Camilla wound her fingers around his and smiled a little sadly. 'Actually, it was my idea in the first place, not yours – remember?'

Until this moment, he'd forgotten that. Of course – it had been her ultimatum, that evening in the rose garden. This recollection in itself was heartening, and useful. 'True. But I know I thought at the time – if this is what it takes … Because I couldn't bear to lose you. Maybe it was all too hasty. I'm worried that you're going to end up hurt and disappointed.'

'So – what are you saying?'

Leo poured some more wine into both their glasses. 'Shall I be perfectly frank? I don't want to marry you, and for you to find a year down the line that I'm not the sort of husband you imagined, that I don't live up to expectations.'

'That could never happen. I love you. I want to be with you, whatever.'

'Well, it's the "whatever" that worries me. I told you I come with no guarantees. I know myself too well. What I'm suggesting is that we forget about the idea of marriage for the moment. Give it time. Let's just enjoy the present, and see where it goes. You're still very young, and in a few years' time you may find that your notions of what you want from life have changed. As you said, your parents aren't likely to be bursting with joy at the idea of you marrying someone like me. Let's leave the rest of the world out of it. This is to do with you and me, nobody else. We can play this any way we like. You needn't give up your flat, or your independence. We can see one another as and when we want. It's our relationship, and we don't need to observe any conventions. They've never been my style, anyway.'

'You don't want to live with me?'

'Of course I want to live with you! You know you could have moved in weeks ago, if you weren't so worried about Jane and your parents. But maybe that's not the right way to find what we both want. We have to treat each other as equals. You don't want to put yourself in a position where your life is simply – well … subsumed into mine.'

'How else is it going to happen? What can I contribute? I'm just starting out, Leo. I have nothing, you have everything.'

'Look, I have a suggestion. I've been talking to a few estate agents recently. I want to get out of the Belgravia flat, find a house somewhere in town which can be more of a home for Oliver – and for you, if you decide that's what you want. It may take time to find the right place. In that time, let's maintain the status quo. No problems with parents or flat-mates. And if you decide you do still want to be with me, be part of the chaos that is my life, then we can make a fresh start together, on equal terms.'

He studied her face. Her smile was slow, thoughtful. 'I'd much rather it was that way. I'd much rather make a new home with you.'

He picked up her hand and kissed the tips of her fingers lightly. 'Exactly. Now that we've sorted that out, let's get the bill.'

An hour later, as they made love, Leo wondered why he was bothering with all this prevarication. She was so intensely delightful in bed, and in every other way. But best to take things slowly – he had her best interests at heart, after all.

The new annexe to 5 Caper Court, where Maurice, Ann, Roger and Marcus had their rooms, consisted of the entire top floor of number 7, the building adjoining number 5 on the west side of Caper Court. It occurred to Leo, who had been largely instrumental in procuring this enlargement of chambers to prevent the necessity of a full-scale move to larger premises, that he hadn't had a proper look at the annexe since it was in its rudimentary stages of development, and he decided, in an idle hour, to pay a visit and have a look at the finished thing.

He went up to the floor above his room and passed

through the new door which had been knocked through from the top floor of number 5 to the annexe. The air was filled with the stark scent of new paint and wood. Leo recalled when, as a flat, this floor had been the home of old Desmond Broadbent, a retired High Court judge, who had lived here with his two little Cairn terriers. Leo had paid a visit only last year, and the sombre habitation had been utterly transformed. None of the proportions of the spacious rooms, or the doors and windows had been altered, and the place retained much old-fashioned charm, but it had been entirely rewired and replastered, with state-of-the-art fittings, lighting and decoration. The annexe consisted of eight rooms – four housing the new tenants and three more soon to be occupied. It had been Roderick's idea that one should be turned into a kind of bedsit, in case any member of chambers – or a client – should ever need to stay overnight. Leo inspected this room, with its trendily utilitarian kitchen and shower, and wondered if and when it would be put to any use. Coming out, he saw that Ann Halliday's door was slightly ajar. He knocked lightly and looked in. Ann was standing with her back to him, sorting through papers on the table next to her desk. Clearly she hadn't heard his knock.

'Hi,' said Leo. 'Hope I'm not interrupting.'

Ann glanced round. 'No. Come in. I've just had a two-hour con. Glad to see the back of them.' She finished arranging her papers and turned to survey Leo. How well he always looked. It wasn't just the handsome features, which seemed to her to have changed little since their days at Bar School together, but their expressiveness, that alert look, charged with interest and expectation. 'What brings you up here?' she asked.

'I came to have a look around, actually. The last time I

was here the place was just bare boards, builders everywhere. How d'you like your room?'

'The room is perfect,' said Ann. 'Maurice seems to have a million and one gripes, but I can't say I have anything to complain about. Except the stairs, perhaps. They keep me fit, I suppose.'

'That's what I like about these buildings. You can't mess around with them too much, putting in lifts and air-conditioning and that kind of nonsense. And yes – the stairs do keep you fit. You're looking very trim.'

Leo said this with practised ease, strolling into the room and glancing around. Ann knew better than to invest the words with any special significance. There had been a time in her youth when, in common with most girls she knew, she would have given anything for a one-to-one with Leo Davies. But years had passed, she had seen the casualties along the way, and now she reckoned that his friendship was more valuable than any casual sexual indulgence.

He propped himself against Ann's desk and folded his arms. 'I'm very glad you've joined us. We used to have some good times, you and I, back at Bar School. What say we re-create those happy times?'

'If you mean staying up till three, listening to Joni Mitchell and drinking too much – no, not even for you.'

'Perhaps something more civilized. Making due allowance for our advanced age. How about lunch?'

'Now?'

'Unless you've had a better offer.'

'Not so far. I'll just put these away. Shall I see if Marcus or Roger wants to join us?'

'No. The company of the young can be hard work, and I feel I've done too much of that lately.'

Ann wondered if this was an oblique reference to young

92

Miss Lawrence, of whom she had heard certain rumours involving Leo. She gave a wry smile. 'Let me get my bag.'

They went downstairs together, making a brief detour to the clerks' room to check for post. Henry was talking to David Liphook, and as he passed Henry's desk, Leo noticed the stacked boxes of white envelopes.

'What's this lot?' he asked.

'Invitations to the chambers' party on the twentieth of next month,' replied Henry. 'Should've gone out last week, only we had a problem with the venue. Couldn't get Inner Temple Garden, so we've had to make do with Gray's Inn.'

'You mean we have to slog all the way up there?' asked David.

'Walk'll do you good, sir,' replied Henry briskly. 'You can always take a cab if it's too taxing.'

'I wasn't even aware we were having a bash,' said Leo.

'Mr Faber's idea. Well, Mr Hayter's originally, but Mr Faber's been overseeing most of the arrangements,' said Henry. 'A sort of "welcome to the new-look Five Caper Court" party. City firms, P&I clubs, judges, all the usual suspects. Mr Faber even suggested a barbecue supper, on top of the champagne and Pimm's. He's very full of ideas, when it comes to PR.'

'I'll bet he is.' Leo turned to Ann. 'I didn't realize Maurice was such a little mover and shaker,' he murmured. 'He seems to have thrown himself into chambers' life with unusual energy.'

'We talked about this party at the last chambers' meeting,' said David. 'Don't you remember?'

'I must have been asleep.'

'Well, Maurice has pretty much sorted it out. He's keen to promote a bold new image for us. Glad someone wants to do it, as long as it's not me. As Henry says, he's bursting with ideas. Even says he's going to re-vamp the chambers' website.'

'Is that a fact?'

'I suspect he's lining himself up to become head of chambers when Roderick pops off.'

Leo was mildly startled. He had no special ambitions in that direction himself, but it irked him to think that some-one so new to chambers should be muscling ahead of people who'd been there many years. Still, if Maurice enjoyed arranging parties and tinkering with websites, let him get on with it.

'Come on,' he said to Ann. 'Let's have lunch.'

Adriana Papaposilakis heard with some satisfaction that Leo had accepted her brief, and a conference was arranged to discuss the case of the *Persephone*. It was to be held in Leo's room at 5 Caper Court, and attended by Miss Papaposilakis, Mr Defereras, Rachel and the junior barrister already instructed in the case, Kate Carpenter.

On the morning of the conference Miss Papaposilakis arrived dead on time. She swept into Leo's room, dressed in one of her trademark designer suits, which managed to make her look both compact and voluptuous at the same time, accompanied by the silent Mr Defereras. Leo rose from behind his desk and extended his hand to Adriana.

While Rachel made brief introductions, Leo surveyed his new client with interest. She was indeed diminutive – no more than five feet tall, at most – but she exuded energy and personality, charging the room with her presence and her light, distinctive fragrance. And she was, he had to admit, extremely lovely, almost to excess. In every aspect of her appearance there seemed to be an element of surplus – in the blondeness of her hair, the extravagance of her very feminine figure, her queenly air, the husky voice, the make-up, the shoes, the jewellery. Leo, as he smiled and shook her hand, marvelled at such an abundance of sensuality in so slight a being.

Miss Papaposilakis, for her part, felt the mildest disappointment when she first set eyes on Leo. He was wickedly good-looking, admittedly, but came across as nothing like the dangerous, reckless lothario portrayed in the newspaper columns of a few weeks ago. His manner was polite, restrained, and in his dark suit and tie in the neat, formal setting of his room, he seemed no different from any of the other barristers she had come across. And then he shook her hand and smiled, and she saw in that smile and in the sharp glance of the blue eyes something much more intriguing and promising. With a little inner shiver of pleasure, Adriana Papaposilakis settled herself in her chair, lifted her chin, and waited expectantly for Leo to begin.

'Well, now, I've been through the papers, and of course I've discussed the case at some length with Miss Dean and Miss Carpenter –' Leo gave a nod in the direction of the junior barrister, a thin, patient girl in her early twenties who, if she was in any way put out that Leo had been instructed as leader in the case, had yet to show it '– and I'm happy to say that I believe we have every prospect of success. That is to say, I think the defendants are going to have a very difficult time establishing that the events which caused the loss of the *Persephone* were anything but accidental. I'm surprised they've been so reluctant to settle. I'm sure we're all familiar with the facts, but it may be useful to summarize them briefly.' Leo glanced down at a couple of pages of his own handwritten notes. 'It appears that the yacht was in harbour at Ventetone in Italy, when a fire broke out in the engine-room in the early hours of the morning of September the twenty-third, two thousand and two. The fire spread rapidly to the accommodation area, where a deck boy died as a result of smoke inhalation. The only other persons on board the boat at the time – the master and the engineer – escaped. We'll discuss their evidence in detail a little later on, but suffice to say for the moment that as a result of the fire the vessel sank at her anchorage. The seat of the fire was in the vicinity of the generator, though the evidence appears to be inconclusive as to precisely where the ignition first took place . . .' Leo thumbed through the file and glanced at a couple of pages before going on. 'Anyway, the expert reports establish that one of the high-pressure diesel fuel supply pipes serving one of the generator's three cylinders had become partially disconnected, and that this was the source of the fuel for the fire. The defendants say that it was the deliberate opening of this injector pipe which caused it. We, on the other hand, maintain that the pipe vibrated open accidentally.'

Leo sat back in his chair. 'Stated baldly, those are the facts of the case. I'll go into the technical aspects more deeply in a moment. As Miss Carpenter has stated in her original opinion, to win their case, the underwriters have a difficult burden of proof to discharge. They have to show that the fire was started deliberately with a view to causing constructive total loss of the vessel, and that it was done with the connivance of her owners.' Here Leo paused to glance at Miss Papaposilakis, but he could read nothing in the depths of those brown, lustrous eyes, which looked straight into his with every appearance of candour. 'Establishing an allegation of scuttling requires strong evidence – strong enough to induce what Mr Justice Coleman described in *The Grecia Express* as "a high level of confidence that the allegation of scuttling is true". I believe there are too many uncertainties here for the other side to induce that level of confidence in court. What motive, after all, could Miss Papaposilakis have for getting rid of the yacht?' Again his eyes met those of Adriana Papaposilakis.

She gave a small smile. 'Precisely. I'm scarcely in desperate need of money. The *Persephone* has long since been replaced by a new yacht for my personal use. The insurance claim was made as a matter of course. It is quite outrageous to suggest that I would arrange for the deliberate sinking of my own yacht, or that any master of mine would agree to it. Why would I do such a thing?' She gave a pretty shrug. 'That is why I have asked you to take this case, Mr Davies. I have every faith that you can win it for me.'

Leo was perfectly convinced that the case could win itself in the very capable hands of Kate Carpenter, but he wasn't going to argue with the passionate warmth which flickered in Miss Papaposilakis's dark eyes as she spoke.

'I'm flattered you think so, Miss Papaposilakis. We shall do our utmost. Now, let's have a look at the witness statements, starting first of all with that of the master, Captain Kollias . . .'

Two hours later, after an exhaustive trawl through statements and expert reports, Leo brought the meeting to a close.

'I think we can leave it there for the present. We still have to put in our skeleton argument – left it rather late, I'm afraid – and Miss Dean will let you have a copy of that as soon as it's prepared. In the meantime, I have to start preparing my examination of the witnesses, so I'll need to see Captain Kollias and Mr Staveris fairly soon. Will we be able to arrange that?' Leo glanced at Rachel.

Mr Defereras leaned forward. 'Captain Kollias is retired now. He lives here in London with his family, so he is available any time you wish to see him.'

'And Mr Staveris?'

'I can arrange for him to come to London in the next two weeks,' said Mr Defereras.

'Good.' Leo put his papers together. He rose, as did Adriana, and they shook hands once more.

'It relieves me to know that you are so optimistic about our chances of success, Mr Davies. As I said before, I am sure you will win this case for me.'

Leo smiled. That slight accent was remarkably sexy, as was everything about this woman. 'Thank you for your confidence. I'll try not to disappoint you.'

'Oh, I'm very sure you won't.'

Rachel tried to watch this exchange dispassionately. After all, here were two people who were past masters at charming the pants off everyone they met. In Leo's case, literally. She sighed inwardly. Leo was too professional to let Miss Papaposilakis work on him at a personal level, and she supposed she should be grateful for that. Rachel really didn't think she could bear to handle this case if she had to watch Leo succumbing to the seductive allure of this insidious Greek midget.

That evening, Leo was lying on the sofa after supper with the *Financial Times*, while Camilla sat cross-legged on the floor, leafing through holiday brochures. Leo had suggested taking a week's break at the end of August, if Henry could clear the way, and Camilla was assessing the various Caribbean options.

'Leo, these places are incredibly expensive. Do you realize?'

'Yes, I realize.'

'I mean, all these five-star resorts. Do you know what a room at this Sandy Lane place costs?'

Leo lowered his paper. 'Forget about rooms. We'll have a suite. Or one of those apartments on the beach, with houseboys and gardeners and maids thrown in. I absolutely refuse to do this on a second-class basis.'

'It's going to cost a complete fortune,' murmured Camilla, turning the pages.

'My dear child, you haven't the first idea what constitutes a complete fortune. It's certainly not the cost of a fortnight's holiday at a decent hotel. I've been instructed recently by a client who could buy the Sandy Lane several times over, and still have change to spare for a cocktail or two.'

'Who's that?' Camilla turned to look at Leo over her shoulder.

'A creature by the name of Adriana Papaposilakis. She runs the Silakis Shipping Line.'

'I've heard of Silakis. They're massive. She must be rolling in it.'

'Somewhat. An amusing woman, in an outrageous kind of way.'

Catching Leo's smile, Camilla turned her attention more fully to this. 'What's so outrageous about her?'

'Hmm. Difficult to say. She has certain . . . qualities.'

'She's attractive, you mean.'

'In a rather overstated way. But yes, definitely personable.'

'Is it a big case?'

'Not particularly. Her private yacht caught fire and sank a couple of years ago, and the underwriters are refusing to pay out. They reckon it wasn't an accident. The case is only worth a few million. She had a perfectly able junior handling it, then out of the blue she asked for me.'

'Why you? I mean – what's the big deal?'

'Oh . . .' Leo cast about for a reason, then shrugged. 'I think perhaps it's become a point of principle for her. Can't stand the thought of being accused of such a thing. Must win at all costs.'

'I'll bet *you're* the big deal.'

'Don't be daft.' Leo raised his paper again, then after a few seconds asked, 'What on earth makes you say that?'

'Oh, come on – don't imagine people weren't intrigued by all that stuff in the papers about you. It's bound to have an effect.'

'Well, the instructing solicitors are Nichols and Co., and with my beady-eyed ex-wife on the case, I don't imagine any Greek hussy is going to be allowed to compromise my manly virtue. So set your mind at rest, and come here.'

Camilla got up and joined him on the sofa, snuggling against him. After the torment of that wretched week following their last argument, she had decided that there was no point in worrying about who or what was going to distract Leo's wayward attentions next. She was just going to have to learn to trust him.

Even though it was midsummer, Sandy spent the first week at Felicity's Clapham flat in a state of near-hibernation. He scarcely got out of bed for the first three days. Then, gradually, he emerged into a kind of torpid life. Felicity would come home from work and find him hunched up on the sofa, watching television. So far as she could tell, he was trying to stay clean. Harbouring a lurking fear that perhaps a heroin habit was the reason for the mess he was in, she'd already had a few furtive glances at his arms for needle marks, but had seen none. But, being Sandy, he must have been doing some drugs while he was on the streets. Maybe he'd been smoking crack. The possibility terrified her. At any rate, he didn't appear to be doing anything at the moment. He didn't have any money. He had signed on, but his money had yet to come through.

At first his presence in the flat didn't seem to impinge on Felicity's own existence at all. Then, gradually, small spores of his aimless, grimy life began to speckle the place – mug rings on the coffee table, his constantly unmade bed, newspapers littering the arms of sofas. She could well imagine them spreading across her life like a fungus before long. Until Sandy's money came through, Felicity lent him some to get by on. She was depressed, but not surprised, to come home from work one evening and detect the unmistakable whiff of dope in the flat.

'Sandy,' she said, taking off her coat, 'I didn't agree to let you stay here just so's you could lie around getting stoned.'

'I'm not stoned,' said Sandy, who was sprawled on the sofa watching television. 'I just needed something to relax with.' He glanced up and stretched out the hand holding the spliff. 'Fancy some?'

Felicity shook her head. 'I don't do it any more,' she replied. 'Waste of time. What have you done today? Did you go down the Job Centre?'

Sandy drew on his spliff and nodded. 'Nothing there I fancied, though.'

'Well, you're going to have to fancy something soon enough. They stop your money if you keep on turning down work.'

'Money's not even started yet.'

'Yeah, well . . .' Felicity went into the kitchen and emerged a moment later. 'I thought you were going to go to the supermarket today. What happened to that list I gave you?'

Sandy scratched his head dejectedly. 'Oh, man – I forgot. Sorry.'

'So what are we meant to eat tonight? There's bugger-all in the fridge. And what about the money I gave you for the shopping?'

Sandy gave her a look of blank innocence. 'I thought that was for me, like. So . . .' He held up the spliff.

'Oh, great. The grocery money gets spent on dope.'

'Look, you don't have to have a go at me as soon as you get in. I said I'm sorry. If you don't want me here I'll leave. I've got my sleeping bag –'

'No, Sandy,' she sighed. 'You're fine here. It's just – well, this isn't forever, you know. It's temporary. You need to get your head together, get a job, and find somewhere of your own. If you don't start trying to make something of your life now, you never will. You're twenty-six, for God's sake –'

'Yeah, yeah. Can you stow it, Fliss? You're coming on like me mum, and I can do without it.' He suddenly dropped his roach in the ashtray and clutched his head with his hands. 'I mean, I have been so low, so bloody low . . . It's like I've got things going round in my head that won't shut up. And now you're going on at me. Everything's getting to me these days. Nobody understands what it's like.'

Felicity realized there was no point in going on, or getting mad at him. Water off a duck's back. She gazed at him, hunched up on the sofa. Poor sod. He looked so pathetic and useless, sitting there all depressed. The dope probably didn't help. How long had he been smoking now? Since he was a teenager. He always said it was less bad for you than alcohol, but she wasn't so sure.

'Right, well,' she said, 'I'd better ring up and order us some pizza.' It was one thing feeding and housing her brother, but she was determined she wasn't going to buy his dope for him. She'd just have to do her own shopping in future.

A few days later, Robert accosted Camilla one morning as she came into the clerks' room. 'Ah, just the lady. I've had Elborne Mitchell on the phone. They've got a big fraud case involving offshore companies registered in Bermuda, and they need someone to go out and take statements. It could take up two or three weeks, but you've got clear space up ahead.'

Camilla's instinct was to say yes instantly – the idea of a trip abroad was very appealing. Then she thought about leaving Leo, and a little empty space seemed to open up beneath her heart. Well, that was stupid. He'd still be here when she got back. It might do her good to be independent of him for a while. Sometimes it felt as though her identity was lost in his, as though, outside of work, her life had little shape except for that which Leo gave it. It was too easy to feel like a child, or a plaything, where Leo was concerned.

'When do they want me to go?'

'They want you out there next week. So it would be a weekend flight.'

'How much?'

'I did a deal. Fifteen hundred a day.'

'I can't really say no, can I?'

On her way upstairs, Camilla passed Leo's room and looked in to tell him.

'I'm going to Bermuda for a few weeks.'

Leo looked up from the papers he was working on. He could tell from her face that she was excited. 'When?' He took off his half-moon glasses.

'This weekend. I haven't got the papers yet, but it's some fraud case Elborne's are handling. Only taking statements. But still. Five-star hotel, the works.'

'Ah, the simple pleasures. You juniors are so easily bought. You look all pink and excited,' said Leo with a smile. 'Which is the way I generally like you.'

There it was – that teasing tone which made her feel rather juvenile. She wished he didn't patronize her, even if it was sweetly meant. She shrugged. 'I'm pleased, of course.'

'As well you should be. At this rate you'll be able to help out with the mortgage on the new house. Which reminds me –' He stretched across his desk for a sheaf of papers. 'Cast your eye over this. I thought we'd go and have a look at it after work.'

'If I'm free,' said Camilla. 'I might be having a drink with friends, or something.'

Leo paused in the act of handing her the house particulars. 'Sorry. Are you?'

'I don't know why I said that. No, of course I'm not.' She felt foolish. It was just that he always assumed she was his, that her time was his . . . She glanced at the particulars. The house was on the borders of Kensington and Knightsbridge, a town house with a large garden. 'Wow. Five bedrooms . . . That's a bit big, isn't it?'

'Not really. Anyway, come back around six and we'll go and have a look at it.'

Leo and Camilla drove across to Chelsea after work. The estate agent, a young woman, was waiting for them outside the house. It was a three-storey detached house, set in a quiet, leafy crescent, separated from the road by a short front garden bordered by black railings. The brass knocker and handles on the dark blue front door gleamed in the evening sunlight, and the little breeze which rustled through the leaves of adjacent trees spoke of quiet prosperity. Leo hadn't mentioned a figure, but Camilla knew that a house of this kind, in this part of London, must be extremely expensive. She could imagine the kind of people who lived round here, and she couldn't see herself ever being one of them.

The estate agent unlocked the door and led them into the house. It was entirely empty, the polished floors gleaming soundlessly, the windows blank, curtainless. The owners, explained the estate agent, had purchased the house a year ago and had never lived in it. They had numerous properties throughout the world. Camilla wandered through the rooms on the ground floor, wondering what kind of person, possessed of what kind of wealth, could buy such a beautiful house and not want to live in it, never setting foot in it, never even wanting to tread through these beautifully proportioned rooms, or open the long windows leading out to the large, sunny garden. Perhaps too much money blunted all desire, all appreciation.

'Would you like me to show you round the rest of the house, or would you rather explore it for yourself?' asked the estate agent.

Leo, standing in the middle of the gleaming, spacious kitchen, equipped to clinical perfection with every state-of-the-art appliance, looked round consideringly. 'We'll have a look on our own, if we may.'

He and Camilla went up the staircase to the first floor. In the quiet, echoing safety of a large back bedroom, Camilla said, 'It's fantastic, Leo. It's the most beautiful house I've ever seen.'

'It is rather good, isn't it?' Leo went to the window and looked down into the garden, at the long, well-kept lawn, at the bright, soft colours of the roses and other flowers, and the mulberry tree which shaded the patio. The owners, even if they hadn't cared to live here, had clearly ensured that everything was perfectly maintained. This bedroom, he thought, would be Oliver's. This one – so that every morning of his young life, whenever he was here, Oliver might wake up to this view, his view, from his own room, and feel a sense of peace and security, of belonging.

Camilla wandered out on to the landing and into another, larger room. She tried to imagine how it should be furnished.

The drawing room, too, and the dining room. She had an idea of the kind of furniture, the way it should all look – but she couldn't picture herself in such a setting. If he lived here, Leo would expect to entertain people, to fill those lovely rooms with people and laughter, and the right food and wine, gleaming candlelight, proper place settings, and . . . Her mind quailed at the thought. She could not see herself managing any of that. Maybe there were twenty-two-year-olds in the world who could, but she didn't think she was one of them. This was the kind of house people aspired to, grew into from a series of less assuming places and stages in life. When she was fifty, perhaps . . . even then, she would probably be totally daunted by the kind of lifestyle befitting such a house.

She wandered into the bathroom connected to the bedroom. It was beautiful. Serene, sophisticated – not things Camilla ever felt. Its pale walls seemed to mock her presence. She thought of the slightly grubby, cramped bathroom she and Jane shared in the Clapham flat. Camilla realized that if ever she had vaguely envisaged the unfolding of her adult life, of making a home with someone, the hazy picture had been of a modest house or flat somewhere, cluttered, cheerful, nothing too ambitious. Not to begin with. Friends to supper, small beginnings, with aspirations to bigger and better. But to be pitched suddenly into this dreamlike, echoing place, with its high ceilings and beautiful fireplaces . . .

The sound of Leo's footsteps interrupted her thoughts. She went back through to the bedroom.

'I wondered where you'd got to.' Leo drew her briefly against him and kissed her forehead, then paced slowly into the bathroom and back out again. 'What do you think?'

'It's lovely,' said Camilla. 'But I do find it a little intimidating.'

Leo smiled. 'What do you mean?'

'It's just so . . . *grand*.'

'This? It's only a town house.'

She shrugged. 'Well, it seems grand to me. I can't imagine it ever being very — very homely. That kitchen, all that stainless steel and polished granite. I just can't see myself in there.'

'It need only be as grand, as you put it, as we want it to be. You decide. If I buy it, you can furnish it.'

'Oh no, I couldn't!' gasped Camilla. 'I wouldn't know where to begin. I don't know about the right kind of furniture, or pictures, or — well, anything.'

Leo shrugged. 'We'd get people in to do it, in that case.' He went out on to the landing and up the staircase to the next floor.

And then, thought Camilla, it wouldn't be like a home at all. It would belong to someone else, with someone else's walls and floors and curtains, the product of someone else's taste and discernment. She wondered if Rachel had chosen everything for the home which she and Leo had shared during their marriage. Probably. Rachel looked like the kind of person who was assured in everything she did.

She followed Leo upstairs. 'How much are they asking?'

Leo turned to glance into her grave, apprehensive eyes. 'Two million — well, thereabouts.'

'Help.'

'But that's not something you need to worry about. Come on.'

They went downstairs to where the estate agent was waiting. They discussed certain aspects of the sale briefly.

'It's a beautiful house,' said Leo. 'And certainly very close to what we're looking for.'

'I have to tell you that there are a number of other interested parties.'

Leo nodded. 'I'm sure there are. We'll think about it. I'll speak to you in the next few days.'

They went down the short flight of steps and through the gate to the pavement. As they got into the car, Leo looked back briefly at the house. It was mad to think that one could choose the first property one looked at, surely. Best to see what else was out there on the market before coming to a firm decision. But he couldn't help giving the house one last, long glance before pulling away from the kerb.

6

Over the following two weeks, Adriana Papaposilakis became a regular visitor at 5 Caper Court. So much so that Michael Gibbon, catching the delicious, tell-tale whiff of her fragrance on his way through the reception area one day, could not refrain from remarking to Leo on the frequency of her visits.

'Oh, you know the old Greeks,' said Leo, as they made their way upstairs. 'They like to have their hands held, to be reassured that their barrister is completely onside, convinced of the winnability of their case.'

'And are you?'

Leo smiled. 'When was I ever not? I really think the insurers are unwise to be fighting this. There's no way they can establish that the fire was started on purpose.'

'So why won't they settle?'

'You know underwriters – completely book-driven. Possibly they're not happy with the Silakis claims record. But we'll see. You never really know with these things until the hearing gets underway. All kinds of stuff can pop out of the woodwork. I've gone through the master's statement with him, and he seems sound enough. I still have to talk to the engineer. He's coming over from Greece next week.'

'Which will doubtless involve yet another visit from Miss Paposil – whatever her name is.'

'Papaposilakis.' Leo smiled. 'Adriana to me, at her insistence.'

'I'll bet.' They had reached the door of Leo's room, and

Leo was about to go in when Michael added, 'By the way, I had a drink with Roderick last night, and it seems pretty certain he's going to be off to the High Court by September at the latest.'

'Which means appointing a new head of chambers. Fine. Anyone, so long as it's not me.' He opened the door to his room. 'See you later.'

Michael carried on upstairs to his own room. Pity, really. And there he'd been thinking that Leo was the perfect man for the job.

The following week saw Henry attending to the final arrangements for the chambers' party, which was to be on Friday evening. By Thursday he felt he had most things under control. Felicity stood patiently by his desk as he went through his list.

'Caterers – fine. Sorted out tables, chairs . . . yes, good. Marquee, drinks . . . yes, fine. Music – Dixieland quartet, not my idea, but Mr Faber thinks it'll go down a treat. Meeting and greeting – here we are.' He turned to Felicity. 'That's your job. You'll have a list of all the guests, and you greet them all as they wander in, tick their names off. That way we know who turns up, and who to target in the future. All part of Mr Faber's marketing strategy.'

'Why me?'

'Because,' said Henry, 'you look so young and lovely. Well, better than Robert, anyway. All part of the PR exercise. Wear your best smile, and something suitable to the occasion.'

'Meaning?'

'You know what I mean. Here, Robert – have you got those guest lists printed out? Fine. You can give Fliss two copies. Then get on to the printers, pronto. Those name badges still haven't arrived.'

Felicity glanced through the list which Robert gave her and sighed. Not her idea of fun, being on her feet all evening, wearing a big cheesy grin for all those solicitors and judges and other assorted riffraff, watching them all get completely trolleyed, and not able to drink more than a glass herself. If she was lucky. Still, if it was good for business, she shouldn't be complaining.

The venue for the party was in Gray's Inn, a quiet, shady garden square surrounded on three sides by chambers buildings, with a gateway at the end. A large marquee had been erected for this and numerous other summer functions, and groups of tables and chairs dotted the lawn. The barbecue, plus a couple of long trestle tables, stood next to the marquee.

The party was officially due to begin at six-thirty, but Henry and Felicity were there well in advance to oversee the caterers, and assist in organizing the squadron of waitresses who were to circulate among the guests with wine and champagne.

'Blimey! How much wine did you order?' asked Felicity, eyeing the cases stacked inside the marquee.

'Fifteen of each,' replied Henry. 'Should be more than enough. Having said that, you could double it and these buggers would still drink the place dry. I'm not sure Mr Faber's idea of the barbecue is such a good one,' he added morosely. 'It'll just make them drink more. Couple of vol-au-vents and a cocktail sausage was always good enough in the past.'

Felicity looked round appreciatively as the lightest of summer breezes stirred the tops of the plane trees and puffed the canvas sides of the marquee. 'I think it's a nice idea. And the little jazz band. Gives it a nice summery feeling, makes it more of a party. And think how good it'll be for business.'

'We've never spent this much on a chambers do before. It had better be.'

Back at 5 Caper Court, Leo was in the throes of a difficult meeting with Adriana Papaposilakis, Rachel, and Pantazis Staveris, the engineer of the defunct *Persephone*. The latter was a swarthy, anxious young man, clad in a new suit, on his first trip to London, and clearly unnerved by his surroundings and the taxing business of trying to present his version of events in halting English. Leo, who would have to take him through his evidence in his examination-in-chief, wanted to ensure that Mr Staveris's account of the loss of the *Persephone* was as simple and direct as possible, and to minimize the possibility of unlooked-for revelations when it came to his cross-examination by the other side.

For over an hour Leo worked him painstakingly and patiently through his statement, until he felt he had done all he could. In his estimation, Pantazis Staveris would make a good witness – his anxiety bespoke candour rather than evasiveness, and his struggle to present his evidence in an unfamiliar language somehow added to his air of reliability.

'Thank you, Mr Staveris, you've been very helpful. I know it's difficult for you, but I hope that the work we have done today will make things easier when we come to the actual hearing.' Mr Staveris nodded, wide eyes fixed on Leo's. 'I shall be calling you after Captain Kollias. My examination-in-chief will be pretty brief, but the other side's cross-examination may last a day or two.' He smiled. 'You have nothing to worry about.'

Mr Staveris nodded again, then glanced at Rachel.

She gave him a smile. 'Right. We'll find a taxi to take you back to your hotel.' Rachel rose and put her papers together.

'Are you going straight to the chambers' party?' she asked Leo. 'We could walk up together.'

Leo glanced at his watch. 'I've got a couple of things I have to attend to first, I'm afraid. I'll see you there later.'

Adriana, who had been leafing through some documents, glanced up at Rachel with her enchanting smile. 'I still have a few things I wish to discuss with Mr Davies, Rachel. Don't let me keep you.'

'Fine. Unless you need to speak to me beforehand, I'll see you at the hearing on Monday.'

Rachel left with Mr Staveris. As she closed the door behind her, she reflected on how such slight torments – not being able to walk to Gray's Inn with Leo, having to leave Adriana in possession of him – were like tiny razor cuts to her soul. She wondered when, if ever, such trivia would cease to matter, or if the minute suffering was destined to last for ever.

For fifteen minutes or so Adriana detained Leo with a detailed consideration of the smoking habits of Mr Staveris, and the possibility that a carelessly disposed of cigarette might have caused the fire. Anxious though Adriana was about this case, Leo knew that this conversation was largely a pretext, a rehash of a previous discussion he and she had had with Rachel. He wondered what was coming. He thought he knew. Sure enough, at the end of it she smiled and said, 'You know, you have this wonderful way of reassuring me. I feel with you everything will be all right. It is not the money that is important to me – it is my good name, my reputation. People think I am very tough, but you know –' she reached out a small, graceful hand and laid it on Leo's arm, pressing it lightly '– I need a strong man sometimes.' Leo was lost for an apt response to this, and she went on, her eyes dark with sincerity, 'You are very solid, very secure, and I don't often meet men like that. You are very good for me.'

Leo decided it would be best to play the baffled professional. He smiled. 'I'm delighted you should think so, of course.'

'I think we are alike. We are both very driven, very successful people.' She took her hand from his arm and rested her chin on it, eyes burning into his. 'Sometimes it can be too much for us. We need to relax.'

Bemused, Leo tried to keep his tone conversational. 'Yes? Yes, very possibly.'

'Have dinner with me. Talk to me. Let us relax together, get to know each other. When people are thrown together in circumstances like these, they should get to know each other. Have dinner with me this evening.'

'Normally,' replied Leo, 'there is nothing I should like better. But I'm afraid I have a previous engagement.'

She shrugged, her gaze still fastened on his. 'Cancel it.'

Leo, whose eyes could not help straying to the few inches of soft, tantalizing cleavage displayed by Adriana's tight little couture jacket, replied, 'I only wish I could. But it's a professional matter. I really have no choice. I'm sorry.'

'That is so disappointing.' She rose, diffusing her light fragrance, gathering her belongings together. Then she gave him a soft smile. 'Some other time, perhaps.'

Leo was relieved that she didn't appear at all piqued by his refusal. The last time he'd rejected the advances of a mettlesome Greek woman, the results had been catastrophic.

'Yes,' he replied. 'Perhaps.' No harm in keeping the possibility open, after all.

Over at Gray's Inn, the first guests at the chambers party began to drift in shortly after half past six. An hour later, by Felicity's count, there were over 120 guests thronging the garden, filling the air with talk and laughter. Little knots of barristers, solicitors, clerks, plus assorted surveyors, under-writers and the odd judge, stood raking over cases and City gossip as waiters and waitresses moved among them, replenishing glasses at a steady rate. In the background, from another world, ran the steady hum of London traffic.

Felicity felt unusually accomplished and efficient as she smiled and greeted the guests. She knew just about every one of them, and it intrigued her to realize how extensive her connections and influence were. Around half past seven it seemed that most of those coming had arrived, and she gratefully grabbed a glass of white wine and temporarily relinquished her duties.

'How are we doing?' asked Henry, squinting down at the list.

'Not bad. About two-thirds, maybe more.'

'That's good, considering the time of year.' Henry glanced at Felicity. 'That's a really nice outfit you're wearing, if I may say so.'

'You may,' said Felicity, gratified. She wandered off to mingle with the guests, and Henry's eyes followed her wistfully. Felicity hadn't gone far before she came across Peter Weir talking to some solicitors. Peter saw her trying to steer herself in the other direction, but intercepted her.

'You can't spend your life avoiding me.'

'Can't I?' Again she tried to move past him, but he wouldn't let her.

'You barely speak to me in chambers. Don't you think it's time we tried to develop a more harmonious working relationship?'

'It suits me just the way it is,' replied Felicity coldly.

'Fliss, don't do this. I've missed you so much since we broke up. Can't we just be friends? At least talk to one another?' He gave his charming, lopsided smile, and she felt a familiar weakening sensation. She tried to remind herself what a bastard he'd been. But the truth was, she didn't want to go on nursing these feelings of anger and resentment. It wasn't her style. She liked to like everyone, and be liked in return.

She shrugged. 'I don't exactly feel very friendly towards you, Peter.'

'Come on, Fliss. We had a thing once, it's finished now – I understand that. There were things I should have told you, and that was my fault. I know that. But we work together, after all, we should be civilized about it. Let's have lunch sometime. Just to sort things out a bit.'

'In your dreams.' She moved abruptly away. It was all very well for Henry to say that she and Peter should try to get on together, but he had no idea how painful it was for her just to have to see him each day. If she started being nice to him, being friendly, it would only end up one place – and that was back in bed. She knew herself, knew her own weakness. Peter was it. And she couldn't afford to make that mistake again.

Sarah Coleman stood by the marquee on the fringes of a group of guests, her third glass of wine in her hand, and sighed inwardly. She'd been here for an hour, and she was bored rigid. God, if there was one thing she hated it was talking shop with City solicitors. At least in another month and a half her pupillage would be finished, and she'd be well shot of this lot. A nice long holiday, and then she would look around for an alternative occupation. Something less intellectually taxing, with an expense account and possibly a car. Armed with her qualifications and her looks, she was pretty confident she could find a job that paid enough, until the right man with the right kind of money came along.

She took a step backwards, detaching herself discreetly

from the group of people she'd been talking to, and scanned the faces. Still no Marcus. Every member of chambers was expected to attend the party, hair neatly brushed and name badge in place, to do his or her bit for the good of 5 Caper Court, but Marcus was just the kind of person who would put his practice ahead of a chambers' marketing exercise. He was probably working right now. Sarah didn't think she'd ever met anyone who grafted quite as hard as he did. She sipped her drink speculatively as she brooded on the thought of those silky, ebony good looks, which turned her on a little bit more every time she saw him. She couldn't decide whether that lofty manner of his was just a pose, or whether he genuinely wasn't interested. She couldn't believe it was the latter. She'd yet to meet a man who didn't succumb to her blend of charm and beauty. Maybe all that arrogance was just a form of come-on.

She sighed again. She didn't even have Leo to while away the tedium. He, like Marcus, had yet to put in an appearance. Well, if Marcus should turn out to be a non-starter, Leo would always do. Dear little Camilla was off on the other side of the world, and in Sarah's experience, Leo was never one to waste an opportunity. If he ever showed up, that was.

She glanced idly around – and her heart turned over. Marcus had arrived without her noticing. He was standing only a few feet away in conversation with a law lord and a couple of brokers, and God, did he look lovely. Oh, for a few hours alone with him, the chance to bring him to his knees, watch those supercilious features soften with sensuality and longing. It had been part of a recurring fantasy of hers for some months.

'Hi.' A voice at her elbow broke into her thoughts. She turned and saw Roger Fry.

'Hello,' she replied, without great enthusiasm. It wasn't

that she especially disliked Roger – that was difficult to do, because he was so amiable, in a mad kind of way – but she didn't exactly go for the geeky, crumpled type. Still, he was a close friend of Marcus, so maybe if she stood and talked to Roger for long enough, Marcus would make his way over.

So conscious was she of Marcus's proximity, and anxious that he shouldn't disappear again before she could speak to him, that Sarah couldn't resist glancing in his direction several times during her conversation with Roger.

Marcus, a few yards away, was well aware of the flirtatious glances of the blonde girl from chambers. He could hardly miss them. What was her name? Sarah? Something like that. Normally he wouldn't have paid a great deal of attention – plenty of women looked at him like that. This evening, however, he was already mildly bored by the fact of this party and by the immediate company, and so amused himself by matching her stare with a languid one of his own. He let his eyes travel slowly, and with overt sensuality, over her face and body, gauging her reaction. Interesting. Quite challenging. Could he be bothered? She was having a one-to-one with old Roger, who probably fancied his own chances. No harm in putting a spoke in that particular wheel. And then, who could tell? She certainly looked like the kind of girl who wouldn't take a lot of persuading.

Sarah, who was doing her best to conduct an unspectacular exchange of small talk with Roger, and at the same time savour the distinctly interested glances of Marcus, was suddenly surprised to hear Roger say, 'You really do have a thing about him, don't you?'

Sarah swiftly removed her gaze from Marcus. 'Who?'

'Marcus. You keep looking over at him.' Roger's eyes, behind his glasses, were frank and guileless.

'No, I don't.'

'Yes, you do. Don't worry. It's an occupational hazard, if you're a friend of Marcus. Women seem to have a thing about him.'

'I don't happen to have a "thing" about him,' replied Sarah. She didn't like to think she could be so easily read. She sipped her wine. When she looked back at Roger he was smiling, and for some reason, that smile was difficult to resist. 'Okay, he *is* very attractive. I'm sorry if I wasn't paying attention.'

'Don't worry. It's a shame, because I was going to ask if you'd like to go out sometime. Maybe this evening, after this is finished.'

Sarah stared at Roger, nonplussed. 'Thanks all the same, but –'

'No, don't worry. It's okay.' Roger shook his head. 'I'll leave the field clear for old Marcus.'

At that moment she glanced over and saw Marcus making his way towards her, and felt a shivering sense of pleasurable anticipation.

She gave him what she hoped was a casual smile. 'Hi. How are you settling into chambers?'

'Hard to tell,' replied Marcus. 'I'm so busy I don't have much time to socialize. Afternoon tea in the common room's really not my scene.'

'Well, I'm glad to hear your practice is healthy, at any rate.'

'Oh, it's always going to be healthy, I think,' said Marcus, with not a little trace of self-satisfaction. 'Not much danger there. Jut a question of matching ambition to talent. At least I'm being better clerked here. I'm having to turn work away, as a matter of fact.'

This guy, thought Sarah, as she sipped her champagne, was truly in love with himself. Normally that would be a bit off-putting, but so much healthy arrogance blended with those knicker-wettingly good looks was somehow a lethal combination.

'I'm told that no barrister can succeed without a good clerk. Where would you be without them?'

The disdainful eyebrow which Marcus raised in reply to this indicated that he wasn't prepared to concede credit for his personal success to any clerk. 'On the subject of clerks,' he replied, 'I've noticed some personal animosity between Felicity and our man, Peter. Or am I mistaken?'

'You didn't know? Felicity and Peter were having a bit of a fling not so long ago – until she found out he was married, that is. It led to a cooling of relations, as you can imagine.'

'I see.' Marcus gave a supercilious little grimace.

'Do I take it from your expression that you don't approve of – how shall I put this? – informal relationships between people in the same chambers?'

'I don't always think it's conducive to workplace harmony,' replied Marcus. Noticing her glass was empty, he crooked a finger in the direction of a passing waitress, who refilled their glasses. 'On the other hand,' he murmured, as the waitress moved away, 'it doesn't do to be too sanctimonious.' He gazed at Sarah and clinked his glass gently against hers, and an instant of total sensuality and understanding flickered between them. Sarah smiled. Oh yes, this evening was definitely going somewhere.

She could tell from the way Marcus glanced swiftly and appraisingly around that he was about to suggest something on the lines of their departure, when a plump, flushed young woman in a red suit laid a hand on his arm. Sarah recognized her as a solicitor from some City firm.

'Marcus, how lovely to see you!' The woman gave Sarah an apologetic glance. 'Excuse me for interrupting –' she turned her attention to Marcus again '– I just had to tell you what a marvellous job you did in that case the other day. The clients were delighted . . .'

Sarah sensed a reluctant but definite shift in Marcus's focus. Obviously he liked hearing his own praises sung. Sarah felt sickeningly annoyed. She stood sipping her wine for a few moments, listening while Marcus condescendingly enjoyed the adulation of the plump solicitor, hoping she was going to go away soon. But the woman hung on, never taking her eyes from Marcus. She clearly wasn't going anywhere in a hurry. Sarah could tell there was no way back into the shiveringly lovely intimacy she and Marcus had been sharing. She felt like a spare part. She glanced around and saw Leo some yards away, engaged in conversation with some old fart, and looking pretty bored. Maybe it would help if she showed Marcus he wasn't the only attractive man she was interested in. Murmuring something inaudible, she moved away. Marcus didn't even glance at her as she went.

Leo had met Ann on his way out of chambers, and they walked together up Chancery Lane to Gray's Inn. He was glad of her company, relishing the contrast of her dry, amusing conversation after an afternoon spent with Adriana. It occurred to him that she looked very pretty this evening, in her understated way.

'By the way,' said Ann, 'I have some news for you. You may be interested to know that I've just been instructed on behalf of Arrow Marine in your scuttling case.'

'Good. Nice to have a friendly face on the other side.' So, thought Leo, the insurers were upping the ante, were they? Ann's brief fee would be in the region of two hundred thousand, and if they were prepared to whack out that kind of money, they must be serious about going all the way to a hearing. 'Have you had a chance to look at the papers yet?'

'No. They're sending them across tomorrow.' They had reached the entrance to the gardens where the party was being held.

'Well, let me know when you've read them, and we can have a drink and a chat. I'd be interested to know what you think.'

'Will do. See you later.' They parted, and Leo helped himself to a glass of champagne and surveyed the throng. He caught sight of Sarah in close conversation with Marcus Jacobs, and felt a flicker of amusement. He could read Sarah even at this distance – that smile, the body language, the tilt of her head – and thought he knew how the evening would pan out for those two. He was conscious, at the same time, of a faint misgiving – she might be the most practised and libidinous twenty-three-year-old he knew, but she had her susceptibilities like anyone else. Marcus had a reputation as a womanizer, and he wouldn't like Sarah to get hurt. Despite the problems she occasionally gave him, Leo had a very real affection for her. Oh well, he thought, glancing away, she would look after herself. She usually did.

He saw Anthony standing by the buffet table, plate in hand, talking to someone whose identity was blocked by a knot of people. Leo was about to go over and join them when the crowd parted and he saw that it was Rachel. No – that would not be a happy little triumvirate, he decided, and steered himself in the direction of Michael Gibbon, who seemed to be having quite a merry time with Mungo Stephenson and Frank Chamberlin, two senior members of the judiciary not noted for their sobriety.

At the buffet table, Anthony and Rachel were helping themselves to food. 'I haven't seen you for months,' said Anthony. 'How are you?'

'Not bad.' Rachel gave Anthony a quick smile, tucking her hair behind her ears. 'What about you?'

'Yes, fine . . . Well, it's been a bit of a strange year, really.' They stood, pausing in uncertainty, on the gravel walk. 'Come on,' said Anthony, pointing in the direction of an empty table, 'let's sit down.'

Rachel, somewhat to Anthony's surprise, had instructed him three weeks previously in a demurrage case, and so it was natural that they should fall into conversation about it this evening. They ate and talked, the evening light fading around them. As Anthony gazed at Rachel's calm, Madonna-like features, the smooth brows, the long, silky black hair, the troubled eyes, he found himself pondering the vagaries of the human heart. He had been deeply in love with this woman just a few years ago, obsessed to the point where even her mute frigidity had had an exquisite appeal, but he'd got nowhere with her. She had been so damaged by adolescent experiences that no one could touch her, reach her – until Leo. It was Leo who had taken with consummate ease that which Anthony never achieved. What a pity such a power to inspire love found itself in such callous hands, he reflected. And how sadly it had ended for all three of them. Anthony watched her, hardly listening to what she was saying, and tested his own heart, wondering how he still felt about her. Love might pass, he realized, but its shadow always remained; the heart retained a memory, an eternal impression of the way in which certain features and a particular voice had once moved it.

He shifted his thoughts, trying to pick up the thread of what she was saying – something about commuting to and from work each day.

'Have you thought about moving back into London? You used to say you liked it. You lived in Fulham, didn't you?'

'That's right. But I don't imagine I'll come back. Charles loves the house, and the countryside. I couldn't ask him to leave. I think it was bad enough for him when he thought he was going to have to sell because of his Lloyd's losses. Besides, there's Oliver to think about. He'll have enough of London life when he's with Leo.'

'How old is Oliver now?'

'He'll be three in October.' Rachel smiled. 'He's fantastic. Funny, and very bright. And beautiful, of course. But as his mother, I would say that.'

'Leo says much the same thing. He talks about him whenever he gets the chance.'

'There you are. Another unbiased opinion.' Her smile softened to sadness.

'I was sorry about you and Leo, you know. Genuinely. Despite everything.'

'Well, that's in the past,' said Rachel quickly. 'Charles and I are very happy.'

'Good. I'm glad.'

There was a hesitant pause, then Rachel asked with diffidence, 'What about Leo? I mean, I don't really get to find out what goes on in his life. He just comes and goes with Oliver. The only clues are the unfamiliar voices on the phone occasionally, when I ring up. Male, female, you never know what to expect with Leo, do you?'

'No,' agreed Anthony. 'He's a law unto himself.' Her eyes were fixed on his. He realized she was waiting. 'I gather . . .' said Anthony slowly, 'that he's been seeing someone in chambers for a while now. Camilla Lawrence. I don't know if you know her.'

Rachel dropped her gaze. 'I've met her. She's – she's very young.' She looked up suddenly again. 'But – didn't you go out with her for a while? I seem to remember –'

'Yes.' Anthony nodded. 'Yes, I did. It was quite serious – well, I thought it was. I screwed things up, though.'

There was silence between them for a while. The sounds of the jazz band drifted across the summer air. Then Rachel murmured, 'Is it habitual, d'you think? Or just coincidental?'

'What?'

'That he annexes people you care for. Makes them his.' Her blue eyes met his.

'I hadn't thought about it, to be honest. Not – not quite in that way. I'm not quite sure what Leo's motives are where I'm concerned.'

'I think I know.' Rachel traced a line in the linen tablecloth with one clean, white fingernail. 'He loves you. And because he can't have you, he'll do what he can to prevent anyone else from having you, even to the point of making your lovers his own.'

After an uneasy hesitation, Anthony replied, 'I try not to think about it. Just take him at face value. It's about all one can do.'

A gust of wind shivered the garden, and Rachel glanced up reflectively at the evening sky. 'I wonder sometimes what it's like to be Leo.'

'Confusing, I imagine.'

And lonely?'

'I don't know. Maybe.'

'Is he serious about this Camilla girl?'

Anthony looked at Rachel. Her eyes were very dark against the paleness of her face. 'I think he might be.' She said nothing, but gazed down thoughtfully at the tablecloth, still running her nail across it, gouging neat creases. 'You have Charles,' he added.

'Yes. But you know how it is, Anthony. You and I – we know better than anyone. With Leo, the thing never finishes, does it?'

His eyes met hers, and he wondered how much she really knew. 'No,' he replied quietly, 'it never finishes.'

'I'm afraid I have to go,' said Rachel. 'Charles is in the States at the moment, and I've got to get back to relieve the poor old nanny. A fourteen-hour stretch with Oliver is enough for anyone.'

'It's been really good to talk to you,' said Anthony. 'And I don't just mean about the case.'

Rachel smiled. 'I know.' She was glad that instructing him had given them both the excuse to repair the damage of a couple of years ago, when Leo had come along and completely put paid to whatever nascent relationship she and Anthony had had. She didn't regret the way things had gone – Leo had thawed her out of that ghastly frigidity, taught her how to set her fears behind her, and made her able to love properly – but she had always felt some sort of guilt where Anthony was concerned. He'd loved her, and she had been very fond of him. She wondered how differently things might have turned out, if it hadn't been for Leo.

'Are you busy on Sunday?' she asked suddenly.

'Not especially. Why?'

'Why don't you come to lunch? It's quite lonely with Charles away, and I'd forgotten how much I enjoy your company. You can meet Oliver.'

'All right – thanks very much. You'll have to give me directions, though.'

Rachel smiled, and opened her bag to search for pen and paper.

Leo, only half paying attention to some long-winded story of Sir Mungo Stephenson's, glanced over to where Rachel and Anthony were sitting on the far side of the lawn. They'd been together for the better part of three-quarters of an hour. He saw Rachel hand something to Anthony as she got up to leave, and the two of them exchanged decorous kisses.

Leo was mildly astonished. He had no idea that they ever spoke much to each other, not since the distant days when, for purposes of his own, he'd seduced Rachel away from Anthony's inexpert clutches. For reasons he couldn't quite fathom, their apparent friendliness irritated him. He waited until Rachel had disappeared, and was about to go over to speak to Anthony – possibly to fathom the mystery, though he hadn't yet decided – when Sarah cruised up. Her face was inscrutable.

'At last,' she said, 'someone decent to talk to. I'm going out of my mind exchanging meaningless small talk with these pinstriped morons.'

'I take it we didn't make much headway with young Mr Jacobs?' Leo couldn't resist asking.

'Young Mr Jacobs is so far up his own backside that I'm surprised he ever sees daylight,' replied Sarah.

'He does exude an air of somewhat remarkable arrogance,' agreed Leo. 'I'm tempted to wonder what particular vulnerability that conceals.'

'Forget Marcus,' she said. She glanced around to make sure no one could overhear. 'Leo, I'm so bored I could kill. And I definitely don't want to eat barbecued beefburgers. Why don't we go and have dinner somewhere? Or better still, go back to yours?' She gave him a glance of practised sensuality, one with which he had long been familiar. Her natural tendencies had been considerably aroused by her brief encounter with Marcus, and if she couldn't have him, Leo would do just as well. 'We haven't slept together in a long time. I'm sure you miss it as much as I do.'

Leo raised an eyebrow. 'A delightful suggestion, but I happen to be somewhat involved with someone at the moment. As you well know.'

'Leo,' said Sarah softly, 'she's several thousand miles away.'

'True, but I have the feeling that if I were to submit to your tempting proposal, it might get back to Camilla. In fact, I'd go so far as to say that you'd make it your business to see that it did. Or am I being wildly unfair?'

Sarah looked at him narrowly. 'I can't believe you've suddenly developed scruples, Leo.'

'Let's just call it a protective instinct. And it's not new. I've actually had it for some time. Particularly where you're concerned.'

She sighed. 'Pity. It would have been fun. See you.'

Leo sipped his drink and watched as she sloped off. True, a few hours in bed with Sarah would have been fun, but of the dangerous variety. Maybe it was that middle-aged thing again, but at the moment Leo felt that he could dispense with danger and excitement in his life. It generally meant trouble, and he was weary of that for the present. He would leave in half an hour or so, and go home and have a blameless early night. He had resisted the advances of two women in the space of one evening, a rare achievement for him, and of this he felt unwontedly proud. Perhaps, beneath Camilla's softening youthful influence, he was becoming a reformed character.

7

Leo came into chambers early on Monday morning to prepare for the first day of the *Persephone* hearing. After an hour's work he went to make himself some coffee, and met Anthony coming upstairs.

'Morning,' said Leo. 'By the way, didn't you say you wanted to have a look at Bill France's article on parametric rolling? I've got a copy of it in my room.'

Anthony made himself a cup of coffee and followed Leo to his room, where he sat down and flicked through the article while Leo finished his work. 'Mind if I borrow this?' he asked after a few minutes.

'Keep it, if you like.'

'Thanks.' Anthony sipped his coffee. He glanced across at Leo's desk, and noticed a framed photograph of Oliver, taken at Stanton. 'You'll have to update that picture pretty soon,' he remarked, gesturing with his cup. 'He's much bigger now, isn't he?'

Leo glanced at the picture, then at Anthony. 'I didn't know you'd seen Oliver recently.'

'Rachel invited me over for lunch yesterday. Oliver was on great form. He's a fantastic kid. You're very lucky.'

Leo nodded. So, Anthony and Rachel's friendship had rekindled to a greater extent than he had imagined. As he put on his jacket he asked, 'How's Charles? I haven't seen him for a while.'

'He wasn't there. He's in the States making some historical documentary.'

Leo began to put his papers together. Presumably nothing significant could be going on between Rachel and Anthony, or he wouldn't have been so frank and forthcoming about spending Sunday with her. He glanced at his watch. 'I'm off to court in a few minutes.'

Anthony stood up. 'Is this the *Persephone* hearing? The first day shouldn't be too much sweat.'

'Normally that would be the case. But the redoubtable Miss Papaposilakis isn't happy with the idea of me giving a quick two-hour outline and Mr Justice Sagewell going off to read the documents. Says she doesn't trust him to read them thoroughly. So I'm going to be on my feet all day giving an exhaustive exposition of our case.' He picked up his robing bag.

'Ann Halliday was talking about the case at lunch last week. I get the impression she's not wild about her prospects of success.'

'Can't blame her. I still don't understand why the insurers won't settle.'

'Who knows? Bet you turn up in twenty minutes' time and the whole thing settles outside the courtroom door.'

'In that unlikely event, Anthony, I'll buy you lunch.'

'You're on.'

'Don't hold your breath.' Leo picked up his robing bag. 'Assuming you lose this bet, what about a game of squash one night this week instead?'

'Fine. Friday would probably be best for me.'

'Right. See you later.'

Anthony went back to his room. He stood at the window, waiting. A few moments later, Leo emerged from below and hurried across Caper Court and through the archway to Middle Temple Lane. Long after the familiar figure had vanished, Anthony remained there, gazing down at the blank flagstones. Leo would never know how much effort it was presently costing him to behave as if everything were perfectly normal between them. As though nothing had ever happened. He dwelt often on that night he and Leo had spent together, without ever being able to share with anyone the profound effect it had had on him. There had been a moment yesterday, after lunch and a couple of glasses of wine, when he had thought he might tell Rachel. She had that peaceful, still way about her which made him feel he could talk to her about anything. But he had let the moment pass. He couldn't trespass on what she clearly still regarded as her own emotional territory. She had talked about Leo far more than an ex-wife in a new relationship should have. Anthony found himself wondering whether she had invited him to lunch not just to while away a lonely Sunday, but because he was someone to whom she could talk about Leo.

He turned away from the window and sat down at his desk. As far as he and Leo were concerned, it seemed to Anthony that he had no alternative but to accept the status quo. Either he allowed himself to blame Leo for the night they had spent together, and the subsequent confusion of feeling which had followed, and let it fester and poison their friendship, or else he put it all in the past and tried to behave with perfect equanimity and friendliness. The latter was clearly what Leo wanted; he himself managed it with perfect ease. But Leo was well practised in matters of self-deception. Of every kind of deception. As he picked up his pen to carry on with his work, Anthony tried to thrust from his mind the third alternative which he knew existed, that frank offer which Leo had made to him – to be sexually available to Anthony on a casual, occasional basis, without any emotional strings, if Anthony so wished. It smacked of that easy promiscuity which Anthony so detested in Leo, and yet he found himself dwelling on it more often than he would have liked.

By the time Leo finished expounding the case of *Silakis Shipping SA v. Arrow Marine plc,* it was four-forty in the afternoon.

'Thank you, Mr Davies,' said Mr Justice Sagewell, a lean-faced, mournful man whose spirit seemed worn down by the cares of his office. 'We shall resume at ten tomorrow morning.'

The court rose, and everyone began to put their papers together and murmur to one another. Adriana came up to Leo.

'That was marvellous!' She put her face up to his and kissed him lightly on the cheek, while Rachel looked on in mild surprise. 'How can we can possibly lose? What is there that the other side can say? I could tell the judge was impressed!'

'Well, let's wait and see, shall we? One side of a case always sounds unarguable, until you hear the other side.'

'No, no – you were wonderful! However –' her manner took on a touch of gravitas '– there are a few things we need to discuss.'

Leo glanced at Rachel expressionlessly, and Rachel guessed what he was thinking. She shrugged. Both of them knew there wasn't a client born who wouldn't want to discuss their case well into the evening, every evening, if they could.

As they emerged from the courtroom into the corridor, Leo said to Adriana, 'I have a few things I need to do in chambers first.'

'That is not a problem.' She laid a hand lightly on his lapel. 'Why don't we meet up in a couple of hours and discuss it over a drink at my hotel?'

Leo's hesitation was momentary. He could hardly refuse a client. 'Fine. Can you manage that, Rachel?'

Rachel met his eye and nodded.

If Adriana was at all piqued at this inclusion of Rachel, she didn't show it. She merely smiled and said, 'Fine. I'll see you both at half past six,' then clacked off down the marble-flagged corridor in her high heels, Mr Defereras following with his burden of files.

'Thanks,' Leo murmured to Rachel. 'I couldn't face being trapped alone with her all evening, being told how to run this case. See you later.' And he made his escape to the robing room, leaving Rachel more than a little pleased. It didn't look as though Adriana Papaposilakis would be making the conquest she had anticipated after all.

Rachel arrived at Adriana's hotel punctually at half past six, and they sat together in the almost deserted bar and spent fifteen minutes in surprisingly agreeable conversation concerning shoes. Clearly Adriana intended to wait for Leo before launching into the gruelling evidential discussion for which she had come prepared, judging by the sheaf of technical documents which she had brought with her. For this Rachel felt thankful. She was already somewhat worn down by the intensity of Adriana's dedication to the minute details of this case. She seemed capable of discussing thermal boundary conditions and fracture stresses in pipework with the same fluency with which she was now ranking the relative merits of Jimmy Choo and Manolo Blahnik. Small wonder, thought Rachel as she sipped her cocktail, that the woman was so well respected in the shipping world, and so wealthy.

When Leo arrived, making his apologies, Adriana's focus switched instantly to work. For a grinding hour and a half they discussed every aspect of the evidence of their witnesses of fact – the master and the engineer – who were due to be examined by Leo over the coming days. Rachel could detect nothing flirtatious in Adriana's behaviour towards Leo, but she got the distinct impression, as the discussion wound itself to a close around half seven, that she was anxious to spend a little more time alone with him.

'I'm sorry to detain you for so long, Rachel,' she said, glancing at her watch. 'I forget you have a baby to go home to. Very thoughtless of me.'

After Leo's earlier remark at the Law Courts, Rachel felt pretty confident that he had no interest in Adriana beyond her case. She began to put her papers together. 'Don't worry. I only hope the discussion was useful.'

'Very.' Adriana smiled her bewitching smile and watched as Rachel rose to go. She turned to Leo. 'You will stay for another drink, yes?'

'I can't, I'm afraid,' replied Leo. He, too, got up. 'Not if you want me wide awake in court tomorrow morning.'

'That is very true,' said Adriana, and nodded. 'You must be at your best. Well – thank you both for coming. I will see you in the morning.'

She bade them a charming goodnight, and swept off to the lift.

Rachel and Leo walked out into the evening air. They stood on the pavement outside the hotel, surveying the traffic.

'Is it really true you haven't got time for another drink?' Rachel asked with a tentative smile. 'I'd like to have a talk about Oliver and the nursery school I've found for him.'

'I honestly can't,' said Leo. 'I do want to talk about it, but Camilla's coming back from Bermuda today, and I know she'll be waiting for me.' He caught the flicker of bleakness in Rachel's eyes. 'Any other night this week. Really.'

She nodded. 'Fine. You have your priorities, of course.'

'Let's get a cab. You can drop me off on your way to the station.' Leo scanned the traffic for the yellow light of a taxi. He hailed one and it drew up to the kerb.

In the taxi, Leo tried to mellow the atmosphere with a little conversation. 'Anthony tells me that he lunched with you and Oliver on Sunday. I'm very jealous.' As soon as he'd said it, Leo knew this was the wrong thing to say. As someone whose very substantial living depended on verbal dexterity, he sometimes marvelled at his own ineptitude.

'If that were true, Leo, we wouldn't all be where we are now.' Her face remained in chilly profile, gazing out at the traffic.

'I meant that Anthony was lucky, seeing Oliver.' He sighed, wondering if conversation between them would ever become less tortured. 'I didn't realize you and Anthony had grown so chummy.'

'We've always been friends,' replied Rachel. 'We were friends before I knew you. I suppose I should find your interest in my personal life touching, however –'

'Okay. Enough.' Leo craned forward in his seat and tapped on the glass to the driver. 'Anywhere here will do.' He turned to Rachel. 'You can pay the fare. Stick it on the *Persephone* file.' He got out of the cab, closed the door, and walked off.

Rachel leaned back and closed her eyes, aching inwardly. Antagonism and resentment – the last things she wanted to express when she was with him, but they always came bobbing to the surface. She experienced a sudden sensation of profound loneliness.

Walking towards Belgravia, Leo's flash of temper subsided and he let his pace slacken. He shouldn't have got out of the cab in that abrupt way. But she really did have the most amazing capacity for confrontation, for aggression. And in the name of what? It had scarcely ever been like that when they were married, except on occasions. Was this what the residue of spent love amounted to? He felt a surge of grateful relief at the thought of Camilla waiting for him, unreproachful, easy in her affection, possessed only of the desire to please him. He must take care to do nothing to change that state of affairs.

When Felicity got home that night, she could hear the noise half-way up the stairs to the flat. Her heart sank. She put her key in the lock and went in. Sandy and four other young men were in the living room, curtains drawn, music centre on, necking vodka. The pungent reek of marijuana hung in the air. Sandy greeted her warily, drunkenly. She sighed and opened the curtains, then the window.

'Come on, Sandy. Tell your mates to piss off back to wherever they came from.' She hauled at his collar and he got to his feet. 'Come on!' she yelled. 'I want them out *now*!'

'Sorry, guys,' said Sandy to his friends. 'My sister's not very hospitable.'

'No, she's bloody not.' Felicity stood, hands on hips, as the young men got up resentfully.

When they'd gone, Sandy closed the front door and came back through. Fliss was straightening furniture and picking up the litter they had left. He regarded her truculently.

'Thanks very much. That was really great, talking to my mates like that.'

Felicity straightened up. She took a deep breath before replying. 'Sandy, when I took you in, I felt sorry for you. Sorry you'd messed your life up yet again. I let you stay here so you could get yourself straightened out, not to give you free board and lodging till whenever. So far, you've done nothing but doss around and take advantage of me. You haven't even tried to get a job. And now you think you can turn my flat into somewhere handy for you and your mates to hang out and get stoned. Well, it's not on. It's simply not going to happen. It's getting to the point where I *don't* feel sorry for you any more. If you don't sort yourself out soon, you can go back to kipping on the streets. I can't prop you up forever. I have a life I want to get on with.' She stopped, gazing at him. 'Sandy, are you listening to anything I'm saying?'

Sandy just stood vacantly in the middle of the room for some seconds, his truculence shifting to self-pity. His eyes met hers. 'Fliss, you won't go to bed just yet, will you?'

'What are you on about? It's only seven o'clock. Of course I'm not going to bed.'

'It's just, being all day on my own, it's doing my head in. I had to get some people round. I can't stand it on my own.' He touched his temples with lightly trembling fingers. 'I keep hearing stuff in my head.'

'What kind of stuff?' Felicity stared at him fearfully.

'Talking. Like it's my head, my brain, but it's other people.'

'Voices?'

'I don't know. A bit like that. And I get scared. I just don't want to be alone.'

'Have you been taking that ketamine stuff you told me about?' demanded Felicity. In one of their heart-to-hearts, Sandy had admitted to his sister that he'd taken ketamine, a horse tranquillizer that induced powerful hallucinations. Felicity's reaction had been a mixture of terror and extreme anger. She had made him promise never to touch anything like that again.

'No,' said Sandy sullenly.

Beneath her exasperation, Felicity felt a mild disquiet. 'Sandy, I have to go to work. If you don't like being on your own, then get a job. Any job. Maybe if you stayed off the booze and the dope, you wouldn't get in this state. I'll make you some coffee. Sit down.'

As she went through to the kitchen, she added, 'I meant what I said, Sandy. You've got to get a job, or you'll have to go.'

As she put the kettle on, and glanced in the fridge to see what she could cook for supper, she found herself wondering whether this was true. What *did* she mean, exactly, where Sandy was concerned? If she kicked him out on the street, he would probably just sink without trace. She couldn't let that happen – could she? At the moment, she had no clear idea. His talk of hearing voices was a bit freaky, but she just put that down to the vodka and dope paranoia. She closed the fridge and sighed, waiting for the kettle to boil. Why was it that all the men in her life were such a total waste of space?

As she was walking from the Tube station the following morning, Sarah caught sight of Leo and Camilla crossing Pump Court together on their way into chambers. She hated seeing them together. She felt little enough where most men were concerned, but Leo was different. It was so utterly galling to think that Camilla had possession of him, almost a physical pain. Still, she reassured herself, it would probably only be temporary. None of Leo's relationships ever endured, not even his marriage. This one would end sooner or later, and Leo's attention would wander back, as it always did. She and Leo had a special connection. They knew each other utterly and intimately, every fault and flaw. She had always had the sense that, no matter what, she and Leo belonged together. It was just a pity she hadn't been able to put a crimp in things while Camilla had been out of the country.

As she dwelt on these consoling thoughts, Sarah heard steps behind her. She turned and saw Roger Fry.

'Hi.' He fell into step beside her. 'I was hoping I'd see you sometime today.'

'Oh? Why?'

'I'm going to the Proms tonight with some friends, and someone's had to drop out. I wondered if you'd like to come.'

Sarah didn't much care for the idea of being a stand-in, and she wasn't madly keen on classical music, but there was always the chance Marcus might be there.

'Who else is going?'

'Myself, Marcus, Tony Foreman – do you know him? Yes, I thought you did. Margot Casement from Three Brick Court, and some friend of hers – and you, if you want the ticket.'

'What's on the programme?' Sarah didn't in the least care, as long as it meant an opportunity to take things a little further with Marcus, but it helped to pretend that she did.

'Mahler's Fifth, and some Russian songs – Mussorgsky, as far as I can recall. It's a while since I made the booking.'

'Okay. I don't mind a bit of Mahler. Thanks.'

'Good.' Roger gave her a smile. 'We're meeting in the Edgar Wallace at six-fifteen. See you then.'

At six-fifteen, after some hasty make-up work in chambers, Sarah hurried to the pub. Her insides had been tight with apprehension all afternoon, not a sensation she was used to. Whatever she might have said to Leo about Marcus's monumental arrogance, there was no doubt that it was this very quality which made him so desperately attractive. That utterly cool confidence, his almost offhand manner with women, made Sarah feel, for once, the anxiety of having the balance of desire weighted against her. Still, she and Marcus had been making pretty good headway at the Gray's Inn party, until the untimely intervention of that friend of his. Maybe tonight they could complete their unfinished business.

Roger and his friends were already at the pub when she

arrived, but no Marcus. Sarah sipped a glass of wine and chatted to the others, one eye on the door. After twenty minutes, Roger glanced at his watch and suggested they'd better get going.

'It's only a few stops to South Ken, but it's a ten-minute walk at the other end.'

'What about Marcus?' asked Margot. Sarah gave her a glance, but didn't reckon there was much competition there.

'Probably got held up in chambers,' said Roger. 'He can make his own way there. We can't hang around for him.'

They arrived at the Albert Hall with fifteen minutes to spare, and loitered in the foyer.

'Why don't you give Marcus a call on his mobile?' someone suggested.

Roger tried. 'He must have it switched off. No point in leaving a message. He knows what time the concert starts.'

So they left Marcus's ticket at the box office and took their seats. Sarah carefully engineered it so that she was next to the empty seat. She glanced around hopefully as the audience murmur subsided and the orchestra tuned up, but there was no sign of Marcus. Sarah resigned herself to the knowledge that he wouldn't show up now, and that she was going to have to sit through an entire evening of Mahler and some dreary Russian songs, all for nothing.

'I'm rather annoyed with Marcus,' said Roger as they left the hall two hours later. 'If he'd known he was going to have a problem with this evening, he could at least have let me know.'

Too right, thought Sarah, whose sense of disappointed expectation had left her feeling dismal and frustrated. She was also bored out of her skull.

'What about a drink?' someone suggested. Sarah had been on the verge of going straight home, but a drink was better than nothing. They found a wine bar, and after a couple of drinks, Roger suggested finding somewhere to eat.

Tony declined, saying he had to be in Uxbridge the following morning, and Margot and her friend said they had to get back to Hampstead.

'That leaves you and me,' said Roger, when the others had gone.

Sarah was about to make her own excuses, but she really was hungry, and besides, she felt in need of a bit of flattering male company to ease her bruised and disappointed ego.

'Where do you suggest?' she asked.

'I think there's a little Italian place near the station,' said Roger. 'Let's try that.'

Dinner with Roger was more amusing than Sarah had expected. She'd assumed from his generally unkempt aspect and often vague manner that he was a bit of an anorak, but his appearance belied a quick and engaging mind. To Sarah's relief, he wasn't much inclined to discuss 5 Caper Court and the personalities therein.

'It's not that I don't like the place,' said Roger. 'I do. I get clerked better than I did at Wessex Street, for one thing, and it's smaller, which I prefer. But at the end of the day it's just somewhere to work. I'm not into chambers' politics the way Maurice is. But then, he's got this inbuilt need to control. Anyway, look – I said I didn't want to talk about chambers. I'd rather talk about you.' He took off his glasses and polished them on the edge of the tablecloth, giving Sarah a smiling, short-sighted glance as he did so. 'Does that sound corny?' She noticed for the first time that his eyes were greeny-grey, and surprisingly soft and gentle.

'A bit. What in particular did you want to know about me?'

Roger replaced his glasses and considered this question

for a few seconds. 'I'm interested to know what kind of person lurks beneath your smart, ultra-cool exterior, and what lies behind that knowing smile you always wear.'

Sarah tossed her blonde hair. 'Maybe what you see is what you get.'

'I doubt it. We're all somewhat vulnerable. That's the only time people get really interesting. When they reveal themselves.'

'Don't think I'm going to get too revealing after a pizza and a glass of Chianti.'

'What about a coffee, then, and maybe another drink? I don't mean here. My place is only five minutes away.'

Sarah wondered if this meant what she thought it did. On the other hand, it could mean nothing. She was curious to know a little more about Roger, who was turning out to be different from her expectations, and after all, if he did try to make a pass, she knew how to deal with it. Years of practice. So she said yes. And when she did so, she thought Roger looked mildly surprised. Since his expression was so often one of bemusement, it was hard to tell.

When they reached the large Kensington mansion block where Roger lived, Sarah said, 'I think I have a pretty good idea what your flat's going to be like.'

'Oh, really? What?' He led the way through the hall and upstairs.

'You.'

'Which is like – ?' They ascended the last steep flight of stairs leading to the top floor. Roger put his key in the front door.

Sarah paused. A mess? She couldn't be quite that rude. 'Much like your room in chambers, I imagine.'

He opened the door and turned to her. For a moment she thought he was going to kiss her, but he merely smiled. 'By which you mean, a complete shambles.' He switched on a light and gestured ahead. 'After you.'

She walked into the hall. 'No, I didn't mean that at all.' She looked around. The flat seemed pretty small — so far as she could see, just a bathroom and a kitchen leading off the short hallway, and another room. Roger led the way into it. It was a large attic room, and it was indeed a mess. Sarah burst out laughing. 'I take that back. It's exactly what I meant.' She looked round. In the corner was an unmade double bed, and next to it a music deck and speakers, and stacks of magazines and CDs. A clutch of unironed shirts on wire hangers hung from the knob of the door of a large wardrobe, sweaters and crumpled clothes spilling from its drawers. Shelves of books lined the walls, and the floor was carpeted with a number of worn, overlapping Persian rugs. A workstation with a computer stood against the opposite wall, and the area was littered with piles of papers and floppy disks. An armchair and a long sofa heaped with shapeless cushions stood in the middle of the room, facing the television, and beneath newspapers and yet more books there sat what appeared to be a coffee table.

Roger dimmed the central light, then switched on a couple of lamps, filling the room with a pleasant glow.

'Have a seat. I'll make the coffee.'

Sarah wandered around the room with curiosity, inspecting the books and CDs, searching for the usual clues. But Roger's interests didn't seem narrow enough to provide any. His taste in books was uneclectic — apart from the standard number of legal textbooks, the shelves contained everything from fiction, plays and poetry to philosophy, travel and archaeology. Two shelves were devoted entirely to film books. His musical tastes seemed similarly catholic — a heavy sprinkling of REM and Red Hot Chili Peppers amongst the Mahler, Beethoven and Mozart, plus a good deal of John Coltrane and Earl Klugh.

'Would you like a glass of wine?' called Roger.

Sarah went through to the little kitchen. It was uncluttered compared to the living room, but Sarah put this down to the non-cooking bachelor tendency. 'No, thanks, no more alcohol. Just the coffee. Otherwise I'll never get up in the morning.' She stifled a yawn. 'I hate getting up early. I really am not cut out for this working life.'

'No?' Roger handed her a cup of coffee and took a carton of milk from the fridge. 'I rather thrive on it.' Sarah held out her coffee and he poured in a little milk.

'That's because you like law. I can't stand it. I only took it up because of my father, and that was a big mistake.'

Roger shut the fridge and followed her through to the living room with his coffee. He cleared a little space among the books and newspapers for their cups. Sarah curled up on the sofa. Roger took off his jacket and tie, chucked them on the back of the chair by the workstation, and sat down in an armchair.

'What did you think of the Mahler?' he asked.

'Not my favourite composer, but I enjoyed it. Thank you for the ticket. I really should pay you.'

Roger made a dismissive gesture. 'I wouldn't hear of it.' He nodded in the direction of the CDs. 'We could have a little more, if you like.'

'I'm not that much of a fan, to be honest. I noticed you've got some John Coltrane. I'd rather hear that.'

This seemed to please Roger. He got up and put on a CD. Low, smoky jazz notes filled the room. Roger sat back down. He sipped his coffee, then observed mildly, 'You only came this evening because of Marcus, didn't you?'

The directness of this startled Sarah. 'Perhaps. Partly. It

doesn't matter.' She picked up her coffee and frowned. 'Why do you always do this? I think it's really strange, asking about me and Marcus.'

'Sorry. We were going to talk about you, weren't we?'

'Were we?'

'Well, I was.' Roger leaned back his head and stared at the ceiling through his glasses.

'Go on, then. Since you hardly know me, this should be interesting.'

'I have my theories.'

'About me?'

'Yes. It comes back to what I was saying earlier, about vulnerability, and the cynical, sophisticated exterior you present to the world.' He glanced at her. 'You really shouldn't, you know. It doesn't suit someone as young as you are.'

Sarah gave a derisive laugh. She kicked off her shoes and tucked her feet beneath her on the sofa. 'Sometimes I don't feel so very young. In fact, most of the time I feel quite world-weary.'

'See? I think it's a façade. A hard exterior hiding the hurt little girl within.'

Sarah stared at him over her coffee cup. 'You are so corny. D'you know that?' Roger shrugged. 'Go on, then,' said Sarah. 'Let's hear more of your theories.'

'I think you play this cool, know-it-all number because you're too afraid to let people near you, in case they find out you're not so assured and confident after all. You come on like you couldn't care less about anything, but it's just a form of cowardice. You say you don't like work, you don't like the law, because at least then it doesn't matter if you fail. You're lazy and off-hand about things, and about people, because enthusiasm and emotion are give-aways. And you don't want to give anything away, do you?'

'My, you're a cheeky bastard.' Sarah eyed him coolly, but his words had perturbed her. No one had ever spoken to her like this. And it had come out of nowhere. She had come back here for coffee, vaguely expecting to have a pass made at her, and instead this guy was sitting here, in his shambolic little flat, conducting a scathing critique of her character.

'So what hurt you so much that you became like this?'

'Nothing hurt me, Roger. You really should practise your low-level psychology on someone else.'

'You mean you've never been in love? Everyone who's been in love has been hurt.'

She was about to make a wry retort, then stopped. Maybe there was something in that. 'Yes, okay. I had a big crush on someone when I was about seventeen. I thought it was love. But I hardly think it warped my character.'

'Don't you? Perhaps not. Tell me about it, anyway.'

Sarah hesitated. Why should she? Then she glanced again at his gentle eyes, large behind his glasses, and decided she would. They talked for over an hour, as the jazz smoked away in the background. Sarah told Roger about her first love, about which she had never told anyone and had never expected to, and then they talked about adolescence, and things that happened, and how long ago it sometimes seemed, and how recent.

'I sometimes wish I weren't grown up,' said Sarah. Roger noticed that her voice had grown softer, reflective. He had noticed a number of gradual changes about her over the past hour. 'There are times when I would quite like it all to be the way it was when I was ten, say, and everything was safe and predictable, and nobody expected things of me, and I wasn't so alone.'

'You forget what ten was like. It was terrifying. It wasn't safe and predictable at all. Well, it was from an adult perspective, but it didn't seem that way then. Forgetting your history homework was such a big damned deal, or not getting picked for the rugby team. Huge, nightmarish issues, blighted little lives.' He shook his head.

'Well, I never expected to be picked for the rugby team,' said Sarah. 'In fact, I steered clear of teams as much as possible. Maybe that's why I don't see my life as a team player in a set of barristers' chambers.'

'You don't have to play it that way at all. I don't. It can actually be a beautifully solitary, self-contained existence.'

'Well, I'm glad you like it. I don't.'

Roger glanced at his watch. 'Come on. I'll ring for a cab. I've got to be in the Court of Appeal tomorrow.'

Sarah untucked her legs and slipped on her shoes. 'Don't bother. I'll walk. It's not far.' She stood up.

'I didn't realize you lived so close. But you can't walk back alone. I'll come with you.' He picked up his jacket from the chair.

'You really don't have to. I'm perfectly safe, you know.'

Roger slipped on his jacket. 'I'd like to.'

They walked much of the way in comfortable silence, the summer night air still mild around them. When they reached Sarah's flat, she said, 'Thanks for the Proms ticket. And the coffee. And the talk.'

'Think nothing of it. Happy to oblige.'

She looked at him as he stood there on the pavement, tall and rumpled and smiling, and wondered if he would make his move now. But instead he merely raised a hand, said, 'See you in the morning,' then turned and walked off down the street.

8

The following day in court the former master of the *Perse-phone*, Captain Kollias, took the stand. He was a squat, middle-aged man with beefy features and a heavy moustache. His voice, when he was asked by Leo to confirm his name and address, was thick and guttural.

'And can you identify this as your sworn statement?' asked Leo, holding the document up to the court. Captain Kollias nodded and confirmed that it was.

'And are the contents true, to the best of your belief and knowledge?'

'Yes.'

Leo sat down, and Ann Halliday rose to her feet and began her cross-examination, taking Captain Kollias through his statement, and through the events of the fateful night two years previously. Captain Kollias confirmed that on 23 September 2002, when the yacht was in harbour at Ventetone, he had been awoken at around 1 a.m. by smoke. A fire had broken out in the engine-room of the yacht. It had taken hold so severely that it was impossible to fight with fire extinguishers. Mr Staveris, the engineer, had similarly been roused by the smoke, and Captain Kollias had ordered the ship be abandoned. Vasillios Fexis, the cabin boy, had died in his cabin.

'You say in your statement that you did not know that Mr Fexis was on board the yacht that night. Why was this?'

'He said he was going ashore to visit friends. There was fiesta that weekend. He said he would not be back that night.' Captain Kollias curled and uncurled his fat fingers.

'But he did in fact return to the *Persephone*?'

'Yes.' Captain Kollias nodded. His face trembled slightly. 'Yes, he came back, and we did not know.'

'What I find strange, Captain Kollias, is that you and Mr Staveris were both woken by the smoke from the fire – as you both say in your statements – but Mr Fexis was not. If it had woken you, why would it not wake up Mr Fexis?'

Captain Kollias spread his sausage-like fingers. 'I do not know. It was a terrible, terrible thing . . .' His voice faltered. 'He was a young boy. Maybe he had too much to drink at the fiesta. If we had known he was on board, we would have –' Here he broke off.

Ann waited for a few seconds. 'You would have . . . ?'

Captain Kollias took a deep breath. 'We would have got him out.'

'Don't you think that perhaps you should have made it your duty to search the accommodation area before the fire took hold, just in case?'

Leo rose to his feet. 'My Lord, I fail to see the relevance of this entirely speculative line of questioning.'

Mr Justice Sagewell nodded. 'I do not think counsel need make these tragic events the matter of too much surmise. Captain Kollias has already stated that he believed Mr Fexis was ashore. What might have occurred had he assumed otherwise is not within the scope of our enquiry.'

'Very good, my Lord.'

Captain Kollias's stolid demeanour had entirely given way, and he sat with his hand covering his face, his large frame visibly heaving with emotion. Ann allowed him a moment or two to collect himself before she pressed on. There was a long discussion of the history of the generator where the fire had occurred, and about its last service prior to the fire two months earlier at Hydra, and Captain Kollias was closely questioned as to the likelihood of the fuel pipe vibrating free. The captain's manner, as he answered these largely technical questions, regained its assuredness. He was unshakeable on every aspect of the circumstances of the fire, and his diffidence in the matter of the engineer's forty-a-day smoking habit hit just the right note of plausibility in relation to the possibility that a discarded cigarette might have caused the fire. Leo could tell, glancing at Mr Justice Sagewell's face from time to time, that the judge found Captain Kollias an impressive witness.

On only one occasion during his cross-examination did Captain Kollias glance in the direction of Adriana Papaposilakis, and since he was answering questions as to the nature of his relations with his employer at the time – which he maintained were always good, and that he was always paid on time – there seemed nothing odd about this. But in catching this single glance, Leo experienced an instinctive flicker of disquiet, born of long experience. After a couple of seconds, however, he decided that the glance had been merely automatic, not one expressive of mutual reassurance. He hadn't been able to tell, from his vantage-point, whether Adriana had returned it or not. In any event, Captain Kollias's evidence had not been shaken, and Adriana and her team of lawyers left court that afternoon well satisfied with the day's proceedings.

After a brief confabulation with Adriana and Rachel outside the courtroom, Leo went off to the robing room to change. On his way out of the law courts, he caught sight of Ann Halliday ahead of him, and caught up with her just as she was about to cross the Strand.

'We still haven't had that drink yet,' observed Leo. 'I want to get an insight into your real feelings about this case.'

'Where this case is concerned, I'm beyond feelings. But I'm up for a drink, certainly.'

'Excellent. Half six?'

'Fine.'

'See you later. I need to get to the bank before it closes.' And he hurried off.

At twenty past six Ann went to the ladies. She combed her hair, then surveyed her features in the mirror. She was glad she'd let Charmaine talk her into having those highlights done – they did look pretty. She essayed a smile, and peered at the fine lines around her eyes that this produced. Then she relaxed the smile and sighed, and dabbed on a little lipstick. The feeling of expectation which bubbled within her was only theoretically pleasurable. In fact, she hated it. It was instinctive, hormonal or something, and she could do without it. Since her move to 5 Caper Court, Leo had sought out her company on a regular basis – that was fine, but he was motivated by nothing more than pure friendship, the fact that they were like-minded people who enjoyed each other's company. It had been that way when they were students. The best of mates, nothing more. The trouble was, one couldn't be around Leo for long without certain primitive impulses rising to the surface. Useless, but unconquerable. Perhaps, raddled old spinster that she was turning into, she should be grateful for this much stimulation. The word was that Leo was seeing Camilla Lawrence, anyway. Ann wondered, as she tucked away her comb and lipstick, what on earth they ever found to talk about. Beyond law or current affairs, she couldn't sustain a conversation with a member of the opposite sex under the age of thirty for more than two minutes at a time – with the exception of Roger Fry, whose mind was eccentric and ageless. No, the best romantic prospect on the horizon at the moment came in the unlikely shape of Stephen Bishop, whose recent shy attentions had both flattered and alarmed her. He was a pleasant enough man, in a portly, solitary way, but she wasn't sure she was that desperate.

She went downstairs and found Leo lounging in reception with a copy of *Lloyd's List*. He glanced up and gave Ann a heart-stopping smile.

'Right.' He chucked the paper aside and stood up. 'Let's go. I'd prefer not to drink in the Temple, if you don't mind. I've had enough of my fellow lawyers of late.'

They took a taxi to Mayfair, to a little bar down a side street. While Leo bought the drinks, Ann sat in one of the comfortable, squashy leather armchairs and surveyed the discreetly lit room, the carefully spaced tables and expensive, muted decor. Just the kind of place Leo would know about.

Leo returned with the drinks and sat down. 'Cheers.' He sipped his Scotch. Ann noticed the fine lines around his mouth and eyes, the slight slackness of the handsome features. Both of them had reached an age where youth was fading fast. She wondered if it was some fault in her own perception which made it seem as though it mattered less to men, or certainly men such as Leo.

'Cheers.' Ann took a sip of her martini. It was deliciously dry. 'So. Not a bad day for you. Captain Kollias did pretty well.'

Leo nodded. 'He stuck to his brief. I just wish every witness would. Mind you, this case is going to rest on the technical evidence, as I see it. I reckon you've got an uphill struggle ahead of you, trying to show the fire didn't start accidentally.'

'Mmm. We'll have to see, won't we? Have you read Toulson's judgment in that scuttling case that was reported just last week? I can't remember the name offhand.'

'The *Delphine*? I wouldn't let that get your hopes up. As I recall, the owner of that particular yacht hadn't paid his crew in months, he had money problems, a yacht which was just running up costs and which he couldn't sell, and which was substantially over-insured into the bargain. He had every motive in the world for sending her to the bottom of the ocean. I don't think my client quite falls into the same category.'

'No, indeed. Miss Papaposilakis is quite something, isn't she? I think old Sagewell likes her more than a little.'

Leo smiled. 'It always helps, doesn't it?'

They discussed the case in a peripheral fashion for a while, then a brief, companionable silence fell over them both. Ann was feeling quite mellow from the effects of her martini.

'I like your hair like that,' said Leo suddenly. 'Have you done something to it?' Ann raised a self-conscious hand, but before she could reply, Leo added, 'Sorry, I shouldn't ask. But it suits you. I remember you used to have very long hair when we were students.'

'We all wore our hair long back then, Leo. You included – down to your shoulders, as I recall.' Ann smiled. 'I believe I may even have some photographic evidence somewhere.'

'I beg you, destroy it, please!'

'Why? You were so good-looking. Half the girls at Bar School were after you.'

'Really? That's not the way I remember it.' Leo drained his Scotch. 'Though there was that desperate female in our tutorial group who used to send me notes all the time. What was her name? Very dark, intense creature, with a big nose.'

Ann laughed. 'Oh, God! Verity! Wasn't she bizarre? Do you remember when she fell asleep once right in the middle of Worsley's tutorial on documentary credits, and started to snore?'

'I don't blame her. Worsley was intensely boring, to say nothing of transferable letters of credit. Ah, dear Verity. I wonder what became of her? I was always bumming fags off her. Talk about taking advantage of her tender feelings.'

'It all seems a long time ago now.'

'We didn't know the half of it, did we? I kidded myself I was working hard, but I suspect I spent far too much time drinking and listening to Led Zeppelin. How I wish I still had the same capacity for frivolity.'

'I don't remember you being especially frivolous, Leo. In fact, I used to think you were sometimes a bit too intense. Always sitting around in the common room having meaningful discussions about life and the universe. I remember on one occasion you became very passionate on the subject of whether or not Wittgenstein was a religious person.'

'Did I now? What a memory you have.' Leo swirled the ice in his empty glass. 'I still think it's a very interesting question. Wittgenstein himself always said he wasn't, but I reckon he had a twin-track approach to God. He didn't think the existence of God could be proved, but then again, I don't think he felt it was necessary. He had this very robust approach to faith. None of your delicate ratiocination for old Wittgenstein.'

'"Is what I am doing really worth the labour? Surely only if it receives a light from above."'

Leo stared at her, nodding. 'I'm amazed you know that quote.'

'Why?'

'Sorry. That sounded rude. I was just surprised. It exactly sums up what I mean. His belief in some kind of external inspiration. I'm sure it's common to most great thinkers. All great minds seem to believe there's a greater mind pushing them from behind.'

Ann pondered this for a few seconds. 'You mean you think Galileo was able to face up to the Pope and the Church, because he was convinced of some external guidance in his exploration of the solar system?'

'Precisely. Or take Newton's religious faith.'

'Or Einstein's in restructuring the Newtonian universe.'

Leo smiled. 'Would you like another drink before we get on to Darwin?'

Ann returned the smile. 'Or David Hume? I think I would.'

Half an hour later, Leo roused himself from the depths of their conversation to look at his watch. 'D'you know, I suggest we carry this discussion on over dinner. What do you say?'

And Ann agreed. Leo thought about calling Camilla to tell her he would be late, but decided it wasn't necessary. It was just dinner with an old friend, after all.

By the end of the week, Ann had finished her cross-examination of the witnesses of fact, and apart from a brief verbal tussle with the over-excitable Mr Staveris concerning his smoking habits, nothing of any great moment occurred. The next stage of the case would involve the lengthy consideration of the evidence of the expert witnesses on both sides, and since this consisted of long and detailed reports and supplementary reports by marine surveyors, metallurgists, fire experts, and two naval architects with special expertise in ship vibration, it was estimated that the case would last some weeks yet.

'I anticipate a certain exasperation on the part of our learned judge,' remarked Leo, while discussing the case with Anthony at the end of the first week. 'There's a repetitive, long-winded element about some of the reports, and Sagewell's not known as the most patient of men.'

'Can't you get the experts together to refine their arguments and get rid of tiresome points?'

'I think we're going to have to. I'll have a word with Rachel about it.' Leo swivelled thoughtfully in his chair.

'How is Rachel?'

'Fine.' Leo gave Anthony a glance. 'Why do you ask?'

Anthony shrugged, and took a few slow paces round the room. 'Just wondered.'

'Well, at any rate, she's doing a sterling job keeping Adriana Papaposilakis off my back. If there's one thing I can do without, it's a client who wants to run the case herself.'

Anthony glanced at his watch. 'Time I got some work done. See you later.'

Anthony went back to his room. Why had Leo given him that look when he'd asked about Rachel? He didn't own her. Not any more. Anthony sat down at his desk. The fact was, he'd been thinking about her, on and off, every day since seeing her last Sunday, wanting to call her. Why? What was the point? She was living with another man. *'Charles and I are very happy.'* He could hear her voice as she'd said that, on the evening of the chambers party. He could picture her features now, that hesitant, watchful look, a glimpse of apprehension behind the eyes. She had a quality which touched him as surely now as it had when he'd first met her; not just a superficial loveliness, but something that went straight to his heart.

There could be no harm in calling and seeing if she'd like to meet up for a drink. He could use the demurrage case as a pretext. He got the impression that, whatever her life might be, however happy she might profess to be with Charles, she was rather lonely. This instinctive knowledge touched a similar chord within himself. Maybe it had to do with the Leo experience. Two damaged people recognizing one another. Bloody Leo. He reached out a hand and picked up the phone, then rang Nichols & Co. and asked to be put through to Rachel. She agreed to meet him for a drink in an hour's time.

They met in a wine bar in Liverpool Street, near Rachel's office.

'I can't stay long, I'm afraid.' Rachel brushed her dark hair behind one shoulder and picked up her glass of wine. 'My nanny usually clocks off at half six, but I asked her to hang on for another hour. She's pretty flexible.'

'I just needed a quick word about that demurrage case. It won't take long.'

For ten minutes or so they talked about the case, until there was no more to be said. After a short silence, Rachel asked, 'You didn't really ask me here to talk about that case, did you? We could have discussed it on the phone.' She looked into his eyes, which were dark and thoughtful, thinking how much she had always liked the boyishness about him, at odds with his tall, muscular frame. She knew that the question was taking them on to dangerous ground, but in that moment she didn't much care. She felt in need of some direct connection, some honest emotion. It had become like a craving over the past few weeks.

'No. No, I didn't.' Anthony dropped his gaze. 'I wanted to see you.' He shrugged. 'Simple as that.' He looked up at her again. 'If you knew this was a pretext, you must have wanted to see me, too. Or am I wrong?'

Rachel opened her mouth to reply, then hesitated. 'Yes,' she said at last. 'I wanted to see you. You're a friend I thought I'd lost. So, you know . . . it's nice to have a drink together.'

But Anthony had no intention of allowing these last lame words to defuse the situation. 'It's more than that. At least, I think it is.' When she said nothing in reply to this, he went on, 'You told me you were happy with Charles. Why do I get the feeling that's not quite true?'

'But it is true. That is . . .' She leaned her head back and closed her eyes briefly. 'The situation – the way we are together. That's happy. Everything's in place . . . It's just that lately, when he comes back from the States, he's only here for a few days, and everything seems disconnected somehow. And there isn't time to put things together . . . And I find I don't want to, necessarily. I don't understand any of it. But externally, theoretically . . . what we have should be enough for anyone.'

'Are you in love with him?'

She gave a laugh, and took another sip of her drink. 'Oh, Anthony. That's not what it's all about.'

'Isn't it?'

'People aren't happy in that way. That's – well, being in love is quite different. What Charles and I have is some kind of . . . well, I suppose the right word would be – contentment. Only –'

'Then why don't you seem contented?'

She looked at him quickly, her eyes almost fearful. There it was again, he thought – that lost, lovely look that turned his insides to water.

'Don't I?' She dropped her gaze, and sat thinking for some seconds. 'You asked about being in love. I haven't felt anything like that since Leo. I don't think I possibly could, ever again. So I don't ask for that much any more, you see.'

'You mean, you tell yourself that what you've got with Charles should be enough?'

'Yes.'

'But you wanted to see me?'

'Yes.'

The intentness of their conversation had brought them

close together over the table. Anthony said softly, 'You know, I want very much to kiss you right now.'

'I think that might be a mistake.'

He said nothing, then after a few seconds sat back. 'You're right. We've both been here before, and –' He broke off, sighed, and glanced at his watch. 'Anyway, you should be getting back to Oliver.'

She nodded, finishing her drink. They rose and left. Anthony walked her to the station. She turned on the escalator and gave him a quick wave, and he hurried off.

On the train she leaned against the window, staring out unseeingly. When he'd said he wanted to kiss her, she had hoped he would. In that moment, she had wanted it. Given the way things had been between them two years ago – the way she had been before Leo had unlocked the sexuality which had lain frozen within her – that was amazing. But Anthony had probably assumed she meant that nothing had changed. Yet it had. Oh, how it had. She closed her eyes. But did it have to be Anthony? The way she felt these days, the sudden spasms of longing for excitement and passion, maybe it could be anyone. In which case, she was being a fool. What was she doing, thinking this way, when she had her happy, stable life with Charles? If she was honest, life with Charles wasn't so happy, and it wasn't so stable. She had known that for some time. When had it begun? When she had refused to go to live in the States with him, while he worked on his documentary series? Possibly. The compromise was for Charles to be away for long stretches of time, then home for short ones. And when they were together, they were cheerful and affectionate and apparently all was well. But her refusal had undermined relations between them. Every single pretext – her job, the difficulty of getting a work permit, not wanting to take Oliver so far from his father – had only underscored the truth: that she was not prepared to make sacrifices to be with him. It could have cost them their relationship, but Charles hadn't let it.

She opened her eyes and stared out at the landscape speeding past. Strange how the conventional picture of a relationship falling apart – rows, petty squabbles, acrimony and ultimate estrangement – was often far from the truth. Things happened more subtly, more sadly. People could still smile, talk, even make jokes, while underneath the whole substance of their world together was undergoing seismic shifts.

As for her feelings for Anthony, they went further than mere physical desire. There was a sense of closeness with someone more of her own age, and that was something she missed with Charles. She'd missed it with Leo, too, whose control had been simply overwhelming. The way Anthony had looked at her this evening, the urgency and intensity of his gaze, seeing only her and wanting only her, had been truly liberating. She had felt singular once more, acutely herself, not anyone's mother or ex-wife or . . . Her thoughts tailed off as reality reasserted itself. She was mad even to think about Anthony in that way. She'd had enough emotional turmoil in her life without inviting more. Things were naturally not perfect with Charles at the moment, because he was away so much. When that situation changed, then probably everything else would. It would get better. She would just have to wait it out.

On her way home from work, Felicity stopped at the minimart on the corner to pick up an evening paper and had a chat with Neelam, the wife of the Indian who ran the shop.

'How's life?' asked Felicity.

'Not so great,' sighed Neelam. She shifted her baby son from one hip to another. 'Sanjay and I are meant to be going to Mumbai next week for a couple of months. We've got the tickets, everything's planned, and now Sanjay's brother, who was meant to be looking after the shop for us, is in hospital. He came off his motorbike at the weekend. He's got a broken arm, pelvis, everything . . . Ankit, his other brother, says he'll come in early and do the morning papers, but he's got to work the rest of the day. The only person who's going to be around is Sanjay's mother, and she can only do so much. She's too old. I mean, she serves in the shop and keeps the stock lists, but there's no way she could take the deliveries and stack the shelves and sort out the freezers.'

'Is there no one else in the family who can help out?'

Neelam shook her head. 'They're all too busy. They would only be able to come in now and again. I really don't want to close up for a couple of months. We'd lose so much business. But I don't see what else we can do.'

Felicity hesitated. Could she see Sandy going in and helping old Mrs Deepak every day? It was worth a shot. Anything, provided he was working. 'My brother's staying with me at the moment. I could ask him to help out, if you like.'

Neelam's eyes brightened. 'Do you think he would?'

'I'm afraid I couldn't guarantee him first thing in the morning. He's not exactly an early riser. But he could help out later on, say from eleven onwards.'

'I wouldn't need him first thing – Ankit'll be here then. But a couple of hours every day to help Sanjay's mum with the heavy stuff – that would be really good.'

Felicity left the shop, charged with resolve. This was Sandy's chance. It might only be a temporary job down the corner shop, but she would lay it on the line to him. Either he took it, made sure he got his lazy arse out of bed each day – ten-thirty surely wasn't too much to ask – and showed he was serious about doing something to help himself and not just sponge off her forever, or she would kick him out. She really would. She meant it. She really meant it.

Sandy wasn't there when she got home. She had arranged to meet her friend Maureen and a couple of other girls for a drink and a spot of clubbing, so she had a shower, followed by a quick sandwich, and went out. She did her best to enjoy herself, but it was an effort. In the end, she gave up. Recent events had become too much for her.

'What's up with you?' asked Maureen. She sat down at the table next to Felicity, who was staring moodily into her drink. 'You've got a face on you like a smacked arse.'

'I dunno, Mo. I'm sorry if I'm not much fun.'

'Come on, what's up? You can tell me.'

Felicity sighed. 'Oh, I feel like life's just stuck on hold at the moment, like everything around me is stopping me moving on. There's Vince in prison, making me feel all guilty and hung up, like I owe him something. I've got my bloody brother sponging off me, and then there's Peter. You don't know what it's like, Mo, having to work eight hours a day with someone who did what he did to me, someone I thought I really loved.'

Maureen knew all about Felicity's romance with Peter Weir, how it had come crashing to earth when she had found out about Peter's wife and children. 'Oh, Fliss, I know – I couldn't believe it when you said he was coming to work where you do. You must really hate having to see that bastard all the time.'

Felicity shook her head miserably. 'That's the stupid part. I like it, him being there. I mean, everyone in chambers likes Peter. He's a really good laugh, plus he's good at his job. I wish he was a really horrible person, so I could hate him properly, but I can't! I mean, just because I hate what he did to me, it doesn't mean I don't still have feelings about him.

That's the problem, you see. By rights, when you break up with someone, that should be the end of it, you don't have to see them any more. You've got some space to get over it. But he's there every sodding day! And if I'm going to work with him, I have to get on with him. And that makes it worse.'

'Yeah, I see your problem.' Mo's troubled vacancy offered no solutions. Then she brightened. 'Tell you what, let me get you another Malibu and Coke. That'll cheer you up.'

By the time she got home later, Felicity's mood hadn't improved. The flat was in darkness. She switched on the lights and slumped in an armchair, relieved that Sandy wasn't there, for once. She just wanted her life back, to be able to live in her own flat without her brother hanging round day and night, to be able to do her job and enjoy her work without the ache of having to see Peter every day.

She made herself some hot chocolate and went to bed. In the early hours, just as dawn was breaking, she heard Sandy come in. Fat chance of him ever getting up to do his job at the Deepaks' shop. Fat chance of anything getting better, ever. She heard voices. Christ, he hadn't brought someone back with him, had he? There was a brief banging of furniture, and Felicity was about to get up, when she stopped, one foot on the floor. From behind the closed door of the living room, she could hear sobbing. Then voices again. There must be someone with him. She listened intently for a few seconds, and realized that she could hear only Sandy's voice. He was talking to himself. But he was talking like he was having a proper conversation. There would be a question, a pause, then his own voice answering, then wavering horribly into cracked sobbing. More questions, and his voice rising, raving. She could hear him moving about, shoving furniture, cursing.

Felicity knew she should go through and find out what was wrong. But she remained there, cold with fear and incomprehension, listening to Sandy's voice as he talked to the voices in his head. That must be who he was talking to. And she was afraid of what he might do if she went through. He didn't sound like anyone she knew. She lay down again in the darkness, pulling the duvet around her, up against her ears, so that the voice became muffled and she didn't have to listen to the senseless words. After a while all sound ceased. She wondered what had happened. Had he fallen asleep in a chair? Gone to bed? Killed himself? She didn't want to know. Whatever was going on, even in her own flat, she couldn't face it right now. She would deal with it in the morning. She closed her eyes and lay there, waiting for sleep, praying for the silence to continue, whatever its cause.

In the morning, she found the living room empty. Despite the noise Sandy had made, the room wasn't in particular disorder. She made two cups of tea and took one into his bedroom. He was lying on his bed, fully clothed, asleep. She set the tea down beside his bed and shook him. He groaned and rolled on to his back. After a moment he opened his eyes.

'Are you all right?' asked Felicity.

Sandy blinked at her. He looked terrible, but possibly no worse than usual. He ran his fingers through his hair. 'What?'

'You came in last night and starting pushing the furniture about. Shouting. Talking to yourself.'

'Did I?'

'Were you drunk?'

He shook his head, and instantly his gaze was blank, uncommunicative. 'I don't remember. No.'

Felicity sat down on the edge of his bed. 'Listen, Sandy,

you were in a bad way last night, and if you can't remember, that makes it even worse. This stuff about voices in your head – maybe you should see someone, get some help.'

He blinked again. 'I'm fine.' He wasn't going to tell Fliss about the ketamine. He glanced at the tea. 'Is that for me?' Felicity nodded. Sandy pulled himself up in bed, reached out for the tea and drank some.

'You're not. You're doing too much dope. It's making you paranoid.'

'That's a laugh. I don't need dope to make me paranoid. I know what's going on.'

'What's that, then? What's going on, Sandy?'

Sandy put down his cup, pushed back the duvet and swung his legs to the floor. 'Nothing you'd understand, Fliss. They're not interested in you.'

She followed him through the flat as he made his way to the bathroom. 'Who's not interested in me?' He closed the bathroom door in her face, and she banged on it. 'You've got to talk to me, Sandy! You've got a problem!' After a moment or two she sighed and went back to the kitchen.

As she was making some toast, Sandy reappeared. He sat down at the kitchen table. 'Sandy, you've got to think seriously –'

'Don't, Fliss. That's all I ever do these days.' He put his head in his hands. After a moment or two, he muttered, 'I'm sorry. Look, I'll go down the Job Centre today. I promise. I really will try to get something. I can't take what's going on.'

Felicity was silent for a moment, then said, 'There's a job going at the Deepaks' shop, if you want it. Only temporary. The Deepaks are going to India for a couple of months, and the person they were leaving in charge has let them down. There's only going to be Sanjay's old mum there, and she can't do much beyond serve in the shop. She needs someone to help with the heavy stuff, taking deliveries, unloading boxes, stacking shelves and things. So I said you might be interested. It won't be much money.' She waited warily for his reaction.

Sandy took his hands from his head and laid them flat on the table, palms down. He nodded. 'Yeah, that'll do. I can do that. When would I start?'

'Next Monday.'

'Does it mean getting up early?'

'No. You wouldn't have to be there till later on in the morning, say around eleven, something like that. But you'd have to be regular. She'll need you every day.'

Sandy stared at the backs of his hands. 'Okay.'

'You mustn't let anyone down, mind.'

'I won't.'

Felicity wasn't sure she believed this, but she had no choice. She left Sandy at the kitchen table, and went to get ready for work. On the way into chambers she thought about Sandy and the job. It was a small beginning, but maybe it would prove significant. If he could just feel better about himself, do a few hours' work every day and bring in a bit of money, no matter how small, he might be on the road to getting himself together at last.

Later that morning, when things were quiet in the clerks' room, Peter came up to Felicity as she sat at her desk. He smiled and leaned down.

'What about that lunch we were going to have?'

She looked up at him, her face cold. 'It's not that easy to make things all right, you know.'

'I know. I'm only asking you to give me a chance. We can be friends, at least.'

She stared back at her computer screen. Right now, she

felt so emotionally fragile that she couldn't handle this properly. She badly needed to be able to tell him to piss off in no uncertain terms. But she couldn't. She looked up at him. 'What for, Peter? What's the point?'

Their eyes made the connection. He let some seconds elapse. 'Because of the way we still feel about each other.'

That was it. By rights, she should have slapped his stupid face. But she sat transfixed, just looking at him. He was doing it to her again. God, she wanted him, and hated him, so badly. How easy it would be to say yes. Part of her longed to, was more than ready to. 'Come on.' His voice was low. 'You don't really hate me as much as you think.'

'Yeah, I do, actually.' She looked away.

'And you know what they say about hate and love.'

Henry came bustling into the clerks' room, and glanced over at Peter and Felicity. 'Got a moment, Fliss?' he called.

Relieved, Felicity got to her feet. 'Yeah, sure.' She gave Peter a glance, and muttered, 'Stick your lunch. You could never be my friend, Peter.'

He watched wistfully as she crossed the room to talk to Henry. That fantastic arse. She really had been about the best he'd ever had, and good company, too. Pity she had these strange ideas about not wanting to be someone's bit on the side. That wasn't the way he'd seen it at all. But he could tell from the look in her eyes that he'd talk her back round. If he knew women, she probably wanted him to. It was only a matter of time, and persistence.

9

The summer weeks drifted by, and the newly expanded chambers at 5 Caper Court settled into a tranquil rhythm. Maurice's early dissatisfactions and restlessness had been soothed by a couple of big-earning cases and the sense that, in playing a significant role in the matter of the chambers party and in the revamping of the website, he had established a certain ascendancy among his fellow tenants. Ann, Roger and Marcus seemed content in their new surroundings and rubbed along harmoniously with the other members of chambers, although Marcus, with his late hours and industrious zeal, remained somewhat aloof. Work appeared to be his consuming passion. His two-seater Alfa Romeo was among the first in the car park in King's Bench Walk each morning, and was often still there late into the evening. To Sarah's frustration, he was rarely around at afternoon tea, and was never to be found whiling away the odd fifteen minutes in idle gossip in the clerks' room, so her fantasies of a growing relationship based on chance meetings around chambers seemed destined to remain unfulfilled.

As July turned to August a heatwave bathed the City, and in the antiquated buildings of the Temple the lawyers sweltered. They flung up their sash windows, rolled up their sleeves, and set piles of papers and briefs flickering and fluttering under the breeze of countless electric fans. Clerks hurrying about their duties paused to loiter and gossip in the cool shade of courtyards and cloisters, lunchtime workers broiled in the sun on the grass in Embankment Gardens, and beneath the summer trees the iridescent waters of Fountain Court danced and splashed.

Sarah was sitting in her room, drafting a statement of case for Jeremy Vane, and hating it. She put down her pen and took a swig from the bottle of Evian water which stood on her desk. Thank God, only four more weeks to go, and she would be out of here. She pulled back her blonde hair in one hand, twisted it up in a knot behind her head, and stuck a pencil through it to hold it in place. She sighed, then stared dispiritedly at the papers in front of her in an effort of concentration.

There was a light knock at the door, and Roger Fry looked in.

'Busy?'

'I should be. Jeremy wants this draft statement of case by the end of the afternoon. But somehow I can't summon up the enthusiasm.' Sarah yawned and gave Roger a reflective glance. 'Roger, tuck your shirt in.'

He looked down, hitched up his trousers and made an ineffectual attempt to straighten his shirt. 'Anyway, I came to ask you – d'you fancy seeing a film tonight?'

'Yes, why not? Who else is going?'

Since the evening of the Proms, she and Roger had become quite friendly, occasionally lunching in hall together, or having a drink after work. Apart from the gorgeous and unattainable Marcus, Sarah regarded him as one of the few interesting members of chambers.

'No one else. Just you and me.'

Sarah hesitated. Was this a date, Roger trying to move things on to another level? She sincerely hoped not.

'What did you have in mind?'

'There's a Portuguese film festival running at the ICA at the moment. That could be quite interesting.'

She returned his guileless gaze. 'Really?'

He shook his head. 'No, that was a small joke. I had the new Samuel L. Jackson movie in mind.'

'Maybe I like Portuguese films.'

'Mmm. Maybe you've never seen one.'

Sarah smiled. 'True. All right, let's go and see Samuel L. Jackson.'

'I'll see you around six. We can have a drink first.'

She nodded. 'Okay. See you later.'

Leo picked up a pen from the box on Henry's desk. He inspected the *5 Caper Court* logo printed on the side, pulled off the cap, then replaced it. 'Whose idea was this? As though I need to ask.'

'Mr Faber's. You lot are meant to hand them around at conferences, solicitors hold on to them, and next time they want to instruct someone, they catch sight of a Five Caper Court pen lying on their desk and think, aha! those are just the boys. Or girls, as the case may be.'

Leo winced. 'I can't go around handing out free pens to people like some *Crackerjack* presenter.'

'Sorry, Mr Davies?'

'Lesley Crowther. Michael Aspel.' Henry looked blank. Leo sighed. 'Don't worry, Henry. It's an age thing.'

'He also has ideas about redesigning the chambers' booklet. Thinks it's a bit staid.'

'Christ, he'll have us advertising on the sides of buses soon.'

'Got to move with the times, Mr Davies.'

'Have we, Henry? I sometimes think I'd be quite happy if they moved without me.'

Leo took his mail from his pigeon-hole and went upstairs to his room. He slung his jacket on the back of his chair and loosened his tie, and began to sort through the letters. The *Persephone* hearing had been suspended for a second day due to Mr Sagewell's indisposition, and Leo was using the spare time to catch up on unattended matters.

A few minutes later his phone rang. It was the surveyor reporting on the Chelsea property. Leo had looked at four other houses since then, but none had been quite as perfect as that in Gratton Crescent. So Leo had put in an offer a couple of weeks ago, and it had been accepted. Now he was waiting to hear what kind of condition the property was in.

'Not entirely good news, I'm afraid,' the surveyor told Leo. 'You may have a problem with subsidence at the back. There's a large mulberry tree close to the house in the garden at the rear of the property, and it's possible the roots have undermined the foundations.'

'Is that going to be expensive?' asked Leo.

'Depends. We really need to dig down to find out.'

Leo sighed. He'd largely expected a property of that nature to be pretty much sound, given the asking price. 'Can we ask the present owners to investigate the extent of the problem? They're the ones who want to sell it, after all.'

'Certainly we can ask them. But you may find you finish up having the work done at your own expense. That's something the estate agent will have to sort out. But look – I'll get a full report out to you in the post this afternoon, and then you can decide what you want to do.'

'All right. Thanks.'

Leo put the phone down. He was still pondering this latest development when Camilla knocked on the door and looked in.

'Robert said you hadn't gone to court.'

'No. Mr Justice Sagewell's still off his cornflakes.'

'Nice to have a day off. Why have you got that brooding look?'

'I've just had a call from the surveyor about the house

in Gratton Crescent. There's a problem with subsidence, apparently. How big a problem, we don't yet know.'

'Oh.' Camilla wasn't sure what kind of response was required. Leo had gone to great pains to involve her in the house purchase, but she was finding it hard to take an absorbing interest. Wandering around these grand properties with Leo, she had difficulty envisaging herself living in any of them.

Leo sighed. 'Still, can't expect these things to go without some sort of hitch.' He smiled. 'Now, is this visit purely pleasure, or business?'

'I just thought I'd let you know that Elborne's are sending me back to Bermuda for another stint. I'm off tomorrow morning.'

'That's a bit sudden.'

'I know. That's why I'm telling you now. So that you can take me somewhere very nice for dinner this evening.'

Leo smiled. 'I'd better book something straight away.'

When she had gone, Leo continued opening his post. From an envelope larger than the rest he drew out a stiff, engraved card. It was an invitation from friends he hadn't seen in some time – Hector and Sonia Treeves – to a party in celebration of Hector's fiftieth birthday in August. A black-tie affair, champagne reception, formal dinner, string quartet – the works. He mused on this, wondering why they had sent it to chambers. Then he realized that the last time he had seen the Treeveses was when he was still married to Rachel, and that they probably had no idea where he was presently living. The Treeveses themselves had a magnificent house in the heart of Mayfair, and Leo had no doubt that this would be an event of some splendour. Camilla would enjoy it. He dropped the invitation into his briefcase, to answer later, and turned his attention to a new set of instructions which had arrived that morning from Richards Butler.

*

'Do you want some popcorn?'

'No, thanks.'

Sarah waited as Roger stood in the queue, watching him with curiosity. Whatever doubts she might have had earlier, this pretty much settled them. No man who had taken her to the cinema on a first date had ever settled down to munch his way through a large bag of sweet popcorn and a medium Coke.

Once in the cinema, he paid no attention to her at all. Not that she expected or liked people to talk to her during a film, but from any man who took her out she was accustomed to some acknowledgement of her existence – a word, or a shared glance or smile. Roger, entirely absorbed in the film, seemed almost unaware she was there.

Two hours later, the credits rolled.

'Excellent,' said Roger, as they made their way out.

'You didn't find it a little low-brow?' asked Sarah, as they stepped out into the dense, warm evening air of Leicester Square.

'Extremely. I'm all for low-brow. Love it.'

'I'm surprised you should say that, given all those movie books on your shelves at home.'

'I don't mean I like that kind of thing exclusively. It's just I'll watch anything. I like Fassbinder as much as, say, the Farrelly brothers. Depends on what mood I'm in. Are you hungry?'

'Yes, I am.'

'Pizza Express all right?'

'I suppose so.'

They talked over pizza about the film, and about films in general. Roger's knowledge seemed encyclopaedic. As she listened, Sarah realized that he reminded her of a boy she knew when she was ten, who'd lived next door to her grandmother. They'd played together all summer long.

Unassuming, mild-mannered and cheerful, the perfect friend. Like the boy, whose name she had long forgotten, Roger treated her in an even-handed, asexual way – which was flattering in one sense, because it meant he valued her company, and baffling in another. Sarah was used to a certain look in men's eyes when they regarded her. No matter how they might try to conceal it, it was always there – desire, sexual interest, call it what you like. She didn't detect that in Roger. Not that she cared. It was just different.

When they left the restaurant it was dark, but the streets were still busy, the pavement cafés crowded.

'What now?' asked Roger.

'Home, I think,' said Sarah. 'I'm doing work for Jeremy all this week, so I'd better not get to bed late. He piles it on.'

'Come on, then. Pity it's so late, or we could have walked through the park.'

'Walk? I can't walk all the way to Kensington – it's miles!'

'So? It's a lovely evening.' And Roger began to amble off in a westerly direction, hands in his pockets. Sarah experienced a few seconds of acute irritation, in which she almost decided to take a taxi and let Roger do as he liked. But something – perhaps the suspicion that if she did, he wouldn't be in the least bothered – made her change her mind. She walked quickly to catch up with him.

Walking home, rather than taking a taxi, was surprisingly pleasant, strolling along next to Roger, chatting, letting the night traffic rush by. After half an hour, they reached Sarah's flat.

'Thanks for the evening,' said Sarah. 'I enjoyed it.'

At this stage in the proceedings, a certain delicate sexual tension would normally have been created, precursory to the customary moves. But Roger merely stood with hands in his pockets and nodded. 'Good.'

Sarah smiled. He was without pretension or self-regard, had no level of sophistication to which she could rise.

'What?' asked Roger, catching the amusement in her eyes.

'Nothing.' She laughed. 'I'm sorry. Nothing. You're just so different from most men.'

'Is there something you were expecting?'

'No, of course not. Like what?'

'Oh . . . Well . . . I imagine most men would have made some kind of pass at you by now.'

'Well, since you mention it, yes – most of them would. But don't worry. It's not mandatory. Thanks again. I'll see you tomorrow.'

She reached up to give him the customary light kiss on the cheek which etiquette demanded. As she did so, he put his arms around her and, with far greater expertise than Sarah would have expected, kissed her properly for some considerable time. Being kissed by Roger wasn't at all what she had anticipated. It was amazing.

'Okay?' asked Roger, with the air of someone who'd done what was expected of him.

'You don't have to sound quite so blasé,' said Sarah, her voice a little faint.

Roger frowned. 'Blasé?' He stared at her for a few seconds. She waited, wondering what he was going to say.

'See you in the morning.' He gave her a smile and walked off.

'Night,' murmured Sarah, somewhat dazed. She went upstairs and let herself in. Her flatmate, Lou, was already asleep. Sarah got ready for bed.

Half an hour later she still lay awake, trying to make sense of Roger, and of her own response to him. Poor guy. He'd kissed her because he thought it was what he should do. It had been nice, but probably only because of the unexpectedness of it. She turned over, closing her eyes. He definitely wasn't her type at all.

By Monday of the following week Mr Justice Sagewell, still looking a little green about the gills, was well enough to resume his duties on the bench, and the *Persephone* hearing got underway again.

'Apparently it was some oysters at the Great Eastern,' whispered a member of the instructing team of solicitors to Leo.

Leo winced. He watched as the judge shuffled his papers in preparation. Seafood poisoning wasn't likely to have improved Sagewell's disposition, choleric at the best of times. A hand touched his shoulder lightly, a light fragrance seemed to envelop him, and he turned to see Adriana Papaposilakis smiling at him.

'Good morning, Leo,' she murmured.

'Morning,' replied Leo, somewhat surprised to see her there. She had been absent for a fortnight, missing much of the tedium of the expert evidence, and he had assumed she wouldn't reappear until towards the end of the case. But here she was, snug and sexy in a blue summer number that showed off a delectable amount of cleavage. His glance flickered from the soft expanse of skin to her blonde hair and mischievous dark eyes.

'Have I missed much?' she asked in a low voice.

'Nothing to speak of,' murmured Leo.

Mr Justice Sagewell shot them a quelling glance, and then addressed Leo's junior counsel. 'Miss Carpenter, I believe you were guiding us through Mr Fellowes' report? Shall we resume?'

As Kate Carpenter rose to her feet, Adriana whispered to Leo, 'I'm only staying for an hour. Perhaps we can meet this evening for a drink to discuss how things are going.' She slipped into a seat behind him.

Since Mr Defereras, Adriana's PA, had sat in quiet watchfulness throughout every hour of every day of the proceedings, and would have reported everything of note to her, Leo was well aware that the need to discuss the progress of the case was the most spurious of excuses. Although he had so far elegantly side-stepped the delectable Adriana's subtle attempts to engineer meetings alone with him, it was getting to the point where another evasion would appear like downright rudeness. He sighed, and made an effort to concentrate as Kate Carpenter questioned the fire expert on the potential ignition point of escaping diesel fuel.

'So, if the pipe had been only partly loosened initially, the release of diesel fuel would have been in the form of a jet, or spray? A kind of atomized mist?'

'Correct. In my experience, such a release can readily be ignited by, for example, a hot surface or an electrical spark, and a fire would develop very rapidly.'

Leo jotted down notes automatically, but a faint drift of perfume clinging to the air kept his thoughts fixed on Adriana. Why shouldn't he have a drink with the woman? She might even cheer him up. He and Camilla hadn't parted on a particularly satisfactory note this morning. He had happened to mention the Treeveses' invitation in passing at dinner last night, assuming she might quite like the idea of dressing up and spending an evening with him in opulent surroundings. But to his surprise she had greeted the prospect with mild indifference, which, on gentle probing, had turned into outright hostility. She had then remarked that on the one occasion when they'd had dinner with friends of his, she hadn't enjoyed herself at all. It had been boring, she'd said, talking to middle-aged people about middle-aged things for hours on end. When Leo had pointed out that she managed to talk perfectly well to him, she had said it wasn't the same thing at all and he knew it. So, he'd asked, why hadn't she said at the time that she'd been bored? Because she'd hoped it was a one-off, and that she wasn't going to have to spend entire evenings with geriatrics on a regular basis.

Leo had never heard her in this vein before. It was a marked contrast to her customary pliancy. Perhaps he'd been wrong in assuming that her natural reserve betokened maturity. She was, after all, only twenty-two. A further gentle enquiry as to whether that meant she didn't want to go to the Treeveses only produced a sulky shrug. Leo had left it at that, and gone on to talk of other things, but the incident had, for some reason, affected the mood of the entire evening. Whatever equilibrium their relationship normally possessed had been disturbed, and when he tried to restore it later in bed, she'd managed to sidetrack the proceedings with a contrite little reference to the Treeveses' party, which had somehow turned into another disagreeable exchange, very close to a row. So much so, that Leo was quite put off his sexual stride, and abandoned any thoughts of lovemaking.

Now she was en route to Bermuda, and Leo had to admit he was mildly relieved. He could do without the arduous business of having to cope with youthful petulance, for a couple of weeks at any rate. He just hoped that last night wouldn't prove to be symptomatic of a growing tendency. A couple of hours of Adriana's sophisticated and mildly provocative company might provide a welcome contrast.

Roger caught up with Sarah as she was leaving chambers at lunchtime.

'Look,' he said, pushing his glasses a little way up the bridge of his nose, 'about last night –'

Oh no, thought Sarah – here we go, a post-mortem about nothing at all. 'What about it?' She carried on walking, Roger falling into step beside her.

'I shouldn't just have gone off like that. It was a bit rude.'

'No, it wasn't.' She gave him a bemused smile. 'Look, Roger, if you're going to let it get to you, perhaps it might be an idea if we kept this friendship platonic.'

'No.' His voice was abrupt. He stopped, and she did too. He touched her arm. Looking at his face, remembering his kiss, she felt an instantaneous desire, a response which she tried to ignore. 'I'd like to see you this evening.'

'All right,' she said at last.

'I'll make us supper.'

'You will?' Recalling the inside of Roger's fridge, this seemed an unlikely scenario.

'Yes.'

She smiled and shrugged. 'What time?'

'Come round about eight.'

'Okay. See you later.' She walked off, hoping he hadn't got the idea that anything more was going to happen. If he had, he was quite wrong. In which case, she should probably just have said no. But she liked being with him, she really enjoyed talking to him. They had a good time together. He was just going to have to accept the fact that it wasn't going to go any further than that.

Adriana, having left the hearing around eleven, returned shortly before the close of proceedings that afternoon, and buttonholed Leo just as he was putting his papers together.

Rachel, standing a few yards away, watched as Adriana chatted to Leo in somewhat closer proximity than was entirely necessary. Clearly Adriana hadn't given up where Leo was concerned. Or perhaps she'd made some headway that Rachel didn't know about. He might have some ongoing relationship with that girl in his chambers, but since when had such considerations ever stopped Leo in the past? Rachel glanced away, wishing she didn't have to care so much what Leo did or with whom he did it. She had been conscious of irritable frustration over the past few weeks, and reluctantly had to admit that it was to do with the fact that Anthony hadn't been near her since their last encounter. Charles had come and gone, was back in the States with his film crew, and Rachel's only wish was that Anthony would ring. She didn't look beyond that event. All she wanted was to know that he still felt the same way about her. That need had filled her, consumed her, over the past fortnight. So why was she getting wound up about Leo and the stupid Greek woman? Habit, that was all. Maybe most ex-wives felt the same way.

When Adriana eventually left the courtroom with Mr Defereras, Rachel came over to Leo.

'Does our client have some concerns that she's not sharing with me?'

'I wouldn't call them concerns, exactly,' replied Leo. 'She wants to have another in-depth discussion about the case over a drink at her hotel.'

'And you're going?'

Leo gave her one of his infuriatingly deadpan smiles. 'It's a job. Someone has to do it.'

'Do you want me to come along?'

'No need. You get back to Charles and Oliver.'

'Charles is in the States.'

'Oliver, then.' Leo picked up his papers. They regarded one another. 'Don't concern yourself, Rachel. This is not your problem.'

'The *Persephone* is as much my case as yours.'

'I don't think the case is what we're talking about, do you?'

Rachel paused, then said bitterly, 'You know, I really feel sorry for that poor, deluded girl you're seeing.'

Leo met her gaze. 'When, Rachel, will you learn to stay out of my affairs?'

'What an ironically appropriate choice of words.' Rachel picked up her briefcase and left before Leo could say anything more.

Leo stood in the empty courtroom, closing his eyes for a few seconds as he fought back his irritation. Then he gathered up his papers and went to the robing room to change. Were it not for Oliver, he could heartily wish that Rachel had gone to the States with Charles. The woman seemed to think she had a duty to act as his conscience, turning her chilly, reproachful eye on everything he did. The fact was, he had no intention of having anything other than a sociable drink with Adriana Papaposilakis.

Leo turned up at Adriana's hotel at half past seven and made his way up to her suite. She opened the door, still clad in the same dress she had been wearing that day, and greeted him with a smile.

'Come in. You're very punctual. I like that in my lawyers.'

Leo glanced round the suite, taking in the size of the place and the opulence of its furnishings, and reckoned it must be the most expensive in the hotel. How many sofas and tables and vases of flowers did one small shipping magnate need, in heaven's name?

He noticed sheaves of papers relating to the case spread out on a low table, giving every appearance that she had asked him here to discuss the case.

'A drink?' Adriana was poised over a small array of bottles and glasses which stood on a small table. No minibars for Miss Papaposilakis, thought Leo.

'I'll have a Scotch, thanks. Just a small one.'

She poured his Scotch, mixed herself a gin and tonic, and brought the drinks over. They sat down on one of the sofas next to the table with the papers on it, maintaining a discreet distance. The context reminded Leo of a Sixties movie. Come to think of it, Adriana even had a Zsa Zsa Gabor quality about her, the way she crossed her shapely little legs and smiled at him over the rim of her drink.

'Cheers,' said Leo.

Adriana raised her glass, took a sip, and, to Leo's surprise, launched without further social preamble into the business of the case. For three-quarters of an hour they dwelt on matters of ship vibration and stress fractures, about which Adriana displayed exhaustive knowledge, until at last Leo was moved to remark, 'You know, I rarely say this to a client, but I think perhaps you're worrying too much about the detail.'

She put down the papers. 'It's habit where business is concerned. I like to be in control of everything.'

'It's only a yacht. You said yourself that you replaced it a year ago. Why invest so much of your personal time and energy in one insurance claim? Leave it to the lawyers. It's what you pay me for.'

'It's because I pay attention to detail that I'm so successful, Leo. That's why I'm a wealthy woman. Anyway, there is a principle at stake here. And a boy died.' A brief silence fell, and then she said, 'Let's not talk about the case any more. I am sure you have had enough of it for one day.' Leo felt he couldn't argue with that. 'Would you like another drink?'

'Let me do that,' said Leo. He took her glass, and went to mix them both another drink. Adriana observed him from the sofa with a meditative smile. He was so delicious, and he had maintained such a tantalizing reserve these past weeks.

She liked to think that was professional discretion, but you never knew with English men – so full of inhibitions. Still, if that scandalous newspaper story about him contained a grain of truth, she suspected Leo didn't have many of those.

Leo sat down again, handing Adriana her drink. She stirred it coquettishly with one finger. 'You know I hired you because of your reputation, don't you?' she asked.

Leo balked at the word 'hired', but let it pass. 'I hope I've lived up to it,' he replied, wondering where this was going.

'Oh, I don't mean your professional reputation.' Adriana smiled. 'I hired you because I was very intrigued by that story the newspaper ran about you.' Leo decided to say nothing to this. He sipped his drink. 'Tell me,' Adriana went on, 'did it do a great deal of harm?'

'Since it was entirely fabricated, I like to think it didn't, no.'

The truth was, Leo had no idea what kind of fallout there had been. Possibly it was too early to tell. Work seemed steady, no one had taken their cases away, though in the immediate aftermath of the newspaper story he had detected a certain embarrassed unease in the demeanour of some clients. Which was perhaps understandable. Henry had been prepared for the worst, but even he now seemed fairly phlegmatic. Leo sipped his Scotch and added, 'Since the story didn't exactly portray me in the most attractive light, I can't see why it would provide you with an incentive to instruct me.'

Adriana smiled. 'I believe you are being deliberately naive, Leo.' Her dark, soft eyes met his, and he wondered whether she was about to make her move. He still hadn't made up his mind as to what he was going to do if and when she did. But after a few seconds Adriana simply gave a little sigh and said, 'It must have been very hard for your family, though, to have such wicked lies spread about you.' She settled back against the sofa cushions, even further away from him. 'You know, I only found out recently that you and Rachel were once married. I had no idea. It must be unusual to have your ex-wife instructing you in cases.'

'It has its advantages and disadvantages.'

'She's a very beautiful girl.'

'Of a kind.' Whatever his feelings about Rachel, he wasn't going to give anything away to Adriana Papaposilakis.

'You have a little boy, haven't you? Tell me about him.'

Leo, bemused by her subtle change of tack, talked willingly about Oliver for a while. He found himself telling Adriana about the unsatisfactory nature of the arrangements when Oliver came to stay, how he had only the garden square in Belgravia to play in, and about his plans to buy a house which Oliver could regard as a proper home.

She nodded. 'You are right. It is so important, a proper home.'

'And where do you call home?' asked Leo.

'That is hard to say. I have too many homes, I suppose. Or too many houses. One in Marbella, on an estate which my father left me. And a château near Cannes, but I'm selling that – I think that Madonna woman is interested in it. And I have a duplex in the Olympic Tower in Manhattan, which I adore. It has a huge swimming pool – and all that way up in the air! But I suppose Greece is my real home. I have a lovely house just outside Athens. Unfortunately, I don't spend enough time there. Work keeps me too busy. In fact, I am in London on business so much these days that I have been thinking of buying a house here. I don't like these hotels. They are too impersonal.' She gave a little yawn and settled herself even further against the cushions. 'Yes, I think a house in England would be nice.'

Suddenly number 2 Gratton Crescent seemed to Leo to

be a very modest proposition compared to Adriana's list of luxurious dwellings. He felt a little flicker of envy, imagining for a moment the sweet possibilities which so much money could buy. That was what being in close proximity to a truly wealthy woman did to you. He put his empty glass on the table. 'You're tired. And I have to be in court tomorrow.' He was about to rise, when Adriana leaned forward and put a hand on his arm.

'Don't go yet. I'm enjoying playing this game.' She took her hand away and sat back. 'I like the way you are with me. Very businesslike, but with a little dash of friendly charm thrown in. Very English. Very cool.'

'I'm Welsh, as it happens,' said Leo, bemused. He stayed where he was on the sofa, wondering how the next few moments would go. He thought he knew.

'But I want to know what lies beneath, what you are really like when you stop being so proper, so charming. That newspaper story must have had a little bit of truth. What are you really like, Leo?' She lay against the cushions, head on one hand, smiling at him.

'Like most men, I suppose.'

'Most men find me attractive, Leo. Most men would have made more of their opportunities, being here in my hotel suite with me, alone.'

'Most men don't have a barrister–client relationship with you.'

'Does that matter so much?'

'It wouldn't be entirely professional for me to do what I'd like to do, no.'

'And what is that? What is it that you'd like to do, Leo?'

How familiar it all was – this sudden heightening of sexual awareness, the familiar, delectable moment of possibility, obscuring all other considerations, total, sensual connection with another person. He had been here many times before, but rarely had the situation seemed so potent, so inviting.

Oh, what the hell. It was going to be difficult to get out of this gracefully, as he had always known it would be. He moved towards her, noting the little flicker of satisfaction in her smile. 'Would you rather I showed you, or told you first?'

Her breathing quickened a little, her body tensing slightly as he slid his hands over her shoulders, down her arms, then traced a line with his finger over the soft flesh at the neckline of her dress. He kissed her mouth, and then her neck. 'Lawyers are meant to be good with words,' she murmured. 'Tell me. Tell me what you want to do to me. Then do it.'

And so he spoke, and she lay back, closing her eyes with erotic pleasure at his words, arching towards him as he unfastened her dress and eased it from her shoulders and down her body. She listened, uttering a small cry of pleasure from time to time as his words mingled with his touch, until at last there were no words, only sensations, and bliss, sheer sensual bliss. Oh, he was everything she had thought he would be, and much, much more. She opened her eyes, watching from among the cushions as he undressed and then lay next to her on the sofa.

'I see you came prepared,' she observed softly, noticing the condom he had produced.

'I had an idea there might be more to this evening than a discussion of the case.'

Adriana smiled and closed her eyes, surrendering herself happily to the prospect of even greater pleasure.

And Leo, though he knew perfectly well that this was the most appalling betrayal of dearest Camilla's trust, couldn't help thinking that what she didn't know couldn't harm her. One had to keep one's client happy, after all.

*

'No, really, I like scrambled eggs.'

'Good.' Roger opened the fridge and took out a box of eggs and a bottle of wine. He opened the wine and poured out two glasses. 'You take this, and I'll bring the food through in a minute.'

Sarah took her glass and the bottle into the living room. She cleared a space on the sofa, chucking the newspapers on to the floor, and sat down. After a while, Roger appeared with two plates of scrambled egg on toast.

He sat down and handed her a plate. 'Cheers.' He took a sip of his wine.

Sarah tried to suppress a smile. 'Do you do much entertaining?'

He glanced at her. 'Sorry. It's not overly sophisticated.'

'It's perfect.'

They ate in silence for a few moments, then Roger said, 'Look, when I apologized for last night, I wasn't actually being as gauche as you imagine.'

'Perhaps these things are best not talked about.'

'What things?'

Sarah put down her plate. 'Roger, I really like you, and we've had some great times. But I have the idea that you kissed me last night because you felt it was expected. I'd actually much rather things went on as before.'

Roger finished his scrambled eggs. 'Okay. I see.' He glanced across. 'Finished?'

She nodded, and he picked up their plates and took them through to the kitchen. Sarah sat back, relieved that the situation had been sorted out with such apparent simplicity. Roger came back through and sat down next to her.

'The thing is,' he said, 'I don't believe you. I don't believe anyone kisses anyone the way you did, without meaning it.'

Sarah was mildly taken aback. 'Actually, you kissed me.'

He frowned. 'That's not the point. You called me blasé. You –' he paused for emphasis '– called *me* blasé. When, in fact, it's the other way round.'

'Sorry?'

'You have these strange preconceptions about yourself. You completely dismiss the idea that there could ever be anything between us.'

Sarah laughed lightly. 'Roger, I'm sorry –'

'The reason I went off last night was because I was annoyed at myself for kissing you. I had meant to take things more slowly. I mean, you're obviously someone who's used to getting what you want as soon as you want it. Which is not always a good thing.'

Sarah gave a gasp of outrage. 'I'm *what*? That is so incredibly . . . ! I can't believe you said that! Whatever I want, it's certainly not *you*!'

'No?'

'No!'

'I don't believe you.'

'Look, Roger, don't make this any –'

He moved towards her and, unable to stop herself, she allowed him to kiss her again, inexplicably overwhelmed with intense longing.

After a while he drew away. He stroked her face with one hand, then traced a slow line with his fingers to her mouth, over her throat, and to the top button of her blouse. He kissed her again on her mouth, her face, her neck, unbuttoning her shirt to caress her shoulders. She closed her eyes.

'Don't worry. Don't think about a thing,' he whispered. 'It's going to be fantastic. I promise you. It really is.'

She allowed herself to be undressed, entirely believing him.

10

On the day that Sandy was due to start work at the Deepaks', Felicity had to fight the urge, half-way through the morning, to ring the flat and make sure he got up in time. He'd been out till two the night before, and there was no guarantee that he'd wake up by ten-thirty. Old Mrs Deepak was expecting him at eleven, when the morning deliveries were in. But in the end Felicity decided this was his life, his job, and if he couldn't get himself up in time, then it would be his problem.

She came home in mild trepidation that evening, and found Sandy watching television.

'Did it go all right?' she asked, taking off her jacket.

'Did what go all right?'

Felicity's heart sank. 'Sandy, you never forgot Mrs Deepak!'

'Course I didn't. I was there.' He yawned and stretched. 'It was a doddle, really. Just carting stuff around and doing the shelves.'

'Good.' Felicity felt immense relief, thinking that that was one day, at any rate.

That had been four weeks ago, and every day so far, without fail, Sandy had gone to his job at the corner shop.

Whatever illusions Felicity might have had about the improving effects upon her brother of regular employment, the truth was that the few hours he spent at the shop made very little difference to his lifestyle. Not that he minded the job. It was a piece of piss, really, humping a few boxes of stock around while old Mrs Deepak stood nodding madly at him, calling him 'a big, strong boy'. Then it was just a question of sitting out the back for an hour or so with a couple of cans of beer sneaked from the stock, reading the paper while old Mrs D rearranged the confectionery out front and watched Indian telly on her little portable behind the counter. Once the late edition of the *Standard* was in and sorted out, he could cop off down the skateboard park, or go to the pub. He'd told Fliss he'd try to stay off the skank, the really heavy dope, but that Jamaican guy, Mazz, always had something, and time hung heavy without the odd spliff. Mind you, he was definitely off the 'k'. That had been good at first, amazing, but he reckoned he'd gone a bit cracked, getting voices and all that stuff. He wanted them to go away, but they were still bothering him. He could be standing in the Deepaks' back shop and he'd definitely hear someone say something. He'd even turned round once, it sounded so clear. But it was in his head. People whispering to frighten him. And they did frighten him. They were watching him, after all. They could see, and tell. And they would. So he had to be careful. He had to do this job, and show Fliss he was okay. And them. He had to show them.

As far as Felicity was concerned, the fact that Sandy was able to hold down any job at all, even a temporary one at the corner shop, was a breakthrough. She had not the vaguest idea what would happen with Sandy once the Deepaks came back from India, but she'd worry about that when the time came. Right now, she had other preoccupations.

It was Carol on reception who told her. 'His wife's left him. Took the kids, and moved out.'

'How d'you know all this?' Felicity stared at Carol wide-eyed over the polished expanse of the reception desk.

'They live round the corner from my sister.' Carol paused

briefly to take a call and put it through, then carried on. 'Her kids go to school with their kids.'

'So why did she leave?'

Carol shrugged. 'No idea. Maybe he's been having an affair. Mind you, if that was it, you'd think she'd have kicked *him* out.' Carol flicked a switch and took another call, and Felicity wandered thoughtfully back to the clerks' room. Peter hadn't said anything to her about his wife leaving. But then, they hadn't said much to each other at all recently, which was hardly surprising, after the way she'd been with him. They maintained a civilized working relationship, which was all that was needed. The trouble was, she still got those little lustful pangs every time she saw him, and that didn't help.

Perhaps Carol was right. An affair on Peter's part was the most likely explanation. But hadn't Peter told her that he and his wife had a sort of 'open' marriage, that each did as they liked? In which case, why would she walk out? Curiosity, mingled with a certain misplaced solicitude, caused her to bring the subject up with him at lunchtime. The clerks' room was quiet. Robert and Henry had both gone out. Felicity and Peter sat at opposite ends of the room, Peter on the phone, Felicity going through figures on her computer screen.

Peter put the phone down. The silence, marked only by the click of Felicity's keyboard, grew around them both. Felicity could stand it no longer. Ostensibly fetching a drink from the water cooler, she stopped by his desk.

'I hear you've been having some problems at home. I'm sorry.'

Peter looked up. He shrugged, but laid down the papers he was going through, ready to talk. 'I suppose Carol told you?' Felicity nodded. Peter leaned back in his chair, clasping his hands behind his head. 'I didn't see it coming, that's for sure.'

'I thought,' said Felicity awkwardly, 'that you and Debbie – well, that is, you told me you had your relationship all sorted out. That you both did what you wanted. That the idea was you wouldn't ever split up.'

'Yeah, that was the theory.' Peter sighed. 'But it seems Debbie couldn't just keep it to having a bit of fun on the side, which I thought was all she was doing. Apparently she's been seeing the same bloke for nearly a year now, and bang – suddenly decides she's going off to live with him. Says they're in love. I should have realized in the first place that the open relationship thing was all crap. Women can't live like that.'

'And men can?'

'I don't know. I thought I could.'

'Only you have to find the right kind of woman to have your little flings with, I suppose. Sorry I couldn't be one of them.'

'Don't give me a hard time, Fliss. I'm missing the kids like hell.'

'I wasn't giving you a hard time. I just don't see how you two ever thought it would work, a relationship where neither person needs to trust the other.'

'Yeah, well, maybe you know more than I do. The truth is that the marriage got a bit dodgy about three years ago, and we decided to give each other a bit of space because we wanted to try to keep things together for the kids. Maybe we thought it would get better. I don't know.' A silence fell between them. At last Peter said, 'Look, the last thing I want is for you to think I'm coming on to you. But you and I were pretty close not so long ago, weren't we?' A pang of sentiment touched Felicity. She nodded. 'And if I'd had my way, we still would be, in which case I wouldn't be sitting at home most nights with a takeaway, drinking too many cans of lager in front of the telly.'

'What about all the women you've been seeing while

Debbie's been getting it together with her bloke? Can't one of them keep you company?'

'I haven't been seeing anyone since you and I split up, Fliss. In some ways, it would have been better if Debbie had walked out a few months ago, while you and I still had something.'

'Before I found out you were married with a family, you mean? I don't think so,' replied Felicity. Her voice was sad.

'Well, it looks like I'll be neither of those things very soon. Anyway, what I was trying to say, without you reading it the wrong way, is that it would be nice to be able to talk to you about it. We could have lunch, or maybe dinner. I could do with the company, to be honest. Someone who knows me, that I don't have to put on an act with.'

Felicity gazed at him. Know him? That was a laugh. She thought she had, once. And she'd been completely taken in. There he sat, giving her that nice crinkly smile, a bit wet round the edges from being dumped by his wife, trying to play the sympathy card, to get her to go out with him and probably into bed. Yeah, that would ease his pain.

'So, what d'you say?' asked Peter.

Felicity took a deep breath. 'Okay. Just to talk.'

'What about tomorrow night?'

'. . . the difference between your theory, Dr Wadsworth, and that of Mr Bullen, is that your theory involves fuel spray coming from an already detached injector pipe, which was subsequently ignited by a spark or engine heat, whereas Mr Bullen's theory involves the ignition of diesel spraying from a loose, but not disconnected injector pipe as it came into contact with the alternator . . .'

Never, ever again would she instruct Leo in a case. Rachel made this resolve as she sat in court, watching him on his feet, listening to the light Welsh cadence of his voice as he conducted his cross-examination of the other side's fire expert. She realized that she could no longer bear the stress of being involved with him in any way. She had no idea what had occurred last night between him and Adriana Papaposilakis, and neither should she care. But there sat Adriana, only a few feet away, scented and serene in her tight little Versace jacket and daytime diamonds, giving off an aura of contented physical repletion which was practically disgusting. Rachel had seen women dart those soft, significant glances at Leo before, and knew what they meant. Of course he had slept with her. Where was the attractive woman, or man, whom Leo could resist?

Until now, working with Leo had seemed worthwhile; it had given her a kind of agonizing satisfaction to be involved with him, seeing and hearing him on a daily basis. But it was becoming unhealthy, and it was making her unhappy. From now on, anyone who wanted to instruct Leo Davies in a case would have to find another solicitor.

'No one doubts that your view is honestly held, Dr Wadsworth, but it must be the case – must it not? – that the most likely concatenation of events is that the nut connecting the fuel injector pipe to cylinder number three of the number one generator worked loose as a result of vibrations which occurred during the grounding of the yacht two weeks prior to this event . . .'

Whatever pleasure she derived from working with him, seeing him on a daily basis, was eclipsed by having to endure her own irrepressible sense of jealousy and anguish at thoughts of his private life. It shouldn't matter to her, but it did. This couldn't go on. When this case was over, she would cut him out of her life, seeing him only when she strictly had to, when he picked up Oliver or dropped him off. In the meantime, she badly needed some emotional distraction, something on which to fix the longings which seemed to flow in her so fiercely these days.

'My Lord, I have no further questions for Dr Wadsworth.'

'Thank you, Mr Davies,' murmured Mr Justice Sagewell.

As Leo resumed his seat, Adriana leaned forward to whisper something to him; Leo, without turning his head, gave the faintest of smiles. Immediately Rachel's feminine instincts picked up on the subtle physicality which bound them, an invisible and intimate connection. She dropped her head, and carried on making her notes in her meticulously neat handwriting, savagely regretting the day she had ever accepted instructions from Miss Papaposilakis.

When court rose at the end of the day, Adriana's legal team and two of their expert witnesses met in Leo's chambers for a brief conference. Afterwards, on her way downstairs, Rachel met Anthony coming out of his room.

'Hi!' He seemed genuinely surprised and pleased to see her. 'What brings you here?'

'The *Persephone*, what else? We're still struggling our way through the expert evidence.'

'Got time for a quick coffee?'

'Why not?'

She went into Anthony's room and stood at the window, gazing out, while Anthony fetched the coffee. He came in, kicking the door shut with his foot, and handed her a cup, setting his own down on his desk.

'Thanks.'

'So, how's it going?'

'The case?' She shrugged. 'I don't see how we can fail. I keep expecting the other side to cave in any day. Leo was on top form today – amazingly enough.'

'Why amazingly?'

Rachel moved away from the window and sat down. 'Because I get the distinct impression that he and our diminutive Greek client were engaged in protracted and intimate discussions last night at her hotel.' She stared down at her coffee, her face stony.

'Right . . .' said Anthony. He observed her for a few seconds, then added gently, 'Don't let it get to you.'

'I spent most of today telling myself that. And it doesn't, really. I mean, it doesn't matter. Only, being around Leo, it's all so –' She broke off, lost.

'I know. He has that effect. You begin to think it would be best if you never had anything to do with him ever again.'

Rachel raised her head quickly. 'You've had that?'

'Yeah, sure. A couple of months ago it got to the point where I was ready to leave chambers. In fact, I even told Roderick and the clerks I was thinking of going.'

'But you didn't.'

'I'm not sure I ever really meant to. Extreme provocation of the Leo Davies variety drove me to make the gesture.'

'Tell me about it.'

'I will, sometime. Not now.' Anthony sighed, then laughed. 'And, paradoxically, guess who talked me out of leaving?'

'It's weird, isn't it? I don't know how any one human being can have that effect. I really hate him sometimes. I vowed today never to instruct him again.'

'You probably will.' They brooded on this for a moment, then Anthony said, 'I'm glad you're here. I wanted to see you.'

'You could have rung.'

'I did think about it. I just had the feeling it might make things . . .'

'What?'

'Difficult. With Charles, and so on.'

'Charles . . .' She stared at her coffee. 'Charles is never there. But I am.' She sighed. 'I'm there. And I don't know what's going on half the time.'

'Meaning?'

She gazed at Anthony for a long, silent moment. 'Come over this Saturday. Come and spend the day, have lunch, see Oliver. I need the company.'

Anthony said nothing for a few seconds, then nodded. 'I'd like to.'

'Good. Come around half eleven.' She glanced at her watch. 'I've got a few things to catch up on. I'd better go. Thanks for the coffee.'

When she had gone, Anthony went over each detail of the conversation. She'd made the move. It was what he'd wanted. He didn't care about Charles, frankly. Well, that wasn't strictly true, but he wasn't the major consideration. What was important was that this time she needed him. After all that had happened two years ago, he couldn't afford to let the balance slip.

Despite the significant change in their relationship, Roger's attitude towards Sarah didn't appear to have altered at all. He was entirely accepting of her, seeming to believe that she must be as happy with him as he was with her. Sarah's feelings were rather more ambivalent. Much as she liked Roger, there were times during the following days when she could hardly believe that she'd ever finished up in bed with someone who bit his nails and wore the same shirt two days running. She knew her friends would think she was mad if they found out she was seeing him. She would see Roger hurrying across Caper Court with his shoelace undone and his robing bag bumping on his shoulder on his way to court, and she would say to herself that she really should tell him to get his hair cut – and then ask herself why she should care about such appalling hair, on such a ramshackle human being. One morning she saw Roger and Leo talking together in the clerks' room, and it set off a flood of mental comparisons from which Roger emerged a poor second, leaving Sarah convinced that whatever had started between her and Roger must be over, that it had been some momentary madness from which she had surely recovered. But that same night found her lying in Roger's bed, quite contented to be there with him, talking and making love.

The whole thing was utterly confusing.

Equally puzzling was Roger's equanimity, the apparent opacity of his feelings for her. She had no idea how deep these ran, and told herself often enough that she didn't much care, either. Sometimes there were sublime and astonishing moments in their lovemaking when it seemed to her that everything unspoken had found its sure and perfect definition – but then, that was just sex. And in Sarah's view, sex was a notoriously poor indicator of true feeling, particularly in men. She decided it was best simply to enjoy the relationship for what it was – whatever it was. She certainly had no intention of getting serious about someone like Roger.

'I should really be doing some preparation for the hearing tomorrow,' said Leo.

Adriana touched one crimson-tipped finger to his mouth, then trailed it down across his neck and shoulder. She smiled. 'This is much more important.'

'I thought one of your chief aims in life was to win this case?'

'It is. We shall. It's been going so well that it looks like winning itself. Don't you think?'

Leo rolled on to his back. 'I never take anything for granted. Neither should you.'

'I think you can afford to relax for one evening.'

'Relax?' He leaned across, drawing down the sheet, and kissed one full, soft breast. 'Since you are the most relentlessly demanding woman it's ever been my good fortune to go to bed with, I wouldn't call this relaxing. And it's the second evening in a row. In fact, I don't know how you talked me into this.'

'I think you do,' murmured Adriana.

'Mmm. Well, in future, weekdays are strictly off limits. That's going to be my working rule.'

'How wonderfully stern and professional of you!' She moved her body against his. 'In that case, you will have to come away with me this weekend.'

'Will I? Where were you thinking of taking me?'

'My friend Lili Vosterliz is having a party at her villa in Tangiers. We can fly to my place in Marbella on Saturday, and you can come with me to the party. There will be all kinds of interesting people there. Rich people. Do you like rich people?'

'When they're paying my exorbitant fees, yes,' replied Leo, as he debated whether or not he should accept this attractive proposition. 'Otherwise, it depends.'

'On what?'

'Well, let's see now. Take you. You're very rich –'

'Very. And I pay your fees.'

'True. But there are other attractions.' He slipped one hand beneath the sheet, and after a few seconds she gave a short, breathless sigh and closed her eyes.

Then she laughed. 'Will you come?'

'Oh, yes,' said Leo, and kissed her. 'I imagine I will.'

*

It was with some bemusement that Leo surrendered himself to Adriana's caprices for the weekend. So far his encounters with fabulously rich people had been confined to those occasions when they came to him in chambers with their litigious anxieties, eager for his help. The prospect of seeing all that affluence and arrogance at play intrigued him.

On Friday evening, while he was working out what clothes to take, Camilla called.

'Hi, how are you?' asked Leo, sitting down on the edge of the bed, absently fingering the mauve silk of a Paco Rabanne tie.

'Missing you,' said Camilla. 'This work's getting rather repetitious. It's Friday afternoon, and all I want to do is catch a plane home and see you.'

'I know,' said Leo, reflecting that it would put something of a spanner in the works if she were to do so. He felt something approaching mild guilt. 'I miss you, too. Still, only another fortnight.'

They talked for a while about Camilla's work, and about chambers, Oliver, and the purchase of the Gratton Crescent house. Then Camilla asked, 'So, what are you up to this weekend? Are you seeing Oliver?'

Leo didn't miss a beat. 'No, he's with Rachel. I'll probably just catch up with a few pieces of work. The *Persephone* hearing is taking up most of my time.'

'Ah – the lovely Adriana. She still hasn't got you into bed yet?'

If anything stupefied Leo more than the remark itself, it was that it revealed just how pitifully little she knew him. The guilt he had failed to feel earlier now hit him hard. Without difficulty, he replied, 'No, she hasn't. Shame on you for thinking it. Makes me wonder what you're getting up to out there.'

Camilla laughed. 'Actually, my assistant is a very sweet young man called Gordon, and I think he's on the verge of asking me out. But don't worry, I won't let myself be tempted.' She gave a little yawn. 'Anyway, I'd better get on with some work. Shall I ring you tomorrow evening, if you're not busy?'

'Why don't you make it Sunday evening instead? There's a film I thought I might go and see tomorrow.'

'Okay. Whatever. I have to go now. I love you.'

'I love you, too. Bye.'

He put the phone down and sat for a few reflective moments, before deciding that it didn't matter. If anything, the deceit saved Camilla from unnecessary misery. By the time she got back, the thing with Adriana would have played itself out. He was certain the affair was as unimportant to Adriana as it was to him, and would be over when the case ended, if not before. It was merely an amusing diversion, just like the coming weekend. Camilla's ingenuous remark about Adriana made him wish, in a way, that he'd never started this affair – but he had, or she had, and he simply had to make the best of it. No point beating himself up over it. He stood up and got on with his packing.

The following morning Leo and Adriana flew in Adriana's private jet to Marbella, where a car met them and took them out to the estate. The house was a spectacular creation, built in three tiers of white stone which sloped back to the hillside, overlooking the shimmering waters of the Costa del Sol. A vast terrace, dotted with orange and lemon trees in stone tubs, stretched all the way round the house, and spread out to embrace a magnificent swimming pool, surrounded by well-tended gardens.

'I had the house rebuilt five years ago,' said Adriana,

leading Leo round the terrace to the back. She slid back a vast glass door and they stepped from the warm sunshine into the cool exterior. 'The original was horrid, very old-fashioned.'

She led Leo through the house, her little heels clacking on the marble floors. A middle-aged woman in a flowered dress came to greet them.

'Ah, Maria – can we have lunch in half an hour? On the terrace by the pool, I think.' She turned to Leo. 'Come – let's go upstairs. We can have a shower first.'

It seemed, however, that Adriana had something else in mind. As soon as they reached the room her mouth was on Leo's, and she was tugging off his clothes. Twenty minutes later, Leo was lying exhausted, watching the hypnotic billowing of the long gauze curtains which separated the bedroom from the balcony beyond. Adriana had gone to shower. Leo thought about joining her, but was apprehensive that it might spark off another lustful session. She certainly was insatiable – a kind of beautiful little female Onassis.

Moments later Adriana padded through, wrapped in a vast white towel, which she discarded as she approached the bed. She nestled next to Leo.

'We could forget about lunch, if you like,' she murmured.

'I don't think so,' replied Leo. 'I'm famished. I only had coffee for breakfast.'

'I don't care. I'd rather stay here for now.' She ran a hand over his chest. 'Don't say no. I'm not nice if I don't get my way.' She smiled, and he was momentarily struck by the expression in her dark eyes.

'No,' said Leo. He sat up. 'My turn to take a shower. And then we'll have lunch. After all, you put your housekeeper to the trouble of preparing it.' And he rose and crossed the marble floor to the adjoining bathroom, wondering if he was going to hear the crash of a flying object from the hand of a small, thwarted shipping tycoon.

Adriana merely lay on the bed, gazing thoughtfully after him.

After lunch, Adriana said, 'Come – I will show you my art collection. Well, a part of it.' She led him downstairs to a specially constructed gallery below the ground floor of the house, and flicked on a small row of lights. Leo wandered in amazement from picture to picture, gazing at each one in turn. Every important painter of the twentieth century seemed to be represented in her collection. He stopped in front of a Picasso, depicting a woman in muted greens and blues, sitting in a chair, head on one hand. Adriana strolled to his side. 'You like it?'

Leo nodded.

'It's of his lover, Marie-Thérèse Walters.'

'I know.' Leo's gaze was fixed on the painting. 'I've seen its sister work, *Nue Aux Colliers*. I was at Christie's the day it was sold, a couple of years ago.'

She glanced at him speculatively. 'You know a little about art?'

'I'm something of a collector myself,' replied Leo. 'But on a more modest scale.' He turned to Adriana. 'The other picture sold for over six million pounds, as I recall.'

Adriana smiled and shrugged. 'It's nice to be able to buy the things one likes.'

Leo inspected the rest of the paintings in silence. They were truly wonderful. It was the closest he had ever come to understanding what it would be like to own such treasures. He estimated that there must be tens of millions of pounds' worth of works of art in this house alone.

'I hope you're well insured,' he observed, taking a long last glance around before Adriana switched off the lights.

'Of course. Now,' said Adriana as they went upstairs, 'I have a little business to attend to, after which I'm going to spend a little time with my masseur, and then I'll get ready for the party. Would you like a massage? Ramon is quite wonderful.'

Leo decided he would content himself with a swim. Afterwards he lay in the green, warm silence of the garden, reading through some papers which he had brought. His attention drifted. He watched small butterflies dipping in and out of the sunshine, flickering over the flowers, and realized suddenly how grateful he was for this respite from his own world. He was able to relax in London – he had the house in Oxfordshire and the flat in Belgravia, and plenty to keep him amused – but since this morning, when he had first stepped into the unashamedly luxurious interior of Adriana's jet, he had a sense of being transported to an idyllic existence far removed from humdrum reality. He let his mind drift over the pleasures encountered so far. The jet, the miracle of dispensing with all the crap of commercial flights at Heathrow and Gatwick, and the hell of other people . . . the private car from the airport . . . Adriana's magnificent house . . . Adriana herself, the compact, sensual perfection of her body . . . making love to her while the gauzy curtains billowed against a Mediterranean sky . . . the unexpected delights of her art collection, savoured like sweets when he was a child . . . a delicious lunch by the pool, prepared by some other, expert hand . . . and not having to clear up afterwards . . .

Leo closed his eyes and let the papers fall from his fingers. He might be comfortably off, with his legal practice and his moderately expensive tastes carelessly indulged, but this world of Adriana's was something else altogether. Work was altogether out of the question. He should concentrate on the bliss of the present, and the knowledge that nothing more arduous was required of him over the next few hours than a helicopter trip from Marbella to Tangiers, to a party stuffed with the rich and famous and amusing, on a warm summer evening far from the cares of home.

'Well?' asked Adriana, as she unclipped the diamonds from her ears several hours later. 'Did you like it?'

'Somewhat,' replied Leo, tossing his jacket aside and lying back on the large bed, which had been made up with fresh linen since they had last occupied it. That was another thing he could get used to. That, and the knowledge that the damp towels on the bathroom floor would have been cleared away and replaced with clean ones.

She sat next to him on the bed, smiling and stroking his face with one finger, her tantalizing scent as fragrant as her breath. He thought he would never tire of the wonderful smell of her. 'What an English thing to say. "Somewhat". What does that mean?'

Leo's mind skated over the people he had met – the fashion designer with white hair, whose fingers trembled as he smoked and from whose mouth poured a staccato series of outrageous stories; the German multi-millionaire who had arrived from his Kenyan estate with half a dozen beautiful women by his side; the hostess herself, a tall, exotic Brazilian in a swirling, iridescent Missoni silk caftan and emeralds, who had orchestrated an evening of magnificent opulence; the divinely beautiful Hollywood actress, the screen epitome of unattainable perfection, who had cornered Leo for twenty minutes and bored him rigid; the wizened ex-politician, a relic of some sex scandal from the Seventies, prowling the party for gossip, a Monte Cristo clamped between his teeth;

the crashingly beautiful young Italian aristocrat who had flashed his blue eyes so often at Leo that both knew perfectly well where, under other circumstances, they would have finished up together . . . And the scent of wealth, the clothes, the jewellery, the sleek cars parked outside, the yachts, the jets, the helicopters – all the trappings that translated human beings from the shabby average to the affluent elite . . . The evening had been transparent and mystifying all at the same time, both electrifyingly stimulating and monstrously tedious.

'Well,' said Leo, slipping the knot of his black tie, 'it convinced me of one thing – that the world of wealthy people is a taste-free zone.'

Adriana laughed. 'Don't you like my friends?'

'I liked young Flavio,' replied Leo, thinking with faint longing of those dangerous blue eyes.

Adriana made a face. 'He is queer. I don't like him and his friends. I don't know how one man can go with another. It's so disgusting.' Adriana slipped Leo's tie from around his neck and began slowly to unbutton his shirt.

'Hmm. I always think it's quite ironic, the Greek attitude to homosexuality,' murmured Leo, wondering whether, if she knew the truth about him, Adriana would be snuggling up quite so cosily. 'But, to answer your question, yes – I did like your friends. Some of them. I liked Lili. She gave a splendid party. Everyone was most amusing. I'm not sure I could live like that, though. A life of endless indulgence and socializing.'

'My life isn't endless indulgence.' Adriana slipped soft fingers beneath his shirt and kissed his neck. 'I work very hard for my pleasures.'

'Indeed you do,' replied Leo, returning her kiss. 'You're a very industrious and energetic girl.'

Adriana fell silent for a moment. Her fingers stopped

stroking Leo's chest. Then she said, 'Sometimes, you know, being rich is quite lonely.'

'It is?' He wound a finger in her blonde hair.

'I don't meet many men of my – what is it you say?'

'Temperament?'

'Mettle. My mettle. I think that is right. Is it?'

'Possibly.'

'Most men are a little afraid of me. Not you. You are your own person. For instance, I am the client, and you run my case for me, but you do it exactly the way you want to. Oh, you pretend to listen to the things I say, but you go ahead with your own ideas. Don't think I don't know.'

'Nonsense. I'm your lawyer. Of course I listen to you.' Leo put his hand over hers, edging her fingers downwards towards the belt of his trousers.

'But you're not afraid of me. I know that. I know it when you make love to me. You are completely in control . . . you know everything I want . . .' Her eyes grew soft, and she shivered a little. 'I sometimes think I would be prepared to beg you . . . Maybe I would like to . . .'

'That can be arranged.' Leo slipped the straps of her dress from her shoulders.

'I never thought I would find a man like you,' she murmured. 'Oh, you know, Leo, I could give you such a nice life.'

'I don't accept gifts from strange women,' murmured Leo, pulling her dress down gently. 'Besides, I have a nice life.'

She pulled away a little, studying his face. 'Nothing like the kind we could have together. We could stay like this. You could work for me. No, you could work *with* me. You could run the legal side of Silakis, make as much money as you want. I need someone as clever as you.' Leo said nothing. She drew herself against him once more, unfastening his trousers. 'I have never wanted a man in my life, until you. I thought at first that I just wanted – well, to take you as my lover. Nothing more.'

'I should remind you,' murmured Leo, shifting slightly to help her, 'that you've only known me for a few days.'

'That's not true. I have known you for some months now. I have watched you, listened to you, and I know we would be good together. We are alike. We amuse one another. There is a great deal we share. We could share much, much more. Everything I have, you could enjoy.'

'I rather think I enjoy the best bits of you already.' Her flimsy underwear was the work of seconds. 'Besides –' He gave a smile, resting his hand tantalizingly on the curve of her stomach.

'What?' Her voice was weak; she was longing to be touched.

'I can't help remembering something you said earlier today.'

'What did I say?' She took his hand and moved it gently downwards.

'You said, "It's nice to be able to buy the things one wants." Or words to that effect.'

This made her pause. 'You think I would buy you?'

'I think you might try.' He watched her, waiting, wondering if this would prompt some minor outburst. He would rather not destroy the delicacy of the moment.

But Adriana merely smiled. 'You are right. I might. But somehow, Leo, I think you are a man who does things only on his own terms.'

'How very true,' he said, covering her mouth with his, and reflecting that those terms could always be negotiated.

When Anthony drove down to see Rachel on Saturday morning, the day was warm and sultry, with a hint of a gathering storm in the air. The house which Rachel shared with Charles Beecham, and from which she commuted daily to her London office, lay just outside Newbury. It was a comfortable, pretty place built of soft ochre stone, and set in a couple of acres of stone-walled garden. It had an air of solidity, of permanence, and Anthony thought he could sense the security which Rachel must feel, living here. He parked his car and got out, retrieving the flowers he had brought from the back seat.

Rachel, who had caught sight of the car turning in at the gateway, came out to meet him, Oliver at her heels.

They exchanged a kiss. Anthony bent down to say hello to Oliver, who returned the greeting with a thoughtful, considering glance, disarmingly like Leo's, then turned and trotted back into the house. 'I obviously didn't make much of an impression last time,' said Anthony, straightening up.

'Don't worry,' said Rachel. 'He's going through a laconic phase.'

But as they went into the house, Oliver reappeared and handed Anthony a book.

Rachel smiled. 'I'm afraid he wants you to read to him. Take it as a compliment. Why don't you go into the garden with him while I finish making lunch? I'll bring you both some lemonade.'

To Anthony's considerable gratification, Oliver put his

small hand in his and led him through the house to the garden, where a rug was spread out on the lawn with a few toys on it.

Oliver instructed Anthony to sit down on the rug, and Anthony did so. The little boy clambered confidingly on to his lap – more gratification – and Anthony glanced at the book he had been given. 'Thunderbirds. Okay, here we go.' He opened the book and began to read.

A few minutes later Rachel appeared with a jug of home-made lemonade and two glasses. 'Thanks,' said Anthony, as she handed him his drink. He tapped the book. 'This is cool. I used to love Thunderbirds.'

Oliver gripped Anthony's chin with small, damp fingers and gently but firmly tried to turn his face back to the book. 'Read,' said Oliver. 'Read de book.'

'All right, mate. Give us a chance.' Anthony took a gulp of his lemonade and turned his attention back to Scott and Virgil.

Half an hour later they ate lunch in the large, cool kitchen. Attempts at conversation between Rachel and Anthony were largely broken up by Oliver's babbled commentary on the state of Tracy Island and the relative merits of Thunderbirds One and Two.

'I'm afraid my son is in the grip of an obsession,' said Rachel, as she cleared the plates away.

'He certainly seems to have inherited his father's intellectual tenacity,' said Anthony.

While Rachel brewed coffee, Anthony dealt gravely with a series of probing questions from Oliver, reaching a crescendo of absurdity which Anthony suspected was designed especially to test him, about the theoretical capabilities of Thunderbirds Four.

'You're very good with him,' said Rachel, smiling, as she

set a small bowl of grapes down in front of Oliver. 'Not many men your age would be so patient.'

'He's fun. I must say, he's got the art of cross-examination down to a fine art, just like his dad.'

'You don't have to keep doing that,' said Rachel abruptly. 'I mean – saying how like Leo he is. I know he is.'

'Sorry,' said Anthony.

She tucked her dark hair nervously behind her ears. 'Forget it. I'm the one who should say sorry. Here, have some coffee.' Since his arrival, it had seemed to Anthony that Rachel's cheerful manner masked a faint unease. It was as though she was grateful for the diversion of Oliver's presence.

When Oliver had almost finished his grapes, Rachel passed a gentle hand over his hair, and looked thoughtfully into his blue eyes. 'Come on, little man – time for a nap.'

She picked him up. He was a small, solid weight against her slender figure. Oliver regarded Anthony pensively over his mother's shoulder, and handed him his last grape.

'Thanks, mate,' said Anthony. The grape was warm, slightly squashed. 'See you later.'

Oliver settled his cheek against this mother's shoulder and allowed himself to be carried upstairs to his cot.

A few minutes later, Rachel came back down. 'Shall we take our coffee into the garden?'

They went out into the sunshine, and crossed the lawn to where a table and chairs stood in the shade of a clump of apple trees.

'When does Charles get back from the States?' asked Anthony, settling in a chair.

'Oh, a couple of weeks, I suppose. He went back last Sunday, so – yes, another fortnight.'

'It must be lonely here without him.' Anthony wasn't quite sure why he was talking about Charles. Perhaps because it was the obvious thing to do. Here they were, after all, sitting in his garden, in his chairs. Rachel was his girlfriend. It seemed suddenly absurd to Anthony that he had ever imagined that any romantic possibilities might arise during this visit.

'I get used to it. Charles being away, I mean. Every time he comes back, it feels more and more like an intrusion. Which is sad, in a way.'

'Well, I imagine it'll get back to rights once he's finished the documentary.'

Rachel said nothing in response to this, merely glanced up at the lichen-covered branches of the trees, narrowing her eyes against the sunlight.

'Actually,' went on Anthony, 'someone gave me one of his books for Christmas. About Assyria. I haven't finished it yet, but it's very good so far.' He felt it impossible to respond to the personal note which she had introduced. It simply didn't feel right.

They talked about Charles's work for a while. It seemed to Anthony that Rachel did so on sufferance. Then a silence fell. Anthony gazed across the fields which sloped away at the front of the house. 'Is that the racecourse over there?' he asked.

'Yes. Charles and I have been a couple of times. It's a pretty course. I'm not that keen on betting, but I quite enjoy the atmosphere.'

'I've never been to Newbury.' It suddenly seemed to Anthony that the afternoon could be quite a long one, if things stayed as they were. 'Why don't we go over, once Oliver's had his nap? I'd really like to see it.'

'I don't know if there's a race meeting on today. I suppose the paper in the kitchen will tell us.'

As she watched Anthony walk towards the house, Rachel

became aware for the first time of her own inner tension. She tried consciously to relax. How stupid she'd been to think anything might happen between them – here, today. He might have said in the wine bar that he wanted to kiss her, but the truth was, this was the last place on earth that he would allow anything like that to happen. Anyway, the fact that he'd kept Charles's name well to the foreground in the conversation indicated where he considered the boundaries lay. She wished she could conquer this aching, insatiable longing – this feeling that something physical must happen to her or she would break, snap. A trip to Newbury would be some kind of a diversion, at any rate. Something to do. She closed her eyes, waiting for him to come back.

His footsteps were so quiet on the grass that she didn't know he was there until he spoke.

'Yes, there's a two o'clock meeting.'

Rachel opened her eyes. 'Let's go, then. Oliver will probably enjoy it.'

'How long does he nap for?'

'I don't let him sleep for more than an hour. Otherwise he's hard to settle in the evenings.' Rachel glanced at her watch. 'I'll wake him up soon.'

They drove to the racecourse in Rachel's car. On the horizon a grey bank of cloud was building up, and an airless pallor seemed to have descended on the countryside.

'Rain by the evening, I suspect,' said Anthony.

'Thank goodness,' said Rachel. 'I don't like this muggy kind of heat. It's so oppressive.' She pointed to her left. 'That's Greenham Common over there.'

Anthony glanced across at the airfield. 'Doesn't that all seem a long time ago?'

'I know.'

Silence fell, the stilted, striving nature of their conversation failing to mask the underlying tension. The combination of the sultry weather, brooding heat lying in wait for the storm, gave the day an unnatural stillness.

Parking was difficult, and they had to walk some distance to the course itself, with Oliver in his pushchair. Once inside, Anthony bought a couple of race cards, and an ice cream for Oliver, and they watched the races. Oliver loved it. At the expense of a proper view of the course, they found a spot on the grass near the rails, so that Oliver could see the racehorses at close quarters. He roared ecstatically as they went thundering to the finish. Anthony put on two modest bets, and won, which spurred Rachel to back something, despite her earlier insistence that she didn't like gambling. She put five pounds each way on an outsider, at odds of twenty-five to one, against Anthony's advice. To everyone's astonishment, the horse won.

'What a fluke!' Anthony couldn't help grinning at the sight of Rachel so pleased and excited. She rarely looked like that, was invariably cool, her emotions carefully banked down.

'I've won a hundred and twenty-five pounds!' squealed Rachel. 'Isn't that appalling?' She bent to give an astonished Oliver a tickle and a squeeze.

'More than that.'

'Why?'

'I don't understand how they work it out, but you get a proportion of what you would have won if it had come second or third. You're so jammy.'

'How brilliant. I like racing.'

'Yes, well – it is possible to lose, you know.'

'But I didn't!'

They collected her winnings, and on the way back Rachel caught sight of the champagne tent. 'Come on. We should celebrate.'

She bought a bottle of champagne. 'Just one glass for me. I'm driving. You can have the rest.'

'I can't drink the better part of a whole bottle,' protested Anthony.

'Then have as much as you want. This is so much fun. I feel very bad and irresponsible.'

'Why?' Anthony smiled as he watched her, thinking that she should be like this more often, lit up with pleasure.

'Exposing my infant son to these licentious pleasures.' She bent down and gave Oliver a kiss.

They watched the next race, and Anthony drank two more glasses of champagne. It seemed a pity to waste good wine. Oliver was evincing a desire to wander off among the crowds, so Rachel put him in his buggy, which he loudly resented. He began to grow fractious. The thunder which had been rumbling on the far horizon for the past hours suddenly cracked across the sky. People kept glancing up at the lowering clouds moving swiftly over the trees towards the racecourse.

'It's going to bucket down in a minute,' said Anthony.

'Should we head back?'

'I think so.'

Much of the crowd had the same idea, and Rachel and Anthony found themselves in a slow sea of people moving through the gates and across the fields of parked cars. The first fat drops of rain began to fall.

'I haven't got anything to cover Oliver with,' said Rachel. 'The rain canopy for his buggy's in the car.'

Anthony had brought a denim jacket, which had been tied around his waist all afternoon. He took it off and spread it over Oliver. The rain fell faster, and people began to run. The sky above was entirely leaden, all trace of the earlier sunshine gone.

'The car's still miles away!' said Rachel.

'Come on!' Anthony broke into a trot, and the buggy bounced across the rain-slicked grass, much to Oliver's delight.

By the time they reached the car, they were drenched, though Anthony's jacket had kept Oliver's lower half moderately dry.

'I've got a towel in the boot,' said Rachel, pushing back wet strands of hair from her face as she collapsed the pushchair. She towelled Oliver's hair dry, and then she and Anthony mopped themselves as best they could. They sat in the haven of the car, watching the downpour, the people hurrying past to their cars, jackets over their heads. A long queue of traffic was heading out of the car park.

'It's going to take ages to get out of here,' said Rachel. 'Everyone's leaving at once.' She sighed and started the engine, and they joined the line of cars.

It took them half an hour to reach the main road, and the rain still showed no signs of stopping. When they reached the house, Rachel got Oliver out of his car seat and made a dash for the house.

'The rug's still out in the garden! I forgot to put it away,' said Rachel.

'Don't worry, I'll get it.'

'Anthony, there's no point —' But he had already gone out to fetch the rug and the toys and the sodden Thunderbirds book.

He dumped them all on the kitchen floor. Rachel was busy divesting Oliver of his damp clothes. She glanced at Anthony. 'You're wet through. You can't stay like that. I'll give you one of Charles's robes and you can put your things in the tumble-dryer.'

She showed Anthony upstairs to Charles's dressing room,

and found a fresh towelling robe. 'Here, this'll do. Bring your wet things down once you've changed out of them.'

Anthony took off his wet outer clothes and slipped gratefully into the thick robe. He walked slowly to the window and looked down at the rain-soaked garden, at the rivulets of water plashing from the gutter on to the flagstones of the patio. He tied the belt of the robe. For some reason – perhaps the weather, perhaps the after-effects of the champagne – he felt melancholy. It had been a good day, despite the disaster of getting caught in the storm, but he wished he hadn't come. Last time, when he'd been here for Sunday lunch, it had been much easier. No expectations. Just a friendly meal. Since then, possibilities had arisen which disturbed them both. The situation was so complex. He wanted to say something, to make some sort of overture – but here in this house, surrounded by the evidence of her life together with Charles, he couldn't begin to contemplate it. He was even wearing the man's bathrobe, for God's sake. He turned and picked up his clothes and went out to the landing. Rachel was emerging from a bedroom, wearing a clean shirt and jeans, tying back her hair. In that moment, as she paused, smiling, he wanted to reach out and touch her, but she merely said, 'I'll put the kettle on. We could both do with some tea.'

As they drank their tea they talked about the race meeting and the excitement of the storm. It was a way of pretending nothing else filled their minds, no unspoken thoughts or undercurrent of feeling.

Oliver, who had been playing with his toys in the living room, came through to the kitchen and demanded a biscuit.

'Just one. I'll be making your tea in a moment,' said Rachel. She reached for the biscuit tin and handed him a custard cream. 'What do you say?'

'Fank you,' murmured Oliver, and trotted back through.

'I'd better be going,' said Anthony, and stood up. 'My things must be dry by now.'

Rachel went to the tumble-dryer. She took his clothes from it and shook them out, then folded and smoothed them. Anthony watched as she did this, watched the slim, white fingers, her preoccupied face.

She handed him his clothes, then said suddenly, 'Why don't you stay? For supper, I mean. It'll be very dull for me otherwise. There's something about Saturday nights – always worse than other nights, for some reason.' Anthony said nothing. 'Unless you're busy, of course. You probably are.'

'No,' said Anthony, 'I'm not busy.'

'Then will you stay?'

'Yes. If you like. Thanks.'

He went upstairs to change. That had been the most threadbare exchange. But then, communication had been reduced to essentials. Someone had to say something relevant, soon.

They spoke very little as Rachel prepared Oliver's tea. Rachel switched on the television in the kitchen, and the news provided some kind of a background. Things began to improve as they prepared supper together. Rachel took steaks from the freezer and defrosted them in the microwave while Anthony made a salad. They were able to have quite a jokey argument about the best way to make a vinaigrette dressing. The cosiness of doing domestic tasks together lent a cheerful superficiality. Rachel left Anthony to grill the steaks while she gave Oliver his bath and put him into his pyjamas. It was seven o'clock.

Rachel came downstairs. 'He wants you to say night night.'

He indicated the steaks. 'These are almost done.'

'I'll take over. Shall I open some wine?'

'Yes, fine.'

Upstairs, Anthony bent over Oliver's cot and gave him a kiss. He stared into blue eyes that were so like Leo's. Then he made a revving sound and said, 'Thunderbirds are *go*!'

'Funderbirds *go*!' replied Oliver in delight, and thrust his small fists skywards. Then his face relaxed, he put his thumb in his mouth, turned his head sideways, and kicked at his quilt with sleepy feet. Anthony straightened up and left the room quietly, switching off the light, leaving the door ajar so that the light from the landing fell a little way into the bedroom.

'How is he?' asked Rachel.

'On his way out. He's such a good little kid.'

'He can have his moments, I assure you. He's not always this easy in the evenings. I think a day at the races has finished him off.'

They were able to talk once more about the race meeting. Rachel had opened some wine, and she brought it to the table with the steaks and salad. Anthony was able to move the conversation effortlessly on to betting, and from there Rachel took it to money, and both were grateful for the apparent ease with which they talked. But there came a moment, at the end of the meal, when the talk trailed away.

'Would you like some coffee?' asked Rachel, to break the silence.

'No, no coffee, thanks,' replied Anthony. 'There's something I want to say.'

Rachel waited, watching him. 'Well?'

'It's been on my mind all day. I have to confess that I came here with the idea that something might happen – that is, I wanted something to happen between us.'

The air in the kitchen seemed to have grown very still. They looked at each other across the table. Rachel felt as though her mind was poised to fly; she had refused to contemplate this moment, and was still reluctant to. 'I think I know that. I think maybe it's why I asked you here.'

Anthony nodded, and said nothing for a few seconds. 'The fact is, we've been dodging the issue all day. And I know why. You have scruples, and so do I.'

'Do we?'

Anthony met her gaze. Her expression was a softer reflection of her earlier pleasure and excitement when she had won her money. He had never seen her look so open and expectant, yet so calm. He felt mildly confused. 'The thing is, I can't just come here, to another man's house —'

'I don't belong to anyone, Anthony.'

Anthony shook his head. 'That's not true,' he murmured.

Rachel stood up and came round the table to where he sat. She rested her hands on his shoulders and he looked up at her. 'I don't care if it's true or not,' she said. 'Do you remember those times when we were seeing one another a few years ago, the times when you wanted to make love to me, and I couldn't let you?'

'I'm not likely to forget.' Anthony gave a little laugh, but it died away swiftly.

'I want to make up for those times.' She bent and kissed him. The gentle touch of her mouth was electrifying.

'I don't want to mess things up,' he said, when she took her mouth away. 'Between you and Charles.'

'That's my business.' Her voice was soft, confident.

He stood up and took her in his arms, and kissed her, and instantly the fierce current of desire within her transmitted itself to him. He could feel the longing which tensed her limbs and warmed her blood, so different from the chilly fear with which she had once repulsed him. When their kiss ended, her voice was breathless, a little broken.

'It won't be in our bed. There's another room. Please. Please. I need you so much.'

He kissed her again, drawing her as close to him as he could. It didn't matter any more where they were, or whose bed it happened in. Nothing in the world existed or mattered except the two of them, at that moment.

Leo arrived back at the Belgravia flat early on Sunday evening. He felt very well indeed, still buoyed up by the events of the weekend. Dropping his overnight bag in the hall, he went into the drawing room and opened one of the long windows which looked down on the garden square. It had been raining in London over the weekend, and the air was fresh and gentle. He let it fill the room. He poured himself a drink and paced the room, glancing at his pictures. Usually they brought a soothing satisfaction, but this evening the sight of them merely stirred a recollection of the treasures which reposed in Adriana's private gallery. All in her keeping, for her to enjoy whenever she wanted.

He sat down in an armchair and leaned back, closing his eyes. It would be easier, of course, if the little Greek princess had meant none of what she said. But he had known many women in his life, and this one was utterly sincere. She wept when he made love to her. She had passion in her voice and in her eyes. He had absolutely no doubt that he could do with her entirely as he wanted. She might be powerful, she might be wealthy, she might be the head of one of the biggest shipping lines in the world, but, quite without any intent or design on his part, she was very definitely his. In the time that was available to him – which was to say, for as long as she was in love with him to the point of desperation – and allowing for a natural mellowing of feeling, he could make her his for good. To do so would involve compromise, a surrender of certain freedoms – but with considerable returns. Would it be so hard to be part of her world? So hard to accept everything she had offered him?

He speculated on the kind of life Adriana and he could have together, the pleasures they could enjoy – the kind they had enjoyed this weekend. There was much to be said for wealth. Suddenly the prospect of slogging away at the Bar for the next fifteen years seemed distinctly unattractive by comparison. He didn't love Adriana, never would, but he liked her well enough. He had no doubt that he could keep her sufficiently happy and satisfied, though the terms would be hers, and the wealth.

As he sat musing on this latter point, and on the difficulties of accepting ancillary status, the sound of the telephone jarred his thoughts. He opened his eyes and glanced at his watch. In all probability it was Camilla, ringing as she had said she would. Small eddies of guilt stirred in him. Not that he didn't love her. He did. It was just that in his present frame of mind, he didn't see how he could possibly speak to her. He swirled the melting ice cubes in the dregs of his drink, and let the phone ring.

Anthony was grateful that the case management conference on Monday morning was relatively straightforward. His mind was still full of the events of the weekend, and as he sat in court with his client and solicitors, he had to force himself to concentrate on the issues. It had been the strangest two days. Recollected moments had almost surreal qualities. Waking in bed in the darkness, momentarily disoriented, listening to the rain drumming on the roof, while Rachel soothed a fretful Oliver in another room. Then Rachel slipping back into bed next to him, the merest touch of her skin setting off again that deep, unsettling desire – quite unlike anything he had ever known before, beyond sex, beyond mere emotion. Then holding her, no more than that, listening to the rain . . .

'Perhaps Mr Cross can give us some guidance as to when Mr Tully will be giving his evidence?'

Anthony looked up with a start, momentarily confused. He glanced down at his papers. His instructing solicitor leaned over and murmured something. 'Um – yes, we would anticipate Mr Tully will be available in the second week of October.'

The judge nodded. Talk drifted on. Anthony's mind slipped back to Sunday. In the morning the rain had stopped, but the sky was overcast. Rachel was quiet. He had stayed for breakfast and lunch, and they had made love again while Oliver slept in the afternoon. Then they had talked about Charles, and Rachel had wept, and Anthony had been bereft of consolation. He couldn't unravel her life for her. All in all, despite this new step in their relationship – or maybe because of that – it had been a miserable Sunday. Everything seemed bleak and touched with guilt. When Anthony left late in the afternoon, they had made no arrangement to meet. Anthony knew he would call her, but now the gesture would seem furtive, clandestine. He had wanted to bring about this state of affairs with Rachel, but now that it existed, it seemed oddly joyless.

The judge's voice broke into his meditations once again. 'No doubt the matters we've discussed can be put into formal words –' The judge glanced in the direction of the downtrodden junior on the other side. 'Mr Foxton, if you would be so kind?' Young Mr Foxton gave a weary sign of assent. 'Good,' said the judge, shuffling his papers together. 'If I could perhaps have that sometime later this after-noon . . . ?' Chairs scraped and people rose. After a brief chat with the client and solicitors, Anthony left the Law Courts and made his way back to Caper Court.

Half-way down Middle Temple Lane he caught sight of Roger Fry crossing Fountain Court. He waited for him.

'I've just been talking to Stephen Bishop,' said Roger. 'Apparently Roderick's going to the High Court sometime in October.'

They passed together through the archway into Pump Court. 'Which means a new head of chambers,' said Anthony. 'I'll bet Jeremy thinks he's in with a good chance.'

'Someone should tell Maurice that. He thinks he's got it sewn up.'

'Seriously? But he's only been with us a couple of months.'

'I admit that Maurice can be a bit blinkered by his own ambitions. But I don't see that it matters how long he's been here. He's the one who's been turning things around in chambers of late.'

'Well, I wouldn't go so far as that,' said Anthony. 'Re-designing the chambers' website is one thing, but he'll have to carry the confidence of the rest of the tenants if he wants to become head of chambers. I don't feel I know him well enough.'

'I can see that. Personally,' added Roger, as they paused at the foot of the steps to 5 Caper Court, 'I would have thought Leo would be the obvious choice, but the word is he's not bothered one way or the other. You can accuse Maurice of being over-ambitious, but at least he's up for it. Anyway, catch you later. I'm going to get some lunch.'

Anthony went into chambers, and through the door to the clerks' room. The mention of Leo's name had unsettled him slightly. As far as his relationship with Rachel was concerned, Leo shouldn't matter in the slightest. But he did. He seemed to overshadow and affect everything.

And there he was, standing in his shirtsleeves by Henry's desk, laughing at some joke of Henry's. Anthony fished his mail from his pigeon-hole and scanned it. Leo sauntered past, and Anthony glanced at him.

'You're remarkably cheerful today,' observed Anthony.

'I am indeed. Had rather an enjoyable weekend. How was yours?'

'Pretty good. I went to the races with Rachel and Oliver. We were doing well, until it began to pour down. Rachel won a packet on some outsider.' Then he added, 'She's probably told you all about it.'

'No,' said Leo, 'she didn't mention it.'

'Oh. Okay.' He was suddenly anxious to get off a subject he wished he'd never raised. Why had he done it? To arouse Leo's ire or interest, get his attention. The old story. 'By the way, did you know Maurice Faber pretty much thinks he's going to be our next head of chambers when Roderick goes off to the High Court in October?'

'That doesn't surprise me,' replied Leo, as they went upstairs together. '*The love of power is the love of ourselves*, or so Hazlitt has it. And God knows, Maurice is vain enough. Not that there's a lot of power in being head of chambers – or glory, come to that. But I suppose Maurice must think he'll acquire both.'

They paused on the landing outside Anthony's room. 'Most people would far rather see you as head.'

'It doesn't interest me. I'm happy doing my work. The whole thing is just another load of PR bullshit in the world of Maurice and his kind.'

Anthony smiled. 'Perhaps you're right. See you.'

Leo carried on upstairs. Anthony had given him two things to think about. On the score of the vacancy which Roderick would leave, what he had said to Anthony was true – he didn't care about it one way or the other. Not for himself. On the other hand, the idea of Maurice Faber, *arriviste* and major ego, becoming head of chambers – well, frankly, he'd sooner see Jeremy doing it. And that was a fairly unpalatable notion, too. Then again, perhaps the whole thing would be an irrelevance by the end of the year. He might not even be here.

As for the subject which Anthony had been so quick to raise, and equally quick to drop – that of Rachel . . . Why mention at all that he'd seen her over the weekend? Guilt? Something approaching it, no doubt. Which could mean that, in Charles's absence, the two of them had got a little thing going. Were they sleeping together? Knowing Rachel, probably not. Which wasn't necessarily a good thing. Set Rachel's delicate moral sensibilities against the thwarted desire of an emotionally susceptible twenty-six-year-old, turn the heat up a bit, and the chances were that Anthony would think he was in love. That was not a desirable state of affairs. Whatever Anthony might imagine he felt about Rachel, Leo wouldn't wish her on anyone, with her martyred soul and pallid lack of emotion. He thought suddenly of Adriana, entirely the converse, warm, sensual and sanguine, and his mind moved away from Anthony and Rachel to his own problems. He was going to have to do some serious thinking in the two weeks before Camilla got back from Bermuda.

I 2

This time it would be different, Felicity told herself. She wasn't going to jump straight back into bed with Peter, just because his wife had left him. She thought she'd shown remarkable self-control that night they'd been out to dinner together. Mind you, she couldn't have had him back to the flat, not with Sandy around. She stared at her computer screen. Who was she kidding? It was nothing to do with self-control. If Sandy hadn't been there, she'd have invited him back. The truth was, she'd have him any time. She glanced up as the door of the clerks' room opened, and saw Peter come in. Her heart did a little flip. What if all this was going to end in disaster again? What if his wife was to come back to him? He'd made it pretty clear that wasn't likely to happen, but still . . . She smiled as he approached.

Peter put his hands on her desk and leaned down. 'Are you busy tonight?'

Wishing like hell that she could say 'Yes,' Felicity shook her head.

'Because a friend's invited me to the opening of this new club up in town. D'you fancy going?'

'Yeah, that sounds good.'

'Great. I'll pick you up around half eight.'

Henry, sitting at his desk going through a pile of papers, had witnessed every nuance of this brief exchange – the way Peter bent down to talk to Felicity, his face close to hers, that soft, lost smile of hers as she looked at him, the way she watched him walk away, the expression in her eyes – one which Henry would have died to have directed at him. Henry could tell it was all back on again, and, frankly, it made him sick. Not that he was jealous. Not a bit of it. He was simply appalled by Felicity's lack of principle. Peter had lied to her, treated her badly, and yet here she was, ready to let him do it to her all over again. She was too easily taken in, that was her problem. Too impressed by good looks and a bit of charm. How could any woman take seriously a man who had highlights in his hair?

Felicity caught his eye, and Henry realized that he had been staring at her. He quickly turned his attention to the documents before him. If anything, it was the professional aspect of it that bothered him. There was always the potential for an upset if people started having affairs in chambers. It could be bad for business. He'd have to keep an eye on things. If it went too far, he might have to have a word with the pair of them. The irony of it was that it had only been a couple of months back that Henry had been telling Felicity to try to get along a bit better with Peter. Henry squared his shoulders and sighed.

Sandy lay on his bed, and felt another uncontrollable shudder run through his limbs. He still felt foggy and stoned in his head, but he kept getting these electric shakes in his body. He shut his eyes. Okay, today had not been a good day. But tomorrow would be better. Mistake, mistake, doing that dope Mazz had given him. Bad mistake. They'd seen him do it. That was when they got in. They'd seen him do it, because they were watching all the time. Were they sitting out there in the other room now, waiting? Yeah. Of course they were. He tried to shut his mind to the sound, but he could still hear them whispering, a sound like a tide surging on a stony beach. Oh, man, they were planning something monster.

He rubbed his face with his hands, and his skin felt leathery and clammy. Shit. He needed something to help him. He'd go down the pub later and see if he couldn't score something. Nothing major, just something to get his head level. Then he'd be fine. Then tomorrow it would all be okay, and – oh, Jesus, fuck, if they would just shut up! He tried not to listen, but they were like in his head. Right inside it!

He rolled on to his side, hunched up, and heard the front door open and close. Fliss was back. He relaxed slightly. They wouldn't hang around once she came in. He heard her footsteps, fingers tapping at the door.

'Yeah?' He rolled on to his back again and folded his arms beneath his head. Relax. Just chilling.

Fliss opened the door and looked in. 'You all right?'

'Yeah, fine.' He tried to make his voice sound clear and normal. 'Just having a bit of a rest.'

'Oh . . . okay. Listen, I'm going out in an hour or so. I'm going to do myself a bit of supper. D'you want some?'

'Yeah, okay.' Nice and normal, nice and normal.

She went away. He listened. Nothing. No one talking. She'd scared them off. He knew she would. They'd gone. For now.

Two hours later, the doorbell rang. Sandy was stretched out on the sofa, barefoot, watching television. He kept shifting restlessly and muttering to himself.

'That'll be Peter,' said Felicity, checking her make-up quickly in the mirror before going to let him in. Peter, she thought, looked heavenly, his blue shirt matching his eyes, a cool, shining contrast to poor Sandy, pimply and unwashed, in his grubby denims and khaki T-shirt.

'I'll just get my bag – won't be a sec. This is my brother, Sandy. Sandy, this is Peter.'

Sandy glanced up and nodded at Peter. Peter nodded back. An instantaneous current of animosity seemed to pass between them. Felicity went off to fetch her handbag and give herself another anxious inspection in the full-length mirror.

Felicity came back. 'Okay. All set.' She looked at Sandy. 'I'll see you later.' She hesitated, then added, 'You will take it easy, won't you? I mean, you won't –'

'Get off my case, Fliss.' Sandy picked up a can of lager from the floor by the sofa and muttered something else that Felicity couldn't hear.

'Yeah, well . . . fine. See you.' Felicity gave Peter a smile. 'Let's go.'

'See you,' said Peter in the direction of Sandy. But Sandy didn't look up or say anything in reply. He took a swig from his can of lager.

'Looks a bit of a dosser, your brother, if you don't mind my saying so,' Peter remarked, as they went downstairs.

'He's not been having a good time lately,' said Felicity defensively. 'He's all right, really. Just a bit low.'

'How long's he staying with you?'

'I don't know. Just till he gets his head together. That's what he says, anyway. It's been hard for him. He was sleeping rough not long ago.'

'Drugs?'

Felicity shrugged. 'Yeah, well, that hasn't helped. But he'll be okay. He really just needs a proper job.'

'Sounds like you're making excuses for him.'

'He is my brother.'

Peter opened the car door for Felicity, and she got in. She loved his good manners. Strapping himself in next to her, Peter remarked, 'He seems a bit weird to me. Did you know he was talking to himself when you were out of the room? I thought he was talking to me at first, then I realized he wasn't.'

Felicity said nothing for a moment. She seemed faintly embarrassed. 'They say dope can make you a bit paranoid. But he told me he's not doing that any more. He's just got a few problems.'

'Personally, I've got no time for people who do drugs. Why would anyone want to screw their brains up like that?'

'Yeah, well, it's easy to be judgmental, but Sandy's had a really hard time.'

'It's not the answer.'

Felicity sighed. 'He knows that. He's sorting himself out.'

'He's a mess. Anyone can see that. You're really getting taken for a ride. You want to learn to be a bit harder, Fliss.'

'He's family, for God's sake!' said Felicity unhappily. 'Anyway, look – can we stop talking about him? I just want to have a good time this evening.'

After an hour or so Sandy put on his trainers, fished around in his sister's bedroom for some change, and went down to the pub. He scored some uppers, which he took in the gents, then bought himself a large vodka. He stood at the bar on his own, eyes fixed on the wide-screen TV. The voices swam in and out of his head. Mostly they were far away, though still distinct. Once, when they got in loud and close, he said something to try to shut them up, then noticed the bloke next to him looking at him strangely. Sandy downed his drink and left.

Back in the flat, he put on his music really loud, and that seemed to help. Loud as possible. Better. Better. Someone in the flat above thumped on the floor a couple of times, but Sandy ignored it. After twenty minutes, the voices came whispering in behind the music, their words tangled indistinctly in the beat. He switched it off and listened intently in the silence of the room. On sudden inspiration he went to fetch a pad of paper and a pen. He sat down on his bed again. That was where he'd been making his mistake. He shouldn't try to shut them out. He should listen, take note. He began to scribble down everything they said to him.

Felicity and Peter sat in Peter's car, a couple of streets away from the club. It was after midnight. Felicity eased herself unwillingly from Peter's arms.

'Come back with me,' said Peter.

'I can't. I don't like leaving Sandy by himself.'

'He's a big boy.'

'I said I'd be back. He has to get up really early to get to the shop. I keep worrying he won't make it one of these days.'

'You've got a life to live, you know.' Peter brushed her neck with his lips, and she shivered. 'I want you so much, Fliss. You don't know how badly I've missed you.'

'Peter, I have to go back.' She gazed into his eyes. 'I suppose you could always come back to mine.'

'And listen to your druggy brother talking to himself through the walls? I don't think so.'

'Don't be such a bastard.'

They kissed for a few minutes, then Peter pulled away and said, 'So how long does this go on? You not coming back to my place because of him, I mean.'

'I don't know. I suppose I'm being stupid. I'm just a bit worried about him at the moment. I'm sorry.' She reached for him and kissed him, but he had lost the mood.

'Come on. I'd better drive you back.'

Twenty minutes later Felicity turned her key quietly in the front door and went in. A light was still on in the living room, but there was no sign of Sandy. The TV was switched off. Passing his room, she saw no light beneath the door and thought he must be asleep.

She climbed into bed and lay in the dark, thinking of Peter, conscious of unsatisfied longing. He was feeling it too, she knew. He hadn't tried to hide how fed up he was. Oh well, maybe it was for the best. Maybe it shouldn't be that easy for him to take up where he left off. Still, she couldn't let Sandy cramp her style for too long.

On Friday afternoon the *Persephone* proceedings finished early, as Mr Justice Sagewell had another appointment.

As they left the courtroom Leo said to Rachel, 'I could pick up Oliver this evening, if you like, instead of tomorrow morning.'

'Yes, that would be fine. Why don't you come around half seven?'

'Right. I'll see you then.'

Leo returned to chambers, intending to read quickly through some papers which had arrived that morning, before going home to shower and change. No sooner had he sat down at his desk than Sarah came into his room.

'Don't you ever knock?' asked Leo mildly.

'Not when I know you're all alone. I saw you come in a few moments ago. I wondered if you felt like going for a drink. We haven't seen much of one another lately.'

'Can't, I'm afraid. I have to pick Oliver up. Anyway, I thought you were usually busy with young Mr Fry of an evening. You always seem to be sloping off together.'

'And?' It piqued Sarah to realize that anyone in chambers was aware of the situation.

'Well, I would hardly have thought he was your type. Not a man overly concerned with the outer image. More the cerebral type. The kind who doesn't bother to iron his shirts.'

Leo's lightly mocking tone touched a raw nerve in Sarah; she certainly wasn't going to admit to Leo the extent of her relationship with Roger. In fact, it suited her pride to deny its existence entirely. 'As it happens, he's not my type. I've seen him for a drink a couple of times, that's all. We are, as they say, merely good friends. And speaking of friends, how are you and the lovely Miss Papaposilakis getting on? Don't tell me you're still holding her at arm's length.'

Leo had to admire her perspicacity. The only problem was that Sarah, in possession of information, was inclined to make mischief where she could. 'She's a persistent woman. I refuse to say any more than that. Besides, she's a client, remember.'

'Oh, come on, Leo.' Sarah hitched herself up on to the window-sill and propped her feet against Leo's desk. 'The client would have to be a Panamanian company before that stopped you. Even then, I'm not so sure. You're sleeping with her. I know you are.'

'Do you?'

'If she was up for it, you couldn't resist it. I know you inside out. Poor old Camilla.'

'You'd do well to keep your idle speculations to yourself.'

Sarah gave him a foxy smile. 'Whom could I possibly tell?'

Leo put on his glasses and untied the ribbon round the brief. 'I think this conversation is closed. Go on – scram. I've got work to do.'

Sarah slipped down from the window-sill. 'I'm sure you have. Not to mention all the strenuous overtime you'll be putting in on the Silakis case.' She kissed the top of his head and sauntered to the door. 'See you.'

Leo sighed reflectively as she disappeared. Strenuous was the word. The fact that Adriana had been absent from the hearing for the past week, occupied with other business affairs, had been something of a relief. He had been grateful for a few days' respite from her exacting physical demands. Still, it would be useful to know when she was going to put in an appearance again. He anticipated problems ahead unless he rationalized his situation.

Two hours later he pulled up in the driveway of Charles Beecham's house. He went through the gate to the back of the house and found the kitchen door ajar. He knocked lightly and went in. Rachel was at the sink, washing some cutlery.

She glanced round as Leo rapped on the door. 'I didn't hear the car. I haven't quite finished putting Oliver's things together. Do you want a coffee?'

'Yes, thanks.' Leo sat down at the kitchen table. Oliver came toddling in, saw Leo, and rushed to him with a squeal of pleasure. Leo caught him up and kissed him, and sat him on his knee. 'What's this you've got?' He took the toy which Oliver offered to him.

'A Thunderbird,' said Rachel, as she made the coffee. 'Thunderbird Two, to be precise. Anthony dropped it off at the office this afternoon. Oliver's recently developed a passion for the things. It started with that book your mother sent him. Anthony was reading it to him at the weekend.'

'Anfony gave me.' Oliver took the toy back from his father and held it aloft.

'That was nice of him.' Leo smoothed the little boy's dark hair. 'You like Anthony?' Oliver nodded. Leo glanced up at Rachel. 'Anthony's here quite a lot, it seems.'

'Hardly.' Rachel set Leo's coffee down on the table. 'He's been to lunch a couple of times, that's all.'

'While Charles is away.'

'As it happens, yes. But then, Charles is away most of the time.' Rachel dried her hands.

'You're sure it's not going to get in the way?'

'What is? Get in the way of what?'

'Your relationship with Anthony. Get in the way of life with Charles.'

Rachel leaned against the sink and regarded Leo. He couldn't tell if her expression was troubled or angry. 'I don't see how it could. I don't exactly have a life with Charles.'

'That's not what you were saying a month or two ago. Everything was sorted out between the two of you. Or so you said.'

'I merely said we were staying together, for the time being.'

'I see,' murmured Leo, and sipped his coffee. He bet poor old Charles didn't quite appreciate the impermanence of the situation. Rachel and Anthony must have got something going, for her to be so defensive and snippy.

'Anyway,' said Rachel, 'you don't have to concern yourself with that. Tell me how you're getting on with your house buying.'

'Not badly. I think I told you the other day that I was waiting to hear whether the vendors would pay to have the subsidence investigated. My chap rang this morning to say that they were prepared to do that, up to a maximum cost of two thousand. So now we just wait and see. I'm hoping it won't be too much of a problem.' He added, 'You'll have to come and see the house sometime. See where Oliver's going to be living when he's with me.'

Rachel nodded. She sipped her coffee in silence for a moment, then said, 'I'll go and get his bag.'

Ten minutes later, she stood on the driveway and waved to Oliver as Leo set off. She remained there for some moments before going back into the empty house. Somehow Leo had divined that there was more to her relationship with Anthony than mere friendship. Had Anthony let something slip in conversation? She could hardly believe that. Maybe she could just put it down to Leo's unnerving forensic skills. Or perhaps she herself had given something away in her look, her manner. As she passed through the hall, she stopped and regarded herself in the mirror. She thought about Anthony, about making love to him, and felt a surge of longing that made her pulse beat faster, watching her reflection to see if any of what she felt was externally evident. A slight flush about her cheeks, nothing more. But then, Leo knew her so well, was adept at reading everything about her.

In the kitchen she picked up Leo's empty coffee mug and took it to the sink. How odd. For the first time, in the wake of Leo's leaving, she didn't feel the usual empty ache. Anthony, it seemed, was capable of doing something which Charles, for all his loving kindness and good humour, never could. He was eclipsing Leo. When she thought of him, it was with a warm, happy desire which made her feelings for Leo – feelings which she had carried around for so long – seem sterile and useless.

Slowly she turned on the tap and rinsed out the mug. She smiled. She had no idea how she was going to resolve the awful complexities of her existence, but at least she had this new knowledge, this new love to sustain her.

The following morning, Sarah was standing on a table in Roger's attic room, resting her arms on the sill of the open casement window, and gazing out across the city skyline. Roger came through from the kitchen with a tray of tea and toast.

Sarah glanced down at him. 'This is amazing. Almost as good as the Millennium Wheel.'

'I wouldn't go that far.' Roger set the tray down by the bed. 'Come and have some breakfast.'

Sarah hopped down from the table and joined Roger in bed. 'Do you do this a lot? Make breakfast for the women in your life?'

'You're doing it again.'

'What?'

'Trying to get me to tell you about all my past girlfriends.'

'I'm not. It's just you're the only man I've ever known who isn't prepared to talk about them. Maybe you haven't ever had any. Maybe I'm the first one.'

'Right.' Roger smiled and pushed his glasses up on the bridge of his nose. 'So tell me – why is it that women always want to know about ex-lovers?' He paused. 'Now, the fact that I can ask that question should indicate you're not the first girl I've been in love with.'

Sarah paused, her mug of tea half-way to her lips, and stared at him for several seconds. 'Is that true?' she asked. 'Are you really?'

Roger took a casual bite from a slice of toast. 'Of course. You must know I am.'

She studied his face, allowing herself a small smile of pleasure. Many men had been in love with her, but another conquest was always satisfying. And this one more touching and pleasurable than most. 'Not necessarily. You're so matter-of-fact about everything.'

'I'm not much good at declarations of undying love.'

'Don't you want to know how I feel about you?' asked Sarah, surprising herself by saying this, since she wasn't exactly sure what she felt.

Roger gave her a speculative glance. 'I have a pretty good idea.' He carried on eating his toast.

Sarah's cheerful mood suddenly evaporated. Something

in his words and attitude had irritated her profoundly. 'Really? And how's that?'

'Much the same way.'

She felt a little flare of anger. 'Sorry. Not quite.' Her tone was abrupt.

Roger put his plate on the floor and lay back. 'Your problem is, you let all kinds of irrelevancies get in the way. You're too busy weighing up what other people think, making bogus judgments about yourself. About me.'

She gazed at him with real hostility. 'What on earth gives you the right to analyse me like this? I happen to know what my own feelings are.'

'No, you don't. All the standards you use to measure feelings are perfectly trite.'

'*What?*'

'They're artificial. How can real feelings stand a chance?'

'Did you just wake up this morning and *decide* to be a complete bastard?'

'I'm not being a bastard. I'm being honest. I love you, so I'm entitled to tell you things you should know.'

'It's a bloody funny way of showing someone you love them.' Sarah untangled herself from the sheets and got out of bed. She began to get dressed, finding her fingers shaking with fury. At least, she assumed that was what it was.

Roger watched her from the bed. 'Where are you going?'

She zipped up her jeans. 'That doesn't concern you. Away from here. I can't believe I've let things go this far. I'm fed up with being patronized.' She glared at him. 'You shamble around in your half-baked world, like bloody Jarvis Cocker . . . D'you think that just because you say you love someone it gives you the right to pull them to pieces and tell them they're emotionally stunted? You are so smug, Roger! Talk about my artificial standards? I sometimes wonder if you've got any at all. You certainly don't dress or act as though you do!' She flung on her jacket and crossed the room, half-expecting him to apologize, or say something to try to stop her leaving.

But Roger merely lay there, mildly surprised. Jarvis Cocker?

Sarah slammed out of the flat. She was right – he was smug. Infuriatingly smug. He'd been smug from the beginning. Love her? Everything he'd just said showed he didn't love her. He wanted to belittle her, to occupy some sort of moral high ground, make out that she was preoccupied with trivia and false values, and that he had the monopoly on all that was genuine. Well, he could be genuine on his own.

Leo was in the Belgravia flat, getting Oliver ready to go out, when the phone rang.

'Leo, darling,' said Adriana's voice. 'Have you missed me?'

'Naturally. It's been the most tedious week without you.'

'Good. I'm glad to hear it. Now, are you busy today?'

'My son's spending the weekend with me. We're just about to go and look at the house in Chelsea that I'm buying. I thought he might enjoy watching the men dig up the foundations. Anyway, what did you have in mind?'

'Something along the same lines, funnily enough. I told you that I'm looking for a house in England, and I have the particulars of a most wonderful place in Gloucestershire. I'm going to look at it this afternoon. Would you like to come, with your little son?'

'I don't see why not. We don't have anything else planned.'

'Lovely.' He could hear the smile in her voice and almost smell her perfume, and felt a glimmer of desire. After the week's respite, the possibility of her gorgeous little body in bed later on this evening was distinctly appealing.

'Give me the address of the house in Chelsea,' said Adriana. 'I can meet you there.'

A couple of hours later, Adriana's car pulled up outside the house in Gratton Crescent. Leo and Oliver, having exhausted the pleasures of watching the workmen dig the trench at the back, were taking a brief tour of the house and saw the car from an upstairs window. Leo, holding Oliver in his arms, watched Adriana step from the car. He was used to seeing her in her business suits. Even in her tight designer jeans and cropped jacket, with her soft hair falling to her shoulders, she looked sleek and expensive. He'd often speculated on how old she was. Mid-thirties, probably. Today she looked much younger.

'She's a pretty lady, don't you think?' he said to Oliver.

The little boy nodded, gazing down. He pointed. 'That man's got a hat.'

'That's her driver. Isn't he smart? And that's a very expensive car. Come on, let's go down and meet her.'

Leo introduced Oliver to Adriana, and then took her on a tour of the house.

'It's perfectly charming,' she said. 'But quite small.'

Leo smiled. 'For you, perhaps. But I think it's quite big enough for my needs.'

'Oh, you would be surprised, Leo, how one's needs can grow. Now, where are you two fine gentlemen going to take me for lunch?'

'I did promise Oliver Pizza Express,' said Leo.

'Very well. Pizza Express it shall be. I suggest we drive back to yours, then take my car for the rest of the day.'

Leo, quite happy to be chauffeured around, thought this was an excellent idea.

*

Adriana was a greater success with Oliver than Leo had expected. She was quite businesslike and direct with him, and not in the least patronizing, and was utterly charmed when Oliver remarked that she smelt nice.

'You have your father's way with women,' laughed Adriana, and stroked Oliver's cheek. Oliver picked up another slice of pizza and ate it with satisfaction, aware that he was getting on all right with this new person.

Observing the interesting chemistry between them, Leo reflected that all males, even those of Oliver's age, must naturally be susceptible to the kind of extravagant femininity which Adriana exuded.

'Do you like children?' asked Leo.

'I like your son. He is intelligent, like you. But I'm not one of those motherly creatures, believe me.'

'Don't you want to create a little Papaposilakis dynasty of your own?'

'No, thank you. I have never wanted babies. My business is my child, and its demands are quite enough for me.'

After lunch, they drove out to Gloucestershire. Adriana produced the estate agent's brochure setting out the house details and read from it in her pretty, light accent. Oliver sat in his car seat with his thumb in his mouth, eyes fastened on her face as she read.

'Clewis and Partners are delighted to offer for sale this exclusive Georgian property, set in an enchanting rural position, with superb gardens and extensive views of the surrounding countryside. Situated near Mapleigh, in Gloucestershire, Boringdon Hall was built by Lord Whiteway in the 1770s and has been extensively refurbished by its present owners. It has its own indoor swimming pool and orangery, six reception rooms, eight bedrooms, a staff wing, and a three-bedroom coach house.'

'Sounds snug,' observed Leo. 'How many times a year would you propose to visit this little pied-à-terre?'

'That depends.' Adriana gave a shrug. 'I'm rather tired of Greece at the moment. The pollution is very bad, even outside Athens. I might decide to live here permanently. It depends on many things.' She closed the brochure and turned her gaze to the passing countryside.

Leo said nothing. He wondered if she was referring to him, to the possibility of persuading him to become a part of her life. He still couldn't decide whether the idea was sublimely attractive, or quite simply ridiculous. Whichever, it had certainly prompted him to review dispassionately the various options which life currently presented, and he had found it a timely exercise. The focus was narrower than he had imagined. Apart from sharing Oliver's life, looking after him and watching him grow up, what lay ahead? Another ten or twelve years of practice, the usual round of cases and clients, then perhaps a seat on the High Court bench. That itself had seemed an interesting enough prospect once, viewed from a distance. Not any more. Leo suspected he wasn't temperamentally suited to being a judge, listening to long-winded counsel and writing his own long-winded judgments. And what of the rest of his life? At present he had a twenty-two-year-old girlfriend of whom he was undoubtedly fond, but to whom, judging from his own present behaviour, he wasn't going to be able to offer the kind of commitment and fidelity which she undoubtedly wanted and expected. He had recently extricated himself from the threat of marriage, and all the domestic impedimenta that that involved, but if he continued with the relationship, he suspected that couldn't be held at bay for too long. The alternative was to revert to his former pattern of behaviour, and take lovers as and when he pleased, of either sex – but how satisfactory could that be, as he slid into middle age, and with Oliver to think about?

He glanced at Adriana's serene profile. She was, by any standards, a remarkable woman. She was beautiful, sexy, clever, rich, cosmopolitan; she was powerful in her own sphere, but delightfully submissive in other ways; she wasn't interested in having children, which was ideal; she shared many of his tastes, and was not, except as a client and in bed, particularly demanding. Above all, she was wealthy, and seemed prepared to share her wealth, and the pleasures it brought, with him. He wasn't in love with her, but she appeared to be with him, and that was good enough. Leo's only misgiving was that he suspected that buried beneath the loveliness, like a stone within a peach, lay a cynical and calculating little heart. Still, that was the quality which made her a shrewd businesswoman, and an indefatigable litigant. Perhaps the same cynicism would make her the perfect partner for someone like himself. Camilla, so innocent and earnest, expected complete fidelity from him. Adriana, on the other hand, might be content with a little less. No, if there was any problem, it was the sacrifice of independence, subsuming his own existence in a world created entirely by Adriana's wealth. Could he handle that? The truth was, he would have no idea how it felt until he tried it.

He reflected idly on these things as they drove through the leafy Gloucestershire countryside, until they reached Boringdon Hall. The driver slowed the car at the entrance gates, and spoke into an intercom. The gates swung open, and they proceeded up a long, tree-lined drive. The house, when it came into view, was imposing yet graceful, and far larger than Leo had expected. The car drew to a halt.

'What do you think?' asked Adriana, as they sat looking out.

'Magnificent,' said Leo. 'Quite beautiful.'

They got out and were met by the estate agent. Leo strapped Oliver into his pushchair, relieved that he looked sleepy and not inclined to run around. This didn't look like the kind of house where they would welcome a boisterous toddler storming through the rooms.

The experience of going round Boringdon Hall felt to Leo exactly like a paid tour of a stately home. The rooms were spacious and light, beautifully decorated and furnished, though in a style somewhat too ornate for Leo's taste. He would arrange things differently – everywhere, that was, except for the library, which struck him as the most beautiful room in the house, filled with gentle light from the large windows overlooking the lawns and gardens. He could imagine the pleasure of spending hours in this room, of mounting the little curved wooden staircase to the gallery which ran around the upper portion of the room in search of some volume, of sitting at the table by the window, working. To work in such a room would be a luxury, in any season of the year. But what work? If his life became part of Adriana's, what work would there be for him to do?

They went slowly through the house, Adriana questioning the agent closely on every detail. They viewed the coach house, the swimming pool, the tennis court and the kitchen garden. They passed down a lawned walk, through wrought-iron gates opening on to a poplar avenue flanked by paddocks, and admired the views over the countryside. They walked back through the gardens, and Adriana thanked the estate agent and asked him to leave them for a little while. She sat down on a bench beneath one of the oak trees and gazed across the lawn to the house.

'Come and sit with me,' she said, patting the bench next to her.

Leo sat down. Oliver was asleep in his pushchair, thumb in mouth, head on one side. Adriana breathed in the air and smiled. 'I like this place. I think it could be quite perfect. It is so English.'

'Do you seriously think you want a place this large?'

'Why not? It's absolutely beautiful. It has atmosphere. The size is immaterial. Don't you think you would like to live here?' She regarded him with thoughtful brown eyes.

'What I want is neither here nor there. This is your adventure.'

'I like that. An adventure. I hadn't thought of it that way.' She reached out a hand and stroked his arm lightly. 'I don't want it just to be my adventure. You know what I said to you in Marbella. I want you in my life. I want to share things with you. This –' she gestured towards the house and its tranquil grounds '– we could enjoy together.'

'Put in vague terms,' Leo replied carefully, 'it's a very attractive idea.' He gazed at the house. 'But I have an existence, I have a job and a life that can't simply be erased. You want to draw me into your world. But what would I be there? How would I fit in? As your lover, your accessory? I'm afraid I'm not available on those terms.'

She smiled. 'You are such a lawyer. You need the fine detail. Very well.' Adriana clasped her hands in her lap. 'Mr Defereras is getting old. He has run the legal side of Silakis shipping line for forty years now. He worked for my father before me. It has been an important and well-rewarded job. He has earned a great deal of money. Now he wants to retire. I need someone to replace him, someone with skill and understanding. Someone who knows the world of shipping.'

'So you're offering me Mr Defereras's job?'

'Not quite. It would be much more than that, in time.' She drew closer to him, and her hand, which had been resting on his arm, touched his face gently. 'If we were as good together as I think we can be, we could run this business together. I need someone. It is very hard and very tiring, sometimes. And lonely.'

'I can't be your partner, Adriana. It's your business, your family business.'

'Leo, you could make of it whatever you want. I am asking you to be with me, work with me, share everything.'

'My life at the Bar is all I've ever done, all I've ever wanted. I don't know that I could leave it that easily. It's my world.'

'That funny, old-fashioned place, with its grey buildings and dreary lawyers? Leo, I could show you a better world than that, much more exciting.' Her soft brown eyes looked into his. 'You know, I am not the kind of woman who gives herself to men. I have never in my life offered myself to anyone, as I am offering myself to you now.' Leo said nothing. She went on, 'Would it be so hard to change your life? What ties do you have that would be so hard to break?'

'There's Oliver.' He had never mentioned Camilla to her, and he wasn't about to start now.

'He lives with you some of the time. Nothing there would change. He could come here, have a home here, or some-where like this. I'm not asking you to come to Greece with me. I can run the business from anywhere. I wouldn't ask you to leave England.'

Leo contemplated her pretty, passionate face. She meant all of this. He didn't flatter himself that he was so exceptional, compared to the kind of men she must have met. What had he done that she should offer herself to him in this way? Perhaps it was simply love after all – a word that hadn't been mentioned so far.

He kissed her face lightly. 'You are a truly extraordinary woman. But I have to be honest with you. This was never intended to be anything more than a brief affair. I always saw it as something that suited us both, for as long as the case lasted. I thought you did too. We're the same kind of people, prepared to take pleasure as and when we find it. Why do you want to turn it into something more serious?'

'I love you, Leo,' she replied simply. 'I am in love with you.'

Leo gazed at her face, its expression fragile, utterly vulnerable, quite different from her usual cool, adamantine composure. It would have been quite easy, in that moment, to say that he loved her too. In a way, he did. But he knew that if this were to have any chance of success, it was not the right thing to say. Not then, and not at any time in the future. A woman like Adriana, so used to getting what she wanted, should not be so easily gratified. It was important that she should remain needy, anxious.

'I'm very fond of you,' he replied gently, 'but I don't love you. It's only fair to tell you that.'

He watched her eyes, and found the response he wanted – a little flicker of fear and apprehension. 'I know,' she replied. 'I don't care. Maybe it's why I love you. It doesn't change anything I've said. I need you.'

Leo looked down at Oliver asleep in his pushchair. He thought for a long moment. 'This isn't easy for me. If I throw in my career at the Bar to come and work for Silakis Shipping, I can't go back. Not easily.' He turned his eyes to hers. 'I need a few days to think about it.'

She gave a soft, happy smile, knowing that he was close to being persuaded. 'I can wait. I shall be in New York all of next week. You can tell me your answer when I get back.'

13

'. . . and, as your Lordship is doubtless aware, in that case the European Court of Justice held *inter alia* that where two actions involve the same cause of action, and some but not all of the parties to the second action are the same as the parties to the action commenced earlier in another contracting state, the second court seised is required to decline jurisdiction only to the extent to which the parties to the proceedings before it are also parties to the action previously commenced . . .'

Anthony, suppressing a yawn of infinite boredom, glanced at Fred Fenton, his instructing solicitor, and wished that he could perfect the same technique of dozing with his eyes open. He could tell from Fred's glazed expression that that was exactly what he was doing. No wonder. As jurisdiction disputes went, this one was pretty dire. As junior in the case, Anthony's role was limited, and it was difficult, on a soporific August Friday such as this, to keep one's attention from wandering. He glanced at his watch. Nearly twelve-thirty. He would be seeing Rachel in half an hour. Two days since he had last seen her, and in that time the ghost of her, luminous and soft and hesitant, had moved constantly in his mind.

The weekend they had spent together had been entirely different from the last. Apart from the fact that Oliver had been with Leo, ensuring Anthony the sublime, concentrated pleasure of Rachel's attention, it was as though they had both decided, silently and independently, to excise all guilt and anxiety from the situation. Charles, out of sight, had stayed out of their minds.

Anthony glanced up. Their learned friend on the other side was still wittering on about anti-suit injunctions, and would probably do so until the lunch break. Anthony's mind drifted over fragments of that perfect weekend. Most perfect of all, being in bed with Rachel.

'This,' he had said to her, 'was something I'd decided two years ago would never happen.'

'Because of me?'

'Because of Leo.'

He had no idea why he'd raised the subject of Leo, but he had.

'Don't talk about him.'

'You still love him, don't you?' Anthony had propped himself up on one elbow and looked into her eyes.

She shook her head. 'I did. It's not that any more. It's like – it's like having been wounded, really badly wounded. The scar may have healed, but it still hurts sometimes.' She sighed. 'Maybe Leo is someone you never quite get over. But if I love anyone, it's you.'

Anthony closed his eyes briefly at the memory of that, the way she had touched his face and looked into his eyes as she said it. Still, even then, he hadn't been able to leave Leo out of it.

'Does he know?' he had asked.

'About us? I don't know. You know what he's like. When he came to pick up Oliver, he seemed to have the idea something was going on. Why? Does it bother you?'

'No. Why should it? This has nothing to do with him.'

And then he had kissed her, and the rest was . . . well, amazing. Anthony let out a sigh, and Fred glanced at him and rolled his eyes, mistaking the sigh for evidence of deep boredom. Anthony smiled faintly in return.

Of course, it hadn't been true. It had everything to do with Leo. Quite why or how, Anthony couldn't work out. But somehow it did. He glanced again at the barrister on the other side, trying to focus his thoughts on the case, but it was hard to tether one's attention to such relentless verbosity.

'. . . and, my Lord, I would submit that there is nothing in the Warsaw Convention to suggest that this rule may be modified under domestic law or otherwise, so as to enable a claim to be brought in some jurisdiction not otherwise permissible under article 28, on the ground that some other defendant is being sued by the same claimant in some other jurisdiction. However, the interpretation of article 28 where the manufacturer is joined as a defendant in addition to the carrier may, as a matter of French law, be different –'

Mrs Justice Miller interrupted him. 'With respect, Mr Griffiths, may I suggest that that aspect of your already lengthy argument might usefully be held over until after lunch? We shall resume at two o'clock.'

The sense of relief as the court rose was almost palpable.

'I was beginning to feel as though I was in a parallel universe,' said Fred, as he and Anthony left the court.

'Or jurisdiction.'

'What are you doing for lunch? Fancy a quick sandwich across the road?'

'Thanks,' said Anthony, 'but I'm meeting someone.'

'Okay. See you later.'

A few minutes later Anthony arrived at the wine bar where he and Rachel had arranged to meet. She was already sitting in a booth next to the window, sipping a glass of wine. Anthony slipped in opposite her.

'I wouldn't normally,' she said, raising her glass, 'but it's Friday. Would you like one?'

'No, I won't. It's difficult enough staying awake in court as it is.' He leaned across and kissed her. 'How are you?'

'Good. I just settled a case this morning. On very favourable terms, too. Nothing like a satisfied client.'

He smiled, surveying her face. She looked so different these days – open and happy, without the drawn, defensive look of a few weeks ago. 'Well done. You deserve to celebrate. Look, I'll go and order some sandwiches. I haven't got long.'

He came back after a few minutes with a plate of sandwiches, and sat down again. 'So, will I see you this weekend?'

Her face clouded. 'Charles is coming back tomorrow.'

'I thought he wasn't back till next week?'

Rachel shook her head. 'He rang last night.' She fell silent, gazing through the window at the street with apprehensive eyes.

Anthony felt as though he'd been kicked in the stomach. He'd spent the last few days thinking about how they'd be together this weekend. This, he supposed, was reality. When Charles was away, it was all pretend.

His words echoed his thoughts. 'Back to real life.'

She shook her head, her gaze still fixed absently on the street. 'It's not real at all. Not any more so than what's happened between us. If anything, less so.' She picked up her wine and sipped it.

'In which case,' said Anthony slowly, 'you have to tell him.'

'It's going to be dreadful. I can just imagine what will happen. He'll be hurt. He'll be agonizingly unhappy. He won't be angry. That's not Charles's style. He probably won't even blame me. He'll blame himself, say he hasn't been fair to me, rationalize it, excuse it, say that he'll jack the series in, that he won't go back to the States, that Oliver and I are more important to him than the work . . .' She sighed, put her head in her hands. 'He's such a good man, and I've done a horrible thing to him. And the worst of it is, I think he'll forgive me.'

'You have to make it clear it's not a question of forgiveness, that it's not just some casual affair.'

'I don't think I can bear to tell him.'

'These things happen.'

She looked up at him. 'No, they don't, Anthony. We *made* it happen. I can't evade responsibility. I let him down, I didn't care enough. I didn't have to let it happen. I had a choice.'

'Possibly.' He reached out a hand for hers. 'But it *has* happened. I'm in love with you. I have been since way back when. And I think you feel the same way.'

'You know I do.'

'In which case . . .' He shrugged.

'It's easy for you. All you have to do is stand back and wait for the dust to settle. I've got to face the awfulness of telling him, of hurting him.'

Anthony offered her the sandwiches, and took one himself. 'Maybe it won't be the way you think. Maybe he's met some charming young researcher out in the States, maybe –' The look in her eyes stopped him. 'Sorry. But these are possibilities, you know. Just because you don't want it to be the case doesn't mean –'

'I'm not saying that! It would solve a lot of problems if he had met someone. It's just the way you –' She stopped, exasperated. 'God, I don't want to argue.'

'There's nothing to argue about. You have to tell him. How does it go on, otherwise? We wait for him to go back to the States and then pick up where we left off? I can't do that. Neither can you. If you think what you've done to Charles is bad, then that would be infinitely worse.'

'I know, I know.' She looked down at her wine. 'I think that's why I needed this. To give myself a bit of courage. Face the fact that I have to do something. The thing is, it would be so much easier if there was no affection, if I had some reason to hate him. I don't. I'm really, really fond of him. And his family. They've been so wonderful to Oliver. They're such a part of his life ... If this involved only Charles and me, it wouldn't be so bad. But it's much more complicated than that. It's going to be like getting divorced from Leo all over again, only worse, because Oliver's old enough to know what's going on.'

Anthony sat in silence for some seconds. 'You're right. I suppose I have got the easy part. I'm not the one who has to make the choices.'

'I've already made my choices.' Rachel sighed. 'Now it's just a question of getting on with it, making sense of a horrible situation.'

'Not all of it's horrible.' He put his hand beneath her chin and drew her face to his, and kissed her for a long moment. 'There is a good side to it.'

She smiled. 'Yes, there is.'

'What about tonight? Can I see you tonight? If he's not coming back till tomorrow —'

'I don't think I can do that. I feel bad enough. It's too close, just before he gets back —'

'Don't worry. I understand.'

She drew a deep breath and sat back. 'God, it's a bit late for pathetic moral subtleties, isn't it? I really, really hate myself. This is not the person I wanted to be.'

'Don't beat yourself up about it. Have another sandwich.' He glanced at his watch. 'I have to get back to court.'

Rachel drained her glass and picked up her bag. 'I should be going too.'

'Will you call me?'

She nodded. 'Of course. If you don't mind, though, it won't be over the weekend. I'll leave it till Monday. I don't know how the next two days are going to be.'

It happened that an official judicial function of some importance, one which required the presence of his Honour Mr Justice Sagewell, *inter alia*, was taking place in the City that day, and so the proceedings in the *Persephone* had been briefly suspended. Leo, who had spent the morning busying himself with other matters in chambers, popped out at lunchtime to pick up some cigars. Coming out of the newsagent's, he glimpsed Anthony and Rachel through the window of the wine bar across the street. He paused for only a few seconds, but that was time enough to see how they spoke, kissed, then spoke again. There was no mistaking their mutual absorption. They looked like two people who were everything in the world to each other. For the moment, at any rate. Experience had taught Leo that nothing in this world lasted for ever.

He had already countenanced the possibility that something was going on between Rachel and Anthony, but hadn't anticipated that actually seeing them together would arouse such disturbing feelings within him. He walked rapidly back to chambers.

He went up to his room, opened his window, took off his jacket and draped it over the back of his chair, then sat down and lit one of the small cheroots which he had just purchased. He leaned back, frowning. So, the smouldering affair had finally ignited. A couple of years ago, Anthony hadn't even been getting past first base. He had Leo to thank for the fact that Rachel was now something more than a frigid Madonna of the Law Courts. Did Anthony allow himself to acknowledge that, or would that be simply too humiliating? At any rate, judging by the brief glimpse of their body language, the relationship between Anthony and Rachel had evidently reached a certain intensity. No doubt the agonizing had begun. Poor old Charles. If there was one chap he really liked, had done ever since the first Lloyd's Names case, it was Charles Beecham. Leo felt genuinely sorry for him.

The telephone rang, interrupting his thoughts, and he picked it up.

When he put it down again a few moments later, all thoughts of Anthony and Rachel had been entirely eclipsed. He put on his jacket, looked into the clerks' room to tell Felicity he was going out for a couple of hours, then walked quickly up to Fleet Street. There he hailed a cab and asked the driver to take him to Charing Cross Hospital in Hammersmith.

Captain Kollias's wife, who had spoken to Leo on the phone, met him in the waiting room outside the intensive care unit. She was a slender Greek woman, pale and composed, but evidently deeply distressed.

'Mr Davies? Thank you for coming. My husband has been asking to see you since he woke up. That was an hour ago. I have been calling you every few minutes . . .' Her eyes filled, and she drew a handful of tissues from the pocket of her jacket.

'Sit down,' said Leo, guiding her to a chair. He sat down opposite her. 'When did the accident happen?'

'This morning. He had been to pick up the car from the garage, and on the way back there was a motorbike coming out of a side street . . .' She pressed the tissues to her eyes.

'How is he?'

'I don't know. Last night they said he was critical, and they operated on him, and today they say he is stable, but I know they are still worried ... He has bad injuries to his chest and his head.'

'Did he say why he wanted to see me?'

She shook her head. At that moment, the door opened and a doctor came in. Mrs Kollias rose to greet him.

'Oh, doctor, this is Mr Davies.'

The doctor shook Leo's hand. 'Mr Kollias has been very insistent about speaking to you, Mr Davies. I'm glad Mrs Kollias managed to get hold of you. Normally, with someone in his condition, I wouldn't recommend that he be disturbed, but I think it's best you see him.' He turned to Mrs Kollias. 'I think, if you don't mind, Mrs Kollias, I'll ask you to wait here.'

She nodded, watching with fearful eyes as Leo and the doctor left the room. On the way down the corridor, the doctor asked, 'Do you know of any special reason why Mr Kollias wants to speak to you so badly?'

'I'm a lawyer, and Captain Kollias – Mr Kollias – has been giving evidence in a case I'm involved in. I can only imagine it has something to do with that.'

The doctor opened a door into one of the intensive care rooms. The light was muted, and the only sound came in regular bleeps from the machines around the bed. The upper part of Captain Kollias's torso was swathed in bandages, as was much of his head. His swarthy face, recognizable only by its thick moustache, was bruised and swollen, with plastic tubing coming from his nose. The doctor leaned over and spoke a few words, and Captain Kollias stirred and opened his eyes. Leo drew up a chair next to the bed, and the doctor left them alone together.

Captain Kollias had closed his eyes again, but his mouth was moving. Leo leaned forward. 'Captain Kollias? Can you hear me?'

Captain Kollias stirred again, and reached out a big, hairy

hand and laid it on Leo's arm. He tried to speak, but his voice was hoarse and Leo couldn't make out his words. He waited. Captain Kollias cleared his throat and tried again.

'Thank you for coming, Mr Davies.' The guttural voice, so clear and resonant in the courtroom, was weak and tired now. He was evidently in a very bad way.

'I'm so sorry about your accident,' said Leo. There was nothing much else he could say. He knew he wasn't here for social chit-chat. He would simply have to wait for whatever it was Captain Kollias had to tell him.

Moments passed. Captain Kollias's eyes ranged round the room, as though he barely knew where he was. Leo presumed he was on some kind of pretty strong painkilling medication, and wondered if he was going to be capable of saying anything much. But after some time his eyes fixed on Leo's.

'This has been so much on my conscience, Mr Davies. If I am going to die, I need to tell you. I am a Catholic, I cannot bear to let this . . .' He breathed heavily, closing his eyes.

'You're not going to die,' said Leo gently. At any rate, he hoped not. In his bowels Leo felt stirrings of fateful apprehension. 'Is this to do with the case?'

'With the *Persephone*, yes,' said Captain Kollias, his voice barely a whisper. 'With the boy.' His face contorted in misery, and large tears squeezed from between his bruised eyelids. 'I did not know he was on board. If I had known he would come back, I would never have done what she asked. Never . . .' Tears rolled down his face and into his moustache.

Leo took a deep breath. He fished in his pocket for a pen. Why was there never paper handy when you needed it most? He glanced around, then crossed the room quickly and opened the door. A nurse was on her way down the corridor.

'Please, I need to write something down. Do you have any paper?'

The girl went to the nurses' station and came back with a notepad. Leo returned to the room and sat down next to Captain Kollias. He leaned close. 'You're talking about Adriana, aren't you? What did she ask you to do? Take it easy, tell me slowly.' Captain Kollias began to speak, and Leo jotted down his words.

'She asked me . . . she asked me to make some accident happen, so the yacht would be destroyed. She wanted to pay me. We talked about it. I said the best way would be a fire. I said I could make it look like an accident.' Captain Kollias stopped, breathing laboriously. Leo waited, pen in hand. He supposed that somewhere, deep in his subconscious, he had been expecting this. Or something like it. For all her charm and loveliness, he had always known the kind of woman Adriana was. He recalled now the single glance which had passed between her and Captain Kollias in court, and understood everything. Everything, that was, except her motive, the reasoning behind such unnecessary mendacity. After a few seconds, Captain Kollias resumed. 'We agreed it would be best to do it when the yacht was in Italy. It was going to be dry-docked. All the crew would be gone, except for Pantazis, and the boy Vasillios . . .' His face contorted again, and fresh tears oozed down his face.

'Pantazis – that's Mr Staveris, the engineer?'

Captain Kollias nodded.

'Did he know what was going to happen?'

'No. He knew nothing.'

'Tell me, as clearly as you can, how the accident, the fire, was arranged. Take your time.'

Captain Kollias nodded. He seemed calmer now that the telling of the tale was underway. 'I had to wait for her to arrange about the paintings first.'

'What paintings?'

'In the yacht, in the main area, she had some very precious paintings. They were in some kind of frame, screwed to the wall . . .' Captain Kollias raised his hands to gesture. 'I had to unscrew them, and she took the paintings away.'

'Where did she take them?'

'I don't know. The yacht was here in England, in a marina in Southampton, two weeks before we were due to sail for Ventetone. She took them away, and then a day, maybe two days later, she brought them back.' He paused for some seconds, struggling for breath. 'She put them back in the frames and I screwed them to the wall again. Then she said it could go ahead. I was paid some money in advance, then I was to receive the rest after it had been done.'

'Did she pay you herself?'

Captain Kollias closed his eyes and rolled his head slowly on the pillow. 'Mr Defereras paid me.'

'How much?'

'Two hundred thousand pounds. A great deal of money. She knew I wanted to retire. I wish now I had not taken it, and that the boy might still be alive . . .' He turned his head on the pillow and wept.

Leo waited. After a few seconds he said gently, 'Tell me how you started the fire.'

Slowly, and with difficulty, Captain Kollias recounted the events of that night in Ventetone, how he had loosened the injector pipe, then run the generator so that the resultant diesel spray would ignite. He had taken the added precaution of collecting some fuel and spilling it in the bilge, and had then thrown in a lighted cigarette end to ensure the fire took hold.

Leo wrote down his words, re-creating the scenario: the loosened fuel pipe, explained away by vibrations created during the grounding incident two weeks earlier; the two different means by which the leaking fuel might have been ignited, either by fuel spraying on to the hot generator or by the idle hand of Pantazis Staveris, engineer and forty-a-day man. He thought ruefully of all those experts who had worked so earnestly, detailing in their reports how very likely it was that the fire was started in one of these ways.

At length Captain Kollias had to stop, his chest rising and falling painfully. Leo read through what he had written down. There it was, in black and white. Adriana had scuttled her own yacht. The paintings destroyed in the fire were copies of originals, and she had claimed the insurance on them, and on the yacht. Why? In her position, why go to such lengths to secure a few million in a fraudulent insurance claim? Perhaps it was simply in the nature of things that people, even people as wealthy as Adriana, should be greedy and petty and conniving. And unlucky.

Captain Kollias gripped Leo's sleeve tightly. When he spoke his voice was low, passionate, broken with misery. 'I swear to God that I would never have done this if I had known the boy was on board! He was supposed to stay with friends that night. When they found his body after, when I realized that if we had searched we might have found him . . . But we could not have known. We could not have known.'

Leo patted his hand – there was no reproach he could make that the man had not already heaped upon himself. Consolation seemed the only natural thing to offer. After a few moments he said, 'You understand the difference this makes to everything? To Miss Papaposilakis's position?'

Captain Kollias closed his eyes wearily. 'I don't care. I tell you so that I can make my peace. I cannot die with this on my conscience.'

Leo suddenly realized with alarm that a patch of red was

seeping swiftly through the layers of bandages covering Captain Kollias's chest. He reached up and stabbed at the red emergency button on the wall above the bed. Within seconds a nurse was in the room, followed by the doctor.

'Mr Kollias is bleeding,' said Leo.

The doctor had already taken over, moving with swift urgency. He and the nurse were dealing with bandages and equipment and monitors as Leo looked on.

After some moments the scene grew calmer. The doctor issued some instructions to the nurse, then came over to Leo.

'Is he all right?' asked Leo.

'For the moment. The strain caused his wound to open. You can't talk to him any more, I'm afraid.'

'No, no, of course. I'm sorry if my visit –' Leo broke off. 'The thing is . . . as I told you, Mr Kollias was a witness in a court case. What he told me today makes a great deal of difference in that case. His evidence is important. How long do you think it will be till he's able to leave hospital?'

'I've no idea. Mr Kollias's condition is still critical, and he's due to have further surgery later today. It's a question of waiting to see how he recovers from that.'

'I see. I'm sorry if my visit has set him back.'

'Don't worry. It would probably have been worse if he hadn't been able to speak to you. He was in quite a state.'

Leo went back to the waiting room. He decided to say nothing to Mrs Kollias about the recent brief drama. She rose anxiously as Leo came into the room.

'Did he talk to you?'

'Yes. Yes, he did.'

'It was important?' Leo could tell from her eyes, her instinctive deference, that she wouldn't think of asking the nature of her husband's private conversation.

'Yes, it was. I'm very glad you rang me. I hope I'll be able to speak to him again, when he's better.'

These last words brought a small smile to her lips. She nodded. Leo pulled out the pen and paper he had been using and jotted down a number. He handed it to Mrs Kollias. 'Here's my mobile number. In case you can't reach me at work. Please, ring me as soon as your husband's well enough to speak to me again.'

On the way back to the City in the taxi, Leo pulled out the notes he had made at Captain Kollias's bedside. He read through them, reflecting on how he was going to play this. It didn't look as though Captain Kollias was going to be up and about any time soon – not before the hearing finished, at any rate – so his evidence would have to be put before the court in a hearsay statement. Before any of that happened, however, Leo would have to deal with Adriana. She was, after all, his client. He was going to have to tell her what Captain Kollias had said, and explain to her that he had a duty to reveal to the court what he had been told.

He rubbed his hands over his face and sighed. Dear God, that part wasn't going to be easy. She wouldn't be the first of Leo's clients to be put in the invidious position of being caught out in a lie. How would she react? If previous clients were anything to go by, she would go ballistic. She would accuse Captain Kollias of having a grudge, of lying for reasons of his own. She would point out that he had already given his evidence, and say that that should be an end of it. Leo, as he was obliged to, would explain to her that he would have to tell the court anyway, and she would doubtless turn on him and accuse him of not doing his best to protect her interests. Clients always liked pulling that one. That would be the usual train of events. Outrage, upset and prevarication – anything but a straightforward admission of the truth –

and then matters would take their course, and that would be the end of the *Persephone* claim. Leo knew, however, that his intimate involvement with Adriana added quite a different dimension to the matter. A most unprofessional one. Adriana might see no need to bluff and bluster. She might simply rely on all that existed between them, and ask him to make it go away. Because that was something he could do. He really could.

Leo gazed out at the traffic. Was there a lawyer born, he wondered, whose first instinct, on being given troublesome fresh information, was not to chuck it straight in the bin? That, he had no doubt, was exactly what Adriana would try to persuade him to do. She knew how close he was to moving from his world to hers. It would seem to her the obvious solution. Forget Captain Kollias had ever told him anything. Let the hearing end without saying a word. If Captain Kollias recovered, the situation could be dealt with without difficulty. With money, probably. A man who believed himself to be dying, with a burning desire to clear his Catholic conscience, was a very different thing from a man recovering from a bad accident and facing the possibility of being charged with giving false evidence. Of course, it would never come to that. Adriana wouldn't let it. She would pay to see that it didn't.

Money. It was what it was all about. Ten million on a fraudulent insurance claim. Why not? It was business, after all. She was a shipowner. It was the way she did things. Second nature. Just as it was second nature to assume that Leo would want part of her wealth, to indulge himself. Working for, or with, Adriana – he could just see it. He would become a second Mr Defereras, making the pay-offs, being involved in all her scams and deals, helping her increase her wealth, and enjoying it with her. That was one thing old

Mr Defereras hadn't done. That was the difference. Leo would live her life, take her money, enjoy the pleasures, and shrug off the lies. What was the big deal? Wasn't much of his personal life conducted on the basis of deceit? He was habitually unfaithful to people he professed to love – Camilla, for instance. Rachel. Anthony. Everyone except for Oliver, the one sacred individual in his wretched life. He confessed himself incapable of fidelity. He had deceived and betrayed on a pretty regular basis. Here was Adriana, offering him a life of wealth and pleasure, on her terms. When she found out what Captain Kollias had told him, that would be the one ultimate term. The easy lie. Not even a lie. Just the option of saying nothing. Where was the difference?

The difference was that, whatever the nature of his personal relationships, he had never lied professionally in his entire career. It had never once crossed his mind. There might be many tainted and corrupt aspects of his life, but work wasn't one of them. Not that he regarded it with any special pride. It was simply an ethic, part of having been a barrister for so many years. He might treat the notion of his responsibilities to other people with amused contempt, but when it came to his duty to the court – that nebulous authority hovering at the back of every lawyer's professional conscience, supreme and unquestioned – he balked. He couldn't do it. Not for the sake of a life of ease and pleasure with Adriana, nor for anything her money could buy. Just as cheating was second nature to Adriana, so it was that Leo knew he had no alternative but to give it all up – Adriana, her case, and any delusions of a life of ease and idleness. Let justice take its course.

And Adriana, when she discovered he was not to be bought? She could, if she wanted, make life quite unpleasant. By becoming involved with her, he had rendered himself vulnerable. A woman who would go so far as to scheme the scuttling of her own yacht, and pursue her false insurance claim even though she had been the instrument of a boy's death, might go to considerable lengths to exact revenge on the person who exposed her. Love, or whatever it was she felt for him, simply wouldn't come into it.

The best way of protecting himself, of course, was to ensure that he wasn't implicated in the disclosure of her fraud. Ideally, he needed to find a way for Adriana to expose it herself. But she had already given her evidence. He pondered this all the way to the Temple, and could find no solution.

By the end of the afternoon, Leo had examined the problem from every angle, but was getting nowhere. At this rate, he was going to have to confront Adriana. Perhaps it would help to talk to Anthony. There was no one else in chambers whom he would sooner trust with the details of his dilemma, and no one else upon whom he would more readily depend to find an intelligent solution. He was going to have to give him a somewhat abridged version of events, making no mention of his intimate involvement with Adriana – he knew from experience how much Anthony detested his libidinous lifestyle, to say nothing of the dim view he would take of his treatment of Camilla.

He was just about to get up from his desk, when the phone rang. It was the surveyor, following up on the weekend's inspection of the foundations at 2 Gratton Crescent.

'Good news about the subsidence. It's not as bad as I thought. In fact, I reckon you could just leave it, not even bother with underpinning.'

'Really? That's a relief,' said Leo. 'So, a clean bill of health?'

'Looks like it. I'll send my report out today.'

Leo rang the estate agent, and by the end of their conversation it had been agreed that contracts could be exchanged over the next few days, and the house would be Leo's by the end of the following week. He put the phone down, reflecting that the timing was fortuitous, since Camilla would be home at the weekend. Would she be pleased? He had no idea. For some reason her enthusiasm for the house had never been as great as his. At any rate, he could set about creating something more like a real home for Oliver. Given the indecisive state of Rachel and Charles's relationship at the moment, that might be just as well. This brought Anthony to mind, and the problem he had been about to put to him just before the phone rang. He got up and went downstairs to Anthony's room. He knocked on the door and looked in.

'Busy?'

'Just about to knock off.'

'Can I talk to you?'

'Sure.'

Leo closed the door and paced around the room for a few seconds, hands in pockets. Anthony watched him, conscious of the acute pleasure that Leo's presence always brought, even when he looked grim-faced and thoughtful, as he did now. It somehow eased his spirit just to see Leo's face and form.

'Some problem?'

'It should be straightforward, but it's not.' Leo sat down, picking up a couple of paperclips from Anthony's desk and twisting them. 'The *Persephone* hearing's almost over, it looks like we'll get judgment in our favour, and today I found out that my wonderful client has been lying all along.'

'The Papaposilakis woman?'

Leo nodded. 'She scuttled her own yacht. Paid the master to start the fire on board.'

'She told you this?'

'Hardly.' Leo explained the circumstances of Captain Kollias's accident, and subsequent events at the hospital.

'Hmm. Not a happy situation.' Anthony leaned back in his chair and clasped his hands behind his head. 'But it's not the first time it's happened to you. Wasn't there that mad Pakistani who doctored the log books in his speed and consumption claim a couple of years back? You just grit your teeth and confront her, tell her you have an obligation to the court, and so forth.'

'Normally, I would. In this case, I'd rather not.'

'Why?'

'She's a volatile creature. Frankly, I'd rather not be the instrument of her downfall, to put it in dramatic terms. I've had quite enough of Greek women turning their wrath on me. I want her exposed, but I'd rather it came from some other angle.'

Anthony pondered this. 'Well, you could always get Rachel to take a statement from the master, and maybe then *she* could speak to the Silakis woman –'

'Hold on a moment,' said Leo. His mobile had begun to ring. He took it from his pocket and answered it. He listened for a few moments, then said, 'I see. I really am so sorry. Thank you for letting me know . . . Yes – yes, I'm glad I had the chance to speak to him. Thank you, Mrs Kollias. I really am very sorry.' He clicked the phone off and looked up at Anthony. 'It sounded like you had the beginnings of a good idea there. But unfortunately that was Captain Kollias's wife. He died a short time ago.'

'Well . . . That's that, then. It's down to you.'

Leo sat in gloomy silence for some moments. 'I suppose I could simply seek not to rely on Captain Kollias's evidence when I make my submissions . . .' He sighed. 'No, that's not going to work, either.'

'You could always ask Rachel to do the dirty deed for you, anyway.'

'How do I explain that away? The woman's my client, after all. I'm going to have to give this some more thought.' Leo stood up. 'This is between you and me, by the way. I'd rather Rachel didn't know until I've sorted it out in my mind.'

Anthony nodded. 'Fine.'

'Speaking of Rachel, how are things between you two?'

Anthony hesitated. It was inevitable, he supposed, that Leo should be interested.

'Fine,' he said.

'I saw you together in Bewley's at lunchtime.'

'Did you?' Anthony watched Leo pace the carpet, wondering what was coming next.

'It's getting serious, isn't it?'

'Look, I'd really rather not −'

'I know. You'd rather not discuss it with me. You don't think it's any of my business. But technically, it is. She's the mother of my son. What happens in her life affects Oliver. What I really want to know is whether this is going to cause a bust-up with Charles.'

Anthony sat in silence for some moments. Leo was right. 'Yes,' he said at last. 'He's coming home tomorrow. She's going to tell him.'

Leo nodded. 'And then?'

'I don't know. I honestly don't know.'

'Well, let me know when you do. I need to know what's happening in my son's life.'

Anthony gazed at Leo. He was evidently angry, but Anthony wasn't quite sure why. Leo certainly didn't love Rachel, so it couldn't be jealousy on his part. Then again, on some subtle level, perhaps it was. Perhaps it was simply that he didn't like two people to whom he had been so close becoming intimate, excluding him. With Leo, one could never be sure what was going on. Anthony spoke evenly. 'I imagine Rachel will let you know everything you need to know when she decides to.'

'Fine. Good. I'll let you get on. Thanks for the chat.'

'Any time.'

14

Sarah's flatmate, Lou, was sitting in her bathrobe by the open window, running her fingers idly through her damp hair and sipping a mug of coffee. She glanced over her shoulder at Sarah, who was sitting at the kitchen table reading the paper.

'So are you going to come or not?'

Sarah shrugged. 'Maybe.'

'You might as well, since you don't seem to be seeing that weirdo Rupert any more.' She swallowed the remains of her coffee. 'Thank God.'

'Roger.'

'Whatever.' Lou went to the sink to rinse her mug. 'Anyway, you'll be missing a good party if you don't come.'

'I said I might.'

'Well, get your act together if you *are* coming. I'm going in half an hour.' She went through to her bedroom to get changed.

Sarah closed the paper. She resented Lou calling Roger a weirdo. She'd only met him once. He wasn't weird at all. In fact, compared to everyone else, with their hang-ups and obsessions, he was remarkably sane. She wished he would ring. He'd been at an arbitration all week, and so she hadn't seen him around chambers, but each day she'd expected him to call to apologize, or to come to her room at the end of the day to suggest a drink, the way he used to. Nothing. Not a word. Okay, she was fine with that. The relationship had probably been on its way out, anyway. In her experience, as soon as someone said they loved you, things got boring. So it was just as well. She might as well go and find something to wear to this party.

Roger lay on his bed in his T-shirt and jeans, barefoot, listening to some moody Oscar Peterson and thinking about Sarah. He gazed up through the skylight window, letting his mind dwell on her features, her lovely body, that trick she had of smiling and glancing sideways, flicking her blonde hair over one shoulder . . . It was his theory that if he did it often enough, that sensation of pain, like a hot wire, would dull eventually.

Maybe he'd been wrong from the beginning. Wrong in thinking that beneath those defences lay a vulnerable, uncertain girl, much in need of love. Perhaps it had been a mistake to think he had touched her enough to make her admit her own pretensions. She didn't want to admit them. She didn't want to be touched. She wanted to stay safely in her world of easy seduction, of soft and cynical options, of material things and people. Okay. But still . . . she had her pride. Not a good thing to have dented it. He should call her. Saturday night, and they could so easily have been here together, on his bed, like those other times. He reached out for the phone, then stopped. It was up to her. She could come back if she wanted. If he had been right, and she was in love with him – if everything he read in her eyes and her smile was true – then she would simply turn up on the doorstep. Things that were meant to happen had a habit of happening. That was what he believed. He closed his eyes.

Three hours later, dressed in her slinky Anna Sui number and her newest and absolutely favourite Jimmy Choos, Sarah was beginning to wonder why she'd bothered. She'd been standing here talking to – no, listening to – this banker in his hand-pressed Levis for what seemed like an age. She should have known by now how deceptive the promise of a party could be. Here they were – the same old Sloaney faces, the same predatory glances, the same old blah-de-blah. If Roger had been here, he wouldn't have been able to stand this bunch of fakes for five minutes . . . She took another slug of white wine, annoyed that he had slipped into her thoughts. The trouble was, being with Roger was one hell of a sight more amusing than being with this lot. She realized she was beginning to feel a little drunk; she'd lost count of the number of glasses of wine she'd had – three? Four? She sighed inwardly and adjusted the smile on her face as she pretended to listen to whatever this jerk in the jeans was saying to her. Then she glanced across the room and saw, with stomach-tightening pleasure, Marcus, in a black open-necked shirt and looking like sex on legs, standing aloof and sultry at the edge of the room. When had he arrived?

'. . . so I've spent ten thousand on the renovations, and netted a fifteen-thousand profit, which isn't bad going. Of course, you have to be a good judge of an area.' The banker felt he was making pretty good headway here. 'So tell me, whereabouts do you live?'

'I'm sorry,' said Sarah with a cool smile, 'I've just seen a friend. Would you excuse me?' She drifted off, leaving the nonplussed banker in her wake.

Marcus saw her coming.

'Well, well.' He bent his head to kiss her cheek lightly. God, thought Sarah, he smelled fantastic. Marcus looked her up and down with a considering smile. 'May I say you look very lovely out of context? Chambers, that is.'

'Thank you.' In that moment, with Marcus's slow-burning smile directed at her, Sarah felt radiantly sexy.

'So –' Marcus cast a lazy glance round the room '– this

all looks incredibly tedious. How many of these people do you know?'

Such fabulous arrogance couldn't work on anyone else, thought Sarah. 'A few. But you're right. It is fantastically dull, so far.'

They stood talking for a while, Sarah doing her best to maintain a semblance of cool. Someone refilled her glass; she scarcely noticed. Marcus, as he talked and sipped his drink, watched her with veiled amusement. She was working so hard to try to appear composed and serene, to conceal her availability. Availability so potent, it was like a scent. She'd been giving off exactly the same signals at that deathly chambers cocktail party a few weeks ago. What had got in the way that night? Anyway, she was certainly unfinished business. He could give this party half an hour or so, see what else turned up, or he could simply save himself the bother and make the most of this opportunity.

He glanced round again, then back at her. 'I thought I might regret coming here this evening.'

'And now?'

He reached out a hand and touched the necklace at her throat. 'Now it's all beginning to seem worthwhile. But I'd still rather get out of here.' His finger strayed to her collarbone and stroked it lightly. 'Wouldn't you?'

Certainly a fast worker, thought Sarah. Not that she minded. Just the touch of him sent little currents of desire through her body. She raised her eyebrows nonchalantly. 'I don't mind.'

'Good,' murmured Marcus. 'Let's go.'

When the night air hit her, Sarah realized she'd probably drunk more than she should have. But she was fine, really. Just right, in fact. She felt a delightful, tipsy shiver of anticipation. She glanced at Marcus, who walked silently next to her, and for an uneasy moment had the impression that he was momentarily oblivious of her presence. She had no sense of connection. Still, she certainly intended to make one.

'My car's round the corner,' said Marcus.

'You drove?'

'Of course.' They stopped, and he opened the door of his sleek Alfa Romeo. 'Taxis really aren't my style. I make it a rule never to have more than one drink at any party.'

They drove through the night in the direction of Docklands. Sarah made a couple of remarks by way of conversation, but Marcus's offhand replies suggested his mind was elsewhere. Sarah gave up and lay back, tipsily contented.

Eventually Marcus pulled up in front of electronic gates, which swung back. He drove into the forecourt of a block of converted riverside warehouse flats, and parked.

'I didn't realize you lived by the river,' said Sarah. The silent drive had made her feel languid. Marcus said nothing. He got out and opened the door for her.

'It's terribly quiet round here,' said Sarah, as they walked to the lift. It only now occurred to her that Marcus hadn't even asked her if she wanted to go back to his place.

'I like it that way,' said Marcus. He pressed the lift button. The lift hummed down and the doors opened. 'I never see my neighbours, which is perfect. I could have bought a place in the Barbican,' he added, 'but that's so yesterday.' Sarah almost laughed.

They stepped out of the lift and crossed the hallway. Marcus slipped a key into his door and gestured for her to go in, flicking a couple of switches.

The flat was one enormous loft space, furnished in minimalist style. Discreetly angled lamps and mirrors cast a glow on the burnished wood floor. Large windows looked out on the panorama of the river, a vista of buildings darkly silhouetted against the London sky, twinkling with lights.

'Drink?' Marcus opened a drinks cabinet of wood and steel and took out a couple of glasses.

'I think I've probably had enough,' said Sarah. She crossed to the window and looked out.

Marcus, on his way to the fridge in the kitchen and dining area, paused to drop a kiss on the back of her neck. Sarah shivered with pleasure. 'Baby,' he murmured, 'we've only just started.'

He hit the ice maker, and chunks tumbled into the glasses. From the freezer he took a bottle of Smirnoff Blue Label and poured out drinks. He handed one to Sarah. She sipped, and felt the icy, sexy touch of the vodka at the back of her throat. Marcus's eyes were on her face. He smiled.

'Come with me.'

She followed him across the room to the far end of the loft, past a sound system and long rows of bookshelves, to his sleeping area. Again he flicked a couple of switches. The bed was vast, bathed in low light. The sheets and pillows were black. Again Sarah stifled the urge to laugh. She glanced around, taking another swallow of her drink. It ran through her limbs like fire. Was there something vaguely ridiculous about all this, or was that just the effect of everything she'd had to drink?

Marcus moved in front of her, touching her throat lightly with his hands, and kissed her. Sarah was surprised at the suddenness of it, but was too aroused and drunk to care. She opened her mouth to his, and immediately felt his hands on her body, insistent, practised, working at the fastening of her dress. Talk about cutting to the chase, thought Sarah through a haze of lust. They'd hardly even spoken since leaving the party, and already he was all over her. Not that she cared. She'd wanted this one for months, and now he was all hers.

Only it wasn't like that at all. It was as though she had almost nothing to do with everything that happened next. In minutes her clothes were on the floor, then his, and their bodies were intertwined on the bed, little gasps and moans of desire stippling the air. But even as he took her, she felt no connection, nothing at all. Even the beauty of his slick, dark skin moving against her own seemed to possess a fake sensuality. Never had she been made love to with such detachment, by a man immersed only in his own pleasure, barely conscious of her existence beyond the fact and availability of her body.

And yet she let it happen. Time passed, and she let him do all that he wanted, feeling throughout as though she were locked away from whatever passionless motives directed his urgent lovemaking. She didn't know this man. She'd thought she wanted him, and she didn't even know him. Such pleasure as there was seemed utterly remote.

'No,' she moaned at last. She lay on her belly, Marcus behind and on top of her. He was breathing deeply and slowly, spent, but still ready to go on. 'Don't. I don't want that.'

Marcus sat up on his haunches. The low light bathed his dark skin. He ran his hands briefly, impartially, over the smooth swell of her buttocks, and climbed off. Sarah lay with her cheek pressed against the pillow. She heard the snap of a discarded condom. Marcus padded to a closet, took out a robe, and slipped it on. He came back to the bed. She thought he might lie down next to her, say something, but he merely picked up his drink and walked across the room.

She rolled on to her side, pushing her hair back from her face. Marcus had settled himself on a long leather sofa some yards away. He sipped his drink, and picked up a remote. Blue light bathed the area where he sat. She could see his perfect profile. He was watching television. The bastard was watching television.

Moments passed. At last she spoke. 'Marcus.'

'What?' He flicked the remote and changed the channel without turning to look at her.

Sarah put her feet on the floor. She picked up her dress and slipped it on, then her knickers. She picked up her Jimmy Choos and walked across to where he sat.

'Is this the way the evening goes?'

'Goes?' He glanced up at her, then back at the television.

She sat down next to him, but not near him. 'I mean, isn't there something . . .' she tried to laugh, but it didn't quite work. Her throat felt a little thick from the alcohol and the recent exertion '. . . something rather impersonal about all this?'

He looked at her, his face a mask of beautiful indifference. He sighed. It was a sigh of boredom. 'Darling Sarah, you got what you wanted. So far as I could tell.' She sat very still. Humiliation pooled within her, numbing her. 'Do you need a taxi?' he asked.

It took a moment for her mind to clear. Her presence here was evidently no more than an unwelcome intrusion. She had served her purpose, and now he would like to be rid of her. Well, what more had she expected? Wasn't it true? Hadn't she got what she'd come for? Through her vestigial drunkenness, she felt a sudden, suffocating sense of shame.

'You're not going to run me home?' She couldn't believe she'd said that. The last thing she wanted was for him to run her home, like some clapped-out tart for whom one had to do the decent thing, whether one liked it or not.

He sighed again in irritation. 'It would be less trouble all round if you took a cab.' He got up, pulling his robe around him, and picked up the phone, stabbing at the buttons. Sarah, dazed, hardly listened as he ordered the taxi, gave the address. He sat down again and picked up the remote. 'It'll be about fifteen minutes. Make yourself another drink, if you like.'

Sarah cast around for something to say or do to salvage her dignity. She felt utterly abased, almost as though she'd been raped. The possibility played briefly in her fuddled mind, then fell away. After a few moments her eyes strayed to the television. It was something to do with Louis Theroux. Blankly she stared at the bespectacled, clever, baffled face on the screen, and thought of Roger. She felt she might cry. She bent down and put her shoes on. For something to do, she went back to the bed and picked up her vodka glass from the bedside table. She stared at the oily remains of the vodka, the sliver of melting ice, then at the rumpled bed, the stupid black sheets and pillows.

She sat down on the edge of the bed and waited. Disjointed voices came from the television. At one point Marcus sniggered. She looked up. He was immersed. She might as well not exist. Her glance strayed around the room. She saw briefs and neatly stacked documents lying on a long lacquered table, evidence of his industrious practice. Everything around her seemed to reinforce her superfluity.

She thought of going downstairs to wait. What dignity would that salvage? She felt so tired. She ached from so much sex. A longing for comfort, for Roger, welled up inside her. She had to steel herself not to cry.

After an age, the bell to Marcus's apartment buzzed. She got up and crossed the long room.

For the first time in twenty minutes, Marcus looked at her. 'Do you need any money?' he asked.

Sarah said nothing. She left the flat and went down to the waiting cab.

*

279

That Monday morning Sandy was due to turn up especially early at the shop, around seven. Ankit, Mrs Deepak's son, had to be in Birmingham and wouldn't be able to do the papers. Mrs Deepak had asked Sandy if he would help out, and he'd said yes. He'd even mentioned it to Felicity over the weekend. But when Felicity got up a little before eight on Monday, she could see no evidence that Sandy was up. His bedroom door was still closed. She knocked on it.

'Sandy? Sandy, d'you know what the time is?'

There was some muffled response, which Felicity couldn't make out. She opened the door and looked in. The curtains were still drawn, and Sandy lay hunched on the bed under his duvet. The floor of the room was strewn with sheets of paper covered in writing. In the stale air hung the unmistakable smell of dope. Several spent spliffs lay in an ashtray on the rug.

'Oh, Sandy . . . Come on, you can't let Mrs Deepak down!' She shook the lumpen figure under the duvet, and Sandy rolled over, blinking his eyes. Deep shadows were etched beneath them, and his hair stuck up in spikes.

'I can't. I can't go out.'

'Come on, Sandy – she's relying on you! If you get up now, you'll still be –'

'I can't go out, Fliss. They'll get me. It's not a joke.' His voice shook with anxiety.

Felicity looked into his eyes. She felt a strange, sinking feeling inside. 'Who will? Who's going to get you?'

'There are people out there, Fliss, who have guns. They have weapons. They want me. They're after me.' He looked and sounded like a small boy. His voice held clear conviction.

'Sandy, no one's after you. Oh, God . . .' Felicity ran her fingers through her hair. She was beginning to feel shaky. 'Sandy, I think you need to see someone. A doctor. All this dope you've been doing is giving you strange ideas.'

'They're real. They're so real. You just don't know.' He curled the duvet round himself and lay back down.

Felicity sighed. 'Look, I can take the morning off. I'll see if I can get you an appointment with the doctor. I'll say it's urgent.' She laid a hand on his shoulder. He didn't move. 'Sandy, I think it's for the best.'

'I'm not going out, Fliss. You think I'm mad, but I'm not. They'll get me. I'm staying here.' His voice was muffled by the duvet.

Felicity took a deep breath. 'Then I'll get the doctor to come here.' Sandy said nothing. She glanced at her watch. The surgery would be open in five minutes.

She stood up and went to the kitchen to make some tea. Then she rang the surgery and asked if the doctor could make a house visit. No, she was told, no house visits until after 6 p.m. If it was an extreme emergency, she should ring for an ambulance or take the person to casualty. Felicity hung up. It seemed there was little she could do immediately. She chewed her thumbnail anxiously. It wasn't as though he was really unwell, apart from his strange paranoia. He seemed unlikely to leave his room today, not in his present frame of mind, so he couldn't come to any harm. And she had so much on at work . . . She would leave him for the moment, see how he was when she got home, and then call out the doctor if she had to.

She went back through to Sandy's room. 'I can't get anyone to come and see you. Not right away.'

'I don't want anyone to see me!'

Felicity sighed. 'I have to go to work. I'll drop in on Mrs Deepak on the way and tell her you're not feeling well. We'll see how you are this evening. For God's sake, don't take any more dope or pills.' Sandy said nothing. 'Will you be all right?' added Felicity anxiously.

It was some seconds before Sandy answered, 'Yeah.'

Apart from the stuff about people being out to get him, Felicity didn't think he sounded too out of it. But he clearly needed some kind of help. Just when she'd thought he might be getting his act together, this had to happen. She sighed wearily, and went to get ready for work, closing his door gently behind her.

Anthony desperately wanted to know how things had gone between Rachel and Charles. He found it impossible to concentrate on work, and several times throughout the morning he was on the brink of calling her. Each time he dismissed the idea, telling himself he would have to wait for her to call him, as she'd said she would.

When at last his private line rang at half past twelve, he snatched up the phone.

'Hello,' said Rachel. 'It's me.'

'How are you?'

'Oh . . . so-so. Tired.'

'Did you speak to Charles?'

Yes.'

'And?'

'I don't really want to talk about it on the phone.'

'Can we meet for lunch?'

'Yes. I won't have long, though. I have a client coming in at two. Can you come up here?'

'Of course.' Anthony glanced at his watch. 'I'll set off now.' He hesitated. He needed to get some faint idea of how things had gone. 'How did he take it? I mean, just briefly.'

'Briefly? It was awful. I don't think he quite accepts it. He's so . . .' She broke off. 'Oh, Anthony, can we talk about it when I see you? It's making me too upset.'

'All right. Sorry. I'll be with you shortly.' He hung up, put on his jacket, and went downstairs.

Leo was on his way into chambers, having come from a long morning at the *Persephone* hearing, and met Anthony just as he was crossing Caper Court. Anthony greeted him hastily in passing. Leo glanced after him. He had a good idea where Anthony was hurrying off to. It had been evident from his manner during their conversation last Friday evening that his relationship with Rachel had reached some kind of critical juncture. Very likely Charles had now been told, and Anthony was about to find out how matters stood. Strange, thought Leo, to be on the outside looking in. Whatever was going on between Rachel and Anthony affected him, but was at the same time entirely remote from him. He wondered, as he mounted the steps to chambers, when he would be told of whatever changes were about to take place in Oliver's life.

He went into the clerks' room, fished his mail from his pigeon-hole, and went back out through reception. Sarah was coming downstairs. She passed Leo and murmured hello.

'Hey,' said Leo. He paused at the foot of the stairs. Sarah turned to look at him. 'Come on,' said Leo. 'Upstairs.'

Sarah followed Leo up to his room. Leo opened the door. Sarah went in, and Leo closed the door behind him. Sarah leaned against a bookcase.

Leo chucked his letters on to the desk. He put his hands in his pockets and regarded her closely. He'd seen Sarah in every variety of mood, including the filthiest of tempers, but never had he seen her so lacking in essential life and warmth. 'So – what's wrong?'

'Nothing. I had a bad weekend.'

'D'you want to tell me about it?'

Sarah gazed at Leo, at the chiselled features so handsome above the white bands and starched collar of his court attire, the silver hair brushed back from his temples, the intense blue of his eyes as he studied her face. He was probably the one person in all the world who possessed the clearest understanding of everything about her, but she believed the state of her feelings at present was beyond even his sympathy.

'Not really. I had a mildly abasing experience at the weekend, that's all.' She paused for a moment, then, with an effort at her customary coolness, added, 'I imagine you think that's nothing new for me, but this one left a particularly bad taste in the mouth.'

'Was it to do with Roger?'

She shook her head, and found her eyes filling with tears. God, the one thing she had never done was cry in front of Leo. She took a deep breath in an effort to stem her tears, but her voice shook when she spoke. 'I've been a bit stupid where Roger's concerned. I think I rather underestimated him.'

'A lot of people do.'

She brushed her eyes with the back of her hand. 'Anyway, it's nothing to do with him. Well, not directly. If you must know, I got a bit drunk at a party, and I had a one-night stand with Marcus – not the pleasantest of experiences – and I'm feeling pretty hellish about it.' She steadied her voice. 'I don't expect your sympathy. You'd probably say it's just the kind of thing I normally do, but I just wish . . . I just wish, for once, that I'd –' She broke off, dipping her head to hide her misery.

Leo gazed at her reflectively. 'Well, at least you're contrite. Which, for you, is something of a novelty. But we all do things we live to regret. Believe me, I know. Don't give yourself such a hard time. Roger doesn't have to know. I abide by the belief that what people don't know needn't hurt them.'

In spite of her tears, Sarah managed a wobbly, challenging smile. 'You wouldn't by any chance be referring to Camilla and the small matter of Miss Papaposilakis, would you?'

Nothing like being comradely in misfortune, thought Leo. 'Let's just say that I've always been too easily tempted for my own good. As regards our relative situations, I'd say you and I would both do well to treat discretion as the better part of valour – don't you think?'

'The thing with Marcus ... I suppose I did it partly because I had a bust-up with Roger last weekend, and he hasn't been near me since.'

'Whatever your argument was about, I suppose it goes without saying that you were in the right?'

'No. Since you ask, I wasn't. I thought I was, but I realize everything he said about me was quite correct.'

Well, well, thought Leo in surprise. Someone had actually managed to chasten the audacious Miss Coleman. And Roger Fry, of all people. 'In which case, you should apologize, instead of standing here feeling wretched. And forget about your aberration with Marcus Jacobs. Think of all the other deplorable things you've done – many of them with me, I might add – and learn from your mistakes.'

Sarah gave a weak smile. 'Good old Uncle Leo.'

'Ever ready with a sympathetic ear. Go on, I have some things to do before I go back to court.'

Sarah sniffed and rubbed her nose with her finger, feeling better. 'How's your case going?'

'Well, let's just say that I don't think it's going to turn out quite as everyone expects.'

'Sounds exciting.'

'As exciting as insurance claims get.' He watched her go, pleased that she looked rather less forlorn. For a moment he felt almost fatherly – not something he'd ever thought he

285

would feel where Sarah was concerned. Then he sat down and picked up the phone, preparing to draw up a list of all the colour copying firms in the port of Southampton.

Anthony paced around the reception area of Nichols and Co., waiting for Rachel. At last she emerged from the lift. The sight of her lifted his heart. She looked, he thought, a little paler and more drawn than usual, but the smile she gave when she saw him seemed to light her from within.

'I'm not particularly hungry,' said Rachel, as they stepped out into the sunshine of Bishopsgate. 'I'd rather just go somewhere and talk, if that's all right.'

'Fine,' said Anthony. 'We don't have long, anyway. I can always pick up a sandwich on the way back to chambers.'

They walked along the pavement to St Botolph's Church and into the gardens, where office workers sprawled on the grass with their lunch. Rachel and Anthony found a quiet spot and sat down on the grass.

'So,' said Anthony, 'tell me everything that happened.'

Rachel sighed. 'I didn't actually tell him until Sunday. When he got in from Gatwick on Saturday morning he was shattered, so he went to bed for a few hours. When he got up, Oliver was around. Charles seemed in such a good mood . . . I just couldn't face telling him. I knew Oliver was going to a party the next day, so I decided I'd wait till then.'

'And?'

'We were sitting in the garden, and I told him. I said I realized I wasn't in love with him any more. I didn't tell him I hadn't ever been, not really. I tried to keep it simple. I told him I'd met someone else.' She put a hand over her face. 'It was just awful. I knew he wouldn't blow his top. Charles isn't like that. He just sat there with the Sunday paper on his lap, looking . . . looking *stricken*. I told him how sorry I was, and how I hadn't meant it to happen, that it just had. I was talking and talking, and when I looked at him again, the expression on his face was . . . sort of . . . unhappy and contained all at once, as though he was determined to stay in control. I thought I knew what was coming. I thought he was going to say it was something we could sort out, that he blamed his assignment in the States, that he should never have left me . . .'

'What did he say?'

'The last thing in the world I expected, really.' Rachel plucked at the grass, her face sad. 'He said – I don't remember his exact words . . . something like . . . "When you said you weren't in love with me any more, I thought you were going to tell me you were going back to Leo."'

'Why would he think that?' asked Anthony, genuinely astonished.

She shook her head. 'I don't know. Anyway, I told him it had nothing to do with Leo. I think I was a little angry. Maybe because I wanted *him* to be angry with *me* . . . He had every reason. But that's not Charles's way. Still, he managed to make me feel pretty dreadful. Which at least is what I deserved. He said that he'd always had the idea I might fall in love with someone, that he'd known I didn't love him in the way he loved me, that he'd wondered how long it would take . . .' She rubbed the plucked blades of grass between her fingers. 'Which was my cue to say that of course I loved him. Which I do. Just not –' She broke off, shrugging her shoulders.

'So, did you discuss moving out?'

'God, no! He asked who it was, so I told him. I thought he might not remember you, but he did. Then we sat in this long, miserable silence for what seemed like for ever. I couldn't think of anything to say. And after a bit he said he was going to have to think about it all for a while, that it was one hell of a shock. He must have been angry, but with Charles that's always . . . Well, it comes out in a sort of awful despair. Moodiness. He got up and went into the house. I didn't know what to do. I'd said it all. It's strange, the way situations never play out the way you think they will. An hour later he went off and picked up Oliver from the party, and the rest of the day was like conducting a kind of ritual. Quite miserable, but normal, if you know what I mean. We half avoided one another, but the usual domestic pattern continued. He went to do some work, I went to bed. I was asleep when he came to bed.' She sighed. 'Then this morning was a frantic rush, as Mondays always are, trying to get myself ready and Oliver fed . . .' She shrugged. 'That's pretty much where things stand.'

Anthony was silent for a few seconds, then said, 'Don't you think you should have told him you couldn't stay with him any more? That would seem the sensible thing. To settle things.'

So far Rachel had recounted the events of the weekend while staring down at the grass, her long hair hiding her face. Now she turned to look at Anthony. 'It's not that simple. I wish it were. I have to wait for him to – to say whatever he has to say about the situation.'

'Why? You know what you want. Why wait? Why not just say you can't go on living with him?'

'Because . . . oh, because I feel so guilty! When I think what I owe Charles . . . He has done so, so much for me and Oliver. When things reached breaking point with Leo, he was a true friend. I was at rock bottom, Leo had just destroyed my world, and Charles was so . . . *decent*. He was funny and kind and he offered to look after me.'

'He was in love with you. He had his motives.'

'Possibly. But the point is, I took advantage of him. Of his good nature. All the time I've been living with him, Anthony, I've known I wasn't in love with him. I thought there would never be anyone after Leo. I stayed with Charles because he made me feel safe and wanted, and because I thought . . . well, maybe this is as good as it gets. How selfish was that?'

'Okay, I see all that. You're grateful for what he did, and now you feel guilty as hell. But what exactly is it that you think you owe him?'

Rachel was silent for a while. 'Time. I think I have to give him the chance to do this his way. He must know, from everything I said, that we can't stay together. But let him be the one to say it, that we should split up. Everyone has their pride. I'm prepared to wait for Charles to make this his decision.'

'And if he doesn't?'

'Then – fine, I'll have to take the initiative. But . . . you know, I don't think you have any real idea how hard this is going to be for me and Oliver. Oliver especially. His little life is just rolling along, he has his nanny, his toys, his friends, his world . . . He's just started at nursery school . . .'

'It has to happen. You know I've always said you can move in with me.'

'I know. But is that really what I should do? Just move from one man's house to another's?'

'It would be temporary. We'll find somewhere together.'

'Oh, Anthony, it's just been the worst two days. I wish I had a more positive idea about what happens next, believe me.'

'You do know. It might take a few days, a few weeks, but you have to leave him.'

Rachel leaned against Anthony and sighed. 'Yes. But let Charles do it his way. It's the least I owe him.'

Camilla was having lunch at a harbourside restaurant with Bob Morris, one of the partners in the Bermudan law firm where she had been working for three weeks.

'You've done a very efficient job,' said Bob. 'I didn't think we'd have it wrapped up this quickly.'

'Thanks,' said Camilla. 'I've really enjoyed being here. But it'll be nice to get back. I thought I'd be here till the weekend, at least.'

'I'll have Marsha check on flights when we get back to the office.' Bob sipped his coffee and smiled. 'Young Gordon's going to be inconsolable for the next few weeks. You made something of an impression there, I think.'

'He's very sweet. And he's been so helpful.' She thought longingly of Leo. Just twenty-four hours and she'd be with him again. Should she ring and tell him she was coming home early, or should she surprise him?

Bob signalled to the waiter for the bill. 'Come on. Let's head back to the office and see about your flight.'

Some time later Bob came to Camilla's office, where she was putting her files together.

'Right, here are the options. There's a flight tomorrow morning at half eight, with a stop-over in New York, which gets you into Heathrow at nine in the evening. Or you can take a direct flight tomorrow evening at half seven, gets in at eight-thirty the next morning your time.'

Camilla reflected. The evening flight would be quicker, and she could have a sleep on the plane. The disadvantage was that she wouldn't get to Belgravia until after half past nine the next morning, by which time Leo would have gone to work. If she got the flight tomorrow morning, she'd be home by late evening. Even if Leo was going out for the evening, she'd be there when he got back, and she could surprise him that way.

'I'll take the one with the New York stopover,' she said.

'Sure?' asked Bob. 'Okay, we'll get that booked for you.'

Felicity came home that evening to find the flat empty. She felt a curious mixture of alarm and relief. On the one hand, it was good that Sandy felt he could go out without being pursued by nameless enemies with weapons, but on the other, she would rather know where he was and what he was doing. She hadn't left him in a stable frame of mind. She went into his room and tidied the bed, opened the window, and started to gather up the sheets of paper which littered the floor. She paused to read them, and the contents weren't encouraging. Stream of consciousness stuff about world forces, sinister designs, the enemy closing in, a good deal of underlining and the occasional word – DESTINY! ESCAPE! – written in heavy, bold letters. She sighed. She had intended to go out this evening with Peter, but she'd have to call it off. She had to be here if and when Sandy came back, and try to sort out the best thing to do with him.

She rang Peter on his mobile and told him she couldn't see him. 'Sandy's gone out somewhere. I have to be here when he gets back, to make sure he's all right.'

'Oh, for God's sake, Fliss. You're not his nanny. Is this the way things are going to be? He goes out for the evening and you drop everything to wait in for him? What the hell am I meant to do?'

'There's no point in getting upset, Peter. I'm staying in, that's all. He was really paranoid this morning. I'm worried about him.'

'He's a waste of time. He's got a drug problem, and you're

making it your problem instead of kicking him out. Which is what I'd do.'

'Yeah, well – he's not your brother, is he? Thanks for being so supportive. You don't care about anyone except yourself.'

'Why should I care about your brother? He's messing up your life, but I don't see why he should mess up mine.'

'It's only one evening, for heaven's sake! Anyway, if you were that bothered, you'd have offered to come round and spend the evening here with me.'

'Oh, right, and have to share the delightful domestic scene when your brother eventually comes home pissed, or stoned, or whatever. No thanks.'

Felicity sighed. 'Fine. Whatever. I'm staying here. I'll see you tomorrow.'

She hung up.

Around midnight, she gave up and went to bed. Three hours later, she was woken by the sound of Sandy coming in. Bleary-eyed, she got up and went through to his room.

'Where the hell have you been? D'you realize I've spent the evening waiting in, because I was so worried about you?'

Sandy sat down on the edge of his bed and tugged off his denim jacket. 'Why?'

'Why? Because you were raving like a lunatic this morning, and because I don't know what's going on! One minute you say you can't go out because the streets are full of people out to get you, and the next you're not here! I mean, what am I meant to think?'

'I don't care,' said Sandy sullenly, taking off his socks and trainers. 'You're not really bothered about me, Fliss. If you were, you'd know the kind of danger I'm in. The kind of danger we're all in.'

'Oh, for God's sake, I've had enough! You've already ruined my evening. And you haven't even said sorry.'

Sandy pulled off his jeans, dumped them on the floor on top of his trainers and socks, and got into bed in his T-shirt and underpants, pulling the duvet round his shoulders. He lay motionless, saying nothing. Felicity, seeing there was no more to be said or done, left the room and went to bed. She had no idea what the next day would bring.

15

Before going to court the following morning, Leo went through to the annexe and knocked on Ann Halliday's door.

'I thought I might catch you before you went to court. Can I have a word?'

'Of course.'

Leo closed the door. He drew a piece of paper from his pocket and laid it on the desk in front of her. 'A couple of things you may wish to consider in relation to our case.' Ann looked at the piece of paper and saw an address written there, together with a couple of dates. 'Now, without wishing to seem too mysterious, I think that you may find it useful to make certain enquiries at that address regarding two drawings – "Woman Bathing" and "The Circus Troupe", both by Degas. I've written the names down, but I think you're already familiar with them.'

'They're the pictures from the *Persephone*. The ones destroyed in the fire.'

'Indeed.' There was a long pause. 'Right,' said Leo with a smile, 'I'll see you in court shortly. By the way –' he paused in the doorway '– are you busy on Saturday?' It had occurred to him that since Camilla wasn't due back till Sunday, he might as well ask Ann if she'd like to go with him to the Treeveses' party. She would probably enjoy it for all the reasons that Camilla wouldn't.

'No. Why?'

Leo told her about the Treeveses' invitation. 'I thought it might be the kind of thing you'd like.'

Ann smiled, filling up with pleasure at the prospect. 'Yes, I'd love to come. Thank you.'

'Good. We can discuss the details later.'

He went out. Ann stood reflecting for a moment, still smiling. Then she turned her attention again to the piece of paper. After a few moments she lifted the phone.

Sarah went straight to Roger's room that morning. She had spent the previous evening debating whether to ring him, but had decided it was best to see him face to face. When she knocked, there was no response. She went to the clerks' room and Felicity told her that Roger had gone to court.

'Can you let me know when he comes in?' asked Sarah.

'Yeah, if I see him,' said Felicity moodily. She was feeling utterly fed up with everyone and everything. All that crap with Sandy last night had left her unable to sleep, and then she'd come into work this morning to find Peter – who clearly took the view that Felicity had got her priorities wrong the night before – snippy and offhand. This was especially galling, since Felicity felt that if anyone had the right to be stroppy, she did.

Henry, sensing the evident coolness between Felicity and Peter, felt encouraged. He hated himself for it, but he couldn't help it.

'How are you getting on with your brother?' he asked, as he passed Felicity's desk.

'I'm not. I thought things were getting better, but I was wrong.' Felicity leaned back in her chair and sighed. 'You know he had a temporary job at that shop down the road? Well, he's more or less blown that. And he's been really funny lately, all paranoid. It's a bit frightening. I don't have a clue what to do.'

'Would you like to talk about it over lunch?'

Felicity looked up at Henry and smiled. She could do with having a heart-to-heart with someone about the situation. It really was getting on top of her. Maureen was sympathetic, but she couldn't offer any practical advice, and Peter – well, apart from last night, every time she'd raised the subject of Sandy he'd made it clear that he couldn't care less, dismissing Sandy as a loser. He didn't seem to realize how much it was affecting her. Or maybe he didn't care. She didn't want to think that. 'Yeah, Henry. That would be nice. I could really do with that.'

'Okay. We can go to the Italian. Haven't been there for a while.'

Felicity glanced across at Peter. He was gazing in apparent absorption at his computer screen, but she could tell he'd taken it all in. Good. She hoped maybe he'd realize that other people were prepared to show a bit of sympathy, even if he wasn't.

Three hours later, just as Sarah was about to go out to lunch, the phone rang. It was Felicity.

'Thought you'd like to know that Roger's just come in.'

'Okay. Thanks.'

Sarah put the phone down and went to Roger's room in the annexe. She found her heart was beating hard; she hadn't realized how wound up she'd been about all this, how anxious she was to put things right. She knocked on his door, and Roger called, 'Come in.'

He was sitting at his desk going through his mail, still in his court attire. The room was its usual clutter of briefs and books, every surface, including the window-sill, piled with documents. Roger glanced up. 'Hi,' he said, then looked back at the letter he was reading.

Sarah sat down in a chair, watching him as he read. Her

heart tightened at the realization of how much she had missed the sight of his kind, easy features, his thoughtful eyes. Eventually he put the letter down and looked at her. He didn't smile, but his expression was in no way cold. It was mildly indifferent.

'I thought I'd come and have a word,' said Sarah. 'I haven't seen you for a bit.'

'No, I've been quite busy.'

'I wondered if you felt like coming for a drink this evening.' Sarah wished he wouldn't make this so difficult. She tried to speak with her usual friendly nonchalance, but her insides felt twisted with anxiety.

'Why?'

She hesitated, then irritation got the better of her. 'Oh, come on. I'm trying to say sorry for what happened a couple of weekends ago. You know I am.'

Roger sat forward, leaning his elbows on his desk, and contemplated her for a long moment, then said, 'Don't bother. It doesn't matter.'

The words should have been reassuring, but his tone was all wrong. Sarah felt confused. 'No,' she assured him. 'It does. All the things you said – you were right. I wanted to say sorry ages ago.'

'I told you, it doesn't matter to me.'

'So . . .' she gazed at him uncertainly '. . . can we forget about it? I mean, can we just pick up where we left off?'

'That's not what I meant. As far as I'm concerned, everything that's happened between us is completely irrelevant. All of it.'

'How . . . how d'you mean? It wasn't that big a deal. It wasn't even much of an argument. I know I shouldn't have gone off like that, but, hey – I've said I'm sorry.' She felt panic rising in small waves. That this man mattered more than anything else in the world was only just dawning upon her. She hadn't expected him to behave like this. A little detached, experienced part of her mind told her to stay cool, that she could handle this situation. She smiled as best she could. 'Come on, don't be horrible. You must have missed me as much as I've missed you.'

'Missed me? Is that why you slept with Marcus?'

Sarah stared at him. Marcus. The bastard. The absolute and complete bastard. She shook her head slowly. 'No, look . . . That was absolutely nothing. It was entirely meaningless, the biggest mistake I've ever made in my life. I was drunk. I was unhappy. It was nothing. Please, please don't think it mattered. I was –'

'Of course it was meaningless. That's the point. That's the point about you. You do whatever comes into your head, because, as you say, none of it matters. None of it has any significance. Me, Marcus, whoever.'

Sarah's voice rose in panic. 'Roger, it was a mistake! Don't compare it with anything that happened between us. That was so, so different! Come on, you said you loved me . . .'

'I did. I thought something so special was going on. I really thought you felt it, too. But you couldn't bear to hear one true word about yourself without walking out on me. Then you went off and slept with one of my friends. And you think it doesn't matter.'

Sarah's gaze moved to the window, the sky beyond. She sensed that something was slipping here, passing out of her control. No, that didn't happen to her. She wouldn't let it. But inside she felt helpless, wordless with panic. She looked back at Roger, lifting her clasped hands slightly from her lap in a conciliatory gesture, resisting the urge to weep and plead. She worked to keep her voice steady. 'Look . . . the thing with Marcus was stupid, unforgivable. I told you – I'd had too much to drink. I didn't particularly want to go to bed with him. In fact, I can't stand him. Marcus is a complete pig.'

'Well, let's give him some credit here. He had no idea I'd been seeing you. He still doesn't. Otherwise it wouldn't have happened. He has some scruples. Which is more than can be said for you.'

'Oh, come on, Roger, don't judge me this way! It was only afterwards that I realized how much I cared about you – only you. I am so, so sorry. But it has nothing to do with us. You can't let someone like Marcus wreck everything between us. Please, Roger.' Her eyes were fastened on his. She took a shaky breath. 'Please.'

'It isn't Marcus who's wrecked things. Mind you, he hasn't helped. Good old Marcus, he doesn't spare the detail when it comes to recounting his sexual exploits. Distasteful, of course, but somehow you just can't shut him up.'

'Roger –'

'Don't. Don't bother. It's a waste of time. I don't want to spin this out any longer. Whatever there was between us doesn't exist, Sarah. Not any more.'

Such finality. Such blankness in his eyes. She wanted to reach out, as if by touch or gesture she might take back what she'd lost. But her hands lay inert in her lap, and her mind was numb. She could think of nothing but that she had destroyed what had been a complex, mysterious and perfect relationship. The sweet and unfathomable human being who had been her friend and lover would never be either of those things again. He was sitting there, a couple of feet away, utterly remote.

Despite the chaos of Sarah's feelings, pride was never far from the surface. She wasn't going to let him see how much this mattered. She stood up and shrugged. With immense self-control, she managed to keep her voice steady, her look calm. 'Okay. If you're going to be stupid about it, fine.' She turned and left the room.

Roger sat at his desk without moving for some moments. Those trivial words summed it all up. The way she regarded everything, including him. The last few minutes had cost him a great deal. He could have believed her. He could have let himself be persuaded – and how badly he wanted to be – that they could start again. But that would have been a waste of time in the long run. She would simply have done it all over again, and he didn't think he could bear to be hurt so badly ever again.

Ann and Leo spoke briefly at the end of the lunchtime break, just as the afternoon's proceedings were about to commence, but she said nothing about the information he had given her earlier. Which, as far as Leo was concerned, was fine. He wanted to maintain his distance, to have no apparent connection to the events which he suspected were about to unfold. Instead, she brought up the matter of electing a new head of chambers.

'Maurice is getting up quite a head of steam,' she said with a faint smile. 'He very much wants to be the new head. What about you? I'd have thought you might have shown a little competitive interest. Don't you mind an *arriviste* like Maurice muscling in on your territory?'

'I hadn't given it much thought,' replied Leo. In fact, he reflected ruefully, until the moment of that revelatory conversation with Captain Kollias last week, it had seemed that 5 Caper Court and its doings might shortly fade into the past and memory. Not any more. He sighed. 'If Maurice wants the job so much, maybe he's the right man for it.'

'I disagree,' said Ann. 'In fact, I think it's that particular aspect of his character which makes him unsuited. It's too much about Maurice, not enough about chambers. Anyway, instead of having a meeting about it, Jeremy's suggested a ballot.'

'Now, there's someone with a competitive instinct. I certainly wouldn't like to see Jeremy as head of chambers. Maybe I should start paying greater attention. I've had my mind on other things lately.'

'And here she is now,' murmured Ann.

Leo glanced round and saw Adriana approaching. Ann gave Leo an arch smile and moved away. How, Leo wondered in those few seconds, did Ann know? Christ, did *everyone* know?

Adriana's voice was soft in his ear. 'I came back from New York two hours ago. Mr Defereras said we are nearly finished, so I thought I should come.' She glanced around and asked softly, 'Are you free this evening?'

At that moment Mr Justice Sagewell made his mournful way in through the side door to the bench. Leo, attempting to look as though he was discussing entirely professional matters with his client, said, 'Possibly. I'll talk to you at the end of the afternoon.'

The afternoon's proceedings consisted of the cross-examination by Kate Carpenter of the last of the expert witnesses. Leo glanced at Ann a couple of times, wondering what she had made of the information he had given her this morning. She was too smart a girl to give anything away. She sat calmly taking notes, giving no indication that anything was about to happen to alter the mundane course of the case. Leo noticed that one of her instructing solicitors was absent, though, which could be significant. With any luck he was sleuthing around Southampton at this very minute. Ann would have to get a move on, if she was going to do anything. Otherwise, in order to prevent Adriana's nasty little fraud from succeeding, he would have to take matters in hand himself. And that was something he dearly wished to avoid. She wanted to see him this evening. Was it wise? On the whole, and all things considered, probably not. On the other hand, it would be unfair not to indulge her. There was every possibility that this might be the last occasion on which he could enjoy that delectable body of hers, and reflect wistfully on what might have been. Leo liked to think he had his sentimental side.

'They're having a meeting tomorrow,' Henry said to Robert.

Felicity picked up on this as she passed by. 'Who's having a meeting?'

'A chambers' meeting,' said Henry. 'Mr Hayter's asked me to be there. They'll be deciding who's to be the new head of chambers in the autumn.'

'God, I hope it's not Jeremy Vane,' muttered Felicity. 'He makes me heave.'

'Doesn't really make much difference to you, does it?' said Robert. 'My guess is it'll be Mr Faber. He's the one who gets things done around here.'

'Oh well, I've got work to do,' said Felicity. 'Can't stand here gossiping.' She went back to her desk. Robert was right – it made no difference to her who was head of chambers, though she thought Leo should be, if anyone. Not that bastard Maurice Faber. He seemed to find something new to complain about every day, whether it was getting his post late because he was in the annexe, or that the lighting in his room was making a funny buzzing.

She sat down. Peter sauntered over. 'You and Henry had a nice long lunch, I notice.'

'Yeah, well, he's a real friend, is Henry. He actually cares about my problems. Not like you.'

'Fliss, the one problem you have at the moment is your brother. The biggest favour you could do him would be to kick him out.'

'You really don't get it, do you? How's that going to help Sandy? What's he going to do on the streets? It's just back to square one.'

Peter shrugged. 'People have to take responsibility for themselves. You're letting him mess up your life, your relationships.'

'You mean, he's cramping your style.'

'You could put it like that, yes. I like to think I come first with you, and that's not the way it feels right now. To be honest, Fliss, I don't really think there's much of a future for you and me until you can sort this out.'

'Don't try your emotional blackmail on me,' said Felicity. But panic rose in her. He didn't mean that, did he? It wasn't fair, it just wasn't fair. 'At least Henry's a bit more sympathetic.'

'Really? And what wonderful practical suggestions did he come up with?' Felicity didn't like to admit Henry had been unable to think of a solution. She said nothing. 'I thought not. You've only got one option, Fliss. I mean it.' He walked off, leaving Felicity to reflect miserably on her dilemma.

At the end of the afternoon, Adriana spoke to Leo. 'So, are you free this evening?' She smiled. 'We have a lot to talk about. At least, I hope we do.'

Leo nodded, conscious that Rachel, standing some distance away, was paying close attention. 'I'll come to your hotel around nine.'

She reflected for a moment. 'No, don't do that. This time, I shall come to you. I've never seen where you live. I would like to.'

Leo hesitated. Was there much evidence of Camilla's presence in the flat? Well, it didn't matter. Not now. 'Fine. I'll make us dinner.' A farewell supper, though she didn't know it.

'You cook as well? You really are a man of parts. Give me your address, and I'll come over in a few hours.'

When Adriana had left the courtroom, Rachel came across, as he had known she would. He gave an inward sigh.

'You're going to miss her when this case is over,' said Rachel. 'Then again,' she added coolly, 'perhaps she'll find other work for you to do.'

'I doubt it,' replied Leo. 'I don't expect to be seeing much of Miss Papaposilakis after this week.'

'Her behaviour a few moments ago doesn't exactly suggest that.'

'Kind of you to take an interest in my private life,' said Leo, heading for the courtroom door. 'How's yours? Charles been put in the picture yet about you and Anthony?'

'Don't be catty, Leo. It doesn't become you.' They walked up the empty corridor in silence, then Rachel gave a sigh. 'As a matter of fact, he does know. I had to say something when he came back at the weekend.'

'Spare me the details. I'm only interested insofar as it concerns Oliver.'

Rachel stopped, and turned to regard Leo. 'That doesn't explain why you're so angry. Because you are – you really are. The truth is, you hate the fact that I'm seeing Anthony. You want to be able to regard him as your property. You've been that way about him since he first came to Caper Court. You'd have seduced him years ago, if you could. I've been married to you, remember, and I know. People come and go in your life. Me, Adriana – Camilla, eventually, poor girl. But it's Anthony you want. You resent my intimacy with him, because it's one thing you'll never have.'

Leo smiled. 'Is that what you think? I'm afraid you're somewhat behind the times. I'd have a word with Anthony, if I were you. Best to be under no illusions. No, if I appear to have misgivings about all this, it's purely out of concern for Anthony, believe me.' Leo crossed the corridor and went into the robing room.

He closed the door behind him and put his papers on the table, leaning against it for a long moment. Perhaps he shouldn't have done that. There was no need for her ever to know about himself and Anthony. It had been vindictive. He straightened up and took off his wig and gown. But she had touched on a truth which he had hardly dared to acknowledge. She had spoken as much out of malice as he had, smug in her possession of Anthony. He pulled off his bands and flung them on the table. What a bloody game this all was. Yes, she was right. He wanted to be the most important person in Anthony's life, the one he was closest to. How realistic was that, given the way he'd behaved towards him? Still, it was the truth, and he detested the fact that Rachel knew it. A few years ago, he might have gone to some lengths to destroy this relationship, if he could. Now . . . Now he no longer had the emotional energy. He sighed, picked up his tie and slipped it under his collar. If only dear Adriana wasn't such a greedy, wily little girl. How differently things might have turned out. He paused before the long mirror, remembering the room in Marbella, the white gauze of the curtains lifting in the breeze from the sea below the cliffs. How sweet life could have been.

Adriana arrived at Leo's flat a little after nine. She was wearing a thin silk dress, cut tight across her breasts, with a significant number of very beautiful diamonds at her throat and her ears. As Leo bent to kiss her, every part of her seemed to exude her special fragrance. It was one of the things he was going to miss most about her.

'You look extremely opulent, even by Belgravia's standards,' said Leo.

Adriana touched the diamonds at her neck. 'You like these? They were my mother's. I had them reset.'

Leo showed her into the drawing room. He had decided they should eat dinner in here, rather than in the somewhat formal and large space of the dining room. A table in the corner of the room was laid for two, with candles burning, and an arrangement of freesias in the centre.

She strolled to the table, smiling. 'How charming this all looks. I believe you are going to be quite a domestic asset, darling Leo.' She bent to inhale the scent of the freesias. 'These flowers smell heavenly.'

'Not as heavenly as you.' Leo took her in his arms and kissed her hair and her face. She was so happy in her presumption; he was very glad he wasn't going to have to bring her face to face with reality. Not tonight. 'Let me give you a glass of champagne, and I'll put the finishing touches to dinner.'

As they talked over the meal, Adriana touched lightly on the subject of their future together. Leo noted the delicacy with which she treated the subject, and realized, despite her earlier remark, that she was less sure of him than she pretended. He kept his response tentative. There was no point in destroying whatever illusions she had. Besides, it might preclude the possibility of sex later, if he were to indicate that he had no intention of becoming part of her entourage. And he did so want to say goodbye properly.

'I am so used to planning ahead, to knowing how things will unfold, that it's a little strange to find everything –' her small fingers plucked at the air as she sought the word

'– suspended. Waiting for you. Waiting to know what will happen with us.' She gazed at him with searching dark eyes.

'That remains to be discovered,' replied Leo. 'Let's get to the end of this hearing before we start worrying about the future.'

She decided to push him no further for the moment. 'I suppose it will be finished by the end of the week?'

'Mmm. I imagine another day or two will do it.'

'I just want it to be over.' She sighed. 'Poor Captain Kollias. His death was a terrible shock. He was a very good friend to me, and such a good master. I sent some money to his family, of course.' She put a small, soft hand over Leo's. 'Thank you for being so supportive over these months. It has been so important to know you've always had belief in me. Belief in my case.'

Leo gazed at her with frank admiration. He longed to know whether it afforded her secret amusement to think she had entirely deluded him, and everyone else, or whether, as happened with so many liars, she had actually convinced herself she was telling the truth. It could hardly be the latter – could it? He would never know. Nor would he ever discover, to his entire satisfaction, why she had perpetrated such a petty and thoroughly unnecessary criminal act, one which had brought about a boy's death. Though he partly understood. She had done it for the simple reason that she could.

'I have always had an unshakeable belief in justice,' replied Leo with a smile.

Adriana, resting her chin on her hand, returned his smile. 'I'm looking forward to showing you the *Persephone*'s successor. I like to think we shall enjoy many happy hours there together.'

'I can think of few things I would enjoy more,' replied

Leo. And he meant it. He raised her hand to his lips. 'One of them, however, possesses more immediate attractions.' He stood up, still holding her hand.

She went with him to the bedroom. She sat on the edge of the bed and slipped off her shoes, gazing at him with wide and expectant eyes. Leo had come to find her expression of undisguised longing somewhat touching. He pushed her gently back upon the bed and lay next to her, and began to kiss and undress her with practised and tantalizing deliberation. When she was utterly aroused, entirely his for the taking, he drew back and gazed at her for a long and wistful moment. She lay in his arms, soft with desire, no longer worldly and sophisticated, merely a passionate and vulnerable woman, and he felt a surge of genuine affection and regret. Still, no point in all that. He ran his hand gently down across her stomach, and she gave a little whimper and arched herself against him. If this was to be the last time he made love to her, he might as well make it a memorable occasion.

Camilla got off the Heathrow Express at Paddington, feeling light-headed with weariness. She wheeled her case to the taxi rank, where the queue was mercifully short. At last she got into a cab, gave the Belgravia address to the driver, and sank back against the seat. Throughout the train journey she'd been hoping that Leo would be in. Now it occurred to her that if he was out, it would give her an hour or two to have a bath and wash her hair, to be entirely and beautifully ready for him when he returned. If she could stay awake that long. She yawned and gazed out at the streets and the traffic, and let her mind go blank.

Fifteen minutes later the cab drew up outside Leo's flat. Camilla got out, paid the driver, and went up the steps. With the key Leo had given her a few months ago, she unlocked the front door and crossed the carpeted hallway to the lift. She took the lift up to the third floor, got out, trundling her case, and unlocked the door of the flat. The light in the hallway was on, but that didn't necessarily mean Leo was in. He often left lights on when he went out. She could hear no sounds, no television or music. She closed the door, set her case down, and slipped off her jacket and hung it up.

'Leo?' She walked down the hallway towards the lights of the drawing room.

Leo, at a truly precipitous moment in his lovemaking, heard the sound of his name, and froze. In the space of several drawn-out seconds, he realized exactly whose voice it was, and what was about to happen. Even if there had been some evasive course of action available to him, he could not have taken it. He turned his gaze to the door and waited, with painful fascination, for what seemed like a strangely long time.

'Leo?' Having scanned the empty drawing room from the doorway, barely taking in the table for two in the corner, Camilla walked the few yards to Leo's study, which was in darkness, and passed on to the bedroom. A low light shone from within, and the door was slightly ajar. Camilla wondered later if she'd had some sixth sense as she pushed it open, but came to the eventual conclusion that until that moment, she remained entirely trusting and unsuspicious. Never would she be so again, not where any man was concerned. The blonde woman lying on the bed next to Leo was entirely naked, except for the diamonds shimmering at her neck. Those, together with her candid sexual languor – for she seemed in too intense a state of arousal immediately to appreciate the situation – gave her the appearance of some extravagant courtesan. Camilla met Leo's appalled gaze. As he rose from the bed, the blonde woman seemed to regain her focus. She too stared at Camilla, who after standing transfixed for a moment, turned blindly back into the hallway.

Leo had her by the wrist. 'Camilla –'

She shook herself free and he grabbed her again. 'Get your bloody hands off me!' Tearfully she fought against his grip.

Leo, who would have dearly liked to be able to pull on his boxer shorts and conduct this scene with some semblance of dignity, tried wildly to think of something to say to redeem the situation, knowing it was beyond hope.

Camilla shook him off again. 'Get – off – me! Bastard!'

'I am so sorry,' Leo said in tones of desperation. He couldn't stay naked in the hallway. 'Wait a minute, please . . .' He went quickly back to the bedroom, glanced at Adriana, who was lying against the pillows with her hand over her mouth, and picked up his boxers. He hopped about for a difficult moment, trying to get them on, and by the time he was back in the hallway, Camilla had grabbed her jacket and opened the front door.

'No, look – hold on. Please.' He didn't think he'd ever spoken with such futility in his life. What in God's name was he meant to say next? This isn't the way it looks? I can explain everything?

Camilla picked up her case and turned to him with a savage, tearful gaze.

'You are the most – despicable – man – I have ever – met!' The words came out jerkily, caught between sobbing breaths.

'I know,' said Leo. 'But . . .'

She yanked her suitcase over the threshold. He watched as she stumbled towards the lift and stabbed at the button. The lift doors opened, and she got in, bumping and jamming her case against the doors, swearing pitifully.

He stood helplessly in the doorway as the lift made its descent. A few seconds later the entrance door slammed. He hoped, fleetingly, that Mrs Gresham wasn't going to come up to complain about the noise. What was Camilla going to do, where was she going to go? She would find a taxi, she would go to her own flat, where she'd barely lived of late, and she would cry all the way there, and beyond. This last knowledge tore at his heart.

He closed the door and went back into the flat. He padded into the drawing room, sat down in an armchair, and put his head between his hands.

A few moments later, Adriana came into the room. She was wearing Leo's shirt. She crossed the room to the drinks cabinet and poured a glass of Scotch, which she handed to Leo.

'Thanks.' Leo looked up and took the drink from her. He couldn't read Adriana's expression.

'I take it that was your girlfriend?'

Leo took a swift swallow of Scotch. 'Yes. She's been abroad for the past few weeks.' No point in any more apologies.

'You were silly not to tell me about her,' said Adriana, with only the mildest note of reproof. Leo supposed he should thank God for her forbearance, at least. What a hellish thing to have happened. And at that particular sexual juncture, too. He grimaced.

'It was never meant to make any difference.' He sighed, feeling a little tired suddenly.

'To you and me?'

Leo glanced at her. If that was what she cared to think, let her. None of it mattered any more. He nodded and drained the remains of his Scotch. 'Something like that.'

'I'm glad to hear it. A pity she had to find out that way.

Still . . .' Adriana took his empty glass from him '. . . at least she knows now.'

Leo gazed at Adriana. It was somewhat ironic, though hardly surprising, to discover that infidelity didn't much trouble her. No kind of double-dealing would, he supposed.

She knelt down and placed her hands on his thighs. She reached up and kissed him, and he smelled her fragrance, mingled with the scent of his cologne from his shirt. 'I think you need a little space.' Leo, marvelling at her tolerance and understanding, nodded.

Adriana got up and went through to the bedroom. She dressed and came back. 'I've rung for my car.'

'I don't understand why you're not angry,' said Leo curiously.

She shrugged. 'Leo, all the time we are together, when we are in bed, whatever . . . I have always known what you felt. Do you think I have ever supposed there weren't other women?' She reached down and touched his face. 'Nothing matters except what you feel for me. Despite what you say, I know you love me. That is why we will work so well together.' The intercom buzzer sounded.

Adriana walked to the door, then turned. 'I'll see you tomorrow in court.'

Leo got up. 'Yes.' He followed her down the hallway to the door. Adriana gave him a brief smile as she got into the lift, and left without another word.

Leo closed the door and went to the bedroom. He picked up the shirt which Adriana had discarded and put it on, then his trousers. He went back to the drawing room, sat down again and closed his eyes. If only Camilla had called to tell him she was coming home . . . But what good would that have done? Wasn't this something that was always destined to happen? She would have been hurt as badly – if not this way, then some other way – in the long run. What was done was past recall. She would never forgive him. Which was probably just as well. She would be better off without him. He just wished he could have spared her such unhappiness. In that moment, he truly detested himself. He sat motionless in the armchair for a long time.

Leo arrived in court the following morning feeling grim. He had spent the intervals between bouts of restless sleep going over and over those hellish few minutes of Camilla's return and her miserable discovery, forced to contemplate the baseness of his conduct through a new and cruel perspective. There was no point, he knew, in trying to see her. Not at present. He must say something at some point, even if only to acknowledge to her how wretchedly he had treated her.

Adriana arrived and slid into the seat behind Leo. Without turning his head, he could detect her presence. The proceedings were about to commence, however, and she had no time to speak to him. Not that Leo cared. He didn't want to discuss the previous night's events.

'Court rise!' intoned the usher. Mr Justice Sagewell swept on to the bench and took his seat.

Well, now,' he said, 'where were we?'

'My Lord,' said Ann Halliday, rising to her feet, 'certain additional matters have recently come to my attention. I would like, with your permission, to recall Miss Papaposilakis.'

A wordless ripple of surprise stirred the courtroom. The judge surveyed Ann over the top of his spectacles. 'This is somewhat unorthodox, Miss Halliday.' He turned to Adriana with infinite courtesy. 'Would you mind . . . ?'

Leo turned round. Adriana appeared surprised, wary. She leaned towards Leo. 'What should I do? Is this all right?' she asked in a low voice.

Leo shrugged and murmured, 'I presume so. I don't really know what it's about.'

Adriana hesitated. Then she rose and walked to the witness stand. She sat down, crossed her legs, directed a soft, confiding smile at the judge, then looked attentively at Ann Halliday. Leo gave a little inward sigh and sat back in his seat.

'Miss Papaposilakis, you have a claim in respect of two Degas drawings which were lost on board the *Persephone*, I believe? In the region of four million pounds?'

'De-gas,' said Adriana, pronouncing the first syllable as in 'the'.

Ann paused, disconcerted. Mr Justice Sagewell leaned forward. 'Miss Papaposilakis is right. Most people mistakenly pronounce the name "Daygas", when in fact it should be "De-gas". As the French would pronounce the syllable.' He gave Adriana a complicit smile. 'I'm a little surprised you didn't know that, Miss Halliday.'

'I must thank your Lordship – and, of course, Miss Papaposilakis – for pointing out my error,' said Ann. Adriana inclined her head with sweet grace and flashed Mr Justice Sagewell another smile. Leo slid forward a little in his chair. He was feeling much better than he had a few moments ago.

'These drawings,' resumed Ann. 'Can you tell the court where and how they were displayed on board the *Persephone*?'

'They were mounted in frames, screwed to the wall of the main cabin.'

'And when did you last see them?'

'They were on the yacht, obviously, before the fire.'

'Yes, but when did *you* last see them?'

Adriana hesitated. 'I can't recall precisely.'

'Would it have been when the yacht was in the marina at Southampton in September two thousand and two?'

'Perhaps. I really don't know. It was a long time ago.'

'You travelled on board the *Persephone* from Nice to Southampton?'

'Yes.'

'And when you left the yacht, the drawings were still there?'

'Yes. They must have been.'

'So you remember now?'

'It's a presumption. Of course they were.'

'How long had they been there?'

'For five years.' Adriana's gaze was fastened intently on Ann's. Her face wore a little frown.

'And Captain Kollias was in your service throughout that time?'

Mr Justice Sagewell scented Adriana's discomfiture. 'Miss Halliday,' he interrupted sternly, 'where is this going?'

Ann picked up a piece of paper from the table in front of her. 'Miss Papaposilakis, perhaps you can help the court with regard to this photocopying receipt.' Adriana stared at the paper in Ann's hand. 'Do you know what this photocopying receipt is for?'

Adriana turned and gave Mr Justice Sagewell an appealing glance. But the judge was busy writing.

'Shall I repeat the question?'

Adriana shot Ann a dark, animal look. 'No. I don't have the least idea what it's for.'

'It's a receipt for the photocopying of two drawings. We have a statement from the gentleman at Sprint Office Services of Southampton, who remembers a blonde woman bringing two drawings to be copied on the second of September. Does that help?' Adriana said nothing. She looked trapped. 'What I am suggesting, Miss Papaposilakis, is that you took these two drawings by –' she paused '– De-gas to Sprint Office Services in Southampton to be photocopied, and that you subsequently substituted the copies for the originals on board the yacht. The only possible deduction the court can make from such actions –'

Leo rose to his feet and interjected smoothly, 'My Lord, if I might request a brief adjournment to discuss the case with my client?'

Mr Justice Sagewell inclined his head grimly. 'Yes, Mr Davies, I think that might be a good idea.'

Leo fixed his gaze on Adriana's face and nodded to her. She left the witness stand and walked with Leo to a side room, leaving the lawyers murmuring behind them.

Leo closed the door.

Adriana turned to him with a face of fury. 'How could you let this happen? Why did you let me answer those questions?'

'I'm afraid I really had no idea what she was going to ask you,' lied Leo. He waited, wondering if Adriana was going to continue to rage and bluster. But she merely folded her arms and stalked up and down the room, still incandescent.

After a few moments she turned to him. 'What am I meant to do? You're my lawyer! You tell me what I'm supposed to do!'

'Well,' said Leo thoughtfully, 'I'm not really sure there's much you *can* do, given the circumstances. Miss Halliday has a receipt for the copying of the drawings. She has a witness who can probably identify you. I think he was the young man at the back of the court.' Adriana said nothing. 'That an owner should trouble to replace two very valuable original paintings with copies only weeks before the vessel is destroyed by fire . . . well, it obviously supports the insurers' contention that there was something suspicious about the loss of the *Persephone*, wouldn't you say? The judge has been listening very carefully, and I can tell you he's formed a pretty bad impression. Which is understandable.'

Adriana lifted her dark eyes to his, and they gazed at each other without expression. Much passed between them in those silent moments. Leo knew she couldn't bring herself to make a clear and unequivocal admission of what she had done. Nor had he any intention of tackling the issue head-on by asking her. There was no need.

'So – what am I to do? Tell me!'

'I think it would be best if I were to go back in and tell the court that you're dropping your claim.'

'Why? Why should I?'

'Because on the evidence as it stands, you have no alternative. You're going to lose, Adriana. If you don't stop it now, there's a chance the judge will hand the papers to the DPP. You don't want that.'

She paced the room. He could tell she was bowing to the inevitable. She turned at last to look at Leo, searching his face for some clue. It must be evident to him what she had done, but he gave no sign of it. She had to know. 'Why don't you just ask me about it?' she said, her voice almost a whisper.

Leo's face was impassive, but he felt almost sorry for her. 'You're my client. I take you as I find you.'

'And afterwards? You and me?'

'Everything comes at a price. You, of all people, understand that. I can't afford this one.'

She looked away and nodded. After a moment she said with some impatience, 'Very well, get it over with.' He turned to the door, and she grabbed his sleeve. 'Is this the worst that will happen?'

Leo was momentarily confused. Was she talking about dropping the case, or the end of their relationship? He thought he would try for the former, and hope. 'If you drop the claim, I doubt it will go any further. I hope not.'

She nodded and took her hand from his arm. A

businesswoman to the last, thought Leo, as he stepped into the courtroom.

A moment later, he addressed the judge. 'My Lord, my client has indicated to me that she wishes to withdraw her claim and pay the defendant's costs on an indemnity basis.' Leo sat down, reflecting that there was much to be said on the complex nature of unprincipled behaviour.

Mr Justice Sagewell nodded. 'Thank you, Mr Davies. Quite understandable.'

Ann Halliday rose. 'My Lord, we accept that. We are pleased that the underwriters' position has been fully vindicated.'

When the court rose, Adriana left the court as quickly as possible, Mr Defereras at her side.

16

Rachel was still stunned. 'How on earth did that happen?' she asked Leo, as people began to leave the courtroom. 'I hadn't the least idea . . . I don't understand how the other side got hold of that receipt.'

'Maybe someone tipped them off,' said Leo. 'You can't scuttle a yacht all on your own, after all. A little technical assistance is generally required.' He gathered up his papers, determined to make a speedy escape. He had no wish to be involved in an extensive post-mortem of the case right now. That could wait till tomorrow. He would greatly relish going over certain aspects with Ann. She had done a concise and expert job in her cross-examination.

As he crossed Fleet Street on his way back to chambers, he met Michael Gibbon.

'You've finished early,' remarked Michael.

'My client's case has just collapsed quite spectacularly,' replied Leo.

'Bad luck.'

'Maybe. Maybe not. Sometimes these things happen for the best. Fancy lunch at Luigi's in a couple of hours? I have a need of conviviality right now.'

'Okay. I haven't had a decent lunch in a while. Better not push the boat out too far, though. There's a chambers' meeting at the end of the afternoon – time to sort out the new head of chambers.' They walked through the gate and down Middle Temple Lane. 'You know, there's a general feeling that people would rather see you as head of chambers than Maurice Faber.'

'Me? You seem to forget I had my name splashed all over the *Sun* not so long ago. I'm hardly the respectable face of Five Caper Court.'

'That's not the point,' said Michael, as they paused in the archway of Pump Court. 'You're liked, and Maurice isn't. He's pushy. The younger lot aren't keen on him, and neither are the clerks. It's not healthy to have someone at the top who isn't generally respected. It would go down well with everyone, in and out of chambers, if you were made head. So far as Roderick is concerned, you're in the running.'

'What about you?'

Michael shook his head. 'I've already told Roderick I'm not interested.'

'I've half a mind to do the same. Who needs the hassle?'

'I wish you'd let me persuade you otherwise.'

Leo smiled. 'Let's see what you can achieve over lunch.' The two men strolled from the archway in the direction of Caper Court.

Camilla was on her way from Temple Tube, crossing Fountain Court, when she caught sight of Michael and Leo in conversation in the archway opposite. She slowed her steps, then sat down on the stone rim of the fountain, not wishing to encounter them. She watched Leo, his robing bag slung over his shoulder, his silver hair catching the light, as he talked to Michael. He seemed his usual self, as though nothing much had happened in the last twenty-four hours to disturb his equilibrium. As if the events of last night hadn't happened. She herself had thought of nothing else, the weight of her unhappiness dragging at her very soul. She realized she had never understood what people meant when they talked about being broken-hearted. She knew now. The physicality of this misery was so intense. It had prevented her from sleeping properly, combining with her jet lag to make her feel dazed and a little unwell. She had had to come into chambers this afternoon, if only for something to take her mind off last night. Last night . . . To think she'd actually made a joke about that Papaposilakis woman getting him into bed. She should really have seen it coming. Hadn't Leo himself warned her about the kind of man he was? She hadn't wanted to believe it. She'd thought she would be the one to change him. What a cliché. He would never change.

Leo and Michael moved beyond the archway into Pump Court, and Camilla watched them go. She saw now that she would have to leave 5 Caper Court and find some other chambers. She couldn't bear to see Leo, day in, day out. She had loved him so deeply, and with such singleness of heart. In spite of everything, she still did and always would. That, perhaps, was the worst part.

Leo had decided that his lunch with Michael at Luigi's would be a spectacularly good one. Recent events, together with the change about to be wrought by the move to Gratton Crescent, and the end of the wretched *Persephone* case, made him want to turn his back on life's realities for a couple of hours at least. Wanton indulgence was the order of the day. At half past three, after a considerable amount of excellent food and two £74 bottles of Dolcetto Bricco Rosso, Leo and Michael rolled out into the sunshine of Covent Garden and began their leisurely walk back to chambers.

'That was very Eighties,' remarked Michael with satisfaction.

Leo, lighting a small cheroot, agreed. 'Nobody lunches properly any more. Probably just as well for the economy.'

'You should have let me split the bill with you.'

Leo shook his head. 'No. My idea. My lunch. A mixture of celebration and valediction.'

'Celebrating what?'

'Well, the fact that that bloody case is over, for a start. Plus, as I told you, I'm moving house.'

'And the valediction?'

'Oh . . . I've had to say goodbye to a couple of things recently. Good things.' Leo thought of Camilla and Adriana, and wondered which of the two might have been the more worthwhile. Too late now. Ironic, though, that he had lost one woman through sticking to his principles, and the other through lack of them.

Michael sensed that Leo had no wish to dwell on these losses, whatever they might be. 'So – have I persuaded you to put yourself forward as the next head of chambers?' he asked.

They were sauntering along the Aldwych in the direction of the Strand. Leo glanced at the familiar surroundings, pondering the question. Apart from Oliver, chambers and work were really the only solid things in his life. They grounded him. And this. All this. The traffic, the people, the buildings, the city through the seasons. He liked the way things were. Did he really want Maurice Faber running the show, presenting his version of 5 Caper Court to the world? Leo felt a flicker of proprietorial jealousy. He had been at those chambers for twenty-five years. He and others – not Maurice Faber – had been responsible for their present success. He had been a tenant under some excellent heads, including Sir Basil, then Cameron, and latterly Roderick. Was he really prepared to sit back and let that upstart Faber take over? He turned to Michael. 'Yes, you've persuaded me. You, plus a mixture of the wine at lunch, this sunny day, and a certain misplaced sentimentality.'

The meeting had been arranged for five-thirty. All the tenants assembled round the long, oval conference table in Roderick's room. Camilla sat some distance away from Leo. He glanced at her once, quickly. He was too enfeebled by his own sense of guilt to look at her again. He would speak to her later, if he could find the courage.

Roderick went through a brief preamble as to the purpose of the meeting, touching on his own imminent departure, and on the recent expansion of chambers, and the future he envisaged.

'There is no orthodoxy in the matter of these things,' he observed, glancing round at the faces. 'The position of head of chambers, as you all know, is very much a nominal one, given that the success of Five Caper Court as an entity depends upon the strengths of its individual members. Seniority is naturally significant. Our most senior and longest-serving members of chambers – Jeremy, Leo, Stephen, Michael – are all amply qualified to take on the role. Maurice, although he joined us only a few months ago, has already demonstrated his sense of commitment, and his enthusiasm for promoting the interests and image of chambers abroad. Being head of chambers is not, however, a position which is to everyone's taste,' added Roderick with a smile, 'and Michael has already let it be known that he would rather not put himself forward. As I have already said, at Five Caper Court we adhere to no rigid form in deciding these matters. Sometimes there is a clear consensus, as when Cameron Renshaw took on the role. At the time that I became head, the matter was made fairly straightforward by the fact that nobody else was interested.' At this there was a little murmur of amusement. 'In the present circumstances, where we have more than two obvious candidates, the most egalitarian method would seem to be to take a vote by way of a ballot. Each person should write the name of their preferred candidate on one of these pieces of paper –' Roderick pushed a little pile of papers to the centre of the table '– and I will give them to Henry to sort out at my desk. Then, with luck, we should have a clear favourite. Does that meet with everyone's approval?'

There were nods of agreement, each tenant took a piece of paper, and each wrote on it as unobtrusively as possible. Then Henry collected the folded slips, took them over to Roderick's desk, and sorted through them. He picked one of the papers from the largest pile and handed it to Roderick.

'Leo Davies,' said Roderick simply. He put the paper on the table with a smile. There was a general murmur of satisfaction, and the atmosphere seemed to relax. 'I think we would all agree the choice is an excellent one.'

Leo was mildly surprised. What had he done recently for chambers, after all, except drag its pristine name through the tabloids? It had seemed to him that Maurice's tireless promotional work and self-publicizing would surely pay off. Still, there it was. He felt pleasantly gratified, and wondered if the votes in his favour had included Camilla's.

He glanced round. 'I'm very touched by your confidence. Thank you. I hope I'll do my best to justify it.'

The meeting broke up. There were smiles and words of congratulation to Leo as they filed out of Roderick's room. Even Maurice managed a slap on the shoulder. 'Not surprised they wanted a familiar face. Well done.'

'Thanks,' said Leo.

'I must have a word with you in the next few days about some suggestions I have for a couple of new chambers' committees. We could do with restructuring in some areas.'

'Fine.' Leo sighed inwardly at the prospect of reining in Maurice's managerial enthusiasms.

He lingered briefly on the stairway as people dispersed. He had to speak to Camilla sometime. Now was as good as any. To his relief she was the last to leave Roderick's room.

She gave Leo an expressionless glance as she passed. He put a hand on her arm. Doors closed below as people went to their rooms. The staircase was empty.

'Please,' said Leo gently. 'Can I have a word?'

'Why?'

'I need to talk to you. Can we go to my room?'

Camilla hesitated, then nodded and followed Leo downstairs and into his room. Leo closed the door. He was about to speak, but before he could, she said suddenly, 'Leo, I need to know something. The Greek woman – are you serious about her?'

'What?'

'Is she the new woman in your life?'

He was touched by the childish solemnity of her voice and look. 'God, no . . . Nothing like that. You were away. She made herself very available. I'm making no excuses. I'm simply telling you how it was. She means nothing to me.' Camilla said nothing, but her shoulders dropped slightly. 'Look,' Leo went on, 'I know no apology could change things. But I owe you one. What I did was unforgivable.'

'Was it?'

This momentarily threw Leo. It hadn't occurred to him that she might be prepared to forgive what had happened, to go on as though it didn't matter. She certainly hadn't given that impression. He'd had the idea that the events of the last twenty-four hours had more or less determined the relationship's future. Or lack of it.

He hesitated. 'By any normal standards, yes. I –'

'But yours aren't normal standards, are they, Leo?'

'No,' he conceded, 'you could say that.' There was a silence. He found it difficult to meet her unwavering gaze. 'So what are you saying? Are you saying that if I tell you how sorry I am, you'll simply be prepared to forget it all?'

Camilla looked at him unhappily. 'I don't think I could ever forget last night, Leo. Not ever. I feel about as badly hurt as anyone could possibly be.' Her eyes, fastened on his, filled with tears. 'I don't think you can imagine the pain you've caused me. I thought you loved me. You told me you did. And despite everything you've done, I still love you. It shouldn't work that way. When someone does the kind of thing you have, there should be no room for anything but hate. But it's not like that. A part of me badly wants you to say that you'll never hurt me again, that you love me so much that you'll never betray my trust, not any more. Will you do that? Will you say that and mean it?'

Leo wanted to lift his hand to brush away the tears which hung on her lower lashes. He wished he could do as she asked, and make sincere and heartfelt promises. He wished so much that he could make her happy in the way she wanted. At last he spoke. 'I'll say it, if you like, if it means that things don't have to be over between us. I'll say anything you want. But I won't mean it. You know that.'

Camilla brushed her own tears away. She spoke shakily. 'It was a stupid question, really. You've always been pretty candid about yourself. Well, as candid as you can be . . .' She glanced away, frowning. 'I just wish . . .' She shook her head. 'I just wish you could have left me alone in the first place. I wish I didn't feel this way.'

'You mean you wish nothing had ever happened between us?' His voice was gentle, curious.

She looked at him. 'No, I don't mean that. I don't mean that at all . . .' She gave a long, miserable sigh. 'I just don't want to *hurt* so much.' There was so much anguish in her voice, she looked so young and pitiful, that Leo wanted to take her in his arms. But that would be a mistake. He knew he must let her take this to its ultimate conclusion, for her own good. Camilla went on, 'I know I have to stop seeing you. I can't handle this kind of relationship. I need trust. I need someone who can make me feel entirely secure. And that's not you.'

In spades, thought Leo. He looked at her sadly. 'If it's any help, I think you've made the right decision. You deserve someone much better. If we let this go on, it would be a disaster in the long run.'

'Yes.'

He touched her cheek with his hand. 'You are a remarkable girl.'

She turned to the door, and as she moved she could tell she was hoping he would say or do something more. Something to change the finality of the situation. For the sake of them both, Leo did nothing. Said nothing. He simply let her go.

Rachel and Anthony had arranged to see each other after work. They met in Finsbury Square, and sat drinking coffee in the sultry evening air at a pavement café. Rachel's manner was subdued.

'Charles and I talked last night,' she told Anthony. 'We agreed things can't go on as they are. Everything is so stilted, so artificial. He's desperately unhappy. He said he doesn't want me to move out, but I told him I didn't see any alternative.' She clasped her hands together, the knuckles white. 'I've never hurt anyone so badly in my life, Anthony. I've had it done to me. I know what it feels like. I never wanted to do it to anyone else.'

'It's done now. Look, you mustn't worry about anything. You can move in with me. The flat's not very big, but there's a room Oliver can have. Then we can look for somewhere together.'

After a moment's silence Rachel said, 'I'm not sure that's a very good idea. I think maybe it's a bit premature. Don't misunderstand me – I love you very much. It's just that we've only been seeing one another for a short space of time. Everything's fine now, but it could change. If we start living together, the relationship doesn't have a proper chance. Apart from anything else, you don't know what it's like, having a toddler around twenty-four hours a day.'

'I like Oliver! I think he's a fantastic little kid!'

'I know you do. That's not the point. I came out of my relationship with Leo and bounced straight into another. Probably not a good idea. But I let it happen. I can't afford to make another mistake. I want to find somewhere of my own, and take it from there. They're making me an equity partner in the autumn, which makes a big financial difference. I'll be able to find a house for Oliver and myself. I'll rent somewhere in the meantime.' She looked up at him, her expression tentative. 'I really think that's the best idea, Anthony.'

Anthony wasn't going to pretend he wasn't a little relieved. He'd had no hesitation in suggesting to Rachel that she move in with him but, much as he was in love with her, he too could foresee problems. He was about to say as much, when Rachel added, 'Besides, there's something else we haven't talked about.'

'What's that?'

'Leo.'

'I don't see where he comes into it.'

She hesitated for some seconds. 'We don't talk about him much. But he's there at the back of both our minds, all the time. I find it a little disturbing, don't you?' Anthony said nothing. Rachel went on, 'It's best to be honest about these things, I think . . . Leo said something the other day that made me realize how little I know about you. About you and him.'

'What did he say?'

'Nothing overt. I said he seemed angry that you and I were seeing one another. I said he couldn't be jealous of you, so he must be jealous of me – having you, I mean. It wasn't a very bright thing to say, I know . . . But what he said next – I can't remember the exact words –' She broke off, regarding Anthony uncertainly. The next words were difficult to say. She spoke them quietly. 'You've been his lover, haven't you?'

There was a long silence. The truth seemed to eddy out slowly, filling the air between them. 'It's not perhaps the label I would use,' replied Anthony. 'I don't know what you'd call it. It was just one night, that's all.' He looked down at the table, tracing a pattern with one finger.

Rachel said nothing. Her mouth felt suddenly dry. She couldn't name the emotion which filled her. There was something almost pornographic in the contemplation of Anthony and Leo together. She let herself dwell on it, filling her mind with the image. Anthony looked up. 'It just about finished me, you know. Finding I could feel that way about another man.' He paused. 'No – that's not entirely right. I always knew what I felt about Leo. I knew what he wanted. I just didn't realize that I wanted it as well.' His gaze dropped, his voice, too. 'I thought I would be ashamed, or something. Something. . . But I wasn't. I hoped it was just the beginning.' He nodded. 'I thought it was. Just shows you, doesn't it? Nothing is ever the way you think it is. Not where Leo's concerned. He doesn't start things. He finishes them. Chokes them dry. Kills them stone dead. Once he's got what he wants, it's all over. So.'

'Why didn't you tell me?' asked Rachel softly.

'Because it has nothing to do with you and me,' replied Anthony, still not looking at her.

'Don't you think so?'

'No. Why?' He looked up now. 'Do you?'

Rachel nodded. 'I think it has everything to do with us. Because you and I both have to ask ourselves – if Leo were to say to either of us right now, "I want you. Come to me" –' she gazed at him '– what do you think either of us would do?'

'I don't know,' said Anthony. He pushed his coffee cup aside and gazed across the square. 'I can't answer for you.'

'No. But you know the truth. Look at me.'

Anthony glanced at her. He shook his head. 'What's the point? What's the point of the question?'

'I wanted to show you. How important he is.'

'He's not. Why do you want him to be?' He paused, gazing into her eyes. 'Would you go to him?

She dropped her gaze. 'No. I love you.'

'Then why bring him into this?'

'Because I wanted to know the truth.'

'So now you know it. Or you think you do.' He leaned forward and put his hands over hers. 'Do you want to let him screw up this relationship?'

'No.'

'Then for once in your life try to forget him. This is about us.' He stroked her fingers. 'Do you believe that I love you?'

She nodded. 'Yes.'

'Then let that be enough.' He leaned across and kissed her. 'Whatever he has been to either of us, that man simply isn't important.'

She nodded, but wondered in her heart whether this would ever be true.

Half an hour later, after they'd parted, Anthony realized

he'd forgotten to tell Rachel that Leo was now head of chambers. She'd find out that bit of gossip in the next couple of days, anyway. He walked down into the Tube station, going over their conversation, wondering how their relationship was going to develop over the next few months. He loved her, he was glad she was leaving Charles, but it was probably best she wanted to find a place of her own. As for the stuff about him and Leo . . . Well, she knew now. It didn't seem to make a difference. She, of all people, knew Leo and the kind of things he could make people do. He mustn't think about that question she had asked. The one about what either of them would do if Leo were to say . . . No – no point in even considering it. These theoretical things were meaningless, anyway.

Felicity got back to the flat. No Sandy. His room was a complete tip, the curtains unopened, the bed unmade, the floor littered with sheets of paper covered in his writing. She certainly didn't intend to read them, that was for sure. She went through to the living room, slipped off her shoes, and made herself a cup of tea. At least Neelam and Sanjay were due back from India tomorrow, so she wouldn't have to go on feeling guilty about how Sandy had let Mrs Deepak down. She settled herself on the sofa and switched on the six o'clock news. What the hell she was going to do next with Sandy, she had no idea. Maybe Henry was right. Maybe Mum and Dad were the people who should take responsibility for him. It might not be what Sandy wanted, but perhaps it would be the best thing for him.

Eleven o'clock came, and Felicity was about to get ready for bed, when she heard the sound of feet thundering up the stairs, and then a furious banging on the front door. She raced to open it. Sandy, staggering, panting, pushed past her into the flat. Felicity closed the door, and Sandy ran into the living room and ducked behind the sofa.

Felicity walked round the sofa. 'Sandy, what the hell's going on?' She stared down at where he lay crouched, one arm raised defensively above his head.

'They're gonna get me, Fliss. They've been after me all day. They're here! Outside! Don't let them in! Please! Don't let them in!'

'Who is? Have you been in a fight?'

'Oh, God . . .' His voice was quivering. 'Oh, God . . . They're all over the streets. They've got weapons, missiles . . . Aaah!!' He ducked again and screamed, terrifying Felicity. She backed away.

'Sandy, there's nobody out there. It's in your head. There's nobody going to hurt you.'

He whimpered, curling himself up. Felicity stood up. This was bad, really bad. She crossed the room. At that moment Sandy got up from behind the sofa, his eyes wild and lost, and picked up the nearest object, which happened to be a hole puncher from the desk where Felicity kept bills and bank statements. He hurled it across the room. 'I'm gonna fight them! They're not gonna get me!'

'Christ!' exclaimed Felicity, and ducked. She knew Sandy wasn't throwing it at her. He wasn't even looking at her, probably wasn't even aware she was there. She glanced up and saw him reach out for something else to throw. He looked completely demented. She ducked again, terrified, and crawled across the room on her hands and knees to the phone. She pulled it down, and sat crouched behind an armchair, her hands shaking, trying to think who to ring. Maureen? She could maybe get her brother round, or her Dad. She dialled the number, but only got Maureen's answerphone. Shit. Objects were crashing round the room. Sandy was shoving the sofa across the carpet for some reason, talking and shouting all the time at his faceless enemy, at the beings in his head who were out to get him. God, had he been on that ketamine again? Felicity gave a little whimper of anguish, badly frightened both for herself and Sandy. 'Calm, calm, keep calm . . .' she muttered to herself.

She stabbed in Peter's number. He would come. Please, please answer . . . Thank God.

'Peter, it's me, Fliss.' Her voice was shaking. 'Can you come over? There's something really horrible going on here with Sandy.'

'What? What kind of thing?'

'I don't know . . .' The room had suddenly quietened. She looked round the side of the armchair and saw the sofa being dragged back into place, Sandy behind it. Digging in and waiting for reinforcements, no doubt. 'He came back a few minutes ago, completely paranoid. He's raving on about people out to get him.'

'Fliss, I told you he wasn't right in the head. I could tell that last time I was round.'

'Peter, he's been violent! I think he could do himself or me some serious harm!'

'In that case, ring the police. Best thing for everyone, if he's locked up.'

'Peter, please, I'd really be grateful if you could come round. I don't want to get the police involved. I don't want him in trouble.' She thought of the dope which Sandy probably had stashed away in his room, to say nothing of other substances.

'It's what he deserves. I've tried to tell you he's not worth it. I don't see what I can do to help, Fliss. I'm sorry.'

'You won't come? You won't even help me?'

'I've got the kids here. I can't do a thing.'

She hung up. She knew Peter didn't have his children there with him. He didn't see them during the week. Not at this time of night, anyway. She felt near to tears. Sandy was at it again, alternately talking and shouting. She thought of Henry. He didn't live too far away. He might know what to do, short of calling the police. She rang his number. What if he was out? But he answered.

'Henry, I'm so glad you're in!' gasped Felicity.

'Fliss, what's the matter?'

'Sandy's gone completely mental. He's got himself behind the sofa, and when he's not throwing things, he's raving on about people out to get him. I'm really frightened, Henry.'

'Give me ten minutes,' said Henry, and hung up. Fliss sat back in relief. She wasn't sure how he could help the situation though. Maybe he could calm things down, think of what to do. At least she wouldn't have to deal with this alone.

Gradually the situation quietened a little. Sandy was still holed up behind the sofa, shouting at the faceless enemy, but he'd stopped throwing things. Felicity had become sufficiently emboldened to crawl round near to him, to talk to him, but he wouldn't come out. The situation, he maintained, was too dangerous.

With relief Felicity heard the doorbell. She went to let Henry in.

'He's still there,' said Felicity, indicating the sofa. 'He won't come out.'

Henry crossed the room cautiously. 'Sandy?'

Sandy screamed, 'Who's that?'

Felicity intervened quickly. 'It's a friend, Sandy. Don't worry, no one's going to hurt you.'

Sandy jabbered frenziedly for a few moments about the enemy and the missiles and dangers that lurked all around, and about how Felicity must keep them away. Henry listened. 'You need to get him to a hospital,' he said quietly. 'He needs looking after. You can't sort this out here.'

'How am I going to do that, Henry? Call an ambulance? Watch him wreck the flat while they try to take him away? I can't do that. He trusts me. He's here because he thinks he's safe. He thinks I'm the one person who's not going to let him down.'

'Right. Okay.' Henry thought for a moment. 'Mind if I make myself some tea?'

'Of course not.' She showed Henry to the kitchen, standing midway between both rooms in anxiety. She waited while Henry, with maddening deliberation, made his tea and drank it. At last he rinsed his cup and said, 'If you don't want him taken away, we're going to have to persuade him to let us take him to the hospital.'

'How are we going to do that?' asked Felicity in exasperation. 'You can see the state he's in! He won't even come out from behind the sofa!'

Henry went back to the living room.

'Sandy?' he said.

Sandy screamed again, 'Who is it? Who is that?'

'I'm a friend,' said Henry. 'I'm here to help you.'

'No one can help! Not even the government! They've got spies everywhere!'

'I'm from the government.'

There was a long silence. Then Sandy said, 'Don't fuck with me. This is dangerous. Don't do that.' After another moment he said, 'Is that right, Fliss? Is he from the government?'

Felicity, wide-eyed, glanced at Henry. She looked back at the sofa. 'Yes. Yes, he's from the government, Sandy. He's here to help.'

'He can't help me. You don't get it. They're out there, and nowhere's safe!'

'I know somewhere safe,' said Henry. 'The government's got a safe place. I can take you there.'

'No, you can't.' Sandy's voice was sullen, but it held a new note. A listening note.

'I can. If you come with me, we can make it there. You'll be completely safe.' A long silence. On sudden inspiration, Henry said, 'You know where I'm talking about, don't you?'

Sandy said slowly, cleverly, 'Yeah, man, I know. I know where you mean.'

Felicity listened in amazement, not daring to say a word.

'Okay, listen. We need to get out of here, and downstairs. Think you can do that?'

Slowly Sandy shuffled from behind the sofa on all fours. His face was pale, slack, but his eyes were focused. They found Henry, and fixed on him. Henry nodded but didn't smile, remaining entirely serious. 'Ready?' he asked.

Sandy nodded, still staring at Henry as though trying to imprint his features. He stood up. 'The government know about this, don't they?'

'That's why they sent me,' said Henry.

He moved towards the door, and Sandy followed. When they reached the landing outside the flat, Henry nodded to Felicity to follow. She picked up her key and closed the door behind her. She was convinced Henry wouldn't get Sandy as far as the street.

They reached the main door of the building, and Henry waved Sandy and Felicity back, while he opened it himself and looked out in either direction. Felicity was astonished by the pantomime.

'Okay!' hissed Henry. He motioned to Sandy and Felicity,

and Sandy shuffled out cautiously into the street behind Henry, never taking his eyes off him.

'Come on,' said Henry, 'I've got a car across the road.'

Sandy shook his head. 'I'm not getting in a car.'

'It's a government car.'

'They wire bombs to them.'

Henry took a deep breath. 'We've got to get there, Sandy. Got to get where we'll be safe.'

Sandy glanced round. 'We'll walk.' He kept looking round, checking the street.

Henry turned to Felicity and said in a low voice, 'How far's the hospital?'

Felicity looked at him frantically. 'A mile, two miles?'

Henry looked at Sandy. 'Okay, Sandy. If you think we can make it, we'll walk.'

They set off down the street, which was relatively quiet at that time of night. Only the odd car went by, which didn't seem to spook Sandy. When they reached the corner, however, he stopped. This isn't going to work, Felicity thought.

'They're going to hear us,' said Sandy. 'On the main road, they'll hear us.'

'We'll walk really quietly,' said Henry.

'We've got to take off our shoes.'

Felicity's eyes met Henry's. 'You're right,' said Henry. 'We'll have to take off our shoes.'

I don't believe this, thought Felicity. The three of them walked down the main road, Sandy looking from right to left, keeping close between Henry and Felicity. They all carried their shoes in their hands. Felicity kept checking the pavement for glass and dog turds. She was convinced that the night traffic would freak Sandy out, that they'd never get there. Or if they did, that Sandy would see it was the hospital and run off screaming into the night.

When they came within sight of the hospital, Henry stopped. 'Right. See the building over there?'

Sandy gazed across at the entrance to A & E. He's not going to buy this, thought Felicity. He's not that mad. But Sandy merely nodded.

'That's it. That's where you'll be safe. You knew this was where we were going, didn't you?'

Sandy nodded. 'Yeah.'

'Come on, then.'

They crossed the car park, Henry in his socks, Felicity and Sandy barefoot. They went through the automatic door to reception. Felicity kept waiting for something to go wrong. They approached the desk. Felicity watched the look of apprehension on Sandy's face with mounting alarm. Any minute now.

Henry looked straight at the receptionist. 'I've brought Sandy,' he said. 'It's right that he'll be safe here, isn't it? He says there are people after him, and I've told him this is a government place, where he'll be safe.'

The receptionist's gaze shifted from Henry to Sandy, then back to Henry.

'That's right,' she said. 'You take a seat over there.'

Henry nodded, and led Sandy to the waiting area, carefully seating him away from the other patients. Sandy's expression was watchful, truculent, but he seemed reassured by Henry's presence.

Almost in tears, Felicity said in a low voice to the receptionist, 'My brother's seriously unwell. He's hearing voices. He's completely paranoid. We had to walk him all the way here. He needs to see a doctor right away. Please, please . . .' She began to weep, not wanting Sandy to see her. They'd got him this far, someone had to help now, but still she didn't want him to see her crying.

*

338

Sometime later, in the early hours of the morning, Felicity and Henry left the hospital. Felicity felt utterly drained. 'I feel I've betrayed him, Henry. Letting them section him. It's like I've abandoned him.'

'Come on, you haven't abandoned him. You've looked after him. He's safe. The doctors will help him. They know what they're doing.'

'That was what he wanted, wasn't it? To be safe.'

'Exactly.'

They stood in the gusty forecourt of the hospital, waiting for the minicab to arrive. When it did, they got in and drove back to Felicity's flat.

'Would you like a coffee before you get back?' asked Felicity as she fished for her key.

'Thanks, but I'd better get back and try to catch some sleep,' said Henry.

Felicity nodded. 'I can't thank you enough, Henry. You were brilliant. I don't know how you thought of all that, getting him to go with you. I never could have. He trusted you so completely.' She smiled. 'But then, anyone would. You're such a nice bloke. Solid gold.'

'Happy to help,' said Henry. He bent his head and kissed her softly, hesitantly on the mouth. Just a brief one, but nice. She didn't seem to mind. 'See you in the morning.'

'Night,' said Felicity, and watched him cross the road to his car. Give her ten Henrys to one Peter any day, she thought. It was at times like these that you found out who your real friends were. She thought of Henry with warmth and grateful love as she went upstairs to clear up the mess in the flat.

On Thursday Leo took possession of the keys to his new house. The contents of the Belgravia flat, which was in the process of being sold, were moved to Gratton Crescent. Leo spent Friday arranging furniture and unpacking boxes. He enjoyed the solitude, sitting in the garden under the mulberry tree with a scrappy lunch of bread and cheese and an apple. He contemplated the garden, picturing Oliver there in a week's time, when he had his room ready. This would be a place of permanence. No more mad fantasies about a life of wealthy and luxury with some Greek heiress, who would probably only have stabbed him in the back in due course. He hoped she was going to pay his bill. Not that he wouldn't always think fondly and wistfully of that voluptuous little body of hers. But for the moment his energies in that direction were pretty much exhausted. What he craved at the moment was simply friendship, companionship, things he had lost with Camilla. He would miss her, because she was an endearing and loving girl, but their future had been uncertain and fraught. No doubt it was for his own good, as well as hers, that things had turned out as they had. She really had been ridiculously young. He thought of Ann Halliday, of the easy and pleasant times they had spent together during the past few months. There was a lot to be said for maturity, for the easy and kindly cynicism of someone who knew you from way back when. He was looking forward to being with her tomorrow evening. He would confide in her the whole bizarre story of Adriana. It would be a relief to share it with someone. Perhaps it would help him to see the ridiculous side of it all.

It was almost midnight when Leo and Ann left the Treeveses' party. Leo opened the door of the taxi for Ann, then got in next to her.

'Thank you. I had a lovely evening. Simply lovely.' Ann sighed and leaned back against the seat. 'The Brahms was perfect. Didn't you think?' She turned to Leo, gazing at his sharply handsome profile, thinking for the hundredth time how well he looked in evening dress.

Leo nodded. 'I'm very glad you came. Very glad indeed.' He turned to smile at her. It was true. Had he taken Camilla, he would have spent the whole evening wondering whether she was enjoying herself or not. Not, more than likely. 'Do you have to go back straight away?' he asked. 'I'd rather like to show you my new house.'

Ann hesitated, a little surprised, then said, 'Yes, I'd love to see it. I shan't stay very long, though.'

Ten minutes later the taxi pulled up outside Gratton Crescent. 'Shall I ask him to wait?' said Leo. 'Taxis can be difficult to find at this time of night.'

'Probably a good idea,' said Ann. After all, it was she who'd said she wouldn't stay long. She'd had no expectations from the very outset, beyond a pleasant evening with an old friend.

Leo opened the door and switched off the alarm. He flicked on some lights. 'Since you don't have long, I'll just show you the ground floor, and the garden. Indulge me – I'm extremely proud of my new property.'

Ann smiled and followed him through the rooms. It certainly was a very lovely house, though it seemed rather large for one person. There had been talk that Leo was seeing Camilla Lawrence. She wasn't in evidence this evening, at any rate. Leo hadn't mentioned anyone else in connection with the house, except his son. He had talked about Oliver quite a lot during the evening, and Ann liked him for that. It was a side to Leo she had never seen before.

As she was admiring the kitchen, Leo opened a cupboard. 'Would you like a drink? I'm having a Scotch, myself.'

'What about the taxi?'

'He's perfectly happy to wait. He's twenty quid up, so far.'

'Leo, you shouldn't have . . .'

'I didn't want you to feel you had to rush off.'

She smiled. 'I'll have a Scotch, too, in that case.'

When he'd made their drinks, Leo crossed to the back of the kitchen and flicked a switch. The entire garden was suddenly bathed in soft light.

'How beautiful!' said Ann, gazing through the window.

'Let's go outside,' said Leo. He unlocked the back door and they stepped out into the fresh summer night. They walked round the garden, discussing the shrubs and flowers. It was, reflected Leo, a constant pleasure to discover the extent of Ann's knowledge and interests. He stood sipping his drink, watching her as she reached up to finger the leaves of a Japanese maple, thinking how pretty the light was on her hair. She was an attractive woman – the more time he spent with her, the more he felt that. He felt a mild stirring of desire, of longing for something that was beyond mere sex. How good it would be to find oneself with someone entirely compatible, easy . . . Life, he had realized of late, threatened to be very lonely.

A small breeze swept the night air, rustling the leaves of the plants, and Ann shivered. Leo stretched out a hand to her pashmina and lifted it lightly on to her shoulder. She turned and smiled, and he let his hand rest there. He contemplated her face, then touched it lightly. When he took her in his arms and kissed her, he felt her whole body tremble slightly.

He drew back after a moment and said softly, 'I could send the taxi away.'

She gazed at him, at the strong lines of his face and the magnetic blue of his eyes. She thought about the tale he had told her this evening of Adriana – their affair, her unscrupulous behaviour. She had wondered at the time why he felt the need to tell anyone. She shook her head slowly. 'No, Leo, I don't think so. It wouldn't do. I'm really not your kind of woman.' She left his arms and crossed the lawn to the house, before he could do or say anything that might make her change her mind. One thing middle age gave you, she reflected wistfully, was an instinct for self-preservation. Leo was too beautiful, and too dangerous. He always had been.

Leo followed her across the lawn and opened the back door for her. Ann went into the kitchen and put her glass down. She turned to him. 'Thank you again, Leo.' She went through the house to the front door, and out to the waiting taxi.

Leo walked between the packing cases and pieces of furniture to the window of the front room. He stood and watched as the taxi drew away, then stayed there for some time, gazing out at the empty street.

CARO FRASER

A PERFECT OBSESSION

Love. Sometimes it feels like there should be a law against it.

But even at a leading firm of barristers you can't legislate for the entanglements of the human heart.

At 5 Caper Court, Leo Davies QC – sexually ambiguous, charismatic and attractive to men and women alike – stirs the hearts of many. There's scheming, sexy Sarah; Anthony, an ex-pupil and friend; charming Gideon, a civil servant on the make; and sweet Camilla, a junior lawyer in Leo's chambers – to name a few. Plenty of opportunities, then, for a silver-haired sophisticate to have fun. But Leo is tiring of his hedonistic lifestyle. Perhaps what he really needs is honest emotion – even love? Could it be that the cool and controlling Leo will fall? But who for . . . ?

In this compelling story of lust, love and jealousy, Caro Fraser once again brings the affairs, friendships and feuds of 5 Caper Court brilliantly to life.

'She writes with panache, exuberance and humour, and never leaves the reader waiting too long for the next emotional twist' *The Times*

CARO FRASER

FAMILIAR ROOMS IN DARKNESS

Harry Day was a national literary treasure, revered for his poetry, novels and plays. But his personal life has remained something of a mystery. When Adam Downing, a young journalist, is appointed his official biographer, he finds that Harry's life holds an abundance of secrets.

But Adam is torn between wanting to protect Harry's reputation and his instincts as a journalist, which drive him to tell the truth at any cost. He will even risk losing the admiration and friendship of Harry's beautiful daughter, Bella. For Harry's biggest secret of all involves Bella; and Adam is well on his way to falling in love.

'Fraser writes with fluent flair. Her irony is light but merciless, benefiting from a good ear for dialogue and a keen eye for masculine vanity' *Daily Telegraph*